After
THE FALL

After the Fall

Eureka in Love Series

Tamara Hart Heiner

Also by Tamara Hart Heiner:
Perilous (WiDo Publishing 2010)
Altercation (WiDo Publishing 2012)
Deliverer (Tamark Books 2014)
Priceless (WiDo Publishing 2016)

Goddess of Fate:
Inevitable (Tamark Books 2013)
Entranced (Tamark Books 2017)

Kellam High:
Lay Me Down (Tamark Books 2016)
Reaching Kylee (Tamark Books 2016)

The Extraordinarily Ordinary Life of Cassandra Jones:
Walker Wildcats Year 1: Age 10 (Tamark Books 2015)
Walker Wildcats Year 2: Age 11 (Tamark Books 2016)
Southwest Cougars Year 1: Age 12 (Tamark Books 2017)
Southwest Cougars Year 2: Age 13 (Tamark Books 2018)

Tornado Warning (Dancing Lemur Press 2014)

Chapter One

LUCE

"Yeah, it's great, Dad. I appreciate you finding me a place."

Luce held the door open with one hand, balancing the heavy box on her hip while cradling the cell phone between her ear and her shoulder. Crumbling stone steps led the way from the concrete sidewalk exterior into the faded brown condo. Even with the curtains pulled back from all the windows, the wood paneling kept the interior dim and enclosed. Glass fixtures enclosed the living room light, adding an orange-ish glare to the galley kitchen next to it.

"I wish you would let me come and help you," her father said, his normally stern voice hinting at something almost like concern.

Not that Luce fell for that. She knew her dad still blamed her for the divorce. "I'm almost done. I've got the last box in my arms. And you've done enough." She fought hard to keep the bitter edge out of her words, not wanting to bring up the sore subject of her new career path. "I'll call you if I need anything."

"Let me know how your first day at the clinic goes tomorrow."

"Sure. Talk to you later."

The call disconnected, and Luce gave an aggravated sigh, letting the phone slide from her shoulder to the floor. She stepped over it and inhaled deeply, trying to get a sense for her new home, but mostly she smelled must and moth balls, a scent that reminded her unpleasantly of her grandma's house. She dropped the heavy box onto the giant rug in the middle of the living room that the previous inhabitant hadn't felt the need to take with them.

Yay. An old condo badly in need of a remodel. This was what she inherited from her broken marriage.

Melodee came in behind her with her arms full of blankets. "Careful with that box!" she said. "It might have some of your pottery in it."

Luce's lip twisted. She never wanted to look at another clay vase or glazed plate again. She kept quiet, though, because she knew Melodee already worried about Luce's mental health. She didn't think the anger at her pottery was "normal."

Like normal was even a real thing.

Melodee pressed a hand against her lower back, the growing bulge of her belly made more evident by the pose. "Was that Dad?" Her long brown hair with reddish highlights, the same color as Luce's, fell in waves across her shoulders. Though four years older, Melodee was shorter by several inches, and there was no hiding her pregnancy.

"Yeah. He just wanted to make sure I got in okay." Luce had left her dad's house in Springdale an hour earlier, just as anxious to get away from his parental care as she was to reestablish herself as as single, independent woman.

Melodee looked around the room at the yellow light fixture

and the dated kitchen behind her. "Nice place. First time seeing it?"

"I came up with Dad to look at places a few months ago. But I told him to just pick one." She could be in a one-room hut in Africa, as long as she was away from Brian.

The desire to redefine herself, to discover her identity as an individual, loomed over Luce, feeding her hands with a nervous energy. She tapped the pads of her fingers against her thumbs. Without meaning to, her eyes turned toward the box labeled "wheel." She could take a glob of clay right now, set up her wheel, get it spinning and spinning while her hands caressed and molded it . . .

Shake it off. She exhaled slowly. "I'm actually looking forward to being by myself."

Melodee favored her with a smile. "I'm sure you are. But dinner's on me, okay? We'll go walk the strip."

The strip? Luce bit back a laugh. The idea of comparing the mile-long shopping center in Eureka Springs with the miles of entertainment available in Vegas was hilarious at best, insulting at worst. "Sure, that would be great. I'll be hungry."

"You know I will be."

Luce waved goodbye and then surveyed the boxes in the living room.

"A new start," she breathed, her eyes locking on the one box she had hauled around for the past six months without opening. She knew the contents by heart: the blanket Brian had given her when they went to the drive-through movie; the stuffed animal he slept with when he was eight years old; the jersey he let her borrow for their first football game.

Silly things, and just things; yet they reminded her of a time when she and Brian were happy. When she had been excited about spending the rest of her life with him.

If only she had known then about his addiction, his need to put the things most precious to him on the line so he could get an adrenaline rush.

Luce didn't need to go through the box. She already knew what to do with it. Squatting down and grabbing it with both hands, she carried it outside and tossed it into the dumpster.

♥

Melodee stopped by a few hours later. The weather was unseasonably cool for late September, and Luce threw on a jacket before heading outside. It would be easier for the two of them to walk twenty minutes to the strip than to take the car and try to find parking downtown. The parking spaces were for the tourists, people willing to pay five dollars because they didn't have any other choice.

"Did you get all unpacked?" Melodee asked as they started down the sidewalk.

Trees covered in lush leaves crowded the walkway, long branches reaching out over their heads and creating a barrier from the wind. Luce glanced up and stared at the different shapes and sizes, the deep dark green color. That shade of green didn't exist in Vegas.

Something unfurled within her, as if her own budding tree was trying to grow in her chest.

"Mostly," Luce answered, turning her gaze back to the sidewalk before she lost her footing. The steep inclines in Eureka could catch even the experienced natives off guard. "It's not like there was much. I just threw a few things in my car and left." She'd only been married a year, after all, just enough time for Luce to lose everything.

Melodee shot her a sideways glance. She shoved her hands into her jean pockets, thrusting her body backward to balance her weight while they walked down the hill. "Have you talked to Brian?"

Luce mimicked her sister's pose as the steep downgrade threatened to make her topple. "No. Not since the court settlement." She'd spent the last year existing in her dad's basement while she went to school in Bentonville, a town thirty minutes away. By throwing her life into her studies, she'd completed a two-year degree in just one.

"Does he know where you are?"

Luce lifted a shoulder. "I hope not. I didn't tell him." And she'd changed her number.

They turned a corner onto Spring Street, and the first shops came into view. Luce's spirits rose at the sight of the little eclectic buildings full of designer jewelry and crafts, funky artifacts, and vintage items. The narrow street continued its curving path, but the colorful stores and waving awnings beckoned them forward. All of the buildings had two or three levels, constructed as they were into the hillside. They staggered beside each other at different heights like stair steps, decades old and built in a Western style, all right angles and brick. Music spilled out of the open bars and restaurants along with the crowds, groups of people dressed in comfortable jeans and casual shirts leaning against the railings and chatting.

Luce let out a soft sigh as a few more leaves unfurled in her chest.

"Sure was nice of Dad to help you score your job at the clinic," her sister said, a hint of something in her voice.

Luce frowned. "Yeah, it was nice of him." Their father was the CEO of the local chain of hospitals and clinics. He'd urged her to finish her nursing degree—urged? More like forced—, and it hadn't taken much for him to secure her a job as an RN. "My life choices have been a big disappointment to him."

"The past few years have been hard on him."

"Hard on him? Try hard on me."

Melodee's hand fluttered in a nervous gesture. "Well, there's no question about that. But—"

Whatever she was trying to say was cut short when they rounded the corner and Melodee smacked into a man coming up the opposite direction, his head turned toward the people with him instead of facing forward.

"Watch it!" Luce gasped, dropping her purse as she reached for her sister.

"I'm so sorry," he said, grasping Melodee's elbows and helping her straighten herself. "I really should slow down going around corners."

"It's okay. I'm fine. Like I keep telling everyone, I'm not fragile."

All Luce could see of their perpetrator was a square jawline and some stubble from at least two-days worth of beard growth. Something about the shape of his jaw reminded her of Brian, and her defenses flared. "You should pay more attention. You could've hurt her."

He turned toward her, the chagrin showing in his light brown eyes. His olive-toned skin evidenced the time he spent in the Arkansas outdoors, and dark brown hair with a slight wave fell back across his forehead, and any similarity to Brian, with his fair, freckled skin and light hair, faded away. "You're absolutely right." And then his eyebrows lifted. "Luce? Is that you?"

Luce squinted, recognizing some familiar features on this man-face. "Connor?" Even as she said it, she knew she had to be mistaken. It couldn't be the same person.

His face split into a smile, revealing a dimple on either side. "Yeah!"

Her mind flashed back to the boy with an acne problem and glasses. "I tutored you in English, right?"

His smile shifted more to the shy grin she remembered. "Turns out I'm more of a math guy."

She'd felt bad for him then, the quiet boy who never spoke to her, not even in tutoring sessions. Apparently he'd outgrown that phase, and his friends snickered and whispered to each other behind him, their eyes on Luce.

Luce glanced at them and her face warmed, embarrassed to have them scrutinizing her. "Hi," she said, inexplicably flustered. "Nice to see you again." He still stood there, gaze intent on her, and she found herself unable to break eye contact. Luce rolled her wrist. "Well, my sister and I are going to get going."

Connor looked behind him at his two friends who stood waiting. "Yeah, of course. I'm on my way back to my mom's story anyway. The one on the corner?"

He pointed, so Luce looked, obligingly, but she couldn't tell which store was his. "Oh."

"I work there," he said, as if he couldn't tell she wanted to leave. "So do you live here now?"

His eyes on her did something weird to her stomach, and Luce forced herself to look away. She hooked her arm through her sister's and pulled her down the sidewalk. "Yes. Bye, Connor."

"Wait!" He bent and grabbed her purse from the sidewalk, then held it out to her. "You almost left this."

Luce tried to keep her stern expression, but she couldn't help giving him a tiny smile as she took it. "Thank you."

At least Melodee had the decency to wait until they had gone a full block before she brought Connor up. "Seriously? You should have been all over that. He was super hot. And a friend of yours from high school!"

"He's not a friend from high school. He's just someone I knew. Six years ago."

"Maybe you should get to know him better."

Connor *had* come into himself quite nicely, a far cry from the scrawny kid who sat silently in the back of the classroom. "I just got out of an ugly marriage."

"A year ago. You can't keep thinking the male species is all evil."

Luce set her jaw, her eyes burning. "Brian was perfect. Remember? He was funny, friendly, the perfect son-in-law. That's why Dad still likes him more than me."

Melodee fell silent. Luce knew her sister had nothing to counter that, but it didn't feel like a victory.

Melodee took her hand. "I'm sorry. But hey, let's look on the bright side. We're at the fudge shop."

Luce exhaled. "You know my weakness."

CONNOR

L uce O'Neil. Connor could not even believe it.

Luce O'Neil, here in Eureka Springs.

He hadn't seen her since high school, and it wasn't as if he'd talked to her then. But he'd noticed her. And even though she'd been nothing but a tutor, she'd always been kind. His secret little crush grew to quite an obsession by the end of their senior year. She had the same long auburn hair, light brown eyes, upturned nose and freckles on her face, but her eyes hadn't glittered quite as brightly. But what did he expect? None of them were carefree teenagers anymore.

And there he'd stood, blabbering like a stupid idiot. Like she cared where his mom's store was.

"Connor." Ty nudged him. "We're going back to your shop, right?"

Behind Ty, Moki snickered. "I think he got bushwhacked."

Connor glanced around and realized he'd walked right past the antique shop. "Oh, yeah, sorry."

"Sure, she was pretty." Ty opened the door and held it while they walked in. He deposited his soda can on the glass counter top and leaned against it. "But seemed like more than that to you."

Connor gave the store a quick once-over, surprised to see it empty and unlocked. His mom had been here when he left. He shoved Tyson off the glass counter and handed him the soda, then wiped the counter down with a cloth, removing the ring of water. He'd known Ty for six years and Moki for three, and they knew him about as well as he knew himself. "We went to high school together."

"And?" Ty pressed, his blond eyebrow almost invisible as it arched into his strawberry blond hair. Moki leaned in also, his braided black hair and olive skin a direct contrast to Ty.

Connor stopped shining the glass and bent toward them. "Okay, yeah, I had a big crush on her. What of it? I had a crush on half the girls in school. At some point or another." Which wasn't exactly true.

"What happened to her?"

"Beats me." Connor shrugged. "Last I heard, she dumped her boyfriend and ran off to a big city."

"And now she's back." Ty scrutinized Connor.

"Now she's back," Connor agreed. "So? I have a girlfriend, and we're happy."

"Sometimes," Moki said.

Ty snorted. "The fire's gone out of that one."

Connor didn't respond. He turned around and organized

the antique porcelain teacups on their matching saucers, wishing once again his mom would let him fill the shop with something newer. Nobody wanted antiques anymore. They wanted modern, sleek, cutting edge. Original. He looked over at his shelf, the one he filled with items from his various travels. She tolerated it, but if he tried to sneak in more than that, she'd remind him of Granny's vision for the store.

"Oh, look at the time!" Tyson said, clapping Moki on the shoulder. "Closing time. We're out of here."

"What?" Connor said. "You don't want to stay and help me clean up?" He hauled another rag out from under the counter.

"Nah." Ty grinned broadly. "Meet us at the Rowdy Beaver tonight. Bring Regina, Amber will be there too. We'll watch the game."

Yeah, but Ty's girlfriend Amber followed him around with the kind of devotion that made Connor's stomach hurt with envy. Regina liked him, but was she devoted? "We'll see if she wants to."

Connor raised a hand in goodbye and began the tedious work of closing the shop. Not hard to count the money in the till today, since only a handful of customers had come in. A little less than three hundred dollars. It would have to do. Hopefully the next day would bring in more.

He picked up the mail under the counter and sorted through it, looking for one thing: the foreign trading post. He sat on the stool and hunched over the magazine when he found it, flipping through pages with a pen in his hand, circling items he thought would sell well. The Christmas retail season would be upon them in a month, and now was the time to get in the decor.

"Hello!"

The back door pushed open at the same time that Connor's

mom poked her head inside. She smiled at him, her natural hair color long hidden by boxes of blond dye.

"Oh!" She giggled as she stepped inside.

Which meant that—

Sure enough, her boyfriend Dave came in behind her, poking her teasingly.

"Oh, Dave," she said, turning and slipping her arms around his neck, "stop that."

Gross. Connor grabbed the bank deposit envelope. "Hey, glad you're here. I was just leaving. You guys can finish closing up." It was his mom's store, after all, and he shouldn't have to babysit it.

"I've got places to be," Dave said, throwing up his hands. "I'll meet you at the winery, Jess?"

"Of course," his mom purred, leaning into him.

Connor averted his eyes from the inevitable kiss, but the noises were unmistakable.

Finally Dave walked out, and his mom plopped down on the stool next to him with a sigh.

"The winery? Again?" Connor said. "Seems you're doing that a lot lately."

"It's what Dave likes to do, honey." She smiled at him patronizingly as if he were a child who didn't understand why dads had to work. "So I like it, too."

"But you don't like it."

"Maybe I'm developing a taste for it."

Connor pressed his lips together before the argument went full force again. There was no point. With the last boyfriend, it had been black and white movies, the one before that, golfing, the one before that, antique cars. He had to admit his mom had become very well-rounded in all of these relationships, but she was never herself.

Not that she knew who she was. She'd been trying to define that person ever since his dad walked out.

"Where were you, anyway? You were supposed to be watching the store," he said, closing the register.

"Dave picked me up an hour ago. I knew you'd stop by before closing."

"So you just left?" Why did he feel more responsible for this place than she did?

"I locked the door," she sniffed.

"No, you didn't."

"Didn't I?" She looked suitably chastised.

"I'm out of here." He handed her the keys. "Don't stay out too late."

"You don't stay out too late." She took the keys and eyed him, the giggly girlfriend quickly replaced by the concerned mother. "Going out with Regina?"

"Maybe."

She softened her voice. "You two been rocky lately?"

"Yeah."

She patted his arm. "I want to see you happy and tied down."

He grunted. Did those two things even go together? Yeah, Regina was nice, but he couldn't really see himself tied down to her. "We're doing fine, Mom."

"What time will you be home?"

"What time will *you* be home?" he returned, shouldering his messenger bag. "I won't be late. I have a few assignments I gotta finish up before the weekend." Connor had gotten his bachelor's degree in art history from the University of Arkansas a year and a half ago, but somehow it didn't prove to be worth much in the job market. Since he didn't plan on being stuck to his mom's/grandma's/great-grandmother's antique shop for the rest of his life, he was taking online classes to get a master's in business management.

The odd thing was, he felt a certain affection for the shop. If his mom would just let him change it. . . . But he knew he'd have to break away and open his own store if he wanted his vision to become a reality.

"A race, then. We'll see who gets home first."

"Me," Connor said, unable to hold back the grin. He hurried to the door to show his mom he meant business.

"Not tonight!" she shouted after him.

"You're opening tomorrow!" he called back.

The back door to the shop closed behind him, and Connor descended the stairs to Mountain Street. His calves tightened as he started up the steep incline to the parking lot, but he was used to it, having lived in Eureka all his life. The backs of shops greeted him, all with steps leading up to them from the street below. Nothing was straight or level in this town. As a kid, it infuriated him not to be able to skateboard or ride his bike around the sharp curves. Now, he couldn't imagine trading this charm and style for anything.

How hard would it be to find a girl who felt the same way?

Probably not Luce. She'd run off to the big city the moment school got out. Couldn't wait to get away from the small-town scene. He shook his head. Why was he even thinking about her?

Connor spent a few hours at home trying to get homework done and study for his Friday exams. But his mind kept wandering back to Luce. Her long reddish brown hair had fallen in soft curls down her back, though her expression had been rather steely. He'd apparently really offended her when he bumped into her pregnant sister.

He checked the time. Nearly eight. Regina would've gotten off work hours ago. Why hadn't she called? Picking up his phone, he dialed her number.

She answered on the fourth ring. "Hello?" she whispered, her voice groggy, as if she'd been sleeping. He pictured her with her white-blond hair tucked into a high ponytail, black eyeliner ringing her eyes. But she was off work now, so maybe she'd let her hair down.

The thought didn't excite him the way it had a few weeks ago.

"Hey, Gee," he said. "You okay?"

"Oh, yeah." She cleared her throat. "You studying like crazy?"

"I was." He rolled his pencil across the notebook. "Moki and Ty invited me out for drinks. I told them I'd think about it. Did you want to go out tonight? Amber will be there."

"You're so sweet." She gave a cough. "I think maybe a patient got me sick. My throat kind of hurts."

"Ah." That explained the husky note to her voice. "I'm so sorry. Should I come over?"

"No, I don't want to give it to you. Besides, aren't you going to ace those exams this time?"

He chuckled slightly. "That's the plan." Last time he'd scraped by with a low B. He definitely didn't want his master's education to be sub-par.

"I'll leave you to it, then. We'll talk tomorrow."

Connor hung up and sent out a quick message to Tyson. If Regina didn't feel up to coming, he didn't really need to, either. Besides, she was right. He needed to score high this time.

LUCE

Melodee walked Luce back to her condo, and Luce unlocked the door before turning to face her sister. "I can find a comfy spot for you on the floor if you want to come in for a bit."

"I'll bring you the extra sofa in our basement."

Luce wrinkled her nose. "You mean the one the dog likes to sit on?"

Melodee gave a brilliant smile. "Yep. That's the one."

"I'll pass."

"Suit yourself."

Luce waved to her sister and went inside. She surveyed the empty kitchen, with only one box on the counter that held all of her plates and pots and pans. She walked through the kitchen into the living room, since not even a wall separated them. Here the majority of her boxes remained, except for the ones labeled "bedroom" that contained all of her clothing. And her pillow and her blankets.

Yes, she was going to need some furniture. A new bed, for

starters. A twin bed, something that left no question in anyone's mind that she was sleeping alone.

Her eyes searched the room and landed again on the box with her pottery wheel. She hesitated. How long would she let Brian haunt her future? With sudden determination, Luce walked over to the box and opened it. She pulled out her wheel and set it up on the floor, since she had no table to work on. Not a problem. She'd worked on the floor before. She set the pedal out in front of her.

It took less than a minute to locate the clays. She pulled one of the dark red ones out and held it a moment, studying it. She flashbacked to the first time she met Brian, how he had raved about her pottery, how he had especially loved the dark red color. He helped her go from a local boutique to a nationwide online store, complete with employees and flat-rate shipping.

The plan was to open franchises and become a recognized brand. He had the financial backing to help her get a good start, and she had enough uniqueness to her pottery to fill a niche that hadn't been met yet. Luce loved throwing pottery and didn't mind if she worked sixteen-hour days to create it.

But even with all her sales, her bank account was always empty. Brian told her she was still operating in the red, with the employees and the accountants and the warehouse fees. He said it usually took five years for a business to make a profit.

She'd believed him. At first.

Luce plied the clay from her hands and dropped it back in its box. Closed it up, then took her pottery wheel and did the same thing.

She stretched herself out into Child's Pose and told herself to go through some yoga moves. Something to get the blood flowing and her mind thinking. But she couldn't seem to pry herself off the floor.

The timer on her phone went off, and Luce got up long enough to find the box of prescription sleep aids. She popped a pill before going to bed in her sleeping bag.

♥

The alarm went off at six o'clock Thursday morning, and Luce let out a loud groan as she reached over and slapped her phone. Her finger managed to hit the snooze button, and she threw her arm over her head, burrowing into her sleeping bag and falling back to sleep.

She jerked her arm off her head and sat up when the alarm went off again. This time there was enough adrenaline running through her system that she didn't hit snooze. The thought that she might be late to her first day at work terrified her. Single, childless, and without her pottery business, this job was all she had left. Her ego could not take the blow if she lost it.

She should have stuck with school and avoided marriage like the plague.

Luce brushed her teeth and threw her hair into a ponytail, then opened the box with all of her scrubs. She bypassed the simple green ones that had been given to her in school and chose instead one of her favorites, the white one with multicolored balloons on it.

From the moment she locked her front door and got in the car, it only took six minutes to get to the clinic. She parked in the back, then hurried to the Employee Only entrance. She had received all of her necessary credentials a week earlier, and now she used her name tag to swipe herself in.

The convenient care clinic was not a twenty-four/seven emergency room like the hospital. They didn't even open their doors until ten in the morning. The nurses were expected to make sure the lab was prepped and the rooms cleaned and sterilized, ready for the first round of patients, before then. The first hour tended to be one of their busiest, as people who had been sick all night and didn't want to go to the ER hurried into convenient care, hoping for a cheaper bill.

"You must be new." A pretty black girl with curly hair and green eyes and a plastic tub in her arms smiled as Luce stepped inside. She had to be wearing contact lenses, because that shade of green couldn't be natural with her skin tone.

That was so Eureka Springs. Total nonconformity, and a huge lean toward the creative side. It was a city of artists, people trying to create their own unique identity in a world where uniformity was the norm.

"Yeah, I'm new." Luce flashed her own smile. "I love your hair."

"This?" The girl pushed up on her black locks, barely managing to keep her hold on the tub as she did so. "I was just thinking how much I like yours. Such a pretty brown."

"Almost auburn," Luce agreed.

"I'm Caroline." The girl extended her hand. Luce took it, giving it a good shake. "I'm one of Dr. Dahler's nurses."

"Luce. Nice to meet you. I am, too. For Dr. Dahler, I mean."

Caroline's smile revealed beautiful white teeth. "You won't see him much except when he hands off patients. Come on. I'll show you the rounds, and you can tell me everything about yourself."

♥

By the end of the morning shift, Luce felt like she'd been working at the clinic for a month. The other nurses and receptionists were very friendly, and even the physicians were welcoming.

Luce took her lunch in the break room, buying a sandwich

and a fruit salad from the deli counter out front. Another woman in purple scrubs sat down across from her.

"I love the balloons," the nurse said. Her name tag read, "Regina."

"Thanks," Luce said. "I'm thinking I need to get some purple scrubs like yours."

Regina flashed a smile. She had her light blond hair pulled into a braid hanging over one shoulder. Even without make up, her blue eyes were large and luminous on her face; she was far too pretty to be a nurse. "I'm Regina," she said. She opened her fruit salad, removed all of the watermelon chunks, and began spearing the grapes with her fork. "Caroline told me you're the new girl. What clinic were you at before here?"

"I just finished my schooling and moved here from Vegas. This is my first placement," Luce said, not offering any more information. She had told a little bit of her story to Caroline, but she didn't feel like rehashing the personal details of her dysfunctional marriage to everyone.

"Oh. Big city. That must've been nice. What brings you here?"

"I grew up here, actually," Luce said.

Regina nodded. "I grew up in Huntsville."

"I've been there," Luce said, picturing the rural city half an hour away with just one main street. "We used to go camping just outside of there." Before her mom died and her dad closed himself off to his daughters.

"Tiny, right? I guess this place isn't much bigger, but it feels like it. Closer to Rogers and Fayetteville, anyway."

Rogers and Fayetteville, the "big" cities in the tiny mecca of northwest Arkansas. "True," Luce said. "Are you an artist?" Eureka was known for its creative ambiance, drawing people from around the nation to the artists' and writers' colonies.

Regina shook head. "I like to dance, but that's it. I've taken lots of classes, but I don't think I have that talent. You know, the one people are born with. The one that makes them great or not."

She knew exactly what Regina meant. She often felt that way about herself. The gene that granted someone success and happiness had landed on Melodee, giving her a beautiful family and a husband with a great career. But Luce it had skipped entirely.

She grunted and unwrapped her sandwich. "Yeah, well, let's hope that at some point the gene for success reveals itself in both of us."

"We can hope, right?" Regina said. She lifted a can of Diet Coke. "Here's to us. Finding the means to achieve our goals."

Luce lifted her glass of water. "To us."

CONNOR

*H*ow you feeling today? Connor texted Regina Friday morning. She'd seemed fine when he saw her on Thursday, but he knew from personal experience that a cold could vanish and reappear overnight.

Fine, she responded. *Already at work.*

Me too, Connor texted back. He stuck the key in the door and pushed open the shop. *Opening again.*

Three days in a row?

Enough with the texting. He punched in the alarm code to the store and dialed Regina's number.

"Hey," she said, answering on the first ring.

"Yeah, I'm opening again," he said without preamble. "Mom's hungover. Again."

Regina made a sympathetic murmur. "But wouldn't you

rather open than close?"

"Beside the point." Connor made the rounds in the store, flipping the sign to "Open" and checking the porcelain and glass fixtures. "She's a grown woman. She should be responsible. This store is her baby, not mine."

"I get it, babe," Regina said. "Hey, can I call you later? Work, you know."

"Yeah, sure," he said. He hung up the phone and counted the money in the till, then shut the cash register.

He drummed his fingers on the counter top, an intangible restlessness rising in his chest. He and Regina were out of sync, operating on different wave-lengths. They needed face-to-face time. Maybe he'd stop by and see her at lunch.

Now all he had to do was hang in there for the next three hours.

The time passed slowly. A woman waved hello when she walked past the store, and Connor waved back, recognizing Mrs. Manning who owned the bead shop a few stores down. How was Kerri was doing? He hadn't talked to Mrs. Manning's daughter in a few weeks.

He closed the shop up at noon and then walked a few stores down to the bead shop.

"Hey, I was hoping you'd be here," he said when he spotted Kerri behind the desk. "How are the plans for the chocolate shop going?"

She looked up and smiled at him, dark brown hair falling around her shoulders, her fingers wrapped in fingerless gloves in spite of the warm weather as she worked on beading a necklace at the lighted table. He'd known Kerri for years, ever since her mom tried to set them up. She'd been diagnosed with rheumatoid arthritis not too long ago, even though she wasn't any older than he was, and Connor felt a certain protectiveness toward her.

"Connor. Nice of you to stop by." The smile dimmed a little bit. "The shop's taking longer to get going than I want. But I still hope to have it up before Christmas."

"You let me know if I can help in any way."

"Thanks. I will."

She started to stand, and he held up a hand. "Don't get up." He went around the counter to give her a hug. "I need some advice."

"Go for it." Kerri raised her eyebrows.

He could see from her face that she'd lost more weight, but somehow Kerri always managed to have a smile. He knew her joints hurt worse every day. He also knew she didn't like to talk about it, so he didn't ask. "It's Regina."

"The girlfriend," Kerri clarified.

"Yes." Connor grinned.

"Problems?"

He heaved a sigh. "Not problems, exactly. But—" He frowned and chewed on his lower lip. "I keep thinking about another girl. Is that bad?"

Kerri looked thoughtful. "Thinking about her, no. But if you act on it, yes."

He nodded. "That's what I thought."

Kerri arched an eyebrow. "But keep in mind, Connor—if Regina had your heart, you wouldn't notice anyone else."

"Thanks, Ker." He bent and gave her another hug, careful not to hurt her. None of his guy friends ever had good advice the way Kerri did.

She patted his back as he pulled away. "Good thing that blind date my mom put us on didn't work out."

"But good thing it happened," he countered, shouldering his bag. "Or I'd have missed out on a friend."

"Keep me posted." Kerri turned her eyes down, already working on the beads again.

♥

"What do you mean, Regina's not here?" Connor furrowed his brow at the young receptionist, her short brown hair pulled into pigtails behind her ears. Why would Regina not be here? She'd told him she was at work. He'd caught her lying to him before, and he wouldn't put up with it again.

The girl looked at him like she wasn't sure what to make of him. "That's right, she's not here. Can somebody else help you?"

"Connor?"

He turned slightly at the sound of his name and started to see Luce coming out of the doctors' hallway, dressed in a nonstandard pink-polka-dots-on-black scrubs.

"Luce!" he said, momentarily forgetting his frustration with Regina. Immediately all his effort to remove Luce from his mind proved fruitless. Even in a ponytail, her hair caught the light in the room, drawing his gaze like a moth to a flame. "You work here?"

"I just started. Can I help you?" she asked. "Do you have an appointment?"

She sounded slightly accusatory. Was she still mad about the crash with her sister? "No, I came to see Regina. But apparently she's not here."

"Regina?" Luce blinked at him. "Oh! Regina." She grabbed a clipboard attached to the wall behind the receptionist and checked it. "She must be at lunch. I think I saw her earlier. Want me to check the break room?"

"Okay." Connor exhaled, some of his annoyance fading. He needed to stop assuming the worst. "If you don't mind." He flashed Luce a smile, hoping it softened his raging entrance.

"Sure." She smiled back, then she stepped through the glass doors and headed down the hall. Connor's eyes followed her, watched the way her hips swayed, making even the shapeless clothing seem fashionable. He pulled his head back as she disappeared from view and drummed his fingers on the counter, his face unexpectedly warm.

A moment later Luce was back. "She must've gone out. Sorry." Her light eyes surveyed his face.

"Yeah, sure." Connor shrugged and avoided her gaze. "Tell her I came by, will you?"

"Sure, I will."

"I'll catch you later." He swiveled to leave, and then spun back. "Oh, hey. I wanted to apologize again about the other day. Hope your sister's baby's okay." He turned and walked out the clinic doors, wincing slightly at his last comment. Hoped her sister's baby was okay? Ugh.

He pulled his phone out. He would try to track down Regina. Maybe there was still time to have lunch together.

Chapter Three

LUCE

"It's Friday, girl," Caroline said, blinking her green eyes with the sultry eyeshadow at Luce as they started the evening clean up. "What are your plans?"

Luce shrugged off the question, spraying disinfectant over the chairs and counters. "I just moved here, remember? I've got nothing."

She tried not to replay in her mind the scene of Connor walking into the clinic. She'd been able to appreciate what Melodee saw in him. When he smiled at her, she'd flashed back to high school, and instead of the handsome man he'd become, she remembered the shy, socially awkward boy who she'd tried to befriend.

For a moment this afternoon, she'd even wondered if he'd come to the clinic to see her.

What a laugh. He'd come for Regina. Who was, apparently, his girlfriend, as Regina had told her when she got back from lunch.

So even if Luce was interested—which she wasn't—she couldn't.

"You're also newly divorced, remember?" Caroline said, mocking her tone. "Let's paint the town before you lose your touch. Or have you already?"

Luce's face warmed. She regretted saying anything about her ex-marriage, but the two girls had gotten a bit chatty today while they waited for the radiologist to analyze a patient's x-ray. Luce put the cleaning spray away and blew a strand of hair out of her face with a puff of air. "Thanks for the offer. Maybe later."

Caroline rolled her eyes. "I've seen your type. It's always later."

They started down the hall while Luce frowned and mulled over those words. "Okay," she said. "Let's meet for lunch tomorrow."

"Girl," Caroline said, "you don't pick up guys at lunch."

Luce grinned. "But it's a start, right?"

"Whatever." Caroline heaved her eyes upward and shook her head. "Fine. Lunch tomorrow. And then we hit the town. But I have to warn you, I'm on call at the hospital. They might need me, they might not."

"Sure." Luce glanced at her. "I haven't heard you say much about guys. Are you dating anyone?"

"No," Caroline said, and the word came out so crisp and hard that Luce raised an eyebrow.

"I take it that's a bad thing?"

Caroline's expression softened, and she looked chagrined. "Sorry."

They stopped at the coat rack, and Luce slipped on her windbreaker, then shouldered her purse. "Something happen?"

"Well." Caroline shrugged, hands stuffed in her pockets. "Everyone here knows, so I guess I should tell you. I'm married."

"So?" Luce flipped her long hair out from under her jacket. "Is that bad?" Her eyes went to Caroline's naked ring finger.

"I didn't want to be insensitive. Not after what you told me."

"Please. No one needs to tiptoe around me. And most marriages don't end up as miserable as mine did." *Only about half.*

"We're separated," Caroline said. "So maybe mine will."

Luce sucked in a breath, the pain of her own recent separation and divorce clubbing her in the chest. "I'm sorry."

Caroline shrugged. "Don't be. We had issues. I kicked him out."

Caroline's voice didn't invite more inquiries, and Luce zipped her lips, fully aware of what it was like to not want to talk about it. *Shake it off, Caroline,* she thought, sending her friend mental encouragement.

They said goodbye in the parking lot, and Luce's thoughts once again rolled backward to when Connor stepped into the clinic.

Total idiot. Such a dolt.

To think Connor was looking for her when he just wanted to see his girlfriend.

Melodee called while she pulled on her seatbelt. "Hey, if you're not doing anything, you should come over for dinner."

Luce hesitated. She didn't want to start using her sister's family as a crutch, or develop the unhealthy habit of spending all of her time with them. "No, that's okay. I'll figure something out."

"Right. Are you going to sit on your kitchen floor and eat

out of a cardboard box? I won't even ask how you're going to cook something. Or did you find your can opener and SpaghettiOs?"

Luce laughed. "Okay. I'll come over for dinner." One time didn't mean she was relying on her sister to provide all of her meals, after all.

Her sister only lived ten minutes away on the north side of town, heading from the city toward the lake. They weren't on the lake by any means, but they were close enough that Melodee and her family frequently took a boat out. It was a tradition carried over from when their parents still lived in Eureka Springs. Luce had very fond memories of hot Arkansas summers and hanging out on the boat after water skiing.

She parked her car in the steep driveway, making sure to put on the emergency brake. She barely made it to the front door before it flew open, and Melodee's oldest child Kayla flew out of the house. She jumped in the air so Luce had to catch her.

"Hey, Kayla," Luce said. Kayla had just turned six, but still had all the exuberant energy of a four-year-old.

Jumping down, Kayla took a step backward, shoving her glasses up on her nose. Her blond hair was in a loose ponytail, with errant pieces falling around her face.

Melodee stepped outside, one hand resting on her protruding belly. "Kayla, why are you out here bothering your aunt? Let's get inside."

Kayla's little brother Timothy scooted out the door before Melodee could stop him. He wrapped an arm around Melodee's leg and stuck his thumb in his mouth, peering at Luce with blue eyes beneath his tousled blond curls.

It tugged at Luce's heart. "My word, Melodee, where did you get these children? They are so beautiful."

Melodee led them into the house. "Yes, they are. I'm sure that yours will be just as beautiful."

The remark hurt, though Luce figured Melodee meant to be encouraging. She chose to ignore it, pulling the front door closed behind her. She spotted a bowl of grapes on the counter and grabbed a few. "Does it make you miss Mom?"

Melodee paused by the refrigerator, her back to Luce. Then she opened it and pulled out a head of cabbage. "Yes," she said, bringing the cabbage and a cutting board to the island. "Especially when I have my babies." She pressed her hand to her bulging belly, her eyes glistening. "Then I really wish I had my mother."

Luce lowered her eyes to give Melodee a moment to grieve. "I wish I'd known her better." Their mother died when Luce was only twelve, but Melodee had been sixteen.

"But now I have you." Melodee began attacking the cabbage with force. "To be aunt and grandmother."

"Huh." Luce popped another grape. "Right."

"Kayla," Jay said, tugging on her ponytail, "go get your reading book. Let's practice your words."

Immediately Kayla's shoulders slumped, her mouth curving downward. "Dad," she whined.

"Nope. Go get it."

She sighed and dragged her feet all the way to her bedroom.

"Mommy, can I eat this?"

Luce and Melodee both turned around to see Timothy standing on top of the counter, reaching his hands into the cupboard.

Melodee shrieked. "Timothy, you get down right now!" She moved incredibly fast for a pregnant lady, grasping Timothy around the waist and hefting him back to the ground. "No food! We're going to eat dinner soon!"

Luce bit her lip to keep from laughing.

Kayla's little voice murmured from the living room as she settled into her father's lap, easy reader in her hands. Luce watched Jay, ever so patient as he corrected her words.

"He does reading time," Melodee said, handing Luce a knife and a tomato. "Slice."

Luce did as she was told. "He likes reading?"

"He has more patience than I do."

Timothy joined his sister, climbing up on his dad's other knee, and then onto his shoulder.

"He's a monkey," Melodee said. "He scares me to death."

Luce gave a wistful smile, glancing at them before turning her attention to the tomato.

She was only twenty-four. There was plenty of time in her life to get married and have kids.

But still, as she sat at the counter and watched Melodee and Jay interact with their children, there was only one word to describe the ache in her chest: jealousy.

CONNOR

Connor meant to call Regina when he left the clinic. But his mind wasn't on her. It was on the brunette with the pink polka-dot scrubs.

And then his break was over and he had to get back to the shop. He kept his mind busy, redirecting his thoughts to dredging up information for his classes. As soon as he closed up, he hurried home to get his exams finished and turned in before the deadline. If he aced this economics class, it might give him the leverage he needed to convince his mom to give him the shop.

He'd just submitted the last answer when his phone chirped.

Let's do something tonight, Regina texted. *It's Friday!*

Connor sat at the dining room table in his mother's house, papers spread out around him. He leaned back and stretched his arms before picking up the phone.

What do you want to do? he responded.

Pick me up at eight. I'll surprise you.

That was unusual. Connor wondered what kind of surprise she'd come up with. He dressed in dark jeans and a lightweight sweater. His mom had a couple of kayaks moored at the lake just west of Eureka Springs. Maybe he could convince her to come along.

Regina opened the door to her apartment with a flourish and a smile, dressed only in a tight red tube top and a short black skirt. His eyes roamed over her body, appreciating her curves at the same time that annoyance twisted in his gut. Why couldn't she have given him a head's up on what to wear? Judging from her attire, they were going clubbing.

"Hi!" she said, tossing her hair to the side. She'd added glitter to her face and the long blond curls.

"What's the plan?" he said, feigning ignorance.

She flashed him a very innocent smile. "Abby invited me to Eureka Live again. Is that okay?"

He refrained from rolling his eyes. Abby asked her to go clubbing at least once a week. "Better idea. Invite Abby here and we'll all go out to dinner."

Regina spread her arms wide. "They serve dinner there! It's perfect."

"The food's crap," Connor said, not backing down.

She gave him a pitiful look. "No, it's not. Besides, Abby's on the prowl."

As was everyone else who stepped into a club, especially if they went dressed like Regina was. That tube top was barely holding her in place, and Connor found himself itching to get her to the couch so he could have her to himself. "Let's just stay in. We'll order dinner. Have a nice evening here."

Regina turned and surveyed her apartment, her nose wrinkling as she took in the worn sofa and the mismatched lamps. Then she spun around and placed a hand on his chest. "We can stay in tomorrow. But I told her we'd come. Please? I don't like going either, but I don't want her to feel like she doesn't have anyone."

"All right." Connor growled in the back of his throat. He gripped Regina by her bare shoulders and kissed her. "But you owe me."

"And I'll repay you, I promise," she purred, running her fingers down his chest.

Connor glanced down at his sweater and jeans. Oh well. He was definitely overdressed.

Chapter Four

LUCE

Caroline and Luce went to Sparks Café for lunch, since Luce was craving a pulled pork sandwich and cookies.

"What kind of furniture are you looking for?" Caroline asked.

Luce shrugged. "I don't have anything, actually. When my ex and I split, I let him keep it all. I was so . . ." Luce trailed off and pressed her lips together. "I just didn't want it anymore."

Caroline narrowed her eyes at her. "He really broke your heart?"

"Well, he was my husband," Luce said defensively.

"Yeah, but a lot of people who get divorced find it's because they didn't actually like the person they married."

Luce poked at her pork, declining to comment. Was that what happened with Caroline? True, Luce hadn't liked the person she discovered Brian to be, but the person she thought he was, the person she'd married, she'd been desperately in love with.

Caroline dropped the subject, to Luce's relief. They chatted about work, their coworkers' love lives—Luce couldn't help being especially curious about Connor and Regina, who had been dating for almost four months—things that had changed in Eureka Springs in the past five years. Which wasn't much, really. Stores opened and closed, restaurants came and went, but Main Street remained pretty much the same.

"Come on." Caroline shouldered her purse and stood up. "Let's decorate your place."

They'd only made it a few feet out the door when Caroline's phone rang.

"Uh-oh," she said, checking the number. She sighed after she hung up. "They need me at the hospital."

Luce tried not to feel deflated. "I guess we all get a turn to be on call."

"Yes, well." Caroline gave her a hug. "Do you know where you're headed?"

Luce shrugged. "I think I know my way around." She couldn't help remembering Connor's words when they'd bumped into each other. His mom had a store on the strip. Would he be there?

"Good luck, then. See you Monday!" Caroline waved as she walked away.

Luce considered leaving her car at the cafe and walking to Main, but she decided it was worth it to pay the five dollar parking and be near the stores. Most of the furniture on the strip was eclectic and artsy, but why not? *It's just me now. I can cater to my own eccentric taste.* She found a kitchen table carved from a tree trunk with matching stools. She thought the price agreeable, and they said they'd deliver it. At least she had a place to eat now, though still no place to sleep.

She walked up Spring Street, her eyes acting of their own

accord as they sought out Connor's mom's shop. *Don't go in,* she told herself, but her feet slowed and came to a stop in front of a shop in the corner. A plaque above read, "Keystone Pieces."

Cute.

Luce hesitated only a moment. She was already here; couldn't hurt to see what was inside. Besides, it might not even be his store. She pushed open the door and stepped in, glancing once at the corner as the omnipresent bell jingled.

CONNOR

The bell clanged as a customer walked in. Connor finished wrapping the antique pitcher for the plump, dark-haired woman in front of him.

"Come on in, feel free to browse!" he called in greeting, even as the words clung to his throat. He knew his life held more for him than working as a store clerk. He stuck the last piece of tape on the thick brown paper and put the pitcher in a plastic bag. "Here you go, ma'am."

"Thank you."

He turned his attention to his newest customer. "Luce!" It was almost like his imagination conjured her just when he'd managed to banish her from his mind. "How are you?"

"I'm good," she said. Her hair was down and styled today, and she wore a bit more makeup, a flirty pink color on her lips. "I need to stock my condo and thought I'd check what you have."

"What are you looking for?" He came around the counter. Her flowery scent washed over him, bringing on a total flashback to high school. Did she wear the same perfume? For a moment he felt like a hormone-crazed teenager walking in a love-induced haze.

She stood in place and pivoted, taking in the store. "Everything, really. Furniture. Decorations. Kitchenware."

"You won't find any couches or beds here, but we've got a good variety of lamps. And antique plates, teapots, and spoons are our specialty."

"Hmm." She picked up a China plate and examined it, then replaced it with a Delphi blue one. "My tastes tend to be more modern," she admitted.

"Yeah." His shoulders sagged, disappointed he didn't have something he could entice her with. "We get new things from time to time."

She turned and gestured to the metal works on the wall. "Where do you get these?"

"Oh, those." His pride and joy. He came around the counter, removing his hands from his pockets and taking the giant star with embedded gemstones off-the-wall. "I met a couple of artists on a trip to Africa a few years ago. I'm still in touch with several. About once a year I go down and collect new pieces. They're the highlights of my collection."

Luce's eyebrows rose. "Fascinating. So you buy these directly from the craftsman?"

"That's right."

She moved to the counter and ran her hands over a flat wooden apple he kept on display there. She fingered the multiple intricate rings carved around it. "What is this? Some kind of pot holder?"

"Watch." He stepped around her, brushing her shoulder as he reached past her. He picked up the outer circle and lifted. The apple in the center remained planted on the counter, but the rings around it rose up like stadium bleachers, creating a wooden basket.

Luce gasped. "It's beautiful!"

"Probably my best-selling item. I saw them at a fair in New York four years ago. They were selling for eighty bucks each. I found a local artisan who could make them for me. I sell them for forty."

"I love it. It's not what I'm looking for today, though. Just need some pots and pans, bowls and plates. You know, kitchen things."

"How about this lamp?" He turned her attention to a tall lamp with a leopard-print shade. "Could light up a dark corner of your kitchen. It's a conversation piece for sure."

"How much is it?"

Too much. He pulled off the eighty- dollar tag and stuffed it in his pocket before she saw. "Twenty bucks. It's on clearance."

"I'll take it."

"Great choice." Connor unplugged the lamp and pulled it over to the register. "You won't regret it. Everyone who comes over will want to know the story behind it."

"Is there one?"

"Not that I know of."

"There is now." She smiled at him and then turned her head, but not before Connor saw the pink rush to her cheeks.

Her reaction encouraged him. "Hey, if you need furniture at a good price, I know a few places. I could take you."

Her fingers traced a lace doily on one of the end tables. "That's okay. I'm sure I can find them."

"I'm sure you can too. But sometimes it's more fun with another person."

She stepped nearer to him, fingering the shade of the lamp. "So. Regina. Your girlfriend, huh?"

Heat rushed to his face, and he tried to play it cool. "Uh.

Yeah." He'd almost forgotten.

"Maybe it's better I do my shopping by myself." She handed him a credit card.

Touche. How could he get himself out of this one? He could already imagine her putting a sticker on his head that read, "Player."

"Seriously." He handed her back her card. "I'd love to get together and catch up. Just as friends. I had no idea you're a nurse also."

"It was kind of spur-of-the-moment." A breath sighed out of her lips, and sadness crossed her face before her normal, stoic expression took over.

"I sense a story behind that one."

She took the lamp from him. "Let's just stick with the story behind how I found this wonderful lamp."

"You got it." He rested his hands on the glass case. "I hope you'll come back. Who knows what I might have next time that will catch your eye?"

A wisp of brown hair fell in her face, and she brushed it back. "I will. Thank you, Connor."

♥

He couldn't help it. He knew he should push her from his mind and maybe go find his girlfriend, but instead Connor called Tyson.

"Crescent Hotel, how can I direct your call?"

Oh good, Ty was working the front desk. "I want one of your haunted rooms. And all the champagne in the hotel. For tonight."

"If it wasn't the same ridiculous request you make every time you call, I might not know it was you," Ty said flatly. "Why don't you ever call my cell?"

"You never answer," Connor returned. He exhaled, then

said, "Luce just came in."

"Luce? Oh! The girl from high school."

"Yeah." Connor glanced around the shop, making sure it really was empty. "I swear, Ty, it's like no time passed. I was crazy about her and she never even considered me. Now—"

"You're still crazy about her and she's considering you."

Was she? "Something like that. Maybe she just wanted to buy a leopard-print lamp."

"Why would anyone want to do that?"

He laughed. "I don't know."

"Oh, I gotta go, I've got guests. But hey, Connor, if you feel this strongly, you gotta pursue it. Do what you have to, man."

Connor hung up and drummed his fingers on the counter. *Do what you have to.*

When the day finally ended, he flipped the shop sign to "closed." It had been a decent day. They'd made enough money in the morning that the afternoon slump hadn't hurt so bad. Connor finished up his ten-page essay and made an outline for the next.

And that didn't even begin to add in Luce's visit. He couldn't deny the excitement he felt whenever he thought of her. Was it just a lingering ghost effect from his high school crush?

You have a girlfriend, he reminded himself.

Speaking of which . . . hadn't she said they could have that night-in tonight?

His conscience nagged at him, telling him he owed her some quality time to make up for his cheating thoughts. He locked up the shop and headed down the steps behind the store, already dialing Regina's number.

"Hey," he said when she answered, his voice huskier than he intended. "I just got off work. How about I get sushi from that restaurant you love so much and come over?"

"Oh, Connor, that sounds so sweet," she said, her voice slightly muffled. Other noises battled to be heard through the speaker. "I'm really tired tonight, though. How about tomorrow?" Sounds echoed in the background, loud and thumping, high-pitched and giggly.

"Is there someone with you?" Connor asked, trying not to sound suspicious. She promised she wasn't talking to what's-his-face—Kale?—anymore.

"Oh, no. I just have the TV on pretty loud. Hang on." The phone went dead silent, and a moment later her voice spoke clearly with no noise behind it. "Is that better?"

"Yeah. Hey, I could just come over. You have to eat, right? We may as well do it together."

She yawned. "Not tonight, Connor. I have to work tomorrow and this is my only chance to rest. Let's get together Monday. Dinner?"

"Yeah, maybe." It would be another beautiful late September day. "We could go biking."

"Sure. Let's talk later. See ya, Connor!"

She hung up, sounding a little too perky for someone about to collapse into bed. Connor put his phone away and tried to shake off the constant feeling that she was keeping something from him. He'd grown up believing liars never changed.

He hoped there were exceptions to that.

♥

"Mom!" Connor pushed open the front door of their old Victorian house, taking the two steps necessary to cross from the entry into the kitchen. "I brought dinner!" He put the bags of sushi on the table. Darned if he wasn't at least going to eat well tonight.

His mom appeared in the hallway, her blond hair pulled

into a ponytail at the side and long dangly earrings brushing the shoulders of her fitted brown dress.

"Zip me up, will you?" she said, turning so he could.

"You look nice," he said, already sensing he'd be eating dinner alone. "Going out with Dave?" Just saying the name left a bad taste in his mouth.

"Of course. Where's Regina? I hate to leave you here alone."

"She's tired."

"Too tired for you?" Instantly his mom held up her hands and shook her head. "Sorry. None of my business. I'm sure you guys have things under control."

"Yep." Connor offered no more excuses for his girlfriend. He wasn't sure of anything right now. "Hey, while I've got you." Connor sifted through his messenger bag and pulled out the magazine he'd marked up a few days before. "I was thinking we could carry some pieces like this in the store. This is hand-carved mahogany from Johannesburg, and I happen to know a supplier—"

Her nose crinkled up. "But that doesn't really fit with our antiques."

Connor pushed down a wave of annoyance. "We could have a specialty line, or maybe just call it seasonal. We could try it, right? I can keep the prices low, give us a high profit margin."

She patted his cheek, and Connor jerked his head away.

"Now you sound like a business student," his mom chuckled. "The store's worked great the way it is for generations. Let's not rock the boat, okay? I let you have your shelf. Don't push me."

"Right," he muttered, turning in frustration. "I thought you were putting me in charge of the store."

"In charge of the sales, Connor. Not the mission statement."

"Which is what?" His temper was getting the best of him.

"Buy dead people's things for more than they're worth?"

She set her jaw. "If you want your own store, by all means, open one. But quit messing with mine."

He heaved a sigh and plopped his computer onto the table. *Maybe you should find a new employee,* he wanted to say. "It doesn't make sense, Mom. We can make our visions for the store fit together."

"I don't want to have this conversation anymore. I'll see you later." She stood on her tiptoes and kissed his cheek. "Have a good evening!"

He didn't answer, though he accepted her kiss. She drove him nuts, but after decades of just the two of them (mostly), he could never stay upset with her for long.

The front door closed behind her and the car purred out of the driveway. Connor opened up his sushi rolls and turned on the TV. Maybe he could find a game to watch and not feel so lame to be by himself on a Saturday evening.

LUCE

The call came Monday while Luce was wiping down a room after a patient exam. She glanced at her phone, not recognizing the number, and slipped it back into her scrubs. She'd answer it later.

Jenn, the receptionist, asked her to make copies for one of the nurses, and Luce promptly forgot about the unknown number. Until after her lunch break, when the call came again. Luce held the phone in her hand, staring at the scrolling number as she leaned against the wall. Something about them calling a second time had her heart skipping a beat. It was a California number. Did she know anyone from there?

The call ended, and Luce exhaled carefully, trying to calm her nerves.

Then her phone pinged that a voicemail had come through.

She gripped the phone. She knew she needed to listen to that message, but for some reason she dreaded it. She'd do it after work.

They called again at four o'clock. Luce stopped mid-filing behind the check-in counter and held stock still, listening to the ringing.

Caroline stepped up to the counter. "I need patient chart three-five-seven-nine. Can you grab it for me?"

"Yes," Luce said, but she didn't move.

"Are you okay?" Caroline cocked her head. "You look nervous."

"Someone keeps calling me." Luce pulled her phone out and set it on the counter between the two of them.

Caroline looked down at it. "Is it someone scary?"

"I don't know." Luce licked her lips. "I think it might be my ex."

"Why don't you answer it?"

Luce's insides twisted at the very thought. She closed her eyes, imagining hearing Brian's voice again. And then she imagined that voice snarling at her, accusing her, putting her down. She couldn't take it.

"They left a message." Caroline picked up the phone and held it out to her. "Listen to it. Then decide if you should freak out."

Luce took a deep breath. "Yes. You're right. Thank you." She put the phone away, intent on waiting until her shift was over to listen to the message.

But she couldn't. She could feel it burning a hole in her pocket, searing a cavity in her skin. Luce stepped into the bathroom and pressed the message button, her heart pounding in her chest as the recording began.

"Hi, Ms. Donovan, this is Arthur McCartney. I'm an attorney representing your former husband, Brian Donovan. We have a few details we need to discuss in regards to your holdings. Please give me a call at your convenience . . ."

He went on to rattle off a number, but Luce wasn't listening anymore. She pulled the phone away from her ear and looked at it. It shook in the palm of her hand. This guy had left her another message, but she didn't need to listen to it to understand what was happening. Brian had found her, and he wanted to take more money from her.

Luce's hands trembled as she unlocked the bathroom door and let herself out. Less than an hour until they closed the clinic and she'd be able to leave. She could hold it together that long until she could sit down and talk with Melodee.

Another call came as she locked the clinic doors. She told herself not to look at it, but she couldn't help it. She picked up the phone. This number she recognized, even if she'd deleted it from her phone months ago when the divorce was final. Now she realized she should have blocked it also.

Brian.

She sent it to voicemail. He also left a message.

"You still look like you've seen a ghost," Caroline said. She joined Luce in the hallway as they headed for the exit.

Regina, on the other side, twisted her head around Caroline to study Luce. "What's wrong? Something going on?"

"It's nothing." Luce held the door open for the other girls. "Just someone who keeps calling me, that's all."

"Was it your ex?" Caroline asked.

Regina made a sympathetic noise. "Exes. They think they still own us even after it's over." She zipped up her jacket as a wind blew through.

"Where's Connor tonight?" Caroline asked her.

Luce stopped at her car and took her time putting her things inside, curious what Regina would say.

"Who knows? Probably working. He's determined to make

a new name for that shop."

"Looks like he's succeeding. I've seen a few new things in there."

"Me too," Luce piped up, in spite of herself.

Regina focused her crystal blue eyes on Luce. "Oh, you've been in it?"

Her face warmed. "Yes. Connor helped me pick out a few things for my house."

"He's so sweet that way," Regina said.

Luce opened her door and climbed in. "See you ladies tomorrow."

They waved, but Regina and Caroline stood there chatting after Luce had pulled out of the parking lot. She wondered how many times her name slipped into the conversation. She picked up her phone and sighed, seeing the message Brian had left her. She didn't have the courage to listen to it by herself.

CONNOR

Monday passed by in a blur as Connor finished up a thirty-page paper. Thirty pages. Professors required the darnedest things. He wasn't getting a degree in creative writing; he was getting it in business management. He was pretty sure he could say in two pages everything that he took thirty pages to explain just for the sake of the class. Did they actually want corporate leaders to be long-winded?

He submitted the essay at 5:07 p.m. He stood up and stretched his hands over his head, cabin fever making him fidgety. Grabbing his phone, he called Regina.

"Hey," she said, answering on the second ring. "I can't talk. We're closing up the clinic."

"Are we still doing something tonight?"

"Sure. Pick me up here."

Some of the tightness in his chest eased. That had been unexpectedly easy. "Where do you want to go?"

"You choose. I'm good with whatever. Stop by my apartment and get me a change of clothes, will you?"

"You bet. See you in an hour."

He used the key hidden under the porch light to let himself into her apartment. Regina was a neat freak, and the kitchen and living room hardly looked lived in. Only her bedroom showed signs of life, with clothing strewn across the bed and dresser.

What he really wanted to do was go biking; but he knew Regina didn't have a bike. They'd been talking about going to one of the Artosphere's traveling concerts for weeks, though, and tonight the outdoor music concert was being held on an overlook above Lake Leatherwood.

It might be just what they needed to rekindle their relationship.

Picking out the right outfit was a bit harder. Regina always looked sleek and put together; Connor had no idea what she would want to wear. He finally chose a long-sleeved T-shirt and leggings.

He got to the clinic five minutes before it closed and parked in the back. He watched as the doctors vacated the building first, leaving the nurses and receptionists to close up. Then the nurses trickled out one by one.

He couldn't help it. Luce caught his eye when she walked out, talking to the nurse with the curly hair. Luce didn't see him, which was just as well, because he watched her all the way to her car.

Out of his peripheral vision, he saw Regina coming, and he

turned his gaze toward her. He rolled the window down.

"Hey." She smiled a him as she rested her elbows on the sill. "What are we doing?"

Her smile didn't make his heart skip the way it used to, and he suddenly feared keeping this relationship alive wasn't even a good idea. *Make the best of it*, he told himself. "Hey." He grabbed the plastic sack he'd put her clothes in and handed it through the window. "I thought we'd finally go to the Artosphere."

"The what?" Her slender eyebrows rose over deep blue eyes.

"The Artosphere. Remember? The outdoor music theater?"

"Oh. Is there dancing?"

"Uh. Maybe."

"Okay." She smiled again and took the bag. "I'll change in my car. Be right back."

She could have changed here in his car, but she didn't ask to, and Connor didn't offer. There was a distance growing between them that he didn't feel like bridging.

Although when she emerged from her vehicle in the tight purple shirt and black leggings, he couldn't help admiring her.

"You look hot," he said as she climbed into the passenger side.

She tugged on the shirt and gave him an odd look. "These are like exercise clothes, Connor. They're not for going out in public."

"Really?" How was he supposed to know? "You still look hot."

She rolled her eyes and sighed.

He shrugged and pulled the car out of the lot, then headed into the foothills.

"Where is this?" Regina asked as he began the switchback

turns.

"Overlooking Lake Leatherwood."

"Did you bring bug spray?"

"No." He glanced at her. "That's why your clothes cover you."

She sighed again and dropped the mirror open on the visor. She ran her fingers under her eyes. "I'm going to sweat and my makeup will run."

"It won't be hot when the sun starts to go down. We'll see the sunset over the lake. You'll love it."

A few college kids in orange vests directed traffic, motioning Connor to park with several other cars on a grassy field. Connor waved a thank you and turned off with the others.

"Are we here?" Regina asked, getting out of the car.

"Almost." Connor joined her, shoving his hands in the pockets of his vest jacket. "We have to walk the rest of the way."

Regina glanced down at her feet and then back at him. "These aren't walking shoes."

He took in the flats she'd worn to work. She hadn't had anything better at her apartment. "You'll be okay. It's not climbing. Just walking."

"Connor." She exhaled and looked heavenward as if trying to find the simplest words to explain something to him.

"What, Regina?" he said, getting frustrated. "I didn't get you the right clothes. Sorry. No bug spray. You've got the wrong shoes. Okay. What of it? I thought you wanted to do this."

Some of the hardness went out of her features. "You're right. I'm sorry. Long day at work. I guess I just wanted to sit somewhere air-conditioned and put my feet up."

He ran a hand through his hair. "It's fine." He didn't want to be here anymore, either. Her negative attitude put him off. But they were here. "We don't have to stay long." He put his hand out, and she took it. "We can a least check out the food trucks."

"Food trucks are good." She squeezed his hand, her smile warmer.

Conner returned the smile and let her pull him toward the gathering crowd. But he felt like he was watching the beginning of the end of a poorly made movie.

Chapter Six

LUCE

M elodee met her on the walkway as soon as Luce pulled up.

"What's wrong?" Melodee asked, one hand supporting her lower back. "You sounded all shook up."

Luce exhaled, hoping her smile looked braver than she felt. Her eyes darted to Melodee's stomach, and she felt bad burdening her sister, but who else did she have? "Brian called."

"Oh." Melodee didn't look as horrified as Luce wanted her to be. "What did he say?"

"I don't know. I haven't listened to the message."

"Give it here." Melodee held out her hand.

Feeling sheepish but relieved, Luce placed the phone in her sister's palm. Melodee hit the voicemail button. Brian's voice, though tiny through the speaker, still reverberated in Luce's ears, full of the snarling and spite Luce had so feared. She couldn't make out the words, but there was no mistaking the tone.

Melodee pressed her lips into a thin white line, her eyes narrowing to slits with every word. Then she hung up and held the phone out to Luce.

"Well?" Luce said anxiously, biting down on her lip.

"Well." Melodee met her eyes and placed her hands on Luce's shoulders. "I think it's time you got a lawyer."

Luce could hear the kids and Jay laughing and talking in the kitchen, but all she could think of was this newest threat. She stepped into the house and began to pace the circular rug in the entryway. "What did he say?"

"That he has a lawyer and you owe him money. He found out about your trust fund and he's mad he didn't get any of it."

"It was never our account!" Luce exploded. Brian had already taken everything from her. She added him to all her accounts when they got married. The ones that he didn't flat out run into the ground, he transferred the funds into his own private accounts. He left her bankrupt, and by the time she realized what she had married, it was too late.

Almost.

Luce had one account her parents set up for her as a child, one that she never used and had never added Brian to. And yet every month she sent money to it. Luce was eternally grateful she'd never revealed it to him.

"He says it was illegal for you not to disclose it," Melodee said.

Luce covered her face with her hands. "Was it illegal?" While she hadn't had a lawyer, she'd sought plenty of legal advice. They'd all said the same thing: any accounts she had privately before she got married were still hers.

"Absolutely not," Melodee said firmly. "But you need to get

someone on your side. Someone to reassure you."

She lowered her hands and nodded, letting out a deep breath. She wanted to say she couldn't afford a lawyer. But truthfully, she couldn't afford to not have one. "I guess it's a good thing I have a job."

Melodee favored her with a smile. "And a new, separate account."

♥

Neither Brian nor his lawyer called Luce all week. As the days crept by, her urgency to get a lawyer abated, and some of the anxiety and tension went out of her. She hoped the threat had also disappeared and tried to shove it from her thoughts.

Getting Connor out of them was much harder.

He hadn't come into the clinic since the previous week. Just when Luce started to think maybe they'd broken up, Regina started gushing over their date to the Artosphere, and Luce found herself walking away before anyone could see the jealousy broiling in her chest.

Why now? She hadn't even glanced twice at any of the guys who tried to date her in the past year. Was it because he was unattainable that she had allowed herself to crush on him?

She let herself into her condo and put a bag of groceries on the counter. Time for yoga. Pulling up some music on her phone, she changed from the puppy-covered scrubs into something more comfortable. But even as she dimmed the lights and lowered her body into Downward Dog, her eyes landed on the pottery wheel, still in the box where she had placed it last week.

Shake it off, she told herself, her muscles groaning as she moved into Upward Dog. *Concentrate on breathing.* She closed her eyes. Breathe in. Breathe out. Breathe in . . .

She peeked one eye open, stealing a glance at the pottery

wheel. Still there. She snapped her eye shut.

What the heck. Luce dropped out of her pose, her breath whooshing out of her. Not this time. This time she was going to actually do it.

She turned the lights back on and set up the wheel on her tree-trunk table. The clay was next, along with a bowl of water. Luce moistened it to just the right level so that it was pliable. Then she threw it on her wheel and jammed her foot down on the pedal, spinning fast. This was not about art. This was vengeance. Vengeance on Brian, for threatening her, for taking away her ability to trust. And, if she were honest, it was a way to release her mounting frustrations about a certain man with a store on Spring Street.

She pulled at the clay on the wheel, feeling it twist beneath her fingers. She ran her palms over the lip of it, hollowing out the middle and forcing it up, up, up. She created a long, elegant neck, giving what had been nothing but a lump new form. Making something beautiful.

And then, channeling all the emotion inside her, she thrust her fist into the base, crumpling it like nothing but tissue paper. It wasn't enough. She did it again and again, punching the clay down, raising it up just so she could knock it over. She turned the wheel off and stared at the lump of knobby clay. She cast her eyes around her condo, looking at the bare accommodations. There wasn't much here. It didn't even look like someone lived here.

No wonder Connor didn't notice her. She was a broken person, only a half a soul.

She detested that weak, spineless person.

Luce pounced upon a box of finished pottery pieces. She opened it up, carefully removing a glazed pie plate. It was a deep dish with an ombre of colors bleeding into each other. At her shop she had sold these and matching sets, mugs and plates and bowls. They would fetch a nice price, and they were beautiful. Some of her best-selling items.

Digging deeper into the box, she pulled out two more pie plates, a set of canisters, and a mug. All of them oven proof, dishwasher proof, even broiler proof. She cradled the mug in her hands tenderly, gently, admiring the perfectly curved brim and the tempered glazing.

Then she thrust her arm over her shoulder and threw it as hard as she could at the opposite wall. It hit next to the fireplace, crashing into the brick and shattering into shards of broken stone.

Luce heaved a sob, released by her furious onslaught. She pictured Brian coming into her storefront, hands shoved in the pockets of his board shorts, flip flops slapping the tile floor. The air conditioning pumped tirelessly, cooling the sidewalk outside and inviting shoppers to enter. He'd stood there, blond hair windblown, skin as bronzed as a surfer's, and he'd effusively praised her work. Flattered her. Admired her. Won her over.

She heaved the pie plate, tossing it after its companion. The crash loosed another sob within her. One more pie plate, then another, and then she stopped, surveying the damage. Was it enough to kill the old Luce? She wanted to be stronger, more vibrant, more confident. More independent. Luce pulled her knees up to her chest and wrapped her arms around them. She buried her face in the crevice formed by her legs and cried until her throat ached, until her head throbbed, until her whole body felt as though it had been squeezed into a vice and slowly tightened until there was nothing left of her.

CONNOR

Regina didn't seem to notice Connor's change in moods after the Artosphere. She even invited him to stay over, but he knew a round in the sack would only muddy the waters more. And he needed to think clearly.

They made plans for Friday, and Connor left it at that. He didn't ignore her calls, but he didn't call her, mostly testing to see how his life felt without her.

It felt fine.

Regina called him Friday as he clicked through a website at the store, indulging his guilty pleasure to imagine how he could reinvent the store's image.

"Hey, Gee," he said, settling back and spinning on the stool. "I'm about to close up here. What did you want to do tonight?"

"I'm working the walk-in clinic tomorrow," she told him. "I'm just going straight to bed."

He could hear her heavy breathing as she walked up the flight of steps to her apartment. "I'll get you home by a decent hour. I promise."

"What fun is that?" she laughed. "I better not. I hate being sleepy on Saturdays."

Never bothered her when she wanted to go clubbing. "You're off at noon?"

"Yes."

"How about tomorrow, then?"

"Yeah, that sounds lovely." She hummed, a low and throaty sound. "I'll call you when I get home."

"Okay." He got that nagging suspicion again that she wasn't telling him something.

The two of them needed to have a serious discussion.

When Saturday came around, he was too anxious to wait for her call, and instead headed to the clinic to meet her after her shift ended.

He shouldn't have been surprised to see Luce talking to the receptionist with the pigtails, but he pulled up short by the automatic doors. Just his luck that she would be here today. And she wore blue scrubs with fluffy white clouds on them that made her look dang cute.

Putting on a smile and trying to look calm, he walked over to the family practitioner intake desk.

"Connor," Luce said, putting down the flower pen and smiling at him. Suddenly she didn't look cute anymore, but feminine and alluring. She reached a hand toward his arm but pulled it back.

Not before Connor noticed the motion.

"Hey," he said, eyes tracking to her hand. Was she about to touch him? "Just looking for Regina."

Her brows furrowed together. "Regina?"

"Yeah." Connor avoided looking directly into her eyes even as his face warmed. Did she know he was attracted to her? "My girlfriend?" He tacked on a smile, hoping she'd find humor in the statement.

She cleared her throat. "Sorry if this sounds like *déjà vu*, but, uh . . . she's not here."

He pulled out his phone and checked the time, even though he knew it wasn't noon yet. "Did she call in sick?"

"I—I don't know. Let me find out." Luce pushed open the swinging glass doors behind her and disappeared down the hall.

"I haven't seen her today," the receptionist offered. Jenn, her badge said.

"Thanks," Connor said, then turned away to wait for Luce.

Luce returned holding a clipboard, which she scanned with pursed lips. "She wasn't scheduled to work today."

Connor exhaled. That was not an answer he'd been expecting. "She told me she was," he said lamely.

Luce glanced around as if hoping someone would rescue her from this awkward conversation. "I'm sorry. I can call her if you like."

"I have her number," he all but growled. He turned and strode briskly from the clinic, aware that his exit was rude but too upset to care. His heart hammered with certain knowledge of impending disaster.

Why would Regina lie? What excuse would she have this time?

Whatever it was, she'd be saying it to his face.

Connor made the drive to her complex in a record twelve minutes, then he ran up the steps to her second-story apartment, keys jangling in his hand. He'd spotted her car parked down below, so she had to be here. Television sounds and muted conversations came from the apartments around her, but Regina's was silent.

He knocked on the door, politely, not wanting to make a scene. "Regina?" he called.

No answer. He reached into her porch light and pulled out the spare key, then let himself in.

All the lights were off, the curtains pulled shut. He closed the door and flipped on the kitchen light. Neat and tidy. No one had eaten here in awhile; no dishes in the sink, nothing on the counter.

"Regina?" He spoke her name softly as he entered the apartment.

A low groan came from the bedroom. Connor headed that direction, wrinkling his nose at the smell of sweat and vomit.

Some of his anger dissipated; maybe she called in sick the night before. "Hey, it's me. Are you sick?"

She lay sprawled out on her bed, face down in nothing but her underwear and a tank top. She lifted her head when she saw him.

"Connor. What are you doing here?"

"You okay, Gee?" He turned on the bedroom light, but she buried her face in her pillow.

"No lights!" she croaked.

And then Connor understood. "You're hungover."

A muffled response came from under the pillow.

Connor approached the bed and stopped. It didn't make sense that she'd sat at home and gotten drunk.

By herself?

Regina hadn't said another word from the pillow, and he walked through the room to the bathroom. Here he found a short, strapless black dress cast aside on the linoleum floor. A rock sank in his stomach. She hadn't put this dress on to hang out alone.

He turned around and faced the bed, crossing his arms over his chest. "You're cheating on me, aren't you. Is it that guy— Carl? Clyde?" They'd fought over him before, when Connor discovered Regina's friend Carla was actually a guy. She'd insisted they were only friends, but his text messages were more than friendly, and Regina finally told Carl to stop calling her.

That had been a tough one, and Connor had almost called it off then. But as far as Connor knew, she and Carl hadn't had any contact in weeks.

She lifted the pillow from her head and pushed herself up. Black makeup lined her bloodshot eyes and was smudged around her eye sockets, and her perfect curls from the night before were broken and stiff. "You mean Kyle? No, you've got this wrong." She groaned again and winced, pressing a hand to her forehead.

Connor worked hard to keep his voice under control. "Oh. So it's a different guy this time." His fury pounded in his temples, but if he yelled at her, she'd shut down. And what was the point? "How long?" Now all those nights when she didn't want to get with him made sense, all the times she'd said she wanted to go to bed early. The indignity, the disrespect, infuriated him. The least she could have done was break up with him first.

But what did he expect? Total honesty. He should have broken up with her after the first lie.

When she didn't answer, he made for the door. "I'll see myself out."

"Connor, wait." She stumbled out of the bed, grabbing the wall for support. With her pretty face so marred by black makeup, she looked more like an evil witch than a vulnerable girl. "I'm not seeing anyone. I'm not cheating on you. I just—I like to go clubbing."

Her words came out in a rush, and Connor waited for them to make sense. When they didn't, he said, "What?"

"I like to go clubbing." She blinked at him. "I've been going to the club in Rogers."

He pictured his girlfriend dancing by herself at the club in that sexy black dress. No, not by herself. He re-imagined the picture, this time with several horny boys bumping and grinding around her. Working to keep his voice under control, he said, "When?"

"Almost every night. Sometimes I go to Eureka Live." She sighed. "I love to dance. I like to drink."

"But you told me you hate clubbing."

"Because you do!" she exclaimed. "You really didn't give me a choice, if I wanted to date you!"

As flattering as that was, it wasn't true. "I never said you couldn't go clubbing. Just not by yourself."

"You said everyone who goes is shallow."

He admitted it sounded like something he'd say. "What of it? Prove me wrong, then! So all those times when you said your brother had an emergency, were you going clubbing?"

She whirled her fingers, her expression guilty. "He owns the club in Rogers. I get in for free."

His initial shock was wearing off, and he couldn't help feeling a bit hurt. She'd met Kyle at a club. "After Kyle, you promised you'd never go without me. People only go there looking for one thing."

"Not everyone." She lifted her chin, an attempt at feistiness crossing her rumpled features. "That's not what I'm looking for. I just go for fun."

He didn't believe her. Any more than he believed Kyle had only been interested in friendship. "Why did you lie to me?"

"Self-explanatory, isn't it? I knew you wouldn't like it."

"Well, of course not!" he snapped. "My girlfriend sneaks off dancing behind my back all hours and texts and calls random guys who she picks up at clubs? What's not to like?"

"I just like to dance and have fun!"

"And there's nothing wrong with that. But I'm done."

Something like panic flickered across her face. "I'm sorry," she said, her tone desperate. "Give me another chance."

"This already was your other chance!" Connor yelled. Immediately he pulled back, regretting the outburst. What else had she lied about? "Well, that's that." He turned away from her.

"Please. No more hiding. Connor, I really like you."

It was too late. He didn't want to draw this relationship out any more. "Try it with Kyle."

"Connor!"

Her voice called after him as he strode down the hall. But he didn't look back.

♥

Connor threw himself into his studies and tried to ignore the gaping hole that used to be a social life and a girlfriend. It had gotten very comfortable, having someone to turn to when he was lonely, an immediate Plus One for activities and events.

This gave himself a chance to regroup. Sunday morning he kayaked on the lake before taking over at the shop in the afternoon. Monday after the shop closed, he and his mom planned a bike ride. He waited for her to put on her windbreaker and biking pants.

"Won't you get cold?" she asked him. October had brought a cold spell to Eureka.

"No," Connor said. "I ride too fast for the wind to catch me."

"Show off." She stuck her tongue out at him.

"See if you can keep up."

The ride invigorated him, got the blood pumping in a hot and heavy way that had nothing to do with women. He pulled out of the seat as the road turned down, letting gravity do the work for him. This had to be what flying felt like. Then he sat and leaned over the handlebars, legs pumping to get back up the hill. He stopped and waited for his mom.

She huffed and panted at the top. "Okay," she gasped out. "I'm a little out of shape. How many miles have we gone?"

"Two. Maybe two and a half. But the restaurant's only a mile away."

She groaned, but he just grinned at her. "Sushi, Mom. Think of what's waiting for you."

"I'm thinking, I'm thinking," she gasped out.

Connor took off again, but he slowed his pace, matching his mom all the way to the restaurant. They locked their bikes outside and left their helmets there, shaking out their hair as they stepped inside.

"Wasn't that awesome?" he said, grabbing his mom's shoulders and giving them a squeeze.

"I have a headache." She pressed the palm of her hand to her temple.

"That's because you can't get through the evening without a glass of wine."

She let Connor order for them, then she lowered her menu to the tabletop. "How are you handling your breakup?"

Connor had just taken a drink of soda, and now he choked. He mopped up the mess with a napkin. "What?"

She narrowed her eyes at him like only a mother can do. "You and Regina."

"How did you know we broke up?"

"I'm your mother, Connor," she said like he was an idiot. "I know everything."

He looked at her, bemused. "I'm doing all right. I knew it wasn't going to work out."

"Someday you'll find the right woman."

"Will I?" He leaned toward her across the table, frustration making him open up. "What girl would do what we just did? Hop on a bike with me? Go out to the lake, hike up a mountain to see a sunset?"

His mother gave a wistful smile. "You're such a romantic."

He shook his head and settled into the booth. "Girls these days are different. They just want makeup and clothes and money. And they don't care who provides it."

She made a tsking noise with her tongue. "If you find a girl at a bar, yes."

He laughed and took another sip of his soda. That was where he'd found Regina, all right, hanging with a bunch of girls at the Rowdy Beaver. "Touché."

"Maybe you should hunt at the gym."

"Maybe." But Connor's mind already flashed on another girl, dressed in scrubs with her hair in a ponytail.

Maybe he should just hang outside the medical clinic.

Their sushi rolls and miso soup arrived, and his mom used chopsticks to scoot a few pieces over to her plate.

"It's not just girls, you know," his mom said softly, surprising him by redirecting the conversation. "Men can be just as fickle."

She was thinking of his dad. Connor clenched his jaw and stared out the window, the slow-burning anger churning up in his stomach like bile.

His dad made her boyfriends look good.

"There's an estate sale this weekend in Bella Vista," she said, her tone anxious as she changed the subject.

Connor followed the new train of thought gratefully. He turned his gaze away from the window and to his food. "There's a sale in Joplin too," he said, tipping his spoon back and slurping his soup. "We could divide and conquer." Both cities were about an hour away, but not in the same direction.

"Don't slurp. It's much more fun to spend time together. We can do both."

"I hate these sales, Mom." Junk they would price up too high and try to convince people to buy so he could clear it off the shelves and make room for more junk. "I'll stay and watch the store."

"We can close for a day. No one will miss us."

He shot a quick glance at her, wondering if she knew how true that was. There was a metal-working shop in Neosho, a small city between Eureka and Joplin. If he could convince her to stop there, it might be worth it. "I'll think about it."

She clucked her tongue at him. "Really, you'd rather stay at the shop?"

"I'll think about it," he repeated.

Tuesday rained all day, normal fall weather, but Wednesday brought the sunshine back. Since he didn't have to take over at the store until lunch time, Connor decided to enjoy the sunshine and walk up Spring Street. He sat outside at a small round table with a "For Sale" sign on it, watching the crowds of people walk down the sidewalk. He was kind of blocking the way, but it amused him to watch people walk around him.

Then he sat up straighter as he recognized the slender girl heading up the sidewalk, just going around the bend next to his mom's shop. Even if she hadn't been wearing white scrubs decorated in little Dalmatians, he knew Luce.

His pulse raced, and he settled back in his wrought-iron chair. He'd thought of her at least once a day since breaking up with Regina, but short of walking into the clinic, he didn't know how to reach her. Yet there she was. Should he go talk to her? He grimaced. She worked with Regina and probably didn't have the best impression of him.

And then she stopped at his mom's store and pushed the door open.

That did it. Connor scraped his chair back across the sidewalk and jogged down to the store. The bell jangled when he stepped inside, but his mom barely glanced at him before returning her attention to Luce.

". . . leopard chair," Luce was saying, pivoting in a circle inside the narrow store.

"To match a leopard lamp?" His mom pursed her lips together, looking nonplussed. "You're better off at a furniture store."

"Yeah, but, everything they have is so—trendy."

"I know what you mean. You need something with character."

"Yes, that's it."

Luce and his mother shared a knowing smile.

Almost hating to interrupt, Connor cleared his throat. "Hey, Luce, how are you?" he said, as if happening upon her by chance.

She swiveled to face him, and the expression she wore was one of someone caught with their hand in the cookie jar. "Oh. Hi."

"You two know each other?" his mom asked, her keen blue eyes zeroing in on Luce with more interest than before.

"Yeah, we went to high school together." Connor shoved his hands in his pockets and leaned against the door. "Luce just moved back."

His mom smiled and thrust her hand out, a predatory grin spreading across her face. "Jessica Thomas. I'm Connor's mom."

Luce looked startled. "Nice to meet you." She shook the tips of the extended fingers.

His mom turned to him. "She needs furniture, Connor, but not the upstyle type from a store. Why don't you take her to one of our vendors?"

"You bet," he said, knowing his mom would have a field day with his answer later but not caring at the moment.

"Oh, I couldn't impose—" Luce began.

"It's not an imposition." Connor stood up straight, dropping his hands to his sides. "I needed to go anyway, see if they have more things for the store. I can take you now, if you have time."

"I can drive—my car's just down on Main Street."

"Mine's behind the store. I'll play you for it." He put his fist out and placed his palm underneath it.

Luce looked at his hands, a smile peeking about her lips, and then she met his eyes. "Are you doing 'rock paper scissors'?"

"Best way to make a decision."

She gave a little laugh, almost a giggle but not quite, and placed her hand on top of his fist. A pleasant shiver tickled into his chest.

"No need," she said. "You win. You can drive."

"Thanks for coming in!" his mom shouted gaily after them.

"Where are we going?" Luce asked, clutching her purse to her shoulder as she made her way down the rickety wooden stairs behind the store. Only because her hand was occupied clasping the strap did he not reach out and take it.

"We have vendors that shop all the estate sales in the area. Rogers, Eureka, Berryville, Bella Vista. If you find something you like, they'll give you a better price since you're with me."

"Oh." Luce lifted her eyebrows, looking suitably impressed. "Well, thank you."

They reached the bottom of the steps, and this time Connor succeeded in wrapping his hand around her arm just above the elbow. "Careful. The sidewalk is uneven here."

"Isn't it everywhere in Eureka?" she joked, but the comment was said with affection instead of derision.

"You like it here?" he asked, guiding her toward the company truck.

"Of course I do. This is my home."

Connor glanced at her. "Me, too. I love it." He wanted to ask her why she'd left it, then, if it wasn't to escape the small-town feel.

She didn't say anything else, just kept her eyes down and focused on the cracked sidewalk in front of them. But she didn't move her arm away from him, and her stature seemed less reserved. He studied the tilt of her head, the lift of her lips. The five years since high school had matured her, filling out her face and giving her the look of a woman instead of a girl. The smile lines around her eyes had faded as if she rarely used them now, but the remnants of the peppy, joyful high school student he'd shyly admired still existed.

As if feeling his thoughts, she lifted her face and smiled. "You've changed since school."

A pleasurable thrill shot through him. "I'm surprised you remember me."

The smile deepened. "You didn't talk much. You were always watching but never speaking."

Connor grunted. "Maybe best you don't remember." He flinched a little, remembering how he'd battled acne and felt his limbs were too long for his body. "I grew into myself."

"You did," she agreed.

"You always planned to be a nurse?"

"No." She stopped when he did at his mom's truck and waited while he opened the door for her. "Still don't plan on it, actually. It's just something to tie me over."

He waited while she got in, then climbed in on his side. "That's a lot of schooling for something temporary. Why nursing?"

She shrugged her shoulders. "I like the scrubs."

He laughed, thinking of the fun prints he'd seen her wear.

"They are cute." She was, at least.

She smiled back. "See?"

He shot her a quick glance before focusing on the road in front of him. "You like working at the clinic?"

She gave him a kind of exasperated look. "It's fine."

About as fine as working for his mom's store, apparently. "What do you really want to do?"

"What about you?" she said, her blue-green eyes narrowing. "You planning to be in the curating of antiques business forever?"

"Curating of antiques?" Connor echoed. He laughed. "Now I remember why you tutored me in English."

She smiled, her shoulders relaxing a bit.

"But no. Not my plan." He put the blinker on as they waited their turn to merge onto the highway leading out to Holiday Island, a retirement village on the lake. "I'm working on my Masters in business. Then maybe I can convince my mom that I actually know what I'm doing with the store."

"Why?"

Loaded question, and he considered how to answer it. "There are a lot of things I'd like to sell, but they don't fit her vision."

"Like what?"

He shrugged. "Well, hand-made goods. Things that aren't always local. I want a rotating selection of ethnic wares. A few years ago I went to Africa and made lots of contacts, I've got loads of really neat things we could sell. And I've got a contact in Italy just waiting for me to send over my flight information —" He broke off. "Those are the things that excite me."

"That's cool," Luce said.

He risked a glance at her and found her studying him carefully. Her cheeks reddened when he caught her eye, but she didn't look away. He looked back out the windshield, a smile pulling at his lips.

"Here we are," he said, finally pulling into the large red barn that had what looked like a perpetual yard sale going on.

Luce paused before getting out, her hand on the door handle. "I'm sorry about you and Regina."

He grimaced. Made sense that she would have heard about it, since they worked together. "Don't be. It wasn't working." And now he had the chance to pursue other people. And that could only be a good thing.

"Still—can't be easy." She pushed open the door and climbed out of the truck before he could help her. He watched her eyes take in the mismatched lamps and bookcases leaning against the barn.

"It's not all a find," he said, joining her and shoving his hand in his pocket before he tried to take hers again. "A lot of it's junk that nobody wants. Like Great-Aunt Junie's pig collection." He wove through piles of rugs and tea cups and porcelain roosters. "But every once in awhile, you find something amazing." He stopped to pick up a teacup, turning it over to look at the manufacture date.

"Like that?" Luce asked.

"Almost." Connor put it down. "With a full set, it would be worth something. By itself, not so much."

"Hang on," she said, her eyes moving past him and into the big red barn. One hand clutched his arm, her fingernails digging in with barely concealed excitement. "Is that—?" Not even finishing her sentence and definitely not waiting for a response, she pushed off him and into the barn.

Connor knew he should examine the roosters to see if anything here had value, but he was much more interested in what Luce had found.

She ran her hands over the painted-white arms of a Victorian sofa, complete with four little legs and fancy white decorative beadings between them.

"The upholstery's a mess," Connor said, joining her. What had once been a cottony blue looked more gray-brown now, complete with stains and even a few holes.

"I can fix it," Luce said.

"You do furniture?"

"No, but that's what the internet's for, right?"

"I can help," Connor said.

She lifted her head. "You do furniture?"

"Ha." He gave a short laugh. "No."

She smiled and turned back to the couch. "It would look lovely with a dark hardwood floor."

"Which you have?"

"No." She sighed and stepped back, admiring it. "But someday. How much do you think it is?"

"Come on." Connor took her hand under the guise of leading her through the stockpiled barn. "This is where we bargain."

♥

"This it?" Connor asked, pulling the truck into the condo parking lot. He surveyed the building. "Looks nice."

"I got it for a good deal," Luce said, a bit stiffly.

Connor glanced at her. She'd been more open and chatty since finding the sofa, but this was one of those moments when he knew she would clam up if he asked the wrong question. Something in her past bothered her. Whether it was family related or a bad relationship, he had no idea.

Nor, he reminded himself, was it any of his business.

He parked the truck and clambered around to the other side to open Luce's door, taking her hand to guide her out. Her smile was back, timidly peeking at him from under lowered eyelids, meeting his eyes before looking away. It was like they had switched roles. Gone was the confident girl he'd known in high school, replaced by someone a little more cautious with life.

She pulled her hand away and grabbed her keys instead. Connor dropped the tailgate on the truck and pulled out a dolly. He wheeled the couch to the front door, which Luce already had open.

"Don't mind everything, it doesn't really look lived in yet," she said.

"No worries," Connor said, though his eyes eagerly surveyed what was visible of the kitchen and living room as he pushed the couch in. Anything he could find that would tell him more about this reticent girl.

A large tree stump took the place of the kitchen table, though it was polished and waxed to a beautiful marbled perfection. Glazed mugs and hand-thrown clay plates sat in piles along the counter, apparently waiting to be put away after being washed. His eyes reached the living room, but he spotted more vases, the colors ranging from sea green to deep red. He raised an eyebrow.

"You like pottery?"

Luce clasped her hands together and pulled her shoulders down as if to make herself smaller. "It was kind of my passion."

It took a moment to put that comment into context. "Wait— did you make these?"

She tugged on her ponytail and nodded.

"But these are—these are beautiful. They look like they're worth a fortune." Already he was picturing a shelf in his mom's store, a line of new products, hand-thrown pottery from a local resident. Of course, they would need a different angle, because potters were nearly a dime a dozen in Eureka Springs.

"Thank you," Luce said.

"Have you ever thought about selling them? Putting them in a store? You know, if you really love to do it, I could help you. You could start your own label, come up with your own unique design."

Her shoulders tightened almost imperceptibly, and Connor knew he had said something wrong.

"I just do this for fun."

"Have you ever thought of not doing it for fun?"

You should stop now. Connor's inner voice warned him that her body language was all wrong to pursue this topic, but for the life of him, the words just kept coming out. "I mean, your work is top quality. We can tweak it here or there, make it your own line, find a good marketing angle." He could feel himself becoming excited by the idea, though her face had gone completely deadpan.

"Thanks for helping me out," she said, moving to the front door and standing beside it.

Obvious dismissal. Connor backpedaled as fast as he could.

"Hey, never mind. I was just thinking out loud." Yeah right, like he could undo the last five minutes of conversation. "I enjoyed hanging out with you. Maybe we could do it again sometime?"

Her eyes flitted toward him, giving nothing away in the short glance. "I appreciate your help, but I'm not new to the area, and I can find my own way around."

Ouch. Her words were a deliberate slam, and Connor couldn't help feeling that they were created strictly to push him away. The egotistical part of him wanted to puff up his pride and take her at face value. But the more emotional side of him panicked, not about to let their interaction end this way.

"Okay, sure. You don't need my friendship. But maybe I need yours."

Her greenish blue eyes widened slightly. "I'm sorry if I was rude. You're just getting out of a relationship, though, and I think what you really need is some space."

The warmth crept up his cheeks, and he shoved his hands into his pockets and turned around before she could notice. How many times would she reject him before he got the hint? "You got it. I'll see you later." Without a backward glance, he let himself out of the house.

Chapter Seven

LUCE

L uce pressed her hot cheeks against the window and watched Connor drive away, grimacing with embarrassment. Why had she spoken to him that way? She liked him. The whole reason she'd stepped into his mom's store was because she'd hoped to see him, especially now that he and Regina were broken up.

But he'd said the wrong thing, and she'd reacted—well, weirdly.

"Urg," she growled to herself. She turned around and glared at the sofa she'd just bought. She'd loved it, but it didn't match the cheap carpeting in her condo, or the dark wood paneling walls.

And now the only thing she'd think of when she saw it was how Connor brought it over and she royally ruined their time together.

It didn't even have anything to do with Connor, and if her heart rate didn't speed up with anxiety every time she thought about Brian trying to take her money, she might not have reacted quite so badly. And she couldn't explain it. If Connor knew her baggage, he'd run as fast as he could to find an easier relationship to invest in.

She picked up her phone and called her sister.

"Hello?" Melodee said.

"I need company."

"Come over for dinner."

Luce didn't need to be told twice. Cooking for one was overrated, anyway.

She helped Melodee set the table, biting her tongue as long as she could. And then she blurted, "I went out with Connor."

Melodee opened the utensil drawer and pulled out the forks without batting an eye. "I thought he had a girlfriend?"

Luce hadn't even realized she'd talked about him that much. "He did. They broke up."

"Did your lawyer say it was okay to date right now?" She placed the forks on the table and stepped back to survey it.

Luce carefully folded the napkin and placed it on the table. She hadn't told Melodee that she never got a lawyer. "Well, it's a moot point. We won't be going out again."

"Maybe a good thing," Melodee said. "He's probably not over his girlfriend yet."

That's what Luce had been thinking, too. So why did she suddenly want to disagree?

"I think you're just fine being single for a while," Melodee went on. "At least until things blow over with Brian and you can think straight."

Luce retreated to the kitchen to grab one of the casserole dishes. "Weren't you the one telling me just a few weeks ago to start looking at other guys?"

"Yeah, but that was before we knew Brian was going to take

you to court. Now you just have to be safe."

"I'll keep that in mind."

Caroline plopped down next to Luce at the sanitizing station at work. "You seem down."

Luce pulled her head out of the clouds and focused on her friend. Caroline wore a green headband over her wild curls, still managing to look serene. Luce heaved a sigh and dried her hands on the paper towels. "I'm fine."

"Not buying it."

"I'm just—" Luce clammed up as Regina walked by, eyes red and face pale. She offered them a wobbly smile before disappearing around the corner.

Caroline lowered her voice. "I don't think she's taking her and Connor's break up so well."

"Apparently not," Luce whispered back. She didn't mention that Connor seemed to be taking it much better.

"Are you working tomorrow?"

"Yes." Luckily the clinic closed at noon on Saturdays. She picked up a patient chart left on the counter and scanned it.

"Me too. Let's do something after."

The idea was appealing. But Luce didn't want to hit the town; she wanted to stand around Connor's shop and wait for him to appear, then apologize for her behavior. Not that she could tell Caroline that. "Okay, yeah."

Caroline squealed and clapped once. "What do you want to do?"

"Come over and let's eat pizza."

The too-green eyes narrowed as Caroline frowned. "That's it?"

"Just some nice quiet girl time." Luce tucked the chart under her arm and gave Caroline a pleading stare. "Please?"

Caroline sighed, resigned. "Fine. If that's all you want. But next time we do what I want."

"Deal."

CONNOR

He'd been burned. Slammed. Totally rejected.

So why was his behavior borderline stalkerish?

Connor purposefully planned lunch with his mom on Saturday at a cafe close to the clinic. If he was lucky, Luce would be working today, and he'd catch her when the morning shift ended.

"I think Dave would like a wedding at the lake, don't you? Should we rent a boat?"

Connor turned his head toward his mother, trying to tune into her words while keeping his eyes on the clinic. His mom was obsessed with weddings, always wanting to discuss her next storybook wedding idea. "Sure. Dave might like that." Connor took a sip of his hot chocolate and made a face. Too bitter. "Has Dave asked you?"

Her lips puckered up in a pout he couldn't miss, even without looking directly at her. "Not yet."

And he wouldn't, just like none of the last boyfriends had. That never stopped his mom from dreaming. He felt sorry for her, so desperate for her fairytale ending that she scared all the candidates away. "Hmm," he said.

"What does that mean, hmm?" She took his chin and forced him to look at her. "Why are you watching the clinic? Is Regina working today?"

"No." He put down his mug, his eyes flitting toward the building again before he faced his mom. "Luce works there."

"Oh, Luce!" His mom brightened. "I like her."

"Yeah, me too," he murmured, looking down at the table. He didn't mean to admit that out loud, but there it was.

The waitress appeared with their lunch, and Connor focused on eating. The clinic closed in half an hour. No point in staring at it the whole time.

"Well," his mom said after they finished eating and stepped outside, "shall we hit Bella Vista or Joplin first?"

"Um."

Out of his peripheral vision, he watched the side door to the clinic open and several people walk out. He straightened up, seeking out the tall brunette who usually wore her hair in a ponytail.

There she was. Hard to miss in the black and pink Polk-a-dot scrubs. He grinned.

"Do you see her?" His mom turned around, and Connor poked her arm.

"Mom! Don't stare."

"Why not? You are."

He couldn't deny that.

"Are you going to say hi?"

He debated it, then shook his head. She'd shot him down pretty emphatically. "Some other time." He palmed his keys. "Let's hit Joplin first."

Chapter Eight

LUCE

"So this is your place?" Caroline followed Luce into the condo and glanced around. She pressed her lips together and bobbed her head. "Dreamy."

"Yeah." Luce gave a laugh and picked up the throw pillow on the floor. "At least I have a couch now." Never mind that every time she looked at it, she thought of Connor. Would she have to go back to his mom's shop just to talk to him?

Caroline plopped herself down on it, resting her legs over the armrest. "And a TV." She gestured to the laptop Luce had set up on an end table by the fireplace. "What's with all the pottery?"

Luce looked at the pieces she'd unpacked, the ones that had survived her rampage last week. "I made them."

"Oh, you're one of those people! What are you working on now?"

Luce hesitated before opening the hall closet and pulling out her wheel. Her newest pie plate sat on top, completed only yesterday. She felt guilty now for destroying her work, but she didn't want to create replacements. Like her life after Brian, she wanted a change. A new style.

But so far this one fell short. It lacked the heart of her old pieces, and even the decorative edging looked more like someone desperately trying to be creative.

"That's pretty," Caroline said, and maybe she meant it. But Luce held herself to a higher standard.

"Thanks," she said, putting the wheel and the pie plate away.

"What will you do with it next?"

"Well, I used to have my own kiln. My own shop, actually, and I'd fire up my pottery right there. But now I'll need to find someone to rent from." If she really wanted to save the piece, anyway. More than likely she'd break it down, but she didn't tell that to Caroline.

"Your own shop? How dreamy! What happened to it?"

A subject Luce did not want to discuss. "I closed it and moved here."

"Are you going to open another?"

She shook her head. "No plans to."

"So, what, your aspirations now are to be a nurse?" Caroline smirked.

"I'm still figuring myself out. Then I'll decide. Maybe I'll go back to school."

The doorbell rang, and Caroline jumped up. "Pizza's here!"

Luce joined her in the kitchen and paid the delivery guy, grateful for the distraction.

"So," Caroline said, ever so casually as she pulled a stringy piece of cheese off the pizza, "what's going on with your ex?"

"Ugh, stupid ex." Luce rolled her eyes. "He quit calling me. I think it's over." A little shudder went down her spine. She hoped it was over. Because the next time she talked to Connor, she didn't want to be worrying about Brian.

"He's out of your life for good?"

"For good."

Caroline eyed her. "Then you can move on?"

"Yes." Connor's face popped into her head, and she sighed.

"Whoa!" Caroline said. "There's already another guy! Do tell!"

"There's no one," Luce said.

Caroline's eyes scanned her face, searching for a hint. "But you want there to be."

Luce considered spilling all. She was dying to tell someone besides Melodee, who continued to frown down at her in a parental way. "We've talked a few times. And there's definitely chemistry."

Caroline clasped her hands together and bounced on the couch. "Can you tell me who?"

"Not yet. It's a bit complicated."

Caroline cocked her head. "I'm dying here, girl."

Luce lifted her chin. "And what's your story? Where's your man?"

Caroline's expression closed off. "He's here in Eureka. We don't talk much."

Luce's smile faded, and she felt bad for bringing it up. "Bad blood?"

"Lots of bad blood," she whispered, and her eyes welled up with tears.

Luce sat on the edge of the couch beside Caroline. "Did he hurt you?"

"We hurt each other." Caroline cleared her throat several times. "Enough about me. Didn't you say we could watch a movie?"

"Oh, yes," Luce said, favoring her with a smile. She recognized a subject change when she saw one. "You'll be the first to see something on my new laptop."

CONNOR

"It's been a week and you're still talking about this girl." Moki lined up behind the pool table in Tyson's basement, aiming his cue at the white ball.

"I can't get her out of my head," Connor said. He smirked as Moki's shot went wide. Putting down his can, Connor gestured for the stick.

"I think I'd take the hint," Moki said, handing him the cue.

"That's because you don't have a romantic bone in your body," Ty said. "I totally get where Connor's coming from. That's how it was when I met Amber. The day I finally convinced her to go out with me, I knew I was set for life."

"And it took you almost six months," Moki said, pointing at Ty and laughing.

"Yeah, well, imagine if I hadn't been persistent."

"Where's Amber, anyway?" Connor asked. "Or is it only guys' nights now that I'm single?"

Tyson shrugged. "I invited her. She didn't answer. Probably odd for her to be here with no other girls. You could fix that."

"I'm working on it," Connor said. "How come Moki doesn't have to get a girlfriend?"

"Me?" Moki sputtered, cookie pieces flying from his mouth.

"There's your answer," Ty said. "It's all on you, bro."

Connor bobbed his head. "How can I get her to give me another chance? I don't even know what I did wrong."

"Baggage," Moki hissed out of the side of his mouth, more cookie spraying the table.

"Quit getting food all over my pool table!" Tyson hollered.

"And what of it? We all have baggage." Connor's shot was golden, and the six-ball fell into the right corner hole.

His phone rang, that particular warning jingle. He gritted his teeth and handed the cue to Ty.

"Not gonna answer that?" Moki asked, nodding toward his singing pocket.

"It's Regina." Connor even gave her a special ring tone so he'd know when it was her. "Why don't I set you up with her? You two can go clubbing every weekend."

"Doesn't sound so bad," Moki said with a shrug.

"Just remember, Moki," Connor said, "never trust a girl who lies to you."

"Yeah, but," Ty said, passing the cue to Moki, "there's a difference between lying about if you did your laundry and lying about where you were last night."

"I know where I was last night," Moki said, making another wild shot. "I have an alibi."

"Lying's lying," Connor said. "If it's what they do, it's what they do." Just like Regina. Just like his father. He accepted the cue from Moki and dropped the last ball into a pocket.

Chapter Nine

LUCE

Luce didn't set her alarm on Sunday. The sunlight streaming through the window beside her bed woke her. She stretched one arm over her head, then grabbed the pillow and tucked it under her ear.

Today. What was she going to do today?

She knew what she wanted. Or rather, *who* she wanted. And she had no intentions of telling Melodee when she saw her at church later.

Luce took her time showering, taking inventory of what else she needed. The shower curtain. Lots of hangers. New clothes? Though she had plenty, she had the urge to throw them all out. They reminded her of the old Luce. She didn't want to have anything to do with that vulnerable, gullible little girl.

She straightened her hair, then sat at the table and made a shopping list. Most items required going to an actual store, rather than a stroll down Spring Street. But she might still be able to find an excuse to get to the strip.

Luce managed to keep quiet about her plans all through the church service. She begged off dinner with Melodee's family and went home when it was over, changing into jeans and a T-shirt before heading to the discount store. The wind blew her hair the moment she stepped out of the car, and as soon as she got into the store, she wrapped the wild strands around a pencil and forced them into a messy bun. She pulled out her list and dropped items into her cart, muttering to herself as she did.

"Not enough forks in the house?"

No way. She had to be imagining Connor's voice, the same way she'd conjured his face in her mind over the past few days.

She turned enough to see that he wasn't a figment of her imagination. He rested against the metal display rack, his lip quirked upward and a playful twinkle in his eyes. Like hers, his hair was windblown and his face a bit chapped as if he'd been jogging.

"What have you been doing?" she asked. "Running?" Her eyes took in the athletic attire, and her face warmed.

"Bike riding. My mom sent me to get some dish soap. Apparently she's out."

She arched an eyebrow. "And you're hoping to find it next to the cheese graters?"

He picked one up. "I already bought some. I was about to leave when I saw you. Thought I'd say hi."

She reached to take the grater from him, but he put it back just as she did, and her hand collided with his. A tingle spread up her palm where his skin met hers, and she withdrew.

Connor looked down at the cheese grater and then back to her. "Did you want this?" he asked, holding it out to her.

"It's on my list," Luce said, inexplicably bashful all of a

sudden. Before he could distract her further, she said, "I wanted to apologize for last week. I was super rude to you."

"How about a do-over?"

She risked a glance to see his brown eyes on her, all seriousness this time. "A do-over?"

"Yeah. I'm gonna ask you out, and this time you're going to say yes."

She couldn't help laughing.

"Saturday," he said. "Craft fair weekend. Come with me." He rested one elbow on the shelf. "Just one day. No commitments, nothing serious. We'll just go out and have fun."

She mulled the idea over. "Will there be fudge?"

He grinned, displaying dimples on either side of his mouth. "You bet."

Craft fairs and fudge, her two weaknesses. She bobbed her head. "Okay."

"Great!" Connor said, straightening up. He looked as giddy as a schoolboy. "Give me your number, I'll pick you up in the morning."

Luce fed him the digits and watched him program them into his phone.

"Saturday, then." He gave her a half smile and started to walk away, then turned around again. "What are you doing tomorrow?"

"Working. I'm off at six, like always."

He didn't seem to hear her, his eyes focused at the front of the store. "Oh, I gotta go! They're gonna tow my bike!"

And he jogged off, leaving Luce to wonder if he was serious or not. She stood on her tiptoes to peer out the storefront, but it was only an employee moving Connor's bike off to the side. She shook her head, unable to keep the bemused smile from her lips.

CONNOR

This was bad. Very very bad.

Kerri watched him pace back and forth in front of the display in her bead store.

"It's like high school all over again," he said. "When I would take the long way to biology just so I could catch a glimpse of her at her locker."

Kerri giggled. "Kind of silly."

"I'm so past silly. I'm like, besmotten."

Now she laughed. "I'm pretty sure that's not a word."

"It is now."

"Kerri?" Her mom poked her head out of the back, but the stern expression on her face softened when she saw Connor. "Oh, hey. I was going to tell Kerri to get back to work, but you're fine."

Connor lifted a hand in a wave. "Thanks."

"Maybe you can help, Mom," Kerri said, swiveling to face her. "Connor really likes this girl."

"Oo." A glint formed in her eyes, and she dropped onto the stool next to her daughter. "I love a good romance."

"Not quite there yet," Connor said, but the two women talked right over him.

"You need to ask her out."

"He already did," Kerri said. "They're going out on Saturday. Connor's question is, would it be okay to call her before then?"

"Of course!" her mom exclaimed.

"She won't think I'm coming on too strong?"

"Connor's liked her for years," Kerri stage-whispered.

That did it. Connor checked his watch. "Lunch is over. I better get back to the store."

The door closing behind him didn't block out their laughter.

He plunged himself into his textbooks at the shop, greeting the few customers that came in with distracted attention. If he closed up right at six, he could meet Luce at the clinic. Just to say hi.

The idea wouldn't get out of his head, and the moment six o'clock rolled around, Connor locked up the shop and hightailed it to the clinic.

He drove by slowly, watching for Luce. He saw her talking to the black girl—Carolyn? Caroline?—who wore her hair like she'd just walked out of the seventies. He waited for their conversation to finish. Only after Luce waved goodbye and headed for her car did he pull around. He parked his car beside hers and got out, trying to look nonchalant.

"Hey," he said, shoving his hands in his pockets.

She paused beside her old maroon Buick and looked him up and down. Apparently she wasn't falling for his casual appearance.

"What are you doing here?"

Following you like a lovesick teenager. "Just driving by. I realized you'd be getting off around now, so I thought I'd say hi."

"Oh. Hi."

He shrugged like it was no big deal. "What do you say we go out tonight?"

"Aren't we going out Saturday?"

"Yeah, then too."

Her fingers toyed with the edges of her scrubs. "I don't know. I told my sister I'd come over, help her out."

"Oh, yeah, the pregnant one. How is she?"

"Still pregnant." Luce's eyes crinkled with mirth. "And she's forgiven you for running her over."

"Whew, I was worried. Okay, then, tell me what you want to do."

She lifted an eyebrow, a mischievous gleam entering her eye. "Yoga."

"Yoga?" he repeated. Was this a test?

Her smile grew bigger. "Yes. And there's a studio nearby that I've been dying to try out. Want to come?"

He squinted his eyes at her. "Are you one of these all-organic girls that doesn't eat meat?"

"Nothing like that." She shot him a teasing grin, tilting her head against the sunlight. "I love red meat."

Why did that make his blood run hot?

"But I do enjoy my vegetables," she admitted.

"What a relief," he said, hoping she didn't notice her affect on him. "What are you doing after yoga?"

She laughed. "Are you too manly for yoga? Or afraid you can't keep up?"

"Oh, I can keep up." On second thought, seeing Luce in yoga pants was worth the pain. "Tonight?"

She arched an eyebrow. "Really? You'd come?"

He shrugged. "I could do it once. For you."

"Tomorrow. Six-thirty in the morning." She reached out her fingers. "Give me your hand."

Connor did so, not about to argue with her.

Luce pulled a pen from her purse and wrote on his palm. "I'll see you tomorrow."

He studied the address she'd written in her slanted handwriting after she drove away. Looked like he'd be doing yoga in the morning.

He never thought he'd be excited to get up so early.

Chapter Ten

LUCE

For once, when the alarm went off at six in the morning, Luce bounded out of bed.

She'd never cared before what her workout clothes looked like, but today they suddenly all seemed too shabby or too revealing. She finally settled on black yoga pants with a turquoise fabric rim around the waist and a matching exercise tank with a built-in bra.

She grimaced at her reflection. Maybe she should add weights into her routine.

Too late for that now! Luce gave a little laugh, a silly giddiness pumping through her veins. She pulled on a jacket, grabbed her change of clothes, and ran out the door.

The yoga studio was upstairs above another store on the strip. Luce let herself into the dimly lit room and saw the instructor had already gotten started. Was she late? A quick glance at her phone showed she wasn't. She unrolled her yoga mat in the back of the room and scanned the attendees. About seven other people—all of them women. They ranged from college-aged to gray-haired. But none of them were Connor.

He'd said he was coming. And it wasn't quite six-thirty yet.

The instructor spoke in what sounded like a French accent, his words soothing and pleasant as he made his rounds through the room. "Hold the Downward Dog pose. Breathe in through your nose. Hold it. Now let it out in three counts. One. Two. Three."

Luce tried to concentrate on her breathing, but her nerves were strung tight. The door behind her creaked, and she swung her head only to see another older lady walk in. She set up her mat next to Luce, and Luce let out another breath as they moved into a different position. He was now officially late. Maybe he wasn't coming. Her heart rate calmed as disappointment replaced her excitement. What had she expected? Guys didn't do yoga.

"Moving into chaturanga," the instructor said, making his way to the back of the room.

Luce moved her body into the plank-like position, leveling her elbows at her ribcage with her palms flat on the mat. She nearly yelped when someone touched the small of her back.

"Nice flat back. Now stretch tall, to the sky, in Upward Facing Dog," the instructor said, dipping his head close to hers. "Don't get distracted. Let your core strength flow through your muscles. Focus on what's right here." He made a small circle over her skin while pulling a fist into his own gut. His accent was oddly clipped and flowing all at the same time, and Luce held her breath until he passed.

"Was that fun?" another voice whispered to her left.

She spun her head, startled to see Connor stretched out next to her in the same pose. She gave a sudden laugh. "When did you get here?"

"A minute ago. Just in time to see you fondled by the instructor."

The way he said "fondled" had her body flushing all kinds of hot. Her eyes darted to his hands, pressed flat against the mat, and the sudden desire rushing through her made her want to roll her mat up and run into the cold air outside.

But the instructor already had them moving into Downward Facing Dog, which Luce had never considered an erotic move until this moment with Connor beside her. What was wrong with her?

Connor grunted, and Luce looked over to see his face twisted in a grimace as his body attempted to master the pose. She burst out laughing, nearly collapsing on her mat. It no longer looked erotic, at least.

"What?" Connor hissed between gritted teeth. "You can't laugh!"

Luce was still giggling when the class ended. The lights came back on, and she wiped down her mat before heading to the front of the room to pay for the class.

"Thank you," she said, handing over the prescribed fee for both her and Connor. "It was fun."

The instructor waved her off. "First time is free. Besides, you are enjoyable to watch."

Now that she could see him in the light, he was stunningly handsome, with olive-toned skin and deep blue eyes. He flashed her a smile, and she knew he was aware of his good looks. "I am Jarrod," he added in a thick accent. Sounded like "Jah-HOOD." "I hope you will be back."

"Sure. It was great." She turned to leave and nearly bumped into Connor, who had appeared at her elbow.

"How much was the class?" he asked, following her to the exit.

"First time's free." His hand floated loosely at his side, and she touched his fingers, almost grabbing his hand. She wrapped her hands around her mat instead. "Thanks for coming."

"It was kind of fun. If you like that sort of thing."

If he'd noticed her groping his hand, he didn't comment, and Luce was grateful. "I'll probably come again. You can too."

Connor glanced over his shoulder, then leaned close to her and whispered, "And listen to that phony accent?"

She told herself not to laugh, but her lip twisted of its own accord. "You think it's fake?"

"There's no doubt."

They stopped at the bottom of the stairs outside, and Luce's grin faded away. "I guess I better head home so I can get ready for work. But I'm really glad you came."

He stared at her beneath the street light, his expression suddenly quite serious. His hand moved up and down on the strap of his messenger bag, and her heart beat a little harder in her chest. The moment stretched on, but he didn't break eye contact.

"Well, I'll see you," Luce said, finally taking a step backward.

That broke the spell. "Saturday," Connor said.

"I'll wait for your call," she replied, offering one more smile before turning around.

Oh snap. It was out of her hands now.

CONNOR

Connor decided he liked yoga.

Not so much the actually doing it part. His body

certainly didn't. He couldn't even believe all the places that hurt Wednesday morning when he woke up.

But all he had to do was picture Luce's slender body twisting around in the Chattanooga or whatever pose, and he knew he would go again.

He wanted to call her, but he never knew what to say on the phone if he didn't have a reason. So he stuck to text messages.

My body despises yoga.

Her reply, riddled with emojis: *You get used to it.*

Maybe I need to try a French accent.

This time her response was nothing but emojis.

He smiled back at the phone, feeling a surge of affection as if the phone itself had started purring and rubbing his leg.

Would it be weird if he showed up at the clinic again?

Connor was still debating it when Tyson called.

"Come over here. Now."

He could tell from the edge in Ty's voice that something was very wrong. Normally he would tease his friend, make some kind of joke about having the same emotional needs of a teenage girl, but he knew this wasn't the right time.

"I'm just closing up the store. Should I bring something?"

"You mean like something to dull the pain? No thanks. I need to think clearly."

Oh. This wasn't good.

Connor hopped in his car and drove the twenty minutes to Tyson's house.

Moki was already there. He met Connor at the door. "Hey. He's in his room. Just follow the music."

Sure enough, angry Country music with a loud bass note drummed through the house. Connor walked to the bedroom in the back and knocked on the door. Before he could open it, the music abruptly ceased, and the door flew open. Ty stood there, hair sticking straight up as if he'd been yanking on it, eyes bloodshot, face wild.

"What is it?" Connor demanded. "Somebody die? Are you in trouble?"

"It's Amber."

Connor gaped. "Is she okay?" Tyson and Amber had the perfect relationship, even though they had only been together about three months. "What happened?" He braced himself.

"I broke up with her." Ty exhaled.

That he had not expected. "What?" He couldn't believe it.

"She kept a huge secret from me!" Ty burst out, banging his fist on the dresser.

"Oh." Connor drew out the word and steadied himself on the large chair next to Ty's bed. "What happened?" he repeated.

"More like, what did I find out?" Ty growled.

Connor felt a twist of sympathy in his gut. "Was she cheating on you?" He couldn't imagine it. She was an incredibly good actress to fake those looks of adoration and the affection in her eyes every time she looked at him.

He chewed on his bottom lip, studying Connor. "No. That's not it."

"Then what?"

"She has a daughter."

Oh. That did put a twist on things. "She just told you?"

"Yeah. That's why she never wants me over."

Connor nodded as the pieces fell into place. "But still, she told you, right? She came clean."

Ty wrinkled his nose. "It's not about coming clean. I'm not her judge. It's that she hid it for so long. That's something that should've come out when we started dating. Or at least, before we got serious."

"But she did tell you. You would be even angrier if she waited six more months."

"I don't know, man. It's a lot to take in. I mean, she has a kid, for crying out loud. It's not like having a dog."

"Yeah, that's heavy."

They both fell into silence after Connor's profound statement, and then Connor ventured, "So you don't like her anymore?"

Ty shot him a look of pure disdain. "Don't be stupid. I'm crazy about her. But this is kind of a big shock, and I don't know what's worse, finding out I'm expected to be a surrogate father or that she's kept this from me."

"Did she have reasons?"

"No, other than that she wasn't sure how I would take it and she didn't want to introduce me into her daughter's life and cause confusion." Ty made air quotes around the last two words.

"How old is the kid?" Connor asked.

"She's only two. It's not like my presence would've caused some great disruption."

"But you have to admire her thought process. The fact that her daughter came before her relationship with you, that's an admirable trait."

"I'm not ready to hear all the good things about her," Ty growled. "You're the one who always says a lie is a lie."

Connor threw his hands up in a permissive gesture. "I'm not saying to just let it go and pretend like she didn't keep it from you. But maybe give it some time and see if you're willing to accept a little girl into your life." Connor couldn't help the grin that spread across his face. "You'd make an awesome daddy."

"Shut up," Ty snapped, grabbing a book off the dresser and chucking it at Connor. But he looked less perturbed than he had when Connor arrived, more thoughtful now.

Sensing that his work here was done, Connor slapped his hands on his thighs and pushed to his feet. "What have you got to eat? I've been holed up at the store doing schoolwork for the past four hours, and I'm starving."

Ty grunted. "At least I can always count on you to clean out my fridge."

They walked out of the room and caught up with Moki in the kitchen.

"Oh!" Tyson said, leaning against the counter while Connor handed food to Moki, "What's up with your girl?"

"She's not my girl," Connor said. And then a slow grin stole its way across his lips. "But she did agree to go to the craft fair with me on Saturday."

Ty and Moki busted up laughing, Moki resting his head on the fridge door for support.

"The craft fair?" Ty said. "It doesn't get hotter than that."

"Is this a topless craft fair?" Moki added.

Connor knew they were teasing him, but he accepted it. His interest in the arts was a laughable quirk to his friends. To him, it was a desirable attribute, and he hoped Luce had it.

Chapter Eleven

LUCE

L uce caught herself humming several times at work on Thursday and finally managed to shush herself when Regina asked her why she was so happy. The question itself, coupled with the person asking, was enough to splash cold water on Luce's euphoria.

She returned to the yoga studio on Friday and couldn't help her disappointment when Connor didn't show. But they hadn't planned it and she hadn't invited him, so she brushed it off.

Her phone rang that evening, interrupting her audio book while Luce cleaned the kitchen. She picked it up, fully expecting it to be Connor, but her dad's name scrolled across the screen. She huffed, blowing a strand of hair from her face. What did he want? To remind her about the registration deadlines for getting her PhD?

She answered reluctantly. "Hey, Dad."

"Hey, Luce. How are you?"

"Oh, good." She attacked a stubborn spot on the counter with the rag. "Just cleaning."

"Are they treating you well at the clinic?"

"Sure." She gave a shrug. "As well as can be."

"Any word from Brian?"

"Nothing pleasant," she said, putting some snark in her tone.

"Were you pleasant to him?"

"Dad." She let the full weight of warning enter the word.

"Sorry." He exhaled. "Something interesting came across my desk, and I thought I'd pass it on to you."

"Oh?" Luce feigned curiosity.

"I have a list of foreign hospitals that are short-staffed and willing to take on residents with less specialized education. Including nurses. And anything you learn can count as hours when you do start working on your degree."

"Yeah, that's cool."

He paused, and then asked, "Would you like me to arrange it for you? You could leave as early as next month."

"Hmm, I'll think about it." Not. "Thanks for letting me know."

"Just watching out for you, Luce."

He was, in his own way. Luce said goodbye and hung up with a shake of her head. She didn't want to be a doctor.

What was she going to do with her life?

Connor called Saturday morning and offered to pick her up at her condo before leaving for the craft fair, but Luce declined. Instead they made plans to meet at the Mud Street Cafe for brunch. It was a perfect autumn day, and Luce put on a cream-colored dress with lavender flowers and walked the fifteen minutes from her place to the cafe.

She spotted Connor when she opened the door, already

waiting at the hostess station. She went down the stairs, descending into the main level of the café. All of the shops on the east side of the street were below ground level. The original street level had been lower, but a series of floods and landslides convinced the city to raise the street, and as a result, all of the store entrances were below street level.

Where else in America would Luce find such a quirky place?

Her boots clomped against the wooden steps as she approached, and Connor turned slightly at the noise. He smiled when he saw her.

"Hi," he said. He took her elbow, pulling her to the hostess station, his hand warming her skin through the thin fabric of her sweater.

"I've got your table ready," the hostess said, shuffling two menus. "If you'll follow me?"

Connor let go of her and gestured her to walk in front. They stepped past the bar into a dimly lit dining room with brick walls.

"Let's get something warm to drink first," Connor said, opening his menu. "What do you want, Luce? Coffee, hot chocolate?"

She could still feel the warmth from his hand. "I'll take a hot chocolate."

Connor ordered two blueberry scones and two hot chocolates, but his with hazelnut syrup. Luce decided to try that next time. The slightly bitter flavor of the hazelnut would accentuate the sweetness of the chocolate.

He leaned back in his chair while they waited for the food. "Anything you're hoping to find at the fair today?"

She shook her head. "You?"

"I don't have anything specific in mind, but I know I'm looking for things I can sell in my mom's shop." He picked up his fork and tapped it against the table.

Their hot chocolate and scones arrived at that moment, sparing Luce the need to make more conversation. She held the large mug in both hands and took small sips of the beverage. A jittery energy fluttered through her veins. She studied Connor over the brim. He looked deep in thought, his eyes glazed over as he stared into his drink, his lips pressed together in a somber line. He lifted his eyes and caught her staring.

"Sorry," he said.

"For what?" Luce asked, captivated by his brown eyes.

"For not making conversation. Didn't want an awkward silence."

"I enjoy a moment of self-reflection."

A twinkle entered his eye, the corners of his mouth crinkling into a grin. "And on what sorts of thoughts were you reflecting?"

Now the heat rushing to her face had nothing to do with the steaming hot chocolate in her hands. "Oh, you know," she said breezily. "Just wondering if there will be any clothing booths at the fair."

"You can count on it. I suppose that's one thing all girls have in common, a like for clothing."

"In defense of women everywhere," Luce said, "mostly we have a fondness for anything that makes us look and feel good."

"You make polka dot scrubs look good."

He didn't even give her a chance to react to his comment before he scraped his chair back and got to his feet. "You ready for this?" He dropped a handful of bills on the table and extended a hand. "Let's check out that fair."

Luce slowly reached her hand out, and he closed his fingers

around hers.

Connor had paid for her drink and now he was holding her hand.

This was definitely a date.

CONNOR

The drive out to Bella Vista was comfortably quiet as Luce messed with the radio stations in Connor's truck until she found a country station with a good signal. Then she settled back in her seat, bobbing her head in time to the music and staring out the window. Connor sneaked glances at her, marveling at how the auburn color of her hair made her seem like a ray of sunshine sitting next to him in the car.

"We're not going to the War Eagle craft fair?" she asked as they continued down the highway farther away from Eureka Springs.

Connor shrugged. "I don't like it as much."

"Isn't it the biggest?"

"Big isn't always better."

Her lip quirked upward. "I can't wait to see this one, then." She fell silent, staring out the window, humming to herself. "The leaves are so beautiful," she said, the words breathing out of her with the longing of a sigh. "I missed this."

Connor turned down the volume of the radio. "You missed it?"

"Yes." Her finger traced the seal between the window and the door. "When I lived in Vegas, it was hot, and dry, and it's this barren desert that people turned into a concrete idol to worship the sun."

"Why did you go, then?"

For a moment she didn't answer, just continued tracing her

fingers over the door, from the windowsill to the lock button to the handle. "I had dreams. There was a . . ." She hesitated. "An opportunity for me to pursue my craft."

"Your pottery?"

She bobbed her head.

"But you can do that here," he said. He gestured his hand to the road and the rolling hills in front of them. "Look where we're going. The craft fair."

"Yes, but I wanted to be more than just a weekend booth. And I wanted to do it on my own, not in the shadow of my parents, with my father constantly towering over me and implying that whatever actions I did weren't good enough because it wasn't in the career field he chose for me."

Ah, tension. Finally, he was seeing what she really felt. "Which is what?"

Luce faced out the front window, chewing her lip before saying, "Medical."

She didn't want to follow in the footsteps of her father's medical profession, yet here she was, a nurse. What had changed her mind?

There was no more opportunity to pursue the subject, however, as they arrived at the grassy field where the sheriff's department was carefully escorting people to park.

A glimmer of excitement entered her eyes. Connor looked around at the rows and rows of white pop-up tents, enough to make any craft aficionado swoon with expectancy. Her face shone, and she swiveled her head from side to side as if unsure where to start.

"You've been here before, right?" Connor asked, unable to believe someone as artsy as her would have missed this craft fair. "I've been to several in the state procuring wares, and this one is the best."

"Uh, yeah, no. Who was going to bring me, my medical practitioner dad? He spent his whole life trying to get my head out of the clouds." She gave a short laugh.

Which explained why she looked like a child who had stumbled across Toyland.

"What about your mom?"

A flicker of sadness crossed her face, and then it was gone. "She didn't have a say."

The statement left so much more to be explained. "You're in for a treat." He clasped her hand, and he noticed she didn't skip a beat this time, but instead tightened her grip on him as if holding hands were the most natural thing in the world. He tried not to grin like an idiot as he pulled her toward the first row of tents. "Let's get started. Don't worry, we'll stay till you've seen it all."

They started at the first long tent, expanding the length of a parking lot, filled with two rows of craft booths, facing each other so that an aisle formed between them. Luce slipped her hand out of his and stopped at the first booth, displaying necklaces created from gemstones and twisted wires. She fingered a purple amethyst before moving on to the next booth, this one with patchwork quilts in bright primary colors.

"Look at this, it's so beautiful!" she said. A minute later she had paused at another booth, and she gasped as she picked up a fat gourd, decorated to look like a turkey with giant tail feathers coming out the back. "The details! Who has time for this?"

Connor stuck his hands in his pockets and suppressed a smile, as tickled by her delight as she was by the crafts.

They wandered through the artisans for more than two hours before stopping at the row of food trucks to grab lunch. He tried to guess what she would want. A giant chicken salad, maybe, or a Navajo taco, since it had so many vegetables.

But Luce surprised him by ordering one of the giant corndogs.

"You can't really eat that," he said, eyeing the foot-long fried dog in her hand.

She led them to the tent set up with rows of tables just for eating and scooted over to make room for him. Then she set down her bags of purchases. "Watch me."

"I'm watching," Connor said as he bit into his own skewer of alligator meat. The food offerings, so strangely expensive, were always unique and exquisite and somehow perfectly Arkansan. Though he wasn't in the habit of buying at craft fairs, he'd already collected a good number of business cards and contact information. Part of his hopes for his mom's store were updating from being antiques and vintage to more handcrafted and artisan. The store would excel in Eureka Springs, where not only the townspeople but also the tourists craved the creative arts.

Just as Connor had predicted, Luce was not able to finish her corndog. She handed it over to him, and he gladly helped her out.

She pulled her phone out and checked the time before looking at him. "Are you sure you're up for more? We've been here almost three hours already."

He shrugged. "The only thing I have planned today is you."

She lowered her eyes, that little smile playing about her mouth again. The same smile that was starting to drive him crazy.

"Are you doing this just for me? Because it's been lovely so far, and if you have to get back for something . . ."

Connor studied her, wondering why she was giving him an out. They had only seen half the exhibits. "I'm good. But if you're tired, if you're ready to go—"

"Oh no!" she said, cutting him off. "I just want to make sure you're okay being here."

Guaranteed. Connor stood up, grabbing her purchases in his left hand and their trash in his right. "There's lots more to see, so we better get to it."

A cooler wind blew into the area as they left the shelter of the tent. Luce buttoned her sweater and bumped her shoulders up and down, huddling her body closer to itself. Her pale purple sweater didn't look very warm.

"Getting chilly, huh?" Connor wrapped an arm around her shoulders, drawing her into his chest. She didn't object, and he breathed in the scent of her hair, earthy with a hint of apple.

"You never know how October will be," she said. "But I like the seasons."

The sun came out from behind the clouds, dropping a few strands of light and warmth on them as it battled against the wind. Connor slipped his hand from her shoulder and down her arm.

"Seasons are nice," Connor agreed, the warmth bubbling up in his chest having very little to do with the sunshine radiating through the cloth of his shirt.

Chapter Twelve

LUCE

A wordless melody danced through Luce's head as she huddled against Connor's chest, warmth from his sweater spreading across her shoulder. And the way his fingers moved up and down on her forearm sent a liquid delight through her navel.

His touch thrilled her. And she wanted more of it.

He let go of her at the truck, opening her door first and helping her put her bags in. She took a hold of the door frame and hefted herself up, then turned to watch him as he climbed in on his side. She took in those dark eyes, the slight wave to the hair, the scruff around his square jaw revealing that he hadn't shaved that day.

Connor turned the key in the ignition and swung an arm around her headrest, his gaze tracking out the window. Then it landed on her, catching her eye. He smiled, a dimple popping out on his cheek.

"What?" he said. "Do I have mustard on my face?"

Oh, snap. He'd caught her staring. "No." She smiled, not sure what else to say. "Thanks for bringing me here. It was perfect."

"You're welcome, Luce." He held her gaze a heartbeat longer, and Luce wondered if he could hear her thoughts. How she wanted to press her hands against his chest and feel his arms go around her. How she wondered what his lips would taste like.

Maybe he could, because his eyes dropped to her mouth and back to her face, and the temperature in the truck seemed suddenly warmer. He shifted the truck back into Park.

"Come here," he whispered.

She didn't hesitate. She pushed her bags down to the floor and leaned toward him, closing the distance between them. Connor's arm went around her shoulder, turning her body toward his. His other hand brushed her face, fingers lingering on her mouth, sending shivers of delight coursing through her veins. When his mouth finally met hers, the touch was feather soft, as gentle as a child holding a snow globe. A light ignited in her chest, glowing brighter and brighter.

He pulled back, his dark eyes searching hers, questioning.

Luce gripped his forearms, using her hold to bring him back. "Don't stop," she whispered, her heart pulsing in her neck, her stomach, her shoulders. She pressed her lips to his, tasting the saltiness of his lips and feeding the flame in her navel.

His hands moved to her waist, fingering the band of her dress, squeezing the skin of her belly, all while his mouth didn't wander from hers. Luce closed her eyes, reveling in the male touch, losing herself in the heady rush of pleasure.

A loud rapping on the window jarred her out if it. She jerked her head, craning away to see a face in a Smoky the

Bear hat tapping on the fogged-up driver's side window. Face flushed but fighting a grin, Connor pressed a button and lowered the window.

"Sorry, deputy," he said to the stern-faced man who stood there. "We got carried away."

"Get carried away elsewhere," the deputy said, not even breaking a smile.

"You got it." Connor rolled the window up and sent Luce a sheepish grin. "Well. We've been invited to leave."

Luce's body tingled all over even as the rush began to recede. She smiled back at him. "I guess so."

♥

Connor drove Luce home after the fair, and it took all her willpower not to invite him in. But she knew after the way it felt to kiss him in the car, it wouldn't take but a moment in her house to give in to her desires.

Luce wasn't surprised when Connor called her Sunday evening at Melodee's house. She looked at his name dancing across the screen, a smile flirting with her lips.

"Who is that?" Melodee asked. "It's that boy, huh?"

Luce lifted an eyebrow at her sister. "That boy? Like you're my mom protecting me from the local troublemakers?"

Melodee had to laugh. "I'm just teasing you. I take it you had a nice time with *Connor* yesterday?"

Luce put down the phone, suddenly eager to talk to her sister. She'd call him later. "He's so different from Brian, Melodee."

Melodee picked up a pile of books from the sofa and rearranged them on the bookshelf. "Different how?"

"We went to a craft fair yesterday. And instead of standing around looking as if he wished he were anywhere else, Connor actually went into the tents with me."

"Oo, wow," Melodee said.

Luce threw up her hands. "You're failing to see the relevancy. Brian never did that. When we went to the Farmer's Market, even when I'd ask him to come in and look at something, it was like he wanted everyone to know I'd dragged him there and he wasn't happy about it. It made going places so awkward!"

"And Connor didn't make you feel that way."

"No," Luce said softly, picking up her phone again and staring at the missed call. "Nothing about him makes me feel awkward at all."

"Did you talk to your lawyer? Just to make sure?"

"No," Luce replied, annoyance flashing hot in her chest. Sometimes Melodee brought out the rebellious teenager in her. "It's not anyone's business. I'm allowed to date."

Melodee saluted her with a picture book. "Good luck, then! More power to you."

"Thanks." Luce picked up a glass of water from the counter and took a swig, shoving down any nagging doubts. She wouldn't let Brian taint this relationship.

♥

Connor texted Luce as she headed for her car after yoga Monday morning.

Meet for dinner?

She smiled. *Yes!*

Pick you up after work. You can wear your scrubs.

It's balloon day, Luce teased.

Like I said. Everything looks good.

She told herself to act sensible, to not read too much into it, but she knew the euphoria she felt had nothing to do with yoga.

"You're doing it again," Caroline murmured as she checked

off inventory in the back room.

"Doing what?" Luce asked, putting the empty vials back on the shelf.

Caroline smirked at her. "Humming. Just like you did on Friday. Something going on?"

Luce opened her mouth to respond and then closed it, thinking better of it. Perhaps some discretion was advised, considering who else worked in the clinic. "I'm not quite ready to say."

Caroline's eyebrows shot upward. "That sounds very ominous. Either you've committed a crime and you're still looking for your alibi, or you've started a secret relationship."

Luce ducked her head, wishing the smile would stop spreading across her face.

"Since you're not rubbing your hands together like a devious mastermind and you're grinning like crazy, I'm going to venture a guess that this has to do with a guy."

Luce pressed a finger to her lips. "I can't say anything just yet. So keep it on the down low, okay?"

Caroline nodded. "I won't say anything. But if you need someone to confide in, I'm here."

"Okay," Luce whispered.

The supply room door swung open, and Regina pushed her head in. "Is Luce in here? Oh." She frowned at the two of them giggling in a suspicious manner. "You have a phone call. At the front desk."

Luce glanced at Caroline, who raised an eyebrow. Odd. She stuffed her hand into the pocket of her scrubs to make sure she had her phone. A quick glance showed that it was on and she hadn't missed any calls. Why would someone call her at work? Unless they didn't have her phone number?

Or unless they couldn't reach her otherwise because they

were being blocked on her cell?

"Did you catch who it was?" Luce asked, trying unsuccessfully to hide the nervous tremor in her voice.

Regina shook her head. "No, but it's a guy. Do you want me to take a message?"

Luce pushed her hands against her rib cage and shoved downward, as if to move air out of her lungs. "Can you just find out who it is, please?"

Regina looked at her more carefully. "Is there someone you're trying to avoid?"

"Can you just ask, Regina?" Caroline said pointedly.

"Sure." Regina vanished and returned a moment later, her pretty features marred by an annoyed expression. "Said his name is Brian. And he got rather aggressive with me. Said if you don't come to the phone, you'll regret it."

"No! Tell him you were wrong, there's no Luce here!" Now her hands were shaking, and she knew from the heat on her face that her skin would be splotchy.

"Is it your ex?" Caroline asked. "I'll take it for you."

Regina's head swiveled back-and-forth between them. "Should I call the police, Luce?"

Caroline headed for the door. "I'll handle this. Do you have a lawyer? I'll tell him to call your lawyer."

"No," Luce said, realizing now that she should have followed through with Melodee's advice, if only to diffuse a situation like this. "But I'm getting one. You tell him that."

"Got it." Caroline was already gone, the door swinging violently in her wake.

Regina still stood there, but she had her head cocked, studying Luce with a different expression on her face. "When you talked about your ex, you didn't mean a boyfriend. You meant your ex-husband."

Luce bobbed her head in affirmation and closed her eyes, feeling the tears slide out from under her eyelids.

Regina stepped closer and rubbed Luce's forearms. "It's okay. Men are scum. Caroline will make sure he doesn't call again. Let's get you a drink of water. Deep breaths, okay?" She stepped away and filled a plastic cup with water at the sink before returning.

Luce accepted it with shaking fingers. "Thank you," she whispered.

"Don't worry," Regina said. "We've got your back."

Luce took a tiny sip of the lukewarm water, her stomach jittery. And a small part of her brain reminded her that Regina might not be so gracious when she found out about Luce and Connor.

The phone call left Luce too rattled to concentrate on work. All she could think about was getting online and finding a good lawyer. She dropped a syringe so many times during inoculations that Regina came over and relieved her. She spilled a urine sample all over the bathroom, earning a scolding from Dr. Dahler. And she mixed up a patient's chart, nearly getting him a prescription for medicine he was allergic to, but luckily the patient noticed first.

Caroline found Luce in the hallway and clasped her by the shoulders. "You have two more hours to this workday. Are you going to make it?"

Luce let out a long, shuddery sigh. "Yes. I just need to get my head together."

Caroline gave her a squeeze. "I scared him off."

Luce allowed herself a brief smile. "Yes, you did."

Caroline's loud blustering voice had filled the reception area while she told Brian off for making what she called "illegal phone calls" and said Luce was getting a restraining order. Her threats carried enough credibility that Luce was fairly certain nobody would bother her at work again.

Of course, the downside was that now the entire office knew her problems.

"Just hang in there, okay? We'll go out for drinks after work."

Luce nodded. She didn't want to drink, didn't like the way alcohol brought out the anger inside of her. But she wouldn't mind sitting with a friend and crying out her worries.

Somehow she stumbled through the next two hours without destroying any lab results or injuring a patient. Finally the shift ended, and Luce joined the other nurses as they washed their hands in the back after putting away the last of the supplies.

"Are you okay?" Caroline asked for about the hundredth time.

Luce rolled her eyes. "Seriously. It's behind me now. "

"Well, run home and change and I'll come pick you up."

Luce nodded, grateful for Caroline, who seemed to know when to take charge. Her sister did the same thing after their mother's death, mothering Luce when she needed it.

"Regina, I think that's Connors car outside," Jenn, the receptionist, said from up front.

Luce stiffened.

"Really?" Regina said, her brow furrowing as she left the nurses' station and went down the hall.

And just like that, Luce remembered she was supposed to be going to dinner with Connor.

Her eyes went wide as she spun to the nearest window overlooking the parking lot. Regina's voice carried from the lobby.

"You're right! That's his car!"

"I thought they broke up?" Caroline said, moving to join Luce as if there were a show to watch.

"Oh, snap," Luce whispered.

Caroline froze. And then she reared her head back and gave Luce a probing look. "You want to tell me now who you started a relationship with?"

Luce could only shake her head. They should have agreed to meet elsewhere.

"You better say something," Caroline warned. "If Regina goes out there and finds out Connor is here for you, she'll never forgive you for letting her make a fool of herself."

She was right. Luce took a deep breath and rushed into the lobby. She darted to Regina and grabbed her arm right before Regina pushed her way out of the double doors.

"Regina," Luce said, "you should know something."

Regina turned her eyes away from the window and shot Luce a distracted look. "Just a sec, Luce. I'll be right back."

Luce gave her arm a gentle shake. "Connor and I have gone on a few dates."

That got her attention. Regina swiveled fully to face Luce, her eyes scanning her as of searching for a lie, or a joke. "You and Connor are dating?"

"No, no, no, we're not dating we're—we're—" What were they?

Regina's eyes narrowed. "So he's not here to see me. He's here for you."

Luce swallowed. "I just thought you should know before—"

"Before I throw myself into his arms like a freaking idiot?" Regina turned on her heel and marched through the swinging glass doors behind the reception desk and down the hallway.

Luce exhaled. *Shake it off.* That hadn't gone so well.

She turned and headed for the exit, in no mood to go anywhere with Connor.

CONNOR

W hy was it taking so long for Luce to come out? Connor checked the time on the dashboard in his car. He'd been here for ten minutes already. Maybe she hadn't seen his text?

He supposed he could just walk in . . . but Regina worked there, and he could imagine that would be all kinds of awkward.

The back door opened and Luce came out, still in her scrubs, one hand securing her purse to her shoulder while the other shoved the hair out of her face as the wind blew it back at her. She made her way toward his car but kept her eyes averted, and something knotted up in his chest. She didn't look happy.

She came to his side of the car and stopped, so he rolled his window down and put on his best smile.

"Hey. Not getting in?" he said, going for feigned ignorance.

"Hey," she said, crossing her arms over her chest. Her cheeks were flushed, but her lips whitened as she pressed them together. "This was a bad idea. Regina saw you."

He winced in spite of his attempts to look nonchalant. "I hoped she wouldn't notice."

"She might not have if the receptionist didn't say, 'oh, look, there's Connor!'" Luce flapped her arms like a crazy woman and crossed them over her chest again.

"Hey, sorry," he said. "I wasn't trying to cause a problem."

"We created drama! And I have to face her tomorrow at work!"

He bobbed his head toward the passenger side. "Come on

inside. We can talk about this."

"Everyone will see!"

His eyes darted toward the clinic windows. He didn't see any faces, but that didn't mean they weren't all there, staring at the parking lot. "Even more reason to get inside. We're causing a scene."

"Connor, I can't go with you. It looks bad."

He frowned at her. "Regina knows now, right? That we're dating?"

"She knows we went on a date."

"Luce, get in the car. Please? Or you don't want to be seen with me now because Regina found out?"

She hesitated. "I'm really not in the best mood right now. And it just feels wrong."

"Why? She was going to find out at some point."

She finally came around to the passenger side and climbed in, and heaving a sigh.

Connor kept his victory dance in his head. He'd gotten her into the car, but he hadn't gotten her off the battlefield. He drove toward her condo and waited a few minutes before speaking. "Are you mad at me?"

She heaved another sigh. "No. You didn't really do anything wrong. I guess I'm more mad at myself. I should have thought about her."

"We could have met elsewhere, if it would make you feel better. But for how long? Isn't it better she knows now?"

She still had her arms crossed over her chest. "Why are we at my condo?"

"Well, that's up to you, really. I can drop you off and you can fret about Regina's feelings all night. Or you can change your clothes and we can get some dinner. Like we planned."

She hesitated, as if actually considering the first option. She pushed on the door handle. "I'll change my clothes."

Connor's mom called while he waited for Luce to return.

"Connor?" she said in a watery voice.

He couldn't tell if it was from crying or from drinking, but immediately his annoyance flared up. Both were usually caused by Dave, and she always expected him to fix it. "What is it?"

"I got hurt," she sniffed. "Can you come home?"

"You got hurt?" There were so many ways to interpret that, and he didn't feel like playing guessing games. "What happened?"

"We went roller blading—"

Connor groaned, loud enough to express his displeasure. "Mom. Not only do you hate roller blading, but you really suck at it." Last time she'd gone with Dave, she'd skinned up her arm from elbow to wrist.

"I love roller blading," she replied in a high-pitched voice, and he ground his teeth together. That statement was meant for Dave's ears. "But I did fall. I hit my head really hard and it, it hurts."

"Dave can take care of you. He's there, right?"

"Yes, but . . ." Her voice trailed off. "Please?"

Luce was exiting her condo now, dressed in dark skinny jeans and a tight long-sleeved T-shirt. "I'm with Luce. We're going out."

"Oh, bring her!" His mom perked right up. "I'd love to have her over."

Now he heaved his own dramatic sigh. "No promises."

Half an hour later Connor parked his car in front of his mom's old Victorian house, yanking on the parking break so the car wouldn't slide backward on the slanted drive.

"Thanks for being flexible," he said to Luce. "Are you okay?"

She hefted the plastic bag in her hands and favored him with a smile, though it seemed a little weak. "You bought sushi. What more can I say?"

He returned her smile, but that nagging voice whispered to him as he followed her up the walkway. She seemed more bothered by the Regina incident than she admitted.

Would he ever know what a girl really thought?

Noises from a football game on the television greeted Connor when he walked in.

"Just take the food to the table in the kitchen," Connor said, placing his hands on Luce's shoulders and guiding her that direction. "I'm going to check on my mom real quick."

He found her in her room, the lights off, the scent of an herbal tea wafting in the air. "Mom?" He nearly tripped over the ottoman at the foot of the bed and righted himself on the back of a love seat.

She sniffed from the bed. "Hi, honey."

He turned on the lamp and stood next to her. "Are you hurting that bad?"

"Oh, I banged my head," she said. "I'm okay, I think."

"Luce is a nurse. Want her to take a look?"

"I'd love to see her! But she doesn't need to baby me."

"I'll get her." Connor closed the door behind him so his mom wouldn't hear when he laid into Dave. He walked into the living room, planting himself between Dave and the TV. Dave tried to look around him, but Connor moved with him.

Lifting his eyes, Dave looked at Connor. "What?"

"What happened to my mom?" Connor demanded.

Dave shrugged. "She fell and hit her head. I brought her home, got her some ice, helped her to her room. Even made her a cup of tea." Dave looked smugly proud of that. "What are you expecting?"

"Oh, I don't know, for you guys to act responsible! Roller blading without helmets? She's not good at this, Dave, you should know that!"

"She wanted to go!"

Connor threw his hands up and walked out, too mad to continue. Dave didn't respect his mom or her needs. All he cared about were his.

Luce waited in the kitchen when he entered. She stood with her back to the table, her hands stuffed in the back pockets of her jeans, a position that highlighted her curves. "Is your mom okay?"

He focused on her face so he wouldn't stare at her chest. "Yeah, I think so. Could you check her out? Just in case?"

She shrugged. "I'm not a doctor, but sure." She grabbed her purse and went down the hall.

Connor followed her back to his mom's room, though he stayed in the doorway and tried to make himself invisible while they talked together.

"I'm just gonna check you for a concussion, okay?"

"Thank you for coming. It means so much to me."

"Oh, sure, no problem."

"And to Connor, too. He was like a lost puppy before you appeared."

She gave a soft laugh, and his ears burned. Part of him wanted to walk away, but the other part wanted to linger in case anything else was said.

"How bad is your pain?"

"It hurts pretty bad. My head is throbbing."

Luce probed his mom's neck, felt her head, even dug a pen light from her purse and shone it in her eyes. "I don't think you have a concussion, and there's no knot on your head. How about I bring you some Tylenol and you get some rest?"

The blankets moved as his mom's hand fumbled with them, then she pressed Luce's fingers. "Thank you."

"You're welcome."

His mom cleared her throat. "We're going up to Joplin Saturday, checking out an estate sale. Want to come?"

Connor felt a ripple of surprise at the invite. His mom wanted Luce there? She never even let Dave come. She always said it was sacred mother/son time.

"Oh." Luce glanced toward the doorway where Connor stood. "I'm not sure. I don't want to intrude."

"You can see what we do. It'll be fun."

"Okay. Sure, I'll come. Let me get you that medicine." She shuffled out, keeping her head down.

"She's okay?" Connor asked, trailing behind as they went back to the kitchen.

"Yeah." She began opening cupboards at random, presumably looking for medicine. "I think so."

"Here." He opened the medicine cabinet and pulled out the Tylenol.

Her eyes shot toward him before looking away, but in that brief moment he noticed they were moist. "Thanks," she said.

"Hey." He took her arm, turning her to face him. "You're not crying, are you?"

Luce hesitated, avoiding his gaze, but there was no mistaking the clear shimmer over her blue-green eyes. "My mom died when I was twelve."

"Oh. I didn't know. I'm sorry."

"Don't be," she whispered, one tear escaping and rolling down her cheek. "Having your mom around is a nice thing."

Seeing her cry tore something up inside of him, and Connor

wrapped her in a hug, not wanting to witness her pain. "Don't cry, then. Make it a happy thing."

She laughed against his chest. "Okay. You're right." She moved away, shaking the tube of pills. "Let me get these to her."

She still didn't meet his eyes, and he trapped her again, grabbing her forearms and turning her toward him. "This isn't how I pictured tonight. Let me make it up to you."

"This is fine, Connor."

He didn't let go. "I'll do it right this time."

"I have some other things going on this week. But I'll see you Saturday, okay? You can even pick me up."

She kept her gaze lowered, and he got the definite sense she was hiding something.

"You sure?" He let her go and tried to catch her eye, but she avoided him.

"Yes."

"Is there anything wrong, Luce?" He couldn't bear it if she were keeping something from him. He held his breath.

"No." She shook her head.

"Promise?" He tightened his grip, trying to get her to look at him. "You would tell me, right?"

She lifted her face and caught his eye for a second before turning away. "Just remembering my mom."

Was she telling the truth? She could be. He hoped she was. "Okay." He leaned back and nodded down the hall. "My mom's waiting."

~ Chapter Thirteen ~

LUCE

Get a lawyer. Get a lawyer. Get a lawyer.

The mantra ran itself through Luce's head as she cleaned her kitchen after Connor dropped her off. Her hands shook with nervous energy, and she dropped the dish soap into the sink twice while trying to wash dishes.

Connor had been quiet on the drive home, but Luce didn't have the energy to make conversation. She'd done her best to act normal, but even her appetite had been down. Now she tried to quiet her nerves by promising to find a lawyer tomorrow.

Her phone rang, and Luce gasped, the plate slipping from her hands and shattering on the floor. She dug her phone out of her purse, letting out a relieved breath when she saw Caroline's name.

"Hello?" Luce said, falling into a kitchen chair with a sigh.

"You ditched me," Caroline's voice said, rich and slightly teasing through the phone line.

"I'm sorry." Luce sighed again. She pulled her hair from the ponytail holder and ran her fingers through it. "I forgot I had something with Connor."

"It's totally fine. So. Connor, huh?"

Her tone begged for details, but Luce couldn't give any right now. "Yeah. Not the smartest move on my part."

"Girl, he's dreamy. Who can blame you?" Caroline softened her tone. "Are you okay?"

So Caroline heard the stress in Luce's voice. "Not really. I guess I need to get a lawyer."

"I'm sorry, hon. I can recommend a good one to you."

"Can you?" Luce sat up straighter. "That would be great." One less thing to figure out.

"Sure. I'll text you his info."

They chatted a few more minutes before Luce gratefully hung up. Her stomach churned, and she popped open the lid to her meds, hoping to fall into a blissful, dreamless sleep. Two pills later, she turned out the lights and stumbled into bed.

♥

The atmosphere was decidedly frosty when Luce stepped into the clinic. Regina set her clipboard with the day's appointments on the countertop and walked back to the sanitation station without a word.

Luce glanced at Caroline, who gave a shrug and went back to pulling files.

"How are you today, girl?" Caroline asked, keeping her voice low.

"Been better," Luce said, as close as she'd come to admitting her splitting headache, the way her pulse raced, and her irrational urge to call in sick so she could talk to a lawyer. "I guess I need to clear the air with Regina."

"If you want."

Luce hated to have someone upset with her. She watched Regina head to the break room for lunch and gave it all of five seconds before she told the doctor she was going on break as well. She slipped into the break room after the other nurse.

"Regina?"

Regina sipped a mug of coffee at the table. She lifted her head, beautiful even with her large blond curls pulled back into a ponytail. She arched one eyebrow and said nothing.

Without waiting for an invitation, Luce pulled out a chair across from her. "I'm sorry. I should've told you before about Connor."

Regina shrugged. "It doesn't matter. I'm not his girlfriend. And you and I barely know each other."

Ouch. Luce considered Regina a friend, but she realized belatedly she shouldn't be going out with a friend's ex so shortly after they'd broken up.

Regina leaned back in her chair and tapped a finger to her lips. "What does Connor think about your divorce?"

Luce's heart did a little skip. "What?"

"Oh. You haven't told him."

She said it with just the right mixture of concern, her brow furrowed as she studied Luce with what almost seemed like pity.

"Well, no," Luce said, shifting her hips on the hard plastic chair. "But we're just getting to know each other."

Regina turned her blue eyes to her cup and ran her fingers across the rim. "Could be an issue with some guys."

Luce pursed her lips. What was Regina really saying? Would it be an issue with Connor? "We're not serious, Regina. Just having fun. He doesn't need to know my whole back story. And I don't need to know his." *Or yours*, she thought, hoping Regina wouldn't see fit to fill her in on the gory details of their relationship.

"Of course." Regina lifted her cup to her lips, keeping her eyes on Luce.

♥

As soon as they closed the clinic, Luce changed into a conservative black skirt and sweater shirt. Her stomach was a jumbled up bunch of knots as she drove toward the office of the lawyer Caroline had recommended. Would this marriage never be behind her? She brought along all the legal documents from her divorce, as well as copies of bank statements of the accounts in question.

The small receiving room had a warm beverage bar on one wall and a tray of miniature croissants and muffins on the low coffee table. Water trickled from a fountain by the door. Luce clutched her file folder to her chest and took several deep breaths, trying to calm her jittery nerves. One foot bounced up and down against the carpet, a physical manifestation of the jumping her stomach was doing.

A door opened, and a heavyset woman with curly lavender hair walked out. Her slacks and blouse said casual and confident. "Luce Donovan?" she said, and the smile lines around her eyes instantly put Luce at ease.

"Yes." Luce stood up, letting out her breath. She needed to legally get her name changed. She used one hand to smooth her skirt while the other one protectively held onto her file folder.

"Mr. Jorgenson is ready to see you," the woman said with a pleasant smile. "Follow me."

Luce did so, her heart beginning its nervous pitter-patter the closer they moved to the office.

The woman opened a door, stuck her head in, and said, "Here's Mrs. Donovan."

Luce stepped into the office, and a broad shouldered, gray-haired man stood from behind a large mahogany desk.

"Come on in," he said. He clasped her hand in one of his large ones and gave it a good shake. "Have a seat." He gestured to the leather chair in front of his desk.

Luce sat down, placing her folder on top of the desk and flattening it with her fingers.

"How can I help you?" Mr. Jorgenson said. He pressed his index fingers to his lips, studying her with soft brown eyes.

Luce swallowed and looked at the lawyer. "I'm not even sure where to start," she said. "I got a call from my ex-husband's lawyer a few weeks ago saying that they were going to take me to court and try to get money from my personal account. And now my ex is even calling me at work and harassing me. So I just need to see if my money is safe and what I can do to end this."

"When was your divorce finalized?"

"About a year ago."

"And is this a joint account or an account where you both deposited money?"

Luce shook head. "No. This is my private account, I've had it since I was a child. I send a portion of my paycheck over every month."

"Even while you were married?"

Luce's heart sank within her. "Yes."

"More than likely, your money is safe. However, there is the question of the money you were putting in while you were married. We'll need to verify that it was indeed only your money."

Luce's shoulders tightened, and she could feel the defensive anger building within her. "He took all my money," she blurted. "He moved our joint accounts into one with just his name, he took all the profits from my company, I had to close my doors, I lost everything. Everything! And now he's trying to take this. It's the only thing I've got. He can't have it."

Mr. Jorgenson smiled at her, a kindly expression, though his eyes were serious. "I understand your situation. And I'm going to do everything I can to protect your money. But I'm going to need documentation. If he takes you to court, I have to be able to prove that it belongs to you."

Luce sank back into the leather chair, suddenly close to tears. She had been fighting for so many months. Fighting to retake control of the life her husband had torn apart. She just wanted to move on. Why was Brian so intent on destroying her?

"Thank you," she whispered. "That's all I want."

"I need you to sign these papers if I'm going to represent you," Mr. Jorgenson said, pulling out several documents for her. "I'll also need a deposit for a retainer. And while we're at it, I need full disclosure from you. I need to know what happened, I need to know what was settled, and I need to know anything you might have done or be doing that your ex-husband could use against you."

Luce opened her file folder and removed the court documents. "Here's everything from the divorce. It details what we went through, how much debt we had, and how much of our money was put into paying off those debts."

Mr. Jorgenson glanced at her. "And these debts, were they both of yours?"

"No," Luce said, feeling immense relief that he had asked. "None of them were mine. But they were wrapped up in my name, and my money was used to pay them off."

Mr. Jorgenson nodded. "Was there anything in your behavior that could be used against you?"

"I don't see how." She spread her hands out at her sides. "I was faithful to him, I wasn't frivolous with money, I'm not a heavy drinker, I don't get in trouble with the law . . . I don't see that there's anything in my behavior that could possibly be construed as wrong."

"Did you wait until the divorce was final before you started dating again?"

Luce gave a short laugh. "Um, yeah."

The shadow of a smile crossed his lips. "So you haven't dated?"

Luce shook her head. "I didn't date anyone."

"And you're not dating now?"

She hesitated. "I'm seeing someone now. But it's a new relationship."

Mr. Jorgenson stood up and came around the desk. "Then you will be very easy to defend." He handed her a sheet of paper with scribblings on it. "Take this to my receptionist, and she will get you squared away. If he calls you again, you can refer him to me. You don't need to communicate with him or his lawyer at all. I'll do that for you."

Luce almost laughed with relief. It was exactly what she wanted. Somebody else to deal with them. "Thank you. Thank you so much. That makes me feel much better."

CONNOR

Connor didn't call Luce on Tuesday, and she didn't call him.

Maybe her emotion on Monday really was caused by missing her mother.

So why did he feel this distance between them?

The door opened with a jangle just as Connor put the

deposits in the bank bag. "We're already closed," he said, surprised the door hadn't been locked. He was in such a rush to get out of here.

"Good thing I have a key."

Connor looked up and grinned at Tyson. "And what idiot would give a key to you?" His eyes took in Amber hanging out behind Ty, her straight blond hair falling around her shoulders, signature turquoise glasses settled on her nose. His grin widened.

"Someone who's hoping to get a killer deal on the honeymoon suite at the Crescent Hotel," Ty said flamboyantly. He wrapped an arm around Amber's waist and tugged her against him. "There's lots going on at the convention center. Want to come with us? Maybe bring Luce?"

"I'd love to meet her," Amber said. "I've heard so much about her."

"That would be awesome," Connor said, a twinge of disappointment in his chest. "Except I'm loaded with homework. Maybe this weekend we can all get together."

"That sounds perfect." Amber glanced at Tyson and added, almost shyly, "I could bring Raven."

"That's her daughter," Tyson said, something like smug pride entering his voice. "And she's absolutely the most beautiful little girl you ever saw. She's got this black hair—"

Amber laughed and tugged on Ty's arm. "Come on, let's let Connor close up here. He can meet her later."

"You bet," Connor said. "Thanks, guys. I'll catch you later."

They waved and walked out, and Connor couldn't help envying their happiness.

Luce finally called Wednesday night.

"Connor?" she said, her voice sounding timid.

"Yeah, this is my number," he said. He paused as he pulled

his bike from the rack in the garage. He'd been about to leave; he needed something to distract himself from her.

"I haven't heard from you. Was it my turn to call?"

He exhaled, a bit frustrated with her. "You can call anytime you feel like it. We're not taking turns."

"Same for you," she replied. "Or did you not feel like it?"

This felt an awful lot like a disagreement, and Connor abruptly decided not to make it one. "You seemed distracted on Monday. I thought maybe you didn't want to be around me." The fact that she hadn't called only reinforced that theory.

"I'm sorry," she said. "I *was* distracted. Just some family issues, though. I didn't mean to keep you out. I missed talking to you."

"You could've called," he said, leaning his bike against the wall and resting against it.

"I'm not very good at that," she said.

He accepted that, taking her response at face value. "Is everything okay with your family?"

"Yes. I think so."

He pulled his bike from the wall again. "I'm about to go for a bike ride. I could come over."

"I'm almost to my sister's," she said. "But I'll see you Saturday, right?"

"Right. And Luce? Don't be afraid to call."

"Okay," she said, a little laugh in her voice. "You either."

He fastened his helmet on and climbed onto the bike, no longer going on a ride to relieve tension. Talking to Luce lightened him somehow.

♥

"Mom!" Connor rattled the keys by the front door for the hundredth time. "I told Luce we'd be there in ten minutes!"

"I'm coming, I'm coming!" Breathless, she finally came down the hallway, a clutch under her arm.

Connor gawked at her. The pinstriped suit she wore didn't have enough buttons to keep her chest where it was supposed to be. "Why are you wearing that?"

"The deeper my cleavage, the better deal we get," she said breezily, brushing past him and out the door.

Just great. She was in that kind of mood.

They were only a few minutes later to pick Luce up, but Connor had his apology all ready as he knocked on the door.

The words caught in his mouth when she answered. Her hair was up in a high ponytail, a loose blue and red tunic hanging over black leggings. She'd painted her eyes the way girls do and something pink shimmered on her lips. The effect was stunning, and he couldn't take his eyes off her mouth.

"Hi," she said, and he finally found his voice.

"Hey, Luce." He extended his hand, and she took his, her fingers weaving naturally with his. He pulled her closer to him and leaned over her, his eyes drinking her in. Her lips parted, begging for a kiss.

The passenger door of his car flew open, and his mom stepped out. "Luce!" she shouted, waving her hand like she was afraid somehow Luce wouldn't see her. Connor rolled his eyes.

Luce bit back a smile and stepped over to his mom, allowing her to throw her arms around her in a hug.

"Hi," Luce said, hugging her back. "How's your head?"

"Oh, fine, like nothing happened," she said. "Just my ego that's wounded now."

"Mom," Connor said, forcing himself to be patient, "you promised not to jump on her."

"Oh, right, sorry. I just couldn't help myself." She backed

off, running her hands down Luce's shoulders and smoothing her shirt. "I'm just so happy that Connor's found someone."

"Mom," he said again, sharper this time.

She clucked her tongue and raised a finger, then climbed into the back of the car. "Just pretend like I'm not here!" she called out cheerfully.

He grunted. Easier said than done.

♥

By the time they headed home after a few hours of sifting through dead people's precious items, Connor's patience with his mom was gone.

"Mom," he said as she began rustling through the plastic bags in the backseat, "don't touch, please. I have it all organized exactly how I want it in the store."

"It's for my store, Connor," she said, and continued to go through bags.

A giggle escaped Luce beside him. She opened up the fudge she'd purchased and offered him a piece. "Fudge? It's dark chocolate."

If it was meant to be a distraction, it worked. "Actually sounds wonderful."

He tore off a piece, and Luce offered some to his mom before cutting off a chunk for herself with the little plastic knife that came with the fudge. "I love fudge," she hummed. "Maybe I'll open a fudge shop."

"We already have one," Connor murmured, letting the bittersweet chocolate flavor melt on his tongue.

"And it's excellent," his mom piped up. "Those two dames make the best fudge you'll ever eat. Get it? Those two dames." And she laughed raucously.

Oh boy. Connor exhaled loudly.

Luce shrugged. "Can't have too much fudge."

His mom let out a squeal in the backseat. "My phone's ringing. Where's my phone? Found it! Oh! It's Dave! Connor, stop the car!"

"Why, Mom?" he all but snapped. "He's on the phone, not the side of the road. I can drive while you talk."

She didn't spare him an answer. She was already on the phone, gushing to Dave.

Connor held out a hand. "More fudge. Please."

Luce obliged him. "Is she always like this?" she asked, keeping her tone low. Not that his mom noticed, engaged as she was in a lively phone conversation.

"No," Connor growled. He shoved the fudge in his mouth. "She's trying to impress you," he said around it, the sugar melting down the sides of his tongue.

"Why would she do that?" Luce asked, pushing against her seat.

He swallowed the fudge. "Because she knows I am."

Watching Luce's face turn a lovely shade of pink made his admission worth it. Luce looked down and plucked at the edge of her tunic, then looked out the window and cleared her throat several times. Connor smiled to himself.

"Is she like this with her boyfriend?"

Connor lifted one shoulder. "Yeah. She's trying to impress him too. The worse part is—no, never mind."

"What?"

"No, really." He shook his head. He couldn't tell her his deep suspicions: that human beings in general hid or manipulated the truth, were dishonest when it suited them. "It's nothing."

His mom got off the phone and launched into a tirade against Dave for not calling her all day, and Connor effectively evaded all of Luce's further attempts to bring up the subject.

His mom only trailed off when Connor parked the car in front of Luce's condo.

"What are we—oh. You're taking Luce home." She pushed herself between them in the front seat and gave him the evil eye. "Don't you think maybe she wanted to go to lunch or something?"

"Oh, no, it's okay," Luce said, undoing her seatbelt and grabbing the box of dishes she'd purchased. "We snacked at the auction."

"We cook steaks on Sunday!" his mom said. "Come over tomorrow!"

"Yeah," Connor said, facing her, not wanting to let her go. "I can pick you up." He could invite Tyson and Amber, Moki, they could all meet her.

"I'm working tomorrow," Luce said, though she sounded like she wished she wasn't. "Maybe next week."

"I'll hold you to it." He put the car into Park and came around to open her door.

They walked in silence, and he stood behind her while she inserted her key and turned the lock. She pushed open the door and turned around to face him.

"Hey, that was fun. I'd go again. If you asked." She flashed him a teasing smile.

That smile lulled him in, and he placed his hands on her forearms, rubbing them up her shoulders and back down to her elbows. "Thanks for coming." Tightening his grip, he pulled her closer, then pressed his mouth to hers and kissed her, long and slow.

He tried to restrain the kiss, but he'd been yearning for this moment since their last kiss at the craft fair. Immediately a flame of desire leapt to life in his navel. Luce sighed against his mouth. Her fingers wove through his hair, an urgency in her touch as she pulled him closer, pressing her body against his.

He closed his hands around her waist, then used his hold on her to push her away before he lost control right here on the porch.

Luce's eyes opened. She placed her hands on his hips, and then glanced at his car in the parking lot. With a chiding laugh, she released him. "I guess you better go."

Yes, he better. "I like you, Luce," he breathed out. He bent his head and kissed her again, gently this time, luxuriating in the feel of her soft lips against his mouth.

"Oh, good," she joked as he released her. "I'd hate to think you kiss girls you don't like."

He quirked a grin. "Yeah, that doesn't happen." With a wave, he turned around. "It's my turn. I'll call you."

He heard her laugh behind him, and a quiver of delight bubbled up in his gut. He wasn't letting a week go by without kissing her again.

Chapter Fourteen

LUCE

Luce stood in the doorway, watching Connor walk away. She felt her body leaning toward him even as he got in the car and drove off, and she knew she'd be watching her phone for the promised call.

But it was Melodee who called as Luce fussed about her kitchen, setting out her newly acquired kitchen dishes.

"Hey," Luce said, answering the phone with one hand and surveying the red and white checked porcelain plates on the table. A warmth filled her chest as she realized she actually liked the set up. Her kitchen. Her house.

"Hey, yourself," Melodee said. "What are you doing?"

"Hanging out at home." Luce pulled out a stool and sat at her tree trunk table. "Enjoying my day off. What about you?"

"Well, since you're not occupied . . . I think you better come over here."

Only now did Luce pick up on the tension in her sister's voice. "What is it?" she asked, straightening. "Did something happen to Dad?"

"No," Melodee said. "It's easier to show you."

Show her? Show her what? "I'll be right there."

Luce forced herself to drive slowly on the switch-back roads from her house to Melodee's. Her hands white-knuckled the steering wheel, and her heart pounded erratically. She hated the suspense. She didn't even want to imagine what could be wrong. It would have been so much better if her sister had just told her.

She hopped out of the car the moment she parked it and hurried up the walk. "Hello?" she called, letting herself in, not bothering to knock. She headed toward the dining room, where she heard the kids giggling with Jay.

"She's in our room," he said, glancing up from a game of dog pile on the floor or something just as uncomfortable.

"Thanks." Luce waved her hand and continued down the hall to the master bedroom.

The door was closed. She leaned her head against it and knocked. "Mel? It's me."

The door swung inward so quickly Luce nearly toppled.

"Come in," Melodee said, gripping Luce by the arm and hauling her into the darkened room. She closed the door after her.

"What is it?" Luce glanced around. Did this have something to do with the baby? "Are you okay?"

"I'm fine." Melodee took a deep breath and held out an envelope. "This came for you today. By certified mail."

Luce took it, frowning. "All this drama over a letter?" She reached over and flipped a switch, flooding the room with light. "You hide out in here like you're some sort of secret spy."

"The light was bothering my eyes," Melodee huffed. She

gestured at the envelope. "Read it."

Luce turned her attention to the white rectangle. "It's open already."

"That's because I read it. Read it!"

Deciding not to tell her sister how illegal it was to read someone else's mail, Luce removed the single sheet of paper from inside.

To Ms. Donovan,

You are hereby summoned and required to serve upon Mr. Rasmussen, Brian Donovan's attorney, an answer to the complaint that is Hereby served upon you, within 20 days after service is received by you, exclusive of the day of service.

Failure to respond to this summons will result in a judgment by default against you by the plaintiff for the relief requested in the accompanying complaint.

What followed were a list of allegations that made little sense to Luce. The one line that stuck out was at the very end.

Plaintiff is seeking restitution in the amount of $80,000.

"What is this?" Luce gasped out, her blood running cold.

"Brian is suing you," Melodee said flatly. "You need to see your lawyer right away."

"This can't be happening." Luce's hand trembled. She wanted to burn the paper and pretend she'd never seen it, run and hide and make it all disappear. "What do I do? If I just ignore it, will it go away?" Even though she knew it wouldn't, every part of her wanted her sister to respond yes.

"No!" Melodee exclaimed. "You absolutely cannot ignore this. That is the best way for you to admit you're guilty."

"What?" Luce looked again at the amount of money on the paper. "I don't understand."

"Let me make it very clear for you," Melodee said, her tone taking on the superiority of an older sister. "You are being sued. By your ex-husband. For eighty-thousand dollars."

"But that's more money than I got in the settlement!" Luce cried. A tremor built up in her chest, inching out along her shoulders and arms until she felt her whole body shaking. With no children between them, Brian didn't have to pay any child support. And since they had been married less than two years, she wasn't rewarded any alimony, either. The few thousand dollars she'd gotten out of the settlement for wrongdoing was all she had.

"Luce!" Melodee shook the paper in her face. "Did you read the allegations?"

Luce shook her head, her mind spinning. Why was Brian doing this to her? He was the one who had cheated her, he was the one who wanted the divorce. How had someone who had once loved her turned so malicious?

"You need to know what you're up against," Melodee said. She pressed the papers against her dresser, flattening them. "He's accusing you of withholding how much money you had. He says you had secret accounts and money you didn't disclose. Is there any truth to that?"

Her thoughts tripped over themselves, trying to piece together the accusation. Her lower lip trembled, and she blinked hard to keep from crying. How was it just a few hours ago she'd been blissfully and completely happy? "I mean, I have my private account. But he can't touch that, can he?"

"No." But Melodee hesitated, and Luce saw doubt in her eyes. "I don't know exactly, Luce. You need to talk to your lawyer."

"How is he supposed to help me?"

"This letter." Melodee slapped her hand against it. "You have him for something like this. He'll help you answer this complaint and make sure you're not mistreated."

Luce exhaled and nodded. "What else does Brian accuse me of?"

Melodee glanced at the letter, but she didn't have to read it. "He also accuses you of having an affair."

Luce gasped, appalled. "But I didn't!"

Melodee placed a hand on top of Luce's forearm and gave her a little squeeze. "We know that. Brian knows that. This is a scare tactic, Luce. He's manipulating you, trying to get your money just like he did when you were married. Don't give in to him. He knows if he scares you enough, you won't fight. You'll just pay to make him go away."

It was a very tempting prospect. "But not eighty-thousand dollars!"

"Not even five thousand. If anything, turn around and countersue him."

Sue her ex-husband. Her former lover. Her former best friend. Luce had the insane desire to laugh like a crazy woman. And then suddenly she was crying. Why had she not seen this coming when they were dating? How could she have been so blind, so gullible, so naïve?

Melodee's arms went around her, hugging her and consoling her. "It's okay. We're going to get him out of your life for good, and then you never have to look back on this." She pulled back. "Are you still seeing Connor?"

Defensiveness flared up in Luce's chest. "I am. And there's no reason for me not to. I didn't even move here until the divorce had been final for a year. There's no way anyone can say that Connor had something to do with it." Her fingers went to her mouth, and she flushed hot for a moment when she considered what she'd felt when he kissed her earlier.

"Luce, be careful. I'm not saying you're a bad judge of character, but you know what happened last time."

Luce rolled her eyes. "Right. I'm not likely to forget anytime soon." *Unfortunately.*

♥

Luce stayed the rest of the afternoon at her sister's house. She helped her cut the fruit for a salad at dinner, and then she and Melodee sat on the couch and watched her children wrestle with their father. Neither one of them said anything about the letter. Nothing could be done about it until Monday, so Luce tried to push it from her head.

The aroma of the tater tot casserole filled the living room.

"I'm hungry, Mama," little Timothy said.

"Keep playing with your dad. It's not time to eat yet." Melodee turned her attention from her children to Luce. "How's work going?"

Luce shrugged. "Fine. I've made some friends." *And maybe some enemies.*

From where her purse sat on the kitchen counter, the familiar jingle of a cell phone rang out. "Maybe that's one of my friends now," Luce said, unable to quell the sudden rush of panic that fluttered into her heart. Or it might be a lawyer calling to threaten her.

Nonsense, she told herself, *even lawyers take a break on the weekend.*

She retrieved her phone, and a smile pressed itself against her lips when she saw Connor's name. "It's Connor."

"Careful," Melodee warned.

Luce turned her back on her sister and answered the phone. "Hey. I didn't expect to hear from you so soon."

"I know. I had to call and apologize for my mom. She was a little over the top today."

"Oh, no, don't worry about it," Luce said, settling herself comfortably on a stool at the bar. "She's funny."

"She's crazy is what you mean. I can't control her. She's like a toddler running rampant."

Luce laughed. She hadn't known Connor was prone to theatrics. "It really was fine."

"Well, all the same, try not to take anything she said seriously. What are you doing for dinner? Want to meet up?"

"I'm at my sisters house."

"I'll pick you up. What's the address? Or did you want to go home first?"

His offer was very tempting. But still . . . Melodee's words rang in her head. *"I'm not saying you're a bad judge of character . . ."*

But Connor wasn't Brian.

Luce turned slightly at a movement by her shoulder and saw Melodee perched behind her.

"Is everything okay?" she asked, sounding concerned when Luce knew she was just being nosy.

Moving the phone away from her mouth, Luce said, "Connor just wants to know if he should pick me up here or at my house."

Melodee's eyebrows rose. "By all means, let him pick you up here. Don't want to waste time going home if you guys are so anxious to see each other."

It would be impossible not to pick up on the sarcasm in Melodee's voice. But Luce knew she had another motive: she wanted to meet Connor. Luce realized, to her surprise, she wanted Melodee to meet him as well. Turning back to the phone, Luce said, "Just come to my sister's house. I'll text you her address."

♥

Melodee lay on the bed with her feet propped up on a pillow, her belly distended so far that from the closet, Luce couldn't see her face.

"What are you going to wear tonight?" Melodee asked.

"If I knew the answer to that, I wouldn't be sifting through your pre-baby clothes." She pulled out a long-sleeved short purple dress and held it up to herself.

"What's wrong with what you're wearing?"

Luce glanced at the mirror behind her and took in the leggings and tunic. "He's already seen me in this."

Melodee laughed. "Take any of my clothes you want. Chances are I'm not getting back into that even after this baby comes along. I haven't worn anything in there in nearly ten years."

Luce made a mental note to enjoy all of her skinny clothes before she started having babies. She put the purple dress back and pulled out a red one with short sleeves and a cute black belt that buckled at the waist.

"I like this one."

"Try it on," Melodee said, and her hand appeared above the belly, gesturing toward the bathroom.

"Thanks," Luce said. She only tripped on one toy getting into the master bathroom. Luce slipped the red dress over her head, squirming her arms to get them through.

"Are you going to tell him about the letter?" Melodee called from the bedroom. Luce frowned at herself in the mirror.

"I don't really see how that's any of his business."

The bedsheets rustled, and Luce turned her head to see her sister pushing herself to the edge of the bed.

"You haven't even told him about Brian, have you." There was no question in her voice.

Luce rolled her shoulders, trying to work out the stiffness. "We're only just starting our relationship. I think the things like major baggage can wait. If I threw that one down on every first date, I'd never get a second."

"Yes, maybe on the first date. But how many have you been on?"

Luce shrugged. She popped out of the bathroom and gave a little spin. "How do I look?"

"Way too cute. Like someone who's never had a baby."

"Well, that's fair, because I haven't."

The timer dinged in the kitchen, and little voices started a chorus of, "Mom! The timer's going off!"

Melodee pushed herself to her feet. "Sounds like dinner's ready."

Luce followed her sister down the hallway. When the doorbell rang, it played over her nerves like a violin bow across the strings. Why was she so nervous? Did it really matter that much what Melodee thought of Connor?

Yes, apparently. Or maybe Luce just wanted her own opinion validated.

Melodee's husband got to the door before Luce reached the living room. The two men shook hands, and Luce put on a bright smile as she stepped to Connor's side. She noted that he was still wearing his jeans from earlier.

Connor glanced at her and gave her a quick smile before his eyes drifted to her left.

"Connor, this is my sister." Luce took him by the wrist and pulled him away from Jay and over to Melodee. Her sister gave nothing away with the quick look she shot Luce but instead accepted Connor's offered hand.

"Hi," Melodee said, smirking. "I'm glad to meet you. Luce has mentioned you a few times."

"I wanted a chance to meet you face to face. Instead of crashing into you on the sidewalk."

"Hopefully you have more grace with my sister."

Connor glanced at Luce, and even she could see the affection in his eyes. "I'm trying."

Luce worked hard to keep her smile firmly in place. "Anyway. Shall we go?"

"What's your rush?" Melodee asked, a mischievous glint in her eyes. "Wouldn't you rather stay and eat here?"

"Um, no," Luce said, just as Connor said, "That's a really nice invite."

Luce swiveled her head and shot him a glare. "Yes, it's nice," she said. "But we have other plans."

"That's right," Connor said, following her lead. "Some other time."

"Some other time," Melodee echoed, barely able to keep the grin off her face.

Luce grabbed Connor's arm and hauled him from the house.

"What's going on?" he asked, laughing. "Why don't you want to stay with your sister?"

"So she can spend the next hour playing twenty questions with you? I don't think so." Not only that, but Luce was suddenly terrified Melodee might accidentally say something about the letter. Or Brian. *Forget about that*, Luce told herself, pushing it from her mind. She didn't want to dwell on Brian and his nastiness right now.

Connor held the door to his four-door sedan open for her, and Luce inhaled the new-car scent as she pulled her seatbelt on.

"You keep your car so clean," she said.

"I'm only in it for a few minutes each day. Not hard to do."

Luce made a vow never to let him in her car, littered as it was with Styrofoam Sonic cups and candy wrappers.

He turned onto Van Buren and headed toward Main Street. When he didn't turn down it, Luce asked, "Where are we going?"

"I want to take you to this little place over here." He glanced at her. "Is that okay?"

Luce raised an eyebrow. "Sure, of course."

He pulled off into a strip mall and stopped in front of a small shop called "Grandma's Beans and Cornbread."

"Come on," he said, offering his hand. "Nothing says comfort food like beans and cornbread."

That definitely depended on the person.

She let him pull her inside. The little restaurant was set up like a cafe, with red and white tablecloths across the tables and a counter to place orders. Luce hovered behind Connor as he ordered.

Sandwiches and beans. The offerings were simple.

"I'll take the beans and cornbread meal," Connor said. He leaned toward Luce and whispered, "You can't go wrong with that."

"Uh-huh." She scanned the menu, wanting something with vegetables.

Looked like the closest she would get was a wrap. "I'll take a turkey wrap."

"You look nice," Connor said, bobbing his head at her as they sat at a booth. "I like your dress."

"It's my sister's," Luce said. She flattened the skirt and gave a sheepish smile. "I'm a little overdressed."

"You're perfect," he said.

She looked away, not sure what to say to that. Connor didn't seem to filter his thoughts before they left his lips. Did he expect such transparency from her?

"Number twenty-two," the girl behind the counter said, and Connor pushed out of the booth.

A moment later he returned with a tray of food. He placed a

bowl of beans in front of his spot and handed Luce a plate with a wrap.

The aroma of beans and bacon and fresh cornbread wafted over her, and she found herself wishing she'd ordered that instead of her turkey wrap. "Is it good?" she asked.

He favored her with a grin. "You wish you'd gotten this, huh. Try it."

He held out his spoon, and Luce shook her head. "No, that's okay."

"Not a germaphobe, are you?" He quirked an eyebrow. "My mouth's already been on yours. We can share food."

When he put it that way . . . She knew her face was turning pink, but she ignored it and accepted his proffered spoon. The beans held the slightest hint of sweetness with the salty taste of bacon. They were the perfect consistency, soft but not mushy.

"Oh, those might be the best beans I've ever tasted," Luce admitted, handing him back his spoon.

"It's not too late. You can order some."

"Next time." She lifted her wrap. "Tonight I'll have this." She paused and added, "Assuming there is a next time."

"I think you're safe in your assumption."

He turned his attention back to his food, and Luce watched him, affection warming her chest. She wished she had the courage to say everything that came to her mind the way he did.

CONNOR

"**C**an I take you somewhere?" Connor hovered over the passenger door, waiting as Luce got in and buckled her seat belt. He tried not to stare at her revealing neckline.

Luce leaned her head back in the passenger seat and smiled up at him. "I hope so. Unless you planned to stay in the parking lot all evening."

He could think of lots of things to do in the parking lot all evening. "Have you been to the tower before?"

"The old one for watching for forest fires just outside of town?"

"Yeah." Of course she knew it. "That one."

She chewed on her lower lip, thinking hard. "I might have gone there in the second grade."

He got in the car and pulled onto Van Buren Street, already heading west. "It's high time you returned."

They reached the edge of town with the watch tower just as the sun was dipping down the horizon.

"Hurry," Connor said. He ran to the front of the car and flexed his fingers, beckoning for Luce. She slammed her door shut behind her and ran to his side, taking his hand.

The old-fashioned turnstile expected quarters, and Connor had his ready. He inserted several for him and Luce, and then hauled her through.

She laughed as he tugged her up the winding stairs. "Do they have a frequent punch card? You act like you've done this before."

"Quick," he said, already breathless, though whether from running up the stairs or anticipation, he didn't know. "We'll miss the sunset."

The wind increased as they climbed the one-hundred-foot building. Luce pushed her hair back from her face and kept pace with him. He looked out over the horizon and saw the sun already disappearing into the rolling hills.

"There." Connor drew to a stop at the top, pulling Luce into his side. "We almost made it."

"It doesn't matter," Luce said, fighting the strands of hair with one hand. "The after effect is just as lovely."

Indeed, it was. The sun might be gone, but the exquisite colors of pink and yellow melted into the treeline as far as he could see.

And then he didn't want to see it anymore. He turned Luce to face him, saddling his hands on her hips. She didn't resist him. He lowered his head just enough to capture her mouth. Her fingers threaded through his hair, and he drew in a breath before kissing her again, bending her body with his, savoring her taste.

She returned his kiss with just as much ardent fervor. Then she pushed him away with a teasing smile. "You're missing the sunset."

"No, I'm not," he said, never taking his eyes from her face. "It's the best I've ever seen."

She stroked his cheek with the backs of her fingers. "How many girls have heard that line?"

Was he supposed to remember if he'd ever said that to someone? Odds were slight, but there was the possibility. He did know, though, that he'd never brought a girl here before. "My dad used to bring me here before he up and left us. For awhile, I hated it here. It made me think of him. But then I grew up, and I realized, whatever else, when my dad brought me here it was a show of love." He shrugged, his hands finding her waist again and drawing her near. "You're the only other person I've ever brought here."

Her blue-green eyes were soft as they flicked over his face, studying him. "Why me?"

He didn't have an answer for that either. He looked away from her instead, watching the pale colors darken to different shades of blue.

"Where's your dad now?"

He'd been expecting the question, and he answered with no emotion. "I don't know. I never heard from him again." It turned out his dad had another family—no, Connor and his mom were the other family. His dad was still married with a wife and children, and one day he went back to them. His mom only found out when she tried to file for divorce. Ended up not being necessary, since bigamy wasn't legal.

"Have you ever tried to find him?"

"No," Connor said, and this time he put enough hard edge in his tone to end the topic.

She shivered, and he glanced at her, then wove his fingers through hers again. "Let's get you home," he said, softening his voice so she'd know his anger wasn't directed at her.

They were almost to Luce's condo when he remembered her car. "Luce. Your car's at your sister's."

She waved it off. "I'll take the trolley tomorrow and get it."

"You sure?" He pulled to a stop in front of her condo, hand on the transmission stick, ready to thrust the car into reverse.

"I'm here. It's fine."

He parked the car and opened her door before she could, helping her out. "I can pick you up tomorrow, take you to get it." He shoved his hands in his pockets and followed her to the front door.

She unlocked her condo and threw the door open, then tilted her head and looked up at him. "I'll work it out." She stepped inside, turning on lights as she went. "You staying out there?"

He hesitated. It wasn't that late, just after eight. But the blood still ran hot in his veins, and if he followed her inside, he doubted he'd be able to keep control.

Which suddenly made him think of Regina, who had persuaded him to her bed shortly after they met, and then the allure of her body prevented him from really getting to know her.

He didn't want that with Luce. He wanted to know her soul, her spirit, first. With no distractions. Well, minimal. "I should probably go."

"It's early still." She returned to the entryway, leaning against the open door. "We can watch a movie. I have popcorn."

She smiled, and his eyes fell on her lips. Her tongue darted out, wetting them, and he met her eyes. The desire he'd felt on the tower flared up again, and he saw it reflected in her eyes, almost challenging him.

He couldn't back down from that. He put his hands on her shoulders and brushed her lips with his, aware of her small hands on his shoulders. He pushed her back against the wall of her kitchen and kissed her again. Her hands moved down his chest, and she uttered a soft gasp as his lips moved to her jaw.

A fire ignited in Connor's navel, traveling quickly downward, taking over his rational thought. One hand found the hem of her dress and pushed it upward, fingers creeping along her thigh, tracing the bare skin of her hip. She gave a low, throaty groan of pleasure, tossing her head back and exposing the clean lines of her neck and breasts.

Connor broke off the kiss and took a step backward. *Slow down.*

"What?" Luce said, straightening her head and leveling her gaze at him.

"Uh." His face burned when he realized he'd spoken out loud. "Nothing. I just—" He wanted this relationship to last.

He wanted to be sure, and he didn't want to do anything on impulse. "I want to take it slow."

She drew her shoulders forward. "I didn't realize I was moving fast."

"Not you." Definitely not her. "I have to call it a night. I've got some homework to do still."

"Right," she said. Her eyes flicked over his face, a slight crease in her brow. She rearranged the skirt of her dress. "Okay, well, better get going, then."

Now that it sounded like she was kicking him out, he didn't want to go. But the reasons still stood, so he moved backward the two steps out the front door. "I'll call—" he started to say, but she'd already closed the door. "Good night," he said to the condo.

He was no Einstein, but something about that goodbye had felt off.

He walked back to the car, frustrated in more ways than one.

Chapter Fifteen

LUCE

S *low down.*

Connor's words burned into Luce's mind, searing her conscience, mocking her.

Slow down.

What must he think of her? What had she been thinking, letting a man into her life again? Especially now?

Melodee was right.

"Right here, on this allegation, put 'denied.'"

Luce forced herself to the present and focused on what her lawyer was saying.

Mr. Jorgensen pointed his finger next to the typed text of the third allegation. Her hand trembled as she wrote out, in her neatest print possible, "DENIED." She forced herself to focus on the task at hand, because otherwise her mind kept going back to last night.

Slow down.

Embarrassment warmed her neck, and she wished she could

purge Connor from her mind.

"Do I need to clarify anything?" she asked, leaning back and staring at the paper.

Mr. Jorgensen shook his head. "Like your sister said, he has no proof and no reason to accuse you. Mostly he's waiting to see if you'll respond or run and hide. The worst thing you could do is ignore this. He would win by default."

Luce kept her eyes on the paper in front of her, glad he couldn't read her thoughts. Her first instinct had been to ignore it and hope it would all go away. "What if he takes me to court?"

"I can almost guarantee he won't. This is a scare tactic, meant to make you pay so you can avoid being sued."

If this was supposed to scare her, it was working. Luce clasped her hands together. "But why should I have to pay a settlement? He's the one who wronged me."

Mr. Jorgensen gave a tight smile. " And that's why you hired me. First thing we are going to do is issue a counterclaim. Not only will we list off the wrongs he did to you, but we are going to include the distress this frivolous suit is costing you." He paused. "You could even counter-sue. I know your biggest priority is making this all go away. But you have a good case."

That sounded long and drawn out and not fun at all. "Um. I don't know."

"Think on it. I'll work on this counterclaim. In the meantime, itemize everything. Everything he's done to you since the divorce was finalized. Go through your phone records. Every phone call, email, correspondence. I need them all."

Luce nodded, grateful for the assignment. It gave her something to focus on, a distraction from this speed bump in her otherwise pleasant life.

And a distraction from Connor, who she had tried valiantly not to think of since he made it clear on her doorstep that he didn't want this to go the same direction she did. All he wanted was to slow down.

CONNOR

Luce didn't answer Connor's calls on Sunday. By Monday, he had resorted to leaving cheesy messages on her voicemail. When he still hadn't heard from her on Tuesday, he sent off a quick text.

Just wanted to make sure you're OK. Haven't heard from you in a few days.

That, at least, got a response, even if it took a few hours.

I'm good. Staying busy with work.

Well, he knew that was a lie. Regina had often complained about how boring the life as a nurse was, how many of the girls brought their homework or something to work on in the back because there was so much downtime. So either she had a hobby consuming her time, or she just didn't want to talk to him.

His gut told him it was the latter.

Was this what it was like to be in love? To have someone singularly consume your thoughts, and every moment away from them felt like an eternity?

Connor wasn't sure he liked it. At the same time, it was extremely exhilarating.

He worked at the shop, organizing the business cards he'd gathered from the craft fair. He'd been working on his mom, and he was this close to getting permission to set up a line of unique artisans. Expand beyond the token shelf she'd given him.

He must've come on too strong. That had to be it. Great.

The door chimed, and Connor looked up from his business cards. "Feel free to look around, just let me know if I can help you with anything," he said, the words exiting his mouth before he recognized the woman standing there. "Mom!" He checked his watch. Not even noon. "What are you doing here?" And why had she come in the front door?

"I came to take over for you."

"You're closing, right?"

"And you need to talk to Luce." She leaned against the counter and glowered at him with her best Mom-eyes.

"What do you mean?" He hadn't even said a word to her about their failed date.

"You were all fluttery and happy after the auction—"

"I wasn't fluttery—" Connor protested, but she rode right over him.

"Yet ever since Saturday evening, you've been as brooding at a teenager. Something happened between you two, and I demand you fix it."

He couldn't help letting out a laugh. "It only it were that easy."

"What happened? Did you offend her?"

He exhaled. How did she know? "I must have."

His mother gave him a look of tender understanding. "You can't throw your father's sins on every woman you meet. Most people are not deceptive like him, Connor."

Connor could point out a dozen examples to prove her wrong, but that was besides the point. "That's not what happened." And telling his mom would be too embarrassing, so Connor shut his mouth.

His mom pushed off the counter and went behind the register. "I'll watch the store. You go do what it takes to talk to her."

"Okay. Fine. I will." He reached over and gave her a quick hug, and his mom patted his arm.

"Love you too," she said with her trademark teasing grin.

♥

Connor took a deep breath outside the clinic doors, his heart beating erratically. He walked through the automatic doors two minutes before the clinic closed. Caroline glanced up at him and froze, her eyes never leaving his face as he approached the counter.

"Hi," he said, a little unnerved by her stare.

"What are you doing here?" she said, her green eyes narrowing.

"I need to talk to Luce about something. Can you tell her I'll wait outside?"

"Yes," the nurse said slowly. "I'll tell her."

"Thanks." Connor felt as if he turned his back on the enemy. Her eyes seemed to bore a hole through his shirt. He let himself outside and waited, shoving his hands in his pockets and resting against the wall.

Two minutes passed. Three. Five.

Maybe she wouldn't come out. Then what? Would he show up at her house? Her sister's?

Just as he started to plan his next desperate move, the door swished open, and Luce stepped outside.

"Connor," she said, her expression both vulnerable and guarded.

"Hey." He pushed off the wall and stepped toward her, careful to maintain a space between them. "Thanks for coming out."

She didn't answer him, just tilted her head like a little bird and regarded him.

Not a very inviting start. Connor plunged onward before he lost his nerve. "I guess somehow I messed things up?" He'd already rehearsed the apology a million times; why was he stumbling over it now? He raked a hand through his hair and then pressed it down when the unruly waves tried to stand up. "What can I do to fix it?"

"Nothing."

He waited for an explanation, but nothing more came. "So, what, you're just not interested anymore?"

She pursed her lips together. "Are you serious?"

"Yes!" He exhaled in exasperation. "Help me out here. I want to make things better, okay? I'm sorry if I came on too strong. The last thing I wanted to do was offend you."

"*You* come on too strong?"

Now it was his turn to tilt his head at her. "Was that not it?"

She shook her head. "I thought when you said—well, what you said—I thought it was a polite rejection."

He blinked at her. "What?" He unraveled her words in his mind. What had he said? *Slow down.* And now it was his turn to laugh, laugh in relief that it was nothing but a misunderstanding. "Luce, I like you. I really, really like you. This is one relationship that I want to get right. I didn't say I don't want you. I said I want to take it slow. *Slow.*" He enunciated the last word. "But I still want it moving forward." He reached out and laced his fingers with hers, tempted to show her just how much he desired her.

Her cheeks flushed pink. "I get it."

"Is that okay with you?"

She rolled her eyes toward the sky. "I should have just asked you."

"Or answered one of my calls," he teased.

"I'm not used to being able to talk to someone." She let out a slow breath. "You're different than my—than the last guy. We didn't—communicate."

Connor tightened his grip on her fingers. This girl had stolen his heart, and he didn't like the idea of her being with someone else. Ever again. "I'm not him, Luce. Just like you're not any of the girls I've dated. See me for me, okay?"

She paused and then met his eyes, her gaze deliberate. "I do see you."

Chapter Sixteen

LUCE

"How's it going with you and Connor?" Regina asked.

Luce hesitated over the medical history sheet she was filling out, cursing herself for being so lost in a replay of Connor's visit that she hadn't noticed Regina approach. They hadn't spoken in nearly a week. She wondered if Regina had seen Connor come into the clinic, if she knew they'd been out in the parking lot talking.

Fine," she said, trying hard to keep the dreaminess out of her voice. The warmth that oozed through her body at the mention of his name left her all floaty and light-headed. "Things are going fine."

"You have to give me more details than that," Regina pressed, smiling even though her eyes glittered. "Don't hold back just because I'm his ex-girlfriend!"

That was exactly why Luce did not want to share. "We're still just hanging out. Getting to know each other." It felt so stiff and awkward and wrong to discuss this with her.

"Have you kissed yet?" Regina said, leaning in close.

The heat crept up her face. "That's kind of personal, isn't it?"

Regina looked strangely smug. "Only if you don't want someone to know! So you have!" She lowered her voice and whispered, "Have you slept with him?"

"No," Luce snapped, the fog clearing from her brain and anger replacing it. "I just got out of a marriage, remember?" She emphasize the last word. "I'm not stepping into another serious relationship that quickly."

Regina backed up, looking properly chastised. "Sorry." She cast her eyes sideways at Luce. "You're just so different from other girls Connor dated. I thought he had a pretty strict no divorcee policy. At least you don't already have kids."

Regina's words smacked Luce like a slap in the face. They played on all of her insecurities and fears about reentering the dating world. Would she be considered used cargo? Something discarded, to be cast away? Would people see her as a failure, believe her incapable of making a relationship work?

She didn't want to lose Connor simply because she'd made a mistake in her first marriage. She spun away from Regina. Her hand shook as she carried the specimen tray back to the lab. Setting it on the counter by the clock, she took a moment to grab a tissue and press it against her eyes, taking deep breaths.

I am not used, she told herself. *My divorce does not define me. I am still someone worth loving.*

They were the same words her therapist had given her in the weeks after the divorce, when Luce had felt like the scum of the earth, like she just couldn't get any lower.

Was Regina right? Would Connor's opinion of her change if

he knew the truth? She tried to tell herself that if it did, it just meant he didn't deserve her, but the clenching in her chest warned her she was the one who would feel the loss.

She replayed their dates, their conversations, for some clue of Connor's feelings, but she found nothing. It hadn't come up. She hadn't brought it up.

Caroline cornered Luce during her afternoon break and took her outside.

"What's wrong with you? And don't tell me it's nothing, because it clearly is."

Luce shifted her weight from one foot to the other and blinked against the hot rush of tears beneath her eyes. "I'm going to ruin this thing with Connor. I don't even know what I'm doing. I should just break up with him and get it over with."

Caroline snorted. "You think any of us know what we're doing? This is a first time rodeo for all of us! That's life for you."

"But I already have a pretty bad track record. What if I screw up life now because of my past? What if I'm doing it all wrong again?"

Caroline tapped her long manicured fingers against the brick wall surrounding the building. "What's really bothering you?"

Luce threw her hands up. "I don't know! I've still got this crazy stuff going on with my ex, and Regina says if Connor knew about my divorce he would never want to date me, which makes me not want to tell him and at the same time wonder why I'm pursuing this relationship because eventually he's going to find out and it's all going up in smoke."

"Yeah, that's a lot to try to juggle. They say honesty is the best policy."

"They say," Luce echoed. "But is it? If I'm going to lose him either way, should I enjoy the ride or just take off the bandage quickly? I can't even think right now."

"Are you going to break up with him before he even has a chance to figure out why?"

She wasn't going to break up with him. She didn't want to, and it would hardly be fair. He had the right to know first, and they'd see what happened after that.

She exhaled and straightened her shoulders, giving Caroline a smile. "Thank you." Luce pulled out her phone and fired off a text.

My house tonight. Bring sushi.

"What are you doing?" Caroline asked, watching her.

"I'm going to tell him." Luce met her friend's eyes. "If it's going to end, at least we'll both know why."

♥

Connor had a commitment with his friends in the early evening, but he promised to come over as soon as they finished. He invited her along, but Luce declined. She didn't feel like hanging out with other people, especially when she knew she had serious news to break to him.

She didn't mean to take her pill until after he came over, but when her timer went off, she threw it back before even realizing it. "Snap," she murmured, realizing she'd have to fight to stay awake now.

Connor didn't show up until ten, and she knew from the burning in her eyes that she was in trouble. He brought two boxes of sushi, and it was the right combination of flavor and texture to satisfy Luce's hunger without making her feel heavy. But by the time she finished eating, her head felt thick with sleepiness and her eyes wouldn't stay open. Wasn't there something she wanted to talk about?

Connor didn't seem to notice. He took a sip from his soda and examined the mug. "I love this design." His eyes swept up to hers, interest lighting up the dark brown irises. "This is one of yours?"

She shrugged off his admiration. "Yes."

"Do you hate them now?"

She avoided his gaze, sensing the way he scrutinized her, trying to find the missing pieces. She was way too tired to have a coherent conversation about this. "I can't really explain it. They make me think of someone. In a bad way." Her head pulsed.

"A guy?" he asked softly.

"A stupid guy. A non-important guy. You know what?" She took the mug from Connor, her hands caressing the glaze, forever frozen in a downward drip of color. "It's nothing, he's nothing. It's just a mug." She smiled at Connor, feeling strangely liberated by the words. "It's yours now. Whenever I see it, I'll think of you and—and my beautiful leopard lamp."

His eyes swept toward the lamp by the couch and he laughed, though his eyes held concern. "You still have feelings for him?"

Feelings of anger. But Luce shook her head. "No."

"This the same guy who didn't communicate well?"

"Yes." And something else. He'd been her husband. The thought was there, the need to confess, but the words wouldn't come out.

Connor leaned back in his chair. "Could you make a few? For me? For my shop? Just one or two. Please?"

He said it so hesitantly, carefully, like he was afraid of offending her. The thought of having a few items in a shop for someone else when she used to have her own store—

Never mind that. "Yeah, maybe."

Surprise flickered across his face, and then he grinned. "That's great!"

She returned his smiled and bobbed her head, letting it slump forward a little too much. The headache grew worse, and suddenly she craved her bed.

A light touch on the top of her hand directed her attention, and she turned her head just as Connor tugged on her arm, sliding her chair closer to him.

"You're tired. I've kept you up too late."

His arm went around her shoulder, and she relaxed into his chest. He wrapped both arms around her, and Luce shifted her weight from her chair to his body. His lips brushed the top of her hair, and a warm contentment bubbled upward in her stomach. His lips found hers next, and she kissed him back, though she was too sleepy to put much energy into it. She closed her eyes and exhaled, nestling her head into the crook of his neck.

Her body jostled and something soft cradled her head, and Luce's eyes snapped open, a surge of surprise banishing the sleepiness.

"What—?" she whispered, trying to sit up and blinking into darkness.

"Sorry, sorry." Connor's voice came from her left, and she turned toward the open bedroom door, light from the living room drifting into the room and outlining his silhouette. "You fell asleep," he said. "I was trying to put you to bed without waking you. Guess I didn't succeed?"

She closed her eyes, the lull of dreams already beckoning her. Her fingers fumbled across the bedspread until she found his hand. "Thank you." The sad desperate loneliness from earlier was gone, replaced by the illusive sensation that all would be right.

He squeezed her hand and started to pull away, but she tightened her grip. "Don't go."

"You want me to stay?" he whispered, a hint of expectation in his voice.

"Yes."

"My mom will notice if I don't come home," he said, and this time she was sure she heard a pleasant lilt of teasing in his voice. "Besides, your bed isn't big enough for us both."

She would've smiled if she weren't already half asleep. Her conscious decision to get a twin bed to save her from moments like this, to keep her from falling into the arms of another man, was coming back to haunt her. "Couch," she breathed, willing the word out.

His breath warmed her face a moment before his lips brushed her forehead. "Whatever you say."

His steps crossed the carpeted floor, and a moment later the lights turned out. Luce relaxed, content in the knowledge that Connor slept in the other room.

♥

Her alarm went off six hours later. Luce's eyes felt like cotton taped shut beneath sand paper. She grabbed up the phone and silenced the alarm. "It's Sunday," she whispered, relief flooding her body. She rolled over and went back to sleep.

Sunlight streaming through her window roused her, and as much as Luce wanted to return to dreamland, her body demanded she wake up. She sat up and realized she'd gone to sleep in her jeans and sweater. Not quite ready to shower, she changed into a pair of yoga pants and a T-shirt.

Her phone dinged, and she scanned it while she brushed her teeth. A text from Melodee.

Working today?

Nope, Luce responded.

Want us to pick you up for church?

Luce texted back a quick, *Sure,* before spitting and washing her face.

Church wasn't until ten. She could get in a yoga routine before then.

She stepped into the living room and began opening the curtains, letting in the beautiful sunshine and trying to lighten the wood-encrusted room. Such a lovely day for October. Warm days were coming to a close, and the threat of winter lingered on the encroaching weeks.

"Sure looks nice out. Want to spend the day on the lake?"

The male voice coming from her left startled her, and Luce jumped away from the window with a shriek. Her heart batted against her ribcage, and she pressed a hand to her chest as she swiveled to the couch.

"Connor!" she gasped out. Her mind whirled, trying to understand why he was here. What had she forgotten from last night? She remembered sushi and soda and soft kisses, but she couldn't discern what was reality and what was a dream. "You're—you're in my house."

He sat up, his light brown hair ruffled into unkempt spikes and peaks, his eyes crinkling with humor. "Yes. I am."

She gave a short laugh. "Uh—you spent the night."

"You asked me to."

The pieces were falling into place, memories replacing the haze of dreams. She held onto the edge of the couch. Had anything else happened between them? And yet, she'd woken up in her clothes. "I'm sorry," she admitted. "I took a sleeping pill last night before you came over. Some of last night is a blur."

He studied her, his eyes unreadable. "You have trouble

sleeping?"

"Sometimes," she murmured, looking away from his gaze. Why couldn't she just be a normal girlfriend? She'd send him running even without him knowing the truth.

Which reminded her that she was going to tell him. Last night. Her heart skipped into double time, and she fought for a deep breath.

"So what's on your schedule today?" he asked, and she appreciated how he changed the subject. "Looks like yoga?"

"First cereal. Then yoga."

"And then the lake?" He smiled, showing off those dimples again. "I have a few kayaks."

She shook her head. "Church. My sister's picking me up."

"Oh, I love church!" He stood up and stretched. "I'll need to go home and change first."

"You don't have to come with me," she protested.

He dropped his arms and leveled his eyes at her. "Are you politely uninviting me?"

Her face warmed. "You are more than welcome to come."

"And then we'll go to the lake."

She laughed. "All right."

"Great." He grabbed her hand and pulled her against him. She turned her head when he tried to kiss her and gave him a playful shove.

"You can kiss me after you change."

"And brush my teeth, right? That's what you're really saying." He located his car keys on the window sill. "I can take a hint. I'll be back in an hour. Save me some cereal." He grinned at her, and Luce found herself leaning forward, drawn to him in spite of herself. His hand crept up her neck and wound itself through the hair at the nape of her head. He kissed her forehead, then threw his messenger bag over his arm and let himself out of the house.

Luce's heart hadn't stopped pounding from the moment she'd spotted him on the couch. She laid the palm of her hand against her fevered skin, feeling the quickened beat, and suddenly she was more terrified of telling him the truth than she'd ever been of anything in her life.

CONNOR

Connor couldn't keep the humming out of his throat as he brushed his teeth vigorously at home. He smiled to himself as he remembered the expression on Luce's face when she realized he'd slept over.

"Ha!" he said, then ducked his head to spit.

His mom walked past his bedroom, hand to her head, and then she stopped and backed up. She stepped into the room and studied him until he finally turned to face her.

"What?" Connor dried his face and put away the toothbrush. On second thought, he should probably leave it at Luce's. He pulled it back out and clasped it in his fingers. Good thing he had two.

"You're awfully happy." A mischievous glint entered her eye. "Where did you sleep last night?"

"At Luce's." He shimmied past her with a grin. Let her think what she wanted.

She smiled, clasping her hands together and following him into the kitchen. "So things are progressing?"

"Maybe." He dropped the toothbrush into his messenger bag and spread his arms wide. "Do I look dressed for yoga?"

"Yoga? Since when?"

"Since Luce." He leaned over and kissed her cheek. "Don't wait for me."

"Oh, I know better," she giggled, her face rosy.

He shook his head and stepped out the front door. His mom got almost as much delight out of his love life as he did.

He checked the contents of his bag before putting the car in gear. A change of clothes to go to church. A few text books in case he decided to study.

And his toothbrush.

He was ready.

Connor scanned the congregation inside the small chapel, surprised by all the people he knew. He spotted his second-cousin Lilly with her husband, Nate, and she gave him the smile/head bob. Close to Lilly he saw Kerri and her mother. Connor slid down just a tad in his seat. If Kerri's mom saw him with Luce, he'd never hear the end of it.

Luckily Mrs. Manning didn't notice him. The sermon ended and Melodee stopped to chat with a few people while her husband herded the children to the car. Kerri also stopped, leaning against a tall man with dark hair. Her mom slid out of the pew and went down the aisle.

"Come on," Connor said, grasping Luce's hand. "There's someone I want you to meet."

"Really?" Luce looked a little reluctant as he pulled her. "You know people here?"

"Kerri," Connor said, and she turned toward him.

"Connor!" she exclaimed, her eyes widening. "Nice to see you here!"

Grinning, he grabbed Luce's elbow and propelled her toward Kerri like some kind of offering. "I had to wait till your mom left. Luce, this is my friend Kerri. She owns a bead shop on the strip."

"And chocolate shop soon," the man beside her added.

Kerri gave Connor a knowing look and clasped Luce's hand. "Hi. Nice to meet you."

"A chocolate shop?" Luce said, her face brightening. "I'd love to come by when you have it open."

"I'll bring you," Connor said, beaming at them all. He felt like sun rays of happiness must be flowing out of his skin.

"And this is Eric," Kerri said, swiveling slightly to indicate the man beside her.

Now it was Connor's turn for the knowing look. He stopped himself just short of saying he'd heard a lot about Eric. Kerri hadn't embarrassed him, after all. Instead he gave Eric a solid handshake. He glanced around for Lilly and Nate, but they must have already left. Newlyweds.

The thought made him smile.

"We should catch up with my sister," Luce said.

"Great to see you guys," Kerri said.

"Nice to meet you," Luce said.

"We'll all hang sometime," Connor said, allowing Luce to pull him out of the church.

"How do you know her?" Luce asked as they stepped out of the building.

"Our moms are friends. With stores close by, we've known each other forever."

"That's nice. What did you think of church?" Luce glanced up at him as they walked down the steps, the sun reflecting off the pink hue in her cheeks.

"I liked what the pastor talked about." Connor took her hand and tucked it between his arm and his ribcage. "All that stuff about brotherly love and serving our neighbors." He squeezed her fingers. "I especially liked sitting by you."

She peeked up at him. "Do you go to church?"

He shrugged. "I haven't made it a priority. I enjoy church. I should probably make it more important."

They had reached her sister's car now, and Luce stopped a few feet from it. "You should?"

He placed his hands on her hips and sidled her up close to him. "I will."

She rested her hands on his chest. "Why?"

He pressed his lips to the side of her mouth. "Because wherever you go, I will follow." He backed away from her and nodded at Melodee as she came over and opened the van door.

"Are you coming for dinner, Connor?" she asked with a quick glance at Luce.

He shook his head. "I'm going home to change." He wanted to ask Luce if she still wanted to go to the lake, but suddenly he worried about pushing his luck. They'd spent all morning together. Maybe he should let her take a break.

"What should I wear to the lake?" Luce asked.

He grinned, affection warming his chest. "Wear something tight but warm. A long-sleeved T-shirt would work. It'll cool off tonight."

Melodee raised an eyebrow at Luce. "So you're not staying for dinner, either?"

"Um, well."

"Dave's cooking steak," Connor said. "It's Sunday. You guys can all eat at my mom's house."

"No, thank you," Melodee said, laughter in her voice. "It's a nice idea, but your mom doesn't want my kids running around her house."

Melodee was probably right on that point, but Connor didn't want to be rude. "If you're sure . . ."

She waved him off. "I'll take Luce home and you guys can figure out your plans."

"Pick you up at three," Connor said to Luce, giving a last wave and then hurrying to his car.

♥

Luce was sitting on her porch steps when Connor arrived a few hours later. She still wore the light cottony dress with purple flowers she'd had at church, the same dress she'd worn when they went to the craft fair, complete with the thin purple sweater. Connor decided it was his favorite. He parked the car and joined her on the porch steps, dropping down beside her.

"Hey," he said, bumping her shoulder, thrilling at the rush of emotion that swept through him.

"Hi," she said, bumping him back. "Ready to go?"

"Well." He bobbed his head at her dress. "You look great. But I thought we were going kayaking."

She folded her arms across her chest and leveled her gaze at him. "You think I can't kayak in a dress?"

"I don't doubt your abilities. But you might not be so comfortable."

"I'll be fine." She stood up, positioning herself in front of him and placing her hands on his shoulders. The look she gave him was both sultry and mischievous, and Connor's heart immediately began pumping faster. She lowered her hands, and he just watched her, waiting to see what she'd do next.

He didn't expect her to grab the edges of her skirt and lift it over her waist.

His jaw dropped seconds before he recognized a swimsuit underneath, and then he burst out laughing. "Come here, you," he said, taking her hand and pulling her back to the patio steps. She laughed, too, letting go of her skirt and falling against him.

He tightened his arms around her and kissed her. She

responded, inviting him in with her lips, inviting him closer. He pictured the swimsuit on her slender body and moved one hand down her back, tracing her hip and thigh through the thin fabric of the dress. The blood pounded in the base of his skull, and he didn't object when she sat up and rearranged herself, peering at him through hooded eyes as she straddled him, the skirt falling over either side of his legs.

He moved his hands up the slick elastic of her one-piece suit and kissed her greedily, claiming her mouth with his, capturing her lower lip. She elicited a soft moan.

She wasn't making this easy. He put one hand on the concrete patio, ready to push off and carry her into the condo behind them. Forget the lake.

A car rolled into the parking lot, driving around them and parking on the other side of Connor's car.

Luce pulled away, glancing over her shoulder and then climbing off him. "Maybe it's time to go," she said with an impish smile.

"Yeah," was all he managed.

♥

He'd brought his mom's life jacket for Luce to borrow, and though it was a little big, Connor tightened up the straps, holding the life jacket snug against her body while he pulled. She still wore her dress and sweater under the jacket, but it didn't prevent him from feeling the warmth of her skin where his hand brushed against her chest. Perhaps intentionally.

He helped her into her kayak and gave her a push off, then he climbed into his own and paddled after her. The sun was descending in the sky, but at four o'clock in the afternoon there was plenty of daylight left. The day had been mildly warm, but a cooler breeze blew up from the surface of the water. Sheer limestone cliffs lined one side of the lake, grand houses dotting the top, overlooking the drop off and the lake below. Bugs dipped into the green water, leaving small rippling circles behind them.

"I'm impressed you wear a life jacket," Luce said, paddling forward at a leisurely pace. "Most guys I know would be too macho for that."

"I don't think you've known the right kind of guys," Connor said, drifting to her side.

"Yeah," was all she said, and he wondered if she was thinking about her ex, the one who left her with so much baggage.

"Race you to the buoy," he said. And then he leaned forward and began paddling as hard as he could, left then right then left again.

"Hey!" she exclaimed. "That's hardly fair!"

She wasn't far behind him, but Connor didn't let up, slicing his oar into the water and back out, the drops of water chilling as they dripped on his face and down his life jacket, soaking the front of his shirt. He drew up when he arrived and paddled around to face her, taking deep breaths to hide his exertion.

She was laughing and shaking her head. "Didn't think you could beat me if you didn't get a head start, huh?"

"I just wanted to give you a reason to disqualify me."

"Well, you did. You're disqualified. I win." She paddled past him, continuing out into the harbor.

His stomach rumbled that it was nearly dinner time, but he had no choice except to follow Luce farther out onto the lake.

"You said Dave makes steak every Sunday?" she asked, calling to him over her shoulder.

"Just about." He glided up to her, keeping pace with her rowing like a synchronized swimmer. "My mom was a vegetarian before she started dating him. Now she loves meat. Can't get enough of it."

"Huh," Luce said. "I guess she's still figuring out who she is?"

"She is whoever the guy wants her to be," Connor said, his words ringing with a distasteful edge even to his own ears.

"So is it Dave you don't like, or your mom's behavior?"

"Both," Connor growled. "Men like him prey off women like her. She acts so desperate, so eager to please, and they gladly let her."

"Has she always been this way?"

"Ever since my dad left." He shook his head. There was no way to explain the deep levels of that rejection in one sitting. "He took something of her with him. Her confidence, her belief in herself. She's desperate to have someone tell her she's valuable." He would never forgive his father for that, more than anything.

"So it's not even her fault."

"No," he answered softly. "It's not."

"It's not yours, either."

He looked at her, startled. "I never said it was."

"Then don't take it so personally when she doesn't act right."

He did take it personally, but not for the reasons she thought. A small, shameful part of him always wondered why his father went back to his old family. Why he didn't choose Connor and his mother instead.

He looked at Luce. Her eyes were on the shore of an inlet to their right, her lips slightly parted as she sucked in the cool air, her forehead crinkling in concentration. The sun cast a glow about her features, the shimmering light reflecting off the water as if sunbeams and fairy dust held up her kayak.

Something tightened in his throat, and he'd barely considered the words before they escaped his mouth. "I think I love you."

She swiveled her head, eyes widening in surprise. "Wh-what?" she stammered, halting the movement of her oar.

He shrugged. "I just now realized it." Without waiting for her response, he dug his oar into the water and paddled his kayak past her.

❧ Chapter Seventeen ❧

LUCE

L uce was dying to talk about Connor's admission. But he didn't bring it up again, nor did he let the conversation lull, so she was forced to hold his words and ponder them in her heart.

Connor was prepared with towels in his car to dry them off. And an extra sweater when Luce shivered. She pressed the collar to her nose and inhaled, hoping he didn't notice. The musty scent mingled with a hint of cologne washed over her with a feeling similar to being homesick, and she suddenly wanted to throw herself into Connor's arms. But she sat still in the passenger side of the truck while he loaded the kayaks into the bed.

"My friends are coming over for dinner," he said when he climbed back in. "I hope that's okay. Ty and Moki, and Ty's girlfriend, Amber. You'll love her."

Luce bobbed her head. "Sure. That sounds great."

He parked in front of his mom's house. He opened the door

for Luce and gave her a quick kiss on the cheek. "Come on inside." He swept her up the walkway, and Luce barely had the chance to take in the dormant flowering bushes before they walked under a portico covered in ivy and Connor pushed open the front door.

"Luce!"

Luce braced herself for the hug as Connor's mom hurtled into the entryway and threw her arms around her.

"Wonderful to see you," Jessica purred, beaming as she held Luce at arm's length. "My son finally got something right."

Her son. Luce could hardly think of him without remembering his declaration. Her pulse quickened.

"All right, Mom," Connor said, rolling his eyes as he pried his mother's fingers off Luce. But he winked at her. "I think we all agree, she's great. No need to tackle her, though, we want to make sure she comes back later."

"I'll come back as often as you'll have me," Luce said, then she blushed at her honesty.

"Hey, hey, hey!" A young man with light eyebrows and a baseball cap came in from the backyard, already holding an aluminum can and grinning like a madman. He extended his hand, slapping palms with Connor. Then he turned to Luce. "And you must be the lovely Luce."

"I guess that's me," Luce said. "You have me at a disadvantage."

The man glowered at Connor. "You mean he doesn't talk about me as much as he talks about you?"

"Quit embarrassing her." A woman about Luce's age came in behind him, dark blond hair flowing around her shoulders, smiling behind a pair of glasses. A toddler with pigtails clung to her finger. "Hi! I'm Amber. That bear you met a second ago is Tyson."

Luce accepted her hug, relaxing slightly at the presence of another girl. "And who is this?" she asked, crouching in front of the child. She always had a soft spot for kids.

"That's Raven," Tyson said, scooping her away from Amber and holding her with one arm. The little girl reached for his baseball cap, and he plunked it on her head.

Luce arched her eyebrows in surprise. "Oh! You guys are married?"

"No," Amber said, taking Raven away from Tyson. "She's just mine."

"But I claim her too," Tyson said, not letting Amber get too far away.

Connor's arm slid around Luce's waist. "And that's Moki on the deck, helping Dave butcher the cow." He pointed to a dark-skinned boy with beads in his braided hair. "I guess you could say they're my friends."

Luce smiled at that, leaning against Connor and enjoying the feeling of belonging.

"Hey." Dave poked his head in through the open glass doors, pinching a pair of metal tongs together in his fingers. "Steaks are about done unless you want them well done. Surely no one here would kill a good cut of meat that way, though."

"Oh, no, no, we all like them medium!" Jessica waved an arm, her bracelets jangling and her perfume sweeping over Luce as she hobbled across the kitchen in stilted heels. "Let me help you!"

Connor growled under his breath. His eyes shot to hers. "There she goes again. Drives me crazy."

"Connor!" Dave called. "Come help me with this grill!"

"Be right back." Connor kissed her forehead, his lips lingering on her skin. Then he stepped out onto the patio.

Was Luce doing that too? Keeping secrets from Connor so he would like her?

No, she told herself emphatically. She was just waiting for the right moment.

She crossed the living room and stared out the window at the twisty street in front of the house. Most of the leaves still held their full green color, the trees boasting what remained of their summer splendor. But a few were already changing colors, the first hints of copper and red peeking out of the foliage. A subtle reminder that the lively green couldn't last. The bright colors would soon take over, eating away at the green until all the leaves fell, exposing the skeletal tree trunk for what it was.

Luce's fingers tightened around the window sill, and she closed her eyes.

"Luce." Smiling, Jessica joined her at the window and grasped her elbow. "Time to eat."

Luce didn't budge. "Jessica, why does Connor like me so much?"

His mom squeezed her arm. "What's not to like? You're beautiful and lively and creative. Spontaneous, delicate, adventurous. I've never seen him so enamored. The way he talks about you, you'd think you're a goddess."

The words didn't soothe Luce's conscience. "But I'm not perfect."

Jessica stepped back, her eyes scanning Luce's. "Has he made you feel you should be?"

Luce shook her head. "No. I just don't want him to think I am." *Because he'll be disappointed.*

Jessica gave her a bright smile. "Just be yourself. That's all he wants."

Somehow that didn't help. He might think he wanted her

the way she was, but when he found out who she really was, he might not want her at all.

She brushed the dark thoughts aside and joined Connor and his friends at the table on the patio.

♥

After dinner they sat around the table, chatting amicably. Luce couldn't shake her discomfort from earlier, but she nuzzled up close to Connor. His arm slipped around her, tucking her into his body. She felt the vibration under her ear every time he spoke, and she smiled to herself at the way his body jostled when he laughed. Her entire soul prickled, as if it had been asleep her whole life and then woken up all at once.

Dave pulled tight a white bag full of trash. "Gonna take out the trash. Connor, lend a hand?"

Connor started to shift from under her, but Luce knew he didn't want to get up. She pushed forward instead, getting to her feet.

"I'll help."

"No, I got it," Connor protested, but Dave had already handed her a trash bag. He grinned at Connor.

"She's a big girl. I like her."

Connor looked annoyed, and Luce flashed him a smile as she followed Dave through the house to the trash bin by the garage.

"Thanks for your help," Dave said, brushing his hands on his pants. His phone rang and he glanced at it before rattling it at Luce. "Gonna take this."

"Sure." Luce stepped around him, past the dormant flower bushes, and let herself back into the house. She tiptoed across the hardwood dining room, listening for voices. Sounded like Connor and his mom were still on the patio, at least. She saw Tyson and Moki and Amber in the backyard, playing with

Raven. Luce made to go out on the deck when she heard her name.

"I agree Luce is wonderful, but do you worry you're moving too fast?"

"Sure, of course. But she's it. I know it."

His mom made a quiet noise. "I'm so happy for you. I've never seen you the way you are with her."

"Mom, I've been in love with her since high school. It's unreal."

"What's your next step, then?"

Luce took a step backward, hiding in the shadows of the living room and holding her breath.

"There's only one possibility." He paused, and when he spoke again, his voice was softer. "I'm going to ask her to marry me."

His mom laughed and clapped her hands. "Oh, Connor! I'm so thrilled for you!"

From the sounds, his mom kissed his face twice, and Luce pressed a hand to her mouth, equally thrilled and horrified. Her time was up.

She took a few steps backward into the living room, then she stepped forward again, slapping her sandals against the hardwood floor noisily this time. She stepped onto the patio with a big smile pasted to her face.

"Dave had to take a phone call," she said, settling into her chair beside Connor again. "Did I miss anything?"

"Not really," Jessica purred. "Connor was just telling me how wonderful you are."

"Mom!" Connor said.

"What? You should tell her what you told me."

Connor cleared his throat, and Luce didn't want to make him any more uncomfortable than he already was.

"Well, this has been a lovely dinner, but I should probably head home. Those nurses' hours, you know."

"Are you sure?" Jessica asked.

"I'll take you home," Connor said, lifting from his chair as though his pants were on fire.

"What was that about?" Luce said as they stepped into the house, unable to resist teasing Connor at least a little bit.

"Nothing." He lowered his head and kissed her, opening her lips with ease and brushing her tongue with his. His hand closed around the small of her back, cocooning her against him.

"Luce O'Neil," he breathed, resting his forehead against hers. "You're pretty awesome."

Luce's breathing was shallow as she peered up at him, wanting him to capture her mouth again, to carry her to that beautiful yellow bedroom and devour her with kisses. *Keep your cool, girl,* she told herself. "I think you're pretty awesome yourself," she whispered.

He bent his head and kissed her again. When he pulled back, he studied her, the desire swirling with emotion in his eyes. "Is it too soon to tell you I love you?"

Luce traced his lips with her finger. "A few hours ago you weren't so sure."

He laughed. "I think I'm sure now."

She smiled, though a lump formed in her throat, making it hard to swallow. "Wait till you know."

Connor tucked her hand against his thigh and walked her to his car. "Tomorrow, then."

Luce didn't respond as he backed out of the driveway, but the whole way to her house the prickly thought that she needed to come up with a way to tell him about Brian wouldn't leave her alone. Preferably, by tomorrow.

There was one thing she could do for Connor. And after he dropped her off, she set her wheel up on her table and pulled out the clays, ready to create.

♥

Luce smiled at the little boy on the examining table while she took his temperature. "Feeling a little under the weather, huh, bud?"

He didn't reply, just kept his watery eyes on her. His mother sat in a chair in the corner.

"Does he have a fever?" she asked.

"A mild one." Luce jotted his information down on a clipboard, her mind wandering to the box of pottery in the back of her car. She smiled to herself as she thought of how she planned to surprise Connor at work. He'd taken her to Oktoberfest on Tuesday, and she'd had to bite her tongue several times to keep from telling him.

Luce's phone vibrated in her scrubs while she put away the blood pressure cuff, and she straightened up enough to check the caller. Her lawyer. Instantly on high alert, Luce silenced the call and slipped it back into her scrubs. Turning around, she smiled at the boy and his mom. "Dr. Dahler will be in in just a moment."

She told herself she'd call Mr. Jorgensen on her break, but the anxiety played havoc on her nerves, and she couldn't wait.

"I have to call my lawyer," she said to Caroline before stepping outside.

"Everything good?" Caroline asked.

"Who knows," Luce muttered, letting herself out. The weak sunshine filtered through the trees, warming her through the long-sleeved shirt under her scrubs. She leaned against the brick wall and took a deep breath, readying herself.

"Mr. Jorgensen's office."

"Hi," Luce said, gripping the phone tightly. "This is Luce Donovan. I missed a call."

"Let me patch you through."

A moment later, Mr. Jorgensen's voice came over the line. "Ms. Donovan?"

"Yes, this is Luce." Her heart rattled in her chest, and she put a hand to it.

"I've got great news," he said. "I just received an official letter from Mr. Donovan's lawyer. He responded very favorably to my cease and desist, and they have agreed on a settlement in light of the pain and suffering you've had to endure anew because of Mr. Donovan's allegations. If you accept the settlement, you agree to not bring litigations against your ex-spouse for anything he may have done previous to this date, and he agrees to the same."

Luce digested his words. What he meant was, even if she discovered some other way Brian had hurt her, some as-yet undiscovered plot to steal from her, she couldn't sue him. "How much is the settlement?" she asked cautiously.

"Twenty thousand dollars."

Twenty thousand. It wasn't a lot of money, compared to everything she'd lost, and it would go very fast as a single woman. But it was infinitely better than him taking something else from her. It might be enough to open a store again . . .

No, she couldn't think that direction. Her days as an entrepreneur were over. "Where did he even get that money? Never mind, I don't want to know. What do you think I should do?"

"Well, we can refuse the offer and demand more money, if you wish. Or you can take it and this all goes away."

She closed her eyes. "Does it?"

His voice changed from less official to a gentler tone, almost consoling. "Yes, Ms. Donovan. And if he attempts anything like this again, you'll have it in official documents that he is breaking an agreement."

She exhaled and opened her eyes, appreciating for the first time the soft yellow and red hues of the brick exterior. "Okay," she said, a sense of relief instantly washing over her. "I'll do it."

"I'll draw up the documents. Can you come in tomorrow and sign them?"

"Yes, absolutely. I'll come in on my lunch break. Thank you."

"You're welcome. Congratulations, Luce. It's over."

She smiled and blinked back the stinging in her eyes. She hoped it was. She no longer mourned her failed marriage. She didn't even feel angry at Brian anymore. That required too much of an emotional investment. If he called her now, she'd quite coolly and calmly tell him to never speak to her again. He'd lost all power over her.

Pocketing her phone, she took a deep breath and smoothed her hair before going back into the clinic. Suddenly she couldn't wait to see Connor. For the first time, she felt free.

CONNOR

*Y*ou *taking a lunch today?*

Connor was actually just finishing up his PB&J sandwich on Thursday when Luce's text popped across his phone. He shot off a reply.

Just a quick one. Lots of customers today.

As if on cue, the shop door opened, and he looked up with his official smile ready. It broadened when he saw Luce stepping through, wearing her balloon-covered scrubs today.

"Hey! I didn't expect you."

She kept her eyes lowered, though a pleased grin never left her face. "I couldn't sleep last Sunday." She placed a box on top of the counter and opened the flaps. "So I made these."

He'd been about to joke that she'd forgotten to take her sleeping pill, but he forgot to be funny when he saw the complete kitchen set she'd made. The canisters, bowls, and matching mugs were perfectly shaped, yet all had that certain uniqueness indicative of hand-thrown pottery. "You made these all in one night?"

She shrugged modestly. "It doesn't take long." She pushed the box toward him. "Here."

For a moment he didn't understand, and then his eyes widened. "Are these for the store?"

"For you." She closed the flap. "To do what you want with." Her eyes sparkled. "You don't know how hard it was not to tell you. But I wanted to surprise you." She pulled the box back when he reached for one. "I still need to get them fired."

He bobbed his head. "I'll find someone with a kiln. You want to leave them with me?"

"No. I like to glaze them right before they go in. Everyone does it different, right? That's part of what makes them special."

"Sure. I'll call you as soon as I have something."

"Thanks." She stood on her tiptoes and pressed a kiss to his lips. "My lunch break is almost over. I better go."

"You're amazing." He captured her hand, holding tight to keep her from swiveling away.

"So are you," she said, her cheeks flushing. "I'll see you after work?"

"I can't tonight. I have this huge paper I was supposed to do Sunday, but somehow I got distracted and didn't do a thing. And then this really pretty girl asked me take her to

Oktoberfest on Tuesday and I couldn't resist . . ."

She tilted her head and tsked. "You should know better."

"I should." He wanted to pull her back and kiss her again. He wanted her to be his. Forever. "And somehow I haven't had any time since then."

"You've been working a lot." Her light eyes flicked over his face.

"Yeah." Sore spot. His mom had turned almost all of her shifts over to him. She spent every moment with Dave or nursing a headache in bed after their expeditions together. At least it had given him more leverage, and he had her official permission to dedicate one wall to whatever he wanted. "But I'll call you."

She tugged her hand free, but the sparkle never left her eye. "I'll talk to you soon, then."

"Later," he said.

She walked to the door and paused once, glancing back at him. Connor grinned at her, and she smiled before stepping outside.

She seemed lighter, happier. Was it because of him? Did he make her as happy as she made him? He let out a slow exhale, feeling his pulse slowly decrease.

Sticking a "I'll be right back" note on the door, Connor locked the shop and strode a few stores down to Kerri's store.

To his disappointment, she wasn't behind the counter, but her mom flashed him a wide smile.

"Need to buy a necklace for your girlfriend?"

"I don't think that's going to be quite enough," he said, shoving his hands in his pockets and peering into the display case. "I need a ring."

"We have rings. They're over here."

He shook his head, not following her to the other case. "Not that kind of ring. A diamond ring."

He saw the moment she got his meaning, and her hands flew to her mouth with an excited gasp. "Connor! Really?"

He hesitated, pleased by her excitement but still unsure. "Is it too soon?"

She dropped her hands and stepped closer. "How long have you been dating?"

"Dating officially?" He shrugged. "A few weeks. Interested in each other? Well, at least a month." He gave a sheepish smile.

She rested her arms on the display glass, studying him. "That is moving awfully fast. How can you know each other in so short a time?"

"Technically we've known each other since high school."

"And how does she feel?"

Oo boy. Connor exhaled, deflating slightly. "That is a very good question."

Mrs. Manning tapped a finger on the glass. "Find the answer to that first."

"These are beautiful, Luce." Connor watched as Luce arranged her finished pottery pieces on the display shelf in his mom's store. He'd found her a willing kiln, but the magic lay in the way she'd applied the purple and blue glazes.

She pushed a hand through her hair and smiled at them, pride showing in her eyes. "Thanks." She looked over at him, beaming. "Ready to go?"

"Yep." He switched the store sign to closed and led her out the back door. He tried not to dwell on the fact that his mom had only worked one shift in the past week.

Instead he thought about the girl walking next to him, holding his hand, going with him to the tailgating party at

Tyson's house like it was the most natural thing in the world. She even wore a red Arkansas Hogs T-shirt.

A crowd had gathered outside on Tyson's lawn, and the revelry had already started. Laughter from inside spilled out across the street. Connor had to park nearly a block away, but Luce didn't complain.

Did she feel like he did, that he would gladly walk thirty miles as long as her hand was in his?

He wove through the crowds with Luce behind him until he found Tyson, directing traffic in the kitchen while he downed a taco.

"Hey man!" he said, greeting Connor with a hand slap. "Moki's downstairs at the pool table. Got a TV set up there also. There's food, drinks, help yourselves. Good to see you, Luce." He grinned at her. "Amber's here somewhere."

"Thanks," Luce said, but she didn't let go of Connor's hand.

He pulled her in closer and nuzzled the hair behind her ear before whispering, "Let's hang out outside. Less crowded."

"Sounds good to me."

They started out the door just as Ty yelled something about the pregame starting, and suddenly they had to fight against the current. A few people lingered on the lawn, mostly couples, but everyone else went inside. Connor headed over to a white hammock that had been recently vacated. He sat down, and Luce settled into it beside him, sending them rocking.

"It's a little cold," she said.

"That's November for you," he replied, wrapping an arm around her and pulling her back into the depths of the hammock with him.

"I forget," she murmured, laying her head on his chest. "Vegas doesn't really get cold."

"Arkansas does. Maybe we'll even get snow."

The hammock swayed slightly with their weight, neither one of them saying anything. Connor kept both arms around her, holding her securely to him.

"You're going to miss the game," she said after awhile.

"I've got what I came for," he replied.

Silence fell over them, and Connor peered up at the stars as they began to peek through the darkening sky. He heard the cheering in the house, the roaring, and imagined the Razorbacks had either just scored a touchdown or gained some yards. He didn't care. He was right where he wanted to be.

"I think I love you."

Luce's whisper barely reached his ears, drifting by as quietly as the wind through the leaves. But it pricked his heart, sent a warmth soaring through his veins. He squeezed her shoulders in response and pressed a kiss to her forehead. But he kept quiet, not about to break the magic between them.

Chapter Eighteen

LUCE

Luce couldn't remember ever being so happy.

She and Connor were dating and Brian was in her past. Ancient history, as far as she was concerned. The more time that passed, the more it felt like it never even happened.

She clasped Connor's hand tightly as he pulled her down Main Street.

"Where are we going?" she laughed, practically running to keep up with him.

"I told you it's a surprise," he said, shooting her a grin. "You just can't wait, can you?"

The giggle that escaped her was so girly she didn't recognize herself.

Connor pulled up short in front of a jewelry store window. "What do you think of these?"

"These what?" She joined him, peering into the display case at the natural stone necklaces and earrings.

"Not those." He cupped her jaw and turned her face to

another case. "These."

She arched an eyebrow at the rings, her heart giving a little pitter-patter. What did he really mean? "They're pretty. Not so much my style."

"Because you don't like turquoise? Or you prefer diamonds?"

Now her heart nearly ran away from her. "Diamonds can be a bit ostentatious. Right? I like braids. Something more subtle."

"Braids?"

She faced him, and he slipped his hands around her waist, meeting her gaze head on. "Designs."

"Ah, I see. You probably don't like yellow gold, either."

She smiled. "You know me."

"I should have expected as much from someone who buys a leopard-skinned lamp."

She burst out laughing. She laughed so hard she had to press a hand to her side.

"What?" He looked confused, though he laughed also. "What's so funny?"

"I only bought that lamp so I wouldn't look like an idiot for coming into your store."

He pulled her to him and kissed her cheek. "You think I didn't know that?" Giving her hand a squeeze, he tugged her down the street again. "Come on. Your surprise is waiting.

They walked past the cluster of shops on the east side of the street, down past the restaurant and toward the Artists Colony, a collection of huts where prospective artists hawked their wares and hoped to make a name for themselves. He stopped at a crosswalk, waiting while a car rolled by, then hurried them over to an antique shop set up in an old mobile home.

"Are we checking out the competition?" she asked, bemused.

"Just wait."

She was dying of curiosity, but Connor wasn't going to reveal anything.

They walked into the long shop, and Luce paused inside the toasty interior to remove her cap and jacket. Connor let go of her hand and went to the register.

"I have a package here. For Connor Thomas."

"Uh." The awkward teen with too many teeth for his mouth turned around and searched through several bags behind the counter.

"It won't be there," Connor said. "It's probably in the back."

"Okay." The kid gave Connor an odd look and then disappeared into the back of the store.

He returned a moment later, pushing a dolly with a large metal box that resembled a squat refrigerator nestled on top.

Luce gasped in spite of herself. "You found a kiln!"

"Connor Thomas," the kid said, pulling a sticky note off the top. "I'll wheel it out to your car. It's heavy."

"Wait." Luce placed a hand on Connor's arm. "This is yours?"

"No." Connor turned to her, his dark eyes drinking her in. "It's yours."

"Connor!" She tightened her grip. "This must have cost a thousand dollars!"

"I got a good deal." He nodded at the boy. "Follow me."

Her head spun as she followed Connor out to the parking lot, and then she came back to her senses when she saw them loading Connor's mom's truck. "But we walked here," she said.

Connor returned to her, rubbing his hands together and

bobbing his shoulders up and down. "I left the truck earlier. I wanted to surprise you. Much more fun than revealing it at your house."

She grabbed him as he neared, placing her hand behind his head and kissing him hard.

He returned her kiss, then pulled back and peered at her. "I take it you like it?"

Her only answer was to kiss him again.

♥

Connor bounced in his seat like a giddy school boy before Christmas vacation as he drove Luce and the kiln back to her condo.

"I'll help you get this in," he said, dropping the back of the truck and pulling out a dolly. "And then I have to go."

"Oh," Luce said, surprised. "You're not staying?" Lately Connor had taken to sleeping on her couch, which only made her wish she hadn't forced a twin bed upon herself.

Though Connor hadn't pressured her to take their relationship to the next level, which Luce appreciated. She knew she couldn't take that step when she hadn't even told Connor the truth about Brian.

"I can't tonight," he said, but he didn't seem sad about it. Excitement still shone in his eyes, as bright as the moon in the dark sky. "But I'll see you tomorrow."

She trailed him through the house and directed him where to set up the kiln. An eager desire to immediately fire it up and see how it worked had her reaching for it, stroking the buttons that controlled the temperature and the time. "I can't believe it. I can work from here now." She'd call an electrician in the morning, get the proper ventilation and wiring set up. And she'd need to find a nonflammable base somewhere . . .

"Or you can work from my shop. We can move it there if

you want." He put his hands on her hips and turned her around.

She smiled coyly and pressed her hands to his chest. "You sure you don't want to stay? Isn't your mom opening tomorrow? I could be late to work."

"I can't." He pulled her closer, close enough that she felt the length of his body pressed against hers. "There's something I've got to do."

He kissed her, and he let it linger, but Luce sensed him already pulling away, not letting himself get swept up in it. "I gotta go." He let go of her and headed for the door. "But I'll see you tomorrow," he repeated, turning to give her another kiss. He let go of the door, his hands quickly running over her curves, down her hips before he broke away with an audible smack. "I love you." One more quick kiss that left her breathless, and then he was gone.

Luce closed the door slowly, watching him turn the truck out of her parking lot.

What was he up to?

As soon as she faced the living room, she saw the kiln, and warmth and delight welled up in her like brewing coffee. He bought her a kiln.

He really loved her.

CONNOR

He knew what to get her.

The moment Luce said she liked braids, the image of a ring popped into his head. One he'd seen at a metal shop on the strip.

A shop that was already closed.

It had taken all of his will power to act normal while he and

Luce picked up the kiln. Of course no one could buy the ring while the shop was closed. And no one was likely to buy it before his lunch break in the morning, either.

And yet it was that fear that had him hurrying back to Spring Street.

He parked the truck right in front of the shop, glad that at least the late hour meant there wasn't any traffic. Of course, late for Eureka Springs in November meant eight p.m.

He jogged down the sidewalk, just in time to see the owner, Maddie, a white-haired pleasant old lady, chatting with another shop owner as she locked up.

"Hang on, hang on, hang on," he called, jumping the curb and coming to a stop beside her.

Maddie arched an eyebrow and looked him up and down. "Myrtle's boy, aren't you? Something wrong?"

Of course she knew his grandmother. They probably chatted together when Granny ran the shop. "You have something I need. In your store."

"I've already closed up for the day."

"Please?" Connor said, not above begging. "Just let me see if it's still here."

With a huffy sigh, Maddie unlocked the door and let him in, hitting the lights as she did so. "You should tell your mom to keep her store open longer. Traffic slows down after five because half of the stores have closed down."

Connor barely heard her. He stopped in front of the rings and spotted it right away. Of course it was the right one; it was perfect. He should've known the first time he saw it. It was rose gold, shiny and brilliant with a delicate pink hue. It had an open weave, six different strands of metal flowing together to create a uniform, stunning design. And not a single diamond in sight.

"What size is she?" Maddie asked, at his shoulder now.

"I have no idea," he replied.

"Let's go with a six. You can bring it in and get it resized if you have to."

Connor remembered to breathe as she put it in a box and rang it up. His hand trembled when he handed her his credit card.

"We have outer bands you can buy also. You know, for a matching wedding band."

Wedding band. Because that's what this meant—marriage. "Yes," he managed through a suddenly dry throat. "Give me one of those too."

She gave him a smile and added a circular band covered in tiny diamonds, putting it in a different box. He had a sudden worry that Luce might not like the diamonds.

"Are these returnable?"

"If she says no, you can bring it back." She winked at him.

"Thanks," he said, taking the bag with the small boxes. "She won't say no." He hoped.

♥

Connor was bursting to tell someone. He wanted to show the ring off, see what other people thought of it.

But some teeny superstitious part of him worried he would jinx everything if he told. So Connor kept his plans to himself.

He only hoped Luce was going to yoga in the morning, because if he had to track her down at work, this could get really awkward.

Connor lay in his bed rehearsing different ways to ask her to marry him, his heart pounding harder with each passing minute. For the first time he considered that she might actually say no. They had, after all, only been dating each other a little over a month. Never mind that it felt like he'd always loved her. She might not feel the same way.

Could his ego bear it if she said no?

It didn't matter. He had to try. He wanted Luce to be in his life forever, and this was the only way to guarantee that.

When his alarm went off at five-thirty in the morning, his first groggy thought was that he was going to kill whoever set it. He hadn't slept well, and his head pounded.

And then he remembered the ring he'd bought, and a jolt of nervous energy had him tumbling out of bed. He pulled out his sweats and then tossed them back, deciding he needed to give "Ja-hood" a run for his money if he was going to propose at yoga class. Long black running pants and a skin-tight T-shirt would have to do.

He pounded on his mom's bedroom door as he passed, then opened it up and peeked in. "Mom. Remember you're opening the store today."

"Oh, Connor," she groaned from the bed, the room still encased in darkness. "I have such a headache. I closed for you last night. Can't you cover for me?"

The irritation flared up. "No. I already covered for you three times this week. Besides, I have an oral exam at eleven."

"All right, all right." The blankets stirred, and she thrust them aside as she sat up. Even in the dark he sensed her glare. "Where are you going so early?"

"What, my apparel's not obvious?" He grinned across at her. "Yoga, of course."

"Are you sure you're not changing yourself too much for this girl?" she said, but he knew she was teasing.

"Just trying new things. Besides, I'm only going to be with her. Not because I actually like yoga."

"And how is that different than me going roller blading with Dave?" She held up a hand before he responded. "Just saying."

"It's different. That's all," Connor said gruffly, not wanting to discuss it more. They would only argue, and he wanted to hold on to this excited mood. "I'll see you after lunch."

Their brief discussion had made him late. Connor quickened his pace out to the car, then drove as fast as he dared down the quiet streets to Spring Street. Luckily there was very little traffic at six-forty-five in the morning. Feeling a bit self-conscious, he climbed the flight of stairs leading to the yoga studio, then slipped into the back.

The alumni—students? Attendees?—were already on the ground, hovering over the soft mats in the Chattanooga pose or whatever it was. Connor didn't have a mat and only intended to exercise enough to not draw attention to himself. His eyes scanned the room, looking for Luce. Instead he caught the eye of the instructor, who carried himself around the room with his chin up and hands behind his back, practically prancing en pointe from mat to mat. Connor rolled his eyes and then held still as Jarrod made his way over to him.

"Do you need a mat?" he asked, the fake French accent sticky on his tongue.

"No, thanks," Connor said, not letting go of his bag. "I think I'll just watch."

"I remember you," Jarrod said. "You come with pretty brunette last time." His hands made the shape of an hour glass as he spoke.

"Yeah, she's my girlfriend," Connor said, not sure he liked Jarrod's appreciation of Luce.

"Looks like she won't come today," Jarrod said with a glance at his wristwatch.

Was she seriously not here? "Okay." Tightening his grip on

his messenger bag, Connor went to the exit, trying to stomp down his rising disappointment. The ring wasn't going anywhere. He'd get with her tonight.

He nearly collided with a breathless girl who yanked the door open the same time he pushed it out.

"Oh!" she cried, and Connor grabbed her shoulders, recognizing Luce just as she stumbled backward.

"Luce!" He couldn't stop the smile that spread itself across his face. "You're late!" The door closed behind him, leaving the two of them on the landing outside the studio.

"Connor?" She cocked her head, her expression quizzical as she studied him. "What are you doing here?"

"I came looking for you." His heart had started to pound harder in his chest, creating a steady drumbeat that thumped in his neck and ears and head. "But you weren't here."

She leaned against the wall of the building, using her yoga mat as a cushion between her and the bricks, and gave him a sheepish grin. "I was a little too excited to sleep last night. I was setting up my kiln."

He laughed. "That's great. I mean, I'm really glad you like it. I knew it would be easier for you if you had your own, so I put out some feelers, asked people to let me know if they got one. I was surprised it happened so quickly . . ." He trailed off, realizing he'd started rambling. Sweat beaded across his forehead, and he clenched and unclenched his fists. How did a guy go about asking a girl to marry him? He was at a total loss.

And apparently it showed.

"What's wrong?" Luce asked, frowning now in concern.

This was going the wrong direction. He needed to take charge, and now.

"Luce," he said, and then he remembered he was supposed

to get on one knee. Begging, right? Whatever it took. He dropped to one knee, hand fumbling in his messenger bag for the box.

"Connor," Luce said, her eyes going wide. The lamp above the door cast most of her face in shadow, but he imagined at this moment she had an inkling of what he was doing.

Crap, why hadn't he planned out a proper speech? "Luce, I love you and I always will. I don't know what's next in my life. But I know for sure I want you in it." He tried to flip the box open like they did in the movies, all suave-like, but it didn't work so well. He had to use both hands, but finally it opened. "Will you marry me?"

Luce had both hands pressed to her mouth, staring at him. She dropped them and let one hand fall to the open box. "This is beautiful," she gasped out, taking it from him.

"Say yes and you can wear it." *Please say yes. Please please please.*

"Yes," she whispered. Her hand trembled as she handed the box back to him. "Yes, I will."

"Yes!" Connor said. He jumped to his feet and let out a throaty laugh, then grabbed her up in a giant hug. "Here. Let's make sure it fits."

She extended her hand and held very still while Connor slipped the ring on her finger. "When did you buy this?" she asked, holding it up to the light and studying it.

"Last night. After I left your place."

Tears shone in her eyes when she looked at him. "I wish I'd known you better in high school."

He gave her a solid kiss and hugged her again. "It's never too late."

~ Chapter Nineteen ~

LUCE

It's never too late, Connor said.

But he didn't know. He didn't know everything that happened between the time he'd known her in high school and now.

They went to breakfast at Mud Street Cafe, and Connor's happy giddiness was infectious, filling her with warmth and joy. He loved her, and she'd made him happy. He told the hostess, the waitress, the motorcycle gang at the table next to them, everyone he saw that they'd just gotten engaged.

"We'll stop by the shop in a little bit and tell my mom, after it opens," Connor said, eating his ham and broccoli quiche like he hadn't eaten in a month.

Luce smiled and nodded and picked at her food, an uneasiness welling in her stomach. She shouldn't have said yes.

"Do you like the ring?"

"It's stunning." She paused to admire it. "I've never seen

anything like it."

He put his fork down and took her hands. "You're a bit quiet. Am I talking too much? Did I scare you? Is this what you want, Luce?"

She stared back into this eyes, so serious. "This is what I want. More than anything. I'm surprised. I wasn't expecting this." She hoped her smile was convincing.

"But not too much of a shock, I hope?"

The concern on his handsome face only cemented her desire to be with him, this kind-hearted boy who loved her so completely. "I love you, Connor."

He squeezed her fingers, eyes crinkling as the grin returned to his face. "I didn't expect you to say yes unless you did."

Connor drove Luce home to change after breakfast, and then they returned to Spring Street.

"I can't wait to tell my mom," Connor said, clutching her hand in his as he pushed open the door to his mom's shop. "She's going to freak out."

Jessica's scream of delight was so loud that several people walking by outside stopped and peered at the store.

"Mom," Connor said, shushing her with his hand, though, like Jessica, he couldn't wipe the silly smile from his face.

Luce's ears burned with embarrassment, but she told herself to shake it off. What did it matter if everyone knew? It wasn't like someone was going to poke their head inside and shout that she was a fraud.

Because that's what she felt like.

"I love your ring, I love love love it," Jessica said, fawning over the rose-gold band on Luce's finger. "Did you pick it out?"

"Connor did," Luce said, glancing at him and feeling the heat rush to her face. "But he knew exactly what I would like."

Her head swam, and she reached out to grip the counter. This wasn't real. She wasn't really going to marry Connor. He wouldn't really be her husband.

She wanted to it so badly she found it hard to breathe.

Jessica gave her a secret little smile. "He knows you, sweetie."

Luce nodded. But it wasn't true. Connor didn't really know her at all.

"Have you guys picked a date? When's the wedding?"

"Mom, I barely asked her this morning." Connor returned to Luce, slipping behind her and resting his chin on her shoulder. "We have time to figure that out."

"Lots of time," Luce echoed, her heart pounding hard in her chest.

Connor moved in front of her, taking her hand and running his thumb over the engagement ring. "Call in sick. Let's go celebrate."

Luce bobbed her head, unwilling to relinquish this fairy tale before she had to. "Okay. Yes."

Jessica stepped up to her again and kissed both of her cheeks, tears in her eyes. "I'm so happy. You're really my daughter now."

Luce feared her face would break from trying so hard to smile.

❤

Luce enjoyed the weekend with Connor, pretending to be his fiance, but Monday brought reality crashing back as she returned to work.

Her thoughts swirled around in her head like a vicious cyclone, sharp pieces of shrapnel cutting her everywhere she turned. She'd said yes to Connor, given every indication that she would marry him. But she couldn't marry him, not without telling him everything.

And then what? Would he still want her?

She cornered Caroline in the hall in between patients and breathed, "Meet me outside during break." Then she walked away before Caroline could ask any questions.

At almost 10:10 she saw Caroline glance her way before heading for the back parking lot. Luce stalled a minute, checking to see how many patients had checked in and if the doctor was running on time. Then she hurried after her.

"What's up, girl?" Caroline asked, fishing around in her purse for something. She finally retrieved a package of gum and offered a piece to Luce.

Luce shook her head. "Why did Connor break up with Regina?" She tapped her fingers against her thigh and tried to act like it was a casual question.

Caroline's ebony eyebrows arched above her deep green eyes. "Things getting serious with you two?"

Luce squeezed her fingers into a fist and then unclenched them, stretching them out as far as they would go. "Yes. A little scary serious. I don't want to make the same mistakes she did. I've fallen in love with him, and it's so frightening."

"And is he falling for you?"

In answer, Luce reached into the pocket of her scrubs and pulled out the beautiful engagement ring. She didn't dare wear it at work for fear Regina would see it. She cupped it in her palm and held it out, feeling as though she held a lie.

Caroline gasped, pressing her fingers to her lips. Understanding and sympathy crossed her face, and she put her hand on Luce's arm. "I don't know why they broke up, exactly. Regina said she made a mistake, one too many mistakes, and this time Connor wouldn't let it go."

Luce took a breath and exhaled. Connor had given her

chances. That made her feel a little better.

Caroline's eyes scrutinized her. "What are you going to do?"

"Well. I guess I need to find a way to tell him about Brian."

"You mean you didn't tell him?"

"No." Luce shook her head. "I totally planned on it. Weeks ago. But the moment slipped away and—then I got scared."

"Luce, you have to tell him."

"I know," she said softly. "He's picking me up after work. We're together every moment. I'm out of excuses."

Caroline bobbed her head. "Maybe it won't be as bad as you think. Just do it and get it over with."

Do it and get it over with. Luce wanted to throw up at the very thought. What would he think of her? How could she tell him?

♥

The closer it got to closing time and seeing Connor, the more anxious Luce got. Every moment with him was like being on board a ship with the self-destruct activated. And she'd activated it.

Her phone dinged as she cleaned up the nurses' station.

In parking lot, the text said.

Luce ducked her head out and saw Regina and Jenn laughing together in the hallway. She pulled her head back before they caught her spying.

I'll come out in a moment. Stay there, she texted back.

She stalled as long as she could, waiting for Regina to leave.

But Regina wasn't leaving. Now she and Jenn were talking animatedly as they filed print outs together.

"I'm out of here!" Caroline said, waving as she headed for the back door. "See y'all tomorrow!"

Luce gave up. She'd just have to leave quickly. "Me too." She went to the break room and grabbed her purse and jacket.

"I guess I'll go too," Regina said. "Looks like I'm the last one here."

"I'll lock up behind you," Jenn called, her bubbly voice pinging down the hall.

Luce groaned inwardly. Should she stay in the break room, pretend to be busy while Regina left? Or should she hurry out and try to get into Connor's car before she saw?

Her hesitation decided for her. She was still in the break room when Regina stepped in.

"Oh, hey, Luce, I thought you'd gone already." Regina opened her locker and retrieved her things.

"Yeah, not yet." Luce stood still, studying her phone as if absorbed in something important.

"Jenn is locking up. You better head out now."

"Right." Trying to act like that had been her plan all along, Luce followed Regina outside.

Connor's car was parked right next to Luce's. She saw the way Regina's eyes landed on it. There was no getting around this now.

Regina turned to Luce, the skin of her face slightly mottled. "I didn't know you guys were still seeing each other."

"We are," Luce said, hoping Connor would have the good sense to stay in the car.

He didn't.

Connor stepped out, wearing a long-sleeved maroon shirt over khakis. He waved at Regina. "Hi, Gee."

Gee. Jealousy tightened in Luce's navel.

"Hi, Connor." Regina stepped up to him and gave him a hug. "Long time no see. You don't have to be a stranger."

"Sorry. You good?" His eyes swept to Luce, and he extended his hand to her.

Regina's gaze swiveled to Luce and her eyes narrowed.

Cocking her head, Regina said, "So I guess you got it all worked out with your ex?"

Luce's heart began to race. Really? Regina was going to bring that up? "Yes, it's all taken care of," she said, begging Regina with her eyes to let it go.

"Oh, because it sounded so serious, like he was stalking you or something."

Luce made a noise in the back of her throat, and Connor said, "When was this? You never said anything about it."

Luce waved him off, taking his arm and pivoting him toward the car. "It was weeks ago." *Just get in, get in, get in.*

"But your ex got his lawyer involved, right?" Regina pressed. "You were pretty scared. I can't believe you didn't tell Connor."

"Luce," Connor said, concern tightening his features. "If you have an ex-boyfriend messing with you—"

"I don't," Luce interrupted, desperate to leave. "Let's just go, we can talk about this later." *Please please please please.*

"Oh no, it's not her ex-boyfriend," Regina said, and Luce swore she saw a malicious glint in her eye. Luce's fingers fluttered as if to ward off the words about to exit Regina's mouth. "It's her ex-husband."

Connor's face turned toward her, puzzlement on his furrowed brow. "Ex-husband?"

Luce wanted to throw up. She reached for Connor, but he pulled away from her and stepped back, evading her touch.

"Wait, what?" he said, his expression perplexed but his tone demanding an explanation.

"She didn't tell you?" Regina said. "Oh, I'm so sorry! I just assumed if you were still seeing each other—surely she wouldn't hide something like that from you."

Hide. The word sounded nasty and intentional.

"Luce?" Connor said, still sounding unsure.

"Let's just go," she said, trying to take his hand. "We can talk at my place."

He didn't let her grab him. "You were married?"

She closed her eyes, humiliation and anger roaring like a brush fire through her body. She swung around to Regina. "Can you give us some privacy?"

"Yeah," Regina muttered, ducking her head and dashing off.

"Is it true?" Connor demanded. A hard edge had replaced the confusion in his voice.

"Yes," Luce said, an anxious trembling overtaking her body. She wrapped her arms around her torso. "Can we go somewhere else to talk?"

He didn't budge, and she didn't dare step closer, though the only thing she wanted was for him to hold her. "And why did I have to learn it from Regina?"

"I was going to tell you today," she said, realizing how empty the words sounded.

He turned to his car.

"Connor—" Luce began.

He climbed inside and shut the door.

Luce pulled her phone out and dialed Connor's number even as he started the engine.

He declined her call, and it went straight to voicemail. Swallowing back her tears, she swiveled on her heel. By the time she turned the key in the ignition, Connor was gone.

CONNor

The only thing Connor wanted to do was go and get very very drunk.

Instead he focused on the essay test on the screen in front of him, his fingers clenching and unclenching over the keyboard. At least his mom wasn't here to ask him questions or see his anger.

Married. Luce had been married before. She hadn't just had a serious boyfriend or two, she hadn't just suffered a bad break up. She'd shared a home with a guy, taken his name, been his wife. She planned her future with him.

How did he know she wasn't still married?

The facts twisted at his gut, making him insanely jealous and wanting to tear the guy's arms off. But even worse was that she had kept it from him. The thought left him so sick inside he couldn't even focus on his test.

How long had she thought she could keep it a secret? Would he stumble across an old wedding certificate six years into their marriage? Would she finally admit to him that she had said "I do" to someone else before?

Was O'Neil even her last name?

He shook his head, wrapped up once again in his own misery. She was like Regina, lying and twisting facts to mask what she didn't want him to know. Like his mother, changing who she was for the next guy she was desperate to catch.

Like his father, hiding his first family while he created another.

The phone rang again. He knew before he even picked it up that it would be Luce. His chest tightened, constricting around his heart. Every part of his soul wanted to answer, to hear her voice, to feel like this would all be okay. But in his head he knew it wouldn't.

The call went to voicemail, and still he stared at it. He toggled her name and silenced her number.

That didn't help. He only made it through half his essay before he picked his phone up and checked his messages.

Sure enough, she'd left one.

He told himself to delete it without listening, but he couldn't bring himself to do it. Instead he opened his voicemail and played the message.

"Connor, I'm so sorry I didn't tell you." There was a choked, husky quality to her voice, as if she fought tears or couldn't breathe because of them. "Please talk to me. I don't want to lose you. I love you."

Connor's own eyes reacted in response to her obvious emotion, but his closing throat and burning eyes were nothing compared to the pit of emptiness he felt in his heart. He loved her. But he couldn't marry a woman who would keep something like this a secret from him. This was bigger than pretending like she didn't like night clubs while sneaking off to them almost every night, this was bigger than pretending she liked red meat and roller blading to match the person she dated.

Connor listened to her message one more time, wondering why he tortured himself. He knew she loved him. But love wasn't enough.

His finger hovered above the text button. It would be so much easier to just write her a quick note and say they were done. That he couldn't handle her betrayal. But it would also be cowardly, and no matter what she'd done, he had enough respect for her to end things in person. He had planned to marry her, after all.

With that thought knifing through is heart, he opened up the text messaging and typed out, *Will have to talk later. I can't do this right now. Need space.*

He hit send, and it wasn't but a few seconds later that her response came.

OK. I'm ready to talk whenever you are. I'm so sorry.

Connor put the phone facedown in front of him. Judging from the tone of her message, she was hoping for reconciliation, not a break up.

The phone was distracting, sitting there in front of him. His eyes kept looking toward it as he worked on his test. With a grunt of frustration and annoyance, he retrieved the phone and took it to his bedroom. He left it there, closing the door on it as though it were a child needing to be put in timeout. Then he returned to the computer.

Unfortunately, having the phone out of sight did not help him focus any better.

♥

Luce didn't contact him the rest of the evening.

That was what he had asked of her. But he spent every moment hoping she would, making excuses to go to his room and check his phone. He knew it was better she did not because he wouldn't be kind to her. The cold anger stifled the other emotions he felt for her, and even though he missed her painfully, over the top of that was a thick frothy layer of mistrust and fury. Not just anger at what she'd done, but anger at the loss of the future he'd planned.

His mom wasn't home yet even though the store had closed hours ago, but that wasn't much of a surprise. He went to his room and sent her a quick text.

Just making sure you're not passed out on the street somewhere.

It was a harsh thing to say, but he wasn't in a generous mood.

When did I raise such a rude son? Just out with Dave watching the game. What are you doing? You should come join us.

What was he doing? Connor went back to the living room and grabbed the remote, perusing channels until he found something factual to watch. No drama, no frills, no fiction. Just the facts of plain, stark reality. He texted her back. *I'm good. Watching a documentary.*

Is Luce with you?

Connor preferred not to answer that. So he didn't. Instead he dumped his phone on the bed.

He must've fallen asleep watching TV, because when he woke again there was a horrible crick in his neck. Blue light from the TV flipped around the room as the documentary had switched to a late night infomercial. He turned the TV off and stumbled to his bed. A heavy, lethargic feeling consumed his body. Maybe he would follow the suit of bears everywhere and hibernate for the next few months. Bury into a hole and only emerge every few weeks for something to eat. The idea had merit.

Unbidden, an image of Luce curled up in her bed, taking up less than half of the twin mattress, flashed through his mind. She slept like a little squirrel, brownish hair falling over her shoulders and face. She ate like a squirrel too, all those vegetables.

Maybe it was just the lateness of the hour, but he wanted to cry.

Connor slipped under the covers. His hand connected with the cold metal of his phone, and he couldn't help how his heart hammered a little harder as he flipped it over. It was still on silent, and he noticed with something akin to alarm that Dave had called five times, three of those times in the past ten minutes.

Connor tilted up right. His phone showed it was almost three o'clock in the morning. Had his mom and Dave gotten into a car accident? If that man had driven her somewhere while drunk—

But no, it wasn't the police trying to reach him, it was Dave.

Connor returned the call, trying to ignore the anxious flurry in his stomach.

Dave didn't answer the first time. Persistent, even more nervous now, Conner tried again. This time Dave picked up, his voice hushed as he spoke into the phone.

"Connor, I've been trying to reach you for half an hour. You need to come to the hospital. Right now."

Something twisted tightly in Connor's chest, making it hard to breathe. "What happened to my mom?"

"I'm not sure. The doctors are looking after her now. But she's very ill. Connor, you need to come down."

She might die. Dave had not said those words, but Connor heard them anyway. His throat closed up. "I'm on my way."

He threw on some flip-flops and grabbed a jacket, glad he hadn't put on pajamas. Now he rushed out the door in his jeans and collared shirt. There were no people out on the road, and even though Connor drove slightly above the speed limit, the seven-minute drive felt like an eternity. If his mom passed while he was in route, he would never forgive the universe.

Careening into a spot at the hospital near the emergency room, Connor barely put the car into park before he launched himself out of it. He ran into the room and paused at the check in, resting his hands on the counter and taking a deep breath. "Jessica Thomas, do you know where she is? "

"Let me see," the woman with the tired eyes behind the window said. "Yes, here she is. Give me one second to see which room she's in now."

Connor turned away from her and shoved a hand through his hair, swallowing hard. He couldn't lose his mom, not now, not when she was all he had.

He thought of Luce and closed his eyes, wishing she were there. Just her presence, the touch of her hand would ease some of this emotional agony. But he couldn't call her, couldn't lead her on and give her hope where there was none.

"Sir?"

He circled back to the receptionist, blinking rapidly to clear the tears from his eyes.

"She's in the ICU. Are you immediate family? It's after hours."

"Yes. I'm her son."

"Take the elevator on your left up one floor. Room 1120. You'll have to show ID to the nurse on duty."

Connor gave a brief nod before jumping into the elevator. He pounded the button several times before the doors took their sweet time closing. He should've taken the stairs.

The nurse on duty wrote down his information and then directed him to a room just left of the station. It wasn't locked, and he pushed the door open to be greeted by the beeping and whirring of machines.

Dave lay sprawled out in a chair, his legs spread wide, head tilted across the top and mouth open. Connor's eyes glued to his mother, who had a respirator over her mouth and a heart monitor somewhere, judging from the fancy lights on the screen next to her bed. He stepped up to Dave and shook him.

"What?" Dave opened his eyes and gave a start at the motion, then winced and stretched his back. "Connor. You're here. Sorry, I must've fallen asleep."

"Must have. What's going on? What happened? Were you guys in an accident?"

Dave reached his arms above his head and yawned, and then pushed to his feet. "An accident? No, she just kind of went limp when we hanging out. Couldn't move and wasn't making any sense."

"What did the doctor say?"

"They think maybe she had a stroke. She has some bleeding on the brain. I'm not exactly sure. But now that you're here, I'm gonna go."

Connor narrowed his eyes. "Wait, you're not staying?"

Dave gave him a patronizing look. "What for? She's asleep. I won't be missing anything."

Connor suddenly understood. Dave hadn't called because his mom might die; he'd called because he wanted to go home to his comfy bed and sleep. "Go on, get out of here." *You always were a lame-ass boyfriend.* The same could be said for every boyfriend his mom ever had. It wasn't exactly Dave's fault.

"Check with the doctor in the morning," Dave said, gathering his jacket and pushing his arms through the sleeves. "One of those nurses keeps coming in to, what's it called, check her vitals? Anyway, I'll call later and see how she's doing."

"Thanks," Connor said shortly. He was grateful, at least, that Dave had the sense to take his mom to the hospital. But that was as far as Connor's gratitude went.

As soon as Dave left, Connor stepped closer to his mom. He took her limp, cold hand in his and stroked her fingers. "Mom?" he whispered. He half expected a response, but there was not one. He dragged the chair Dave had been sitting in over to the bed, then took her hand again and rested his forehead against the edge of the mattress.

He slept fitfully, dreams and images of people in hospitals and doctors and nurses running around, pushing gurneys, white scrubs flapping as they went. And there was one nurse with black scrubs with pink polka dots. Connor found himself following her . . .

Someone touched his shoulder, jostling him awake. He

blinked groggily and lifted his head. An older man with graying hair and a kind smile looked down at him.

"Hey, there. Are you her son?"

"Yes." He cleared his throat. "How is she? Can you tell me anything?"

"I can't tell you much except she's stable. You'll have to talk to the doctor to get the rest."

"She going to be okay?"

The man gave him a sympathetic look. "I don't know." He placed a blood pressure cuff around his mom's forearm, then asked, "Is there anyone who could be here with you right now? So you're not alone?"

"No," Connor said softly, an ache in his throat. "There's no one."

♥

Connor woke again around six in the morning. He couldn't sleep, between his haunting dreams and worrying that his mother lay there dying. He stood and paced the room, then turned on the television and searched for something mindless to watch. He settled on a silly comedy that was so stupid it was actually laughable.

A low groaning sound percolated behind him, starting at the bed and slowly filling the empty spaces. Connor turned around. His mother had lifted one hand to the side of her face.

"Mom!" Connor rushed to her side.

She groaned again, not as low this time, some of the natural timbre of her voice returning. "Oh," she moaned, drawing the word out like a balloon losing air.

Connor sank into the chair next to the bed, realizing the respirator kept her voice from sounding normal. "I'm going to call the nurse, okay?" he said, making eye contact with her. Though her eyes were puffy, they met his with perfect lucidity. He felt a small squeeze of comfort. That had to be a good sign.

He pushed the call button for the nurse and waited for his arrival. He also sent a quick text to Dave.

"Yes?" the nurse said, stepping into the room, the same smile on his face, though he looked significantly more tired. Connor wondered what he was doing on this shift. Shouldn't he have enough seniority to have a better one? Or maybe he was just getting started as a nurse, finally fulfilling a lifelong dream in the medical field.

Why did everything make him think of Luce?

"She's awake," he said, gesturing to his mom, but the motion was needless. The nurse had turned his attention toward his mom before he even spoke.

"Oh, good. The doctor said to page him as soon as she woke."

He disappeared from the room for a moment, and then he returned. "It's all right, hon, we're going to take good care of you." He stroked her forehead and put the blood pressure cuff on her arm again, then checked her temperature and jotted all of the findings down on his clipboard. "How long ago did she wake up?"

"Five minutes ago."

"Okay." He patted his mom's hand and gave her a smile.

He left the two of them, and Connor settled next to his mom. "Can I get you anything? Another blanket?"

Her eyes scanned the room. She made a gurgling noise in the back of her throat.

"What was that?" Connor leaned closer.

"Loose." She blew out the "oo" sound before adding on the "s," but it only took Connor a moment to catch the word.

Luce.

Not that. His throat tightened and he blinked, turning away so she wouldn't see his face. "She's sleeping, Mom. I'm sure she has to work today. Don't you want me to call Granny?"

His mom began to cry. Her shoulders shook, her voice rasping, tears streaking down her face. "Luce."

Connor panicked. She always kept a positive face, even with all the lousy boyfriends and difficult life of a single mom. "Okay. I'll call her. But she might not answer." For more than one reason. He knew, instinctively, that now was not the time to spill about their break up.

He pulled his fingers from hers and stepped out of the room.

Only for his mom would he break the silence and call Luce.

And yet at the same time, the weaker part of himself felt relief, glad he didn't have to be strong and go through this without her. His mother had provided him the excuse he needed.

Chapter Twenty

LUCE

It took hours for Luce's wounded mind to fall asleep. She blamed herself for this fall from grace. She had thought she'd have time. How was she to know things would get serious so quickly?

How was she to know how much he would mean to her?

Eventually she must've slept, because she woke up to her phone ringing. Her eyelids ripped open, sticky and itchy from crying. She grabbed her phone.

Six-thirty in the morning. She'd slept through yoga.

And it was Connor calling.

Sitting up, Luce cleared her throat and answered. "Connor?" Somehow she doubted he was calling at this time to make up.

"Luce."

Her name whispered across the phone, and she felt his own hurt and anguish. She closed her eyes, and more tears worked their way out from under her eyelids.

"I need you."

She opened her eyes, catching her breath. But he wasn't done talking.

"I'm at the hospital. Something's really wrong with my mom. She's asking for you."

Disappointment that he was calling for his mom quickly melted into concern. She rolled out of bed and opened her closet, searching for jeans and a T-shirt. "I'll be right there."

"Thanks."

Nobody questioned Luce being at the hospital. She used her ID card to bypass the check in desk and made her way to a computer terminal. Jessica was still in the ICU. Her heart did a little flipflop. What was wrong? She took the stairs, running up them as fast as she could.

She came out of the stairwell and immediately saw Connor standing by the elevators. His clothing was rumpled as if he'd slept in it or pulled it off the bedroom floor, and his hair was in disarray, extending in every direction like a little boy. Adding to that impression were his puffy eyes and forlorn expression. It made her stomach ache to know she had caused some of that.

"Connor," she whispered, hesitant.

He turned from the elevator, his eyes lighting up when he saw her. "Luce." His strode to her, his arms going around her, and he pressed his face into her neck. She hugged him, feeling how his shoulders tightened beneath her hands.

"What happened?" Luce asked, ducking away from him enough to see his face.

"I have no idea. I'm waiting on the doctor. It's been an awful night, Luce. I don't think I've ever been more scared."

She squeezed his hands. "I'm here."

"Thank you," he whispered.

"Let's go in and wait for the doctor."

Jessica's eyes landed on Luce the moment she stepped into the room, and immediately tears began to flow.

"Shh," Luce said, releasing Connor and bending over to hug his mom. "You're okay. You're safe." She found a chair next to the bed and sat in it, stroking Jessica's hair and holding her hand. "The doctor will tell us everything."

Sure enough, a light tap came at the door a moment later, followed by it opening. The doctor and his nurse came in. Luce didn't recognize either. The doctor had a full head of sandy brown hair and a kind smile.

"How are we, Miss—" He took the clipboard from the nurse, glanced at it, and looked back up. "Miss Thomas?" Putting the clipboard down on the tray beside the bed, he reached his hands over Jessica's face and gently removed the ventilator.

She sucked in a deep breath as if somehow the device had been inhibiting her breathing rather than helping it. "What happened? Why am I here?" Her voice croaked from disuse, and she swallowed several times.

"What do you remember?" the doctor asked, taking out a penlight and shining it in her eyes. Luce leaned closer. Pupil dilation looked good. Eye reflexes were instantaneous, also.

"The last thing I remember . . . I'm not sure. I remember being at the store, closing it up, but it feels like I did something after that. It's all hazy, I can't say exactly. It's as if I'm just waking up from a dream."

"Your speech is very good, as are the reflexes I tested," the doctor said. "The neurological staff did an MRI last night when they brought you in and we have some inconclusive results, but I'd like to do another before we give a diagnosis."

Luce heard what he didn't say and felt her navel tighten.

The first results were bad, and the doctor wanted to make sure before giving them their sentence. She focused on the wall above the bed, unable to look at either of them for fear they would see what she knew.

"Can you move your other hand?" the doctor said.

Luce turned her gaze to Jessica's hands and watched as the right one gripped the bed sheet. The left hand merely trembled.

"I can see that wasn't easy for you, but you still did it. That's a good sign for rehabilitation. You may have damage to your entire left nervous system." The doctor looked at Luce and cleared his throat. "Are you the daughter?"

"Uh—I—" Luce stuttered.

"Yes," Jessica said. "She's my daughter."

Not for long, Luce thought, and again tears stung.

"But I'm the primary caregiver," Connor said, stepping closer to the bed.

"Well, this is for both of you. She's awake, but it's going to be a busy day of tests. Only one of you should stay here at a time. Make sure she gets rest."

Luce wanted to pull the doctor aside and corner him, ask him her questions, but she simply nodded, keeping her face stoic. "I'll go. I have to get ready for work." Luce bent and pressed a kiss to Jessica's forehead. "Hang in there," she whispered in her ear.

"Come back later?" Jessica said when Luce straightened, her eyes frightened and desperate.

Only if Connor wants. "Of course."

"I'll walk you out," Connor murmured.

They stepped out of the room together and stood in the hallway, Connor with his hands in his jeans pockets and an awkward space between them.

"What do you think?" he asked.

"You want my professional, speculative opinion?" She tried to keep her voice light, but she felt like her soul was quaking.

He inclined his head to a row of chairs by a window. "Let's sit."

They sat down, and Luce clasped her hands together to keep from taking his. "The doctor doesn't want to say until he knows for sure. But that means it could be something—something bad."

He squinted his eyes. "Define bad."

She scanned his face, wanting desperately to hold him. Taking a chance, she grasped his hand, relieved when he didn't pull away. "Something debilitating. Permanent. Even terminal."

"Like what?" His voice cracked on the last word, and he cleared his throat.

"A stroke. A tumor."

His face grew paler. "Can they operate on a tumor?"

"It really just depends," Luce whispered. She wasn't a doctor, but she knew brain tumors were often inoperable. And even if they were, the recovery after such a surgery was long and difficult.

Connor's shoulders slumped, and he wavered a moment before sliding closer to her and dropping his head into her lap. She stroked his hair, grateful that he'd at least accepted her into his life this much, right now. She trembled with hope that this meant he'd be able to forgive her.

♥

The doctor found them by the windows an hour later. It was a little after eight, and Luce would be late to work if she didn't leave, but she couldn't bear to walk away from Connor right now.

"We have the results from her second MRI," the doctor said. "I'd like to discuss them with her while you're present."

Connor had fallen asleep on Luce's leg, and she hated to wake him. This moment with him might be her last. But she knew he was anxious to know the diagnosis, so she nudged him gently.

"Connor. The doctor wants to talk to you."

He sat up, blinking his bloodshot eyes groggily.

"Let's head back to her room," the doctor said.

Connor pushed himself to his feet and started after him. Luce stood as well, heaving a sigh as she shouldered her purse. Probably time to end the charade and leave.

"Wait," Connor said, holding up a hand. Then he turned around. "Luce? Aren't you coming?"

Her chest warmed. He waited until she reached him, and then he looped his fingers through hers. She exhaled, and some of the tightness left her shoulders.

The doctor paused outside of the room. "You'll probably have lots of things to discuss, but she's exhausted. Let's keep this to ten minutes."

Dave was already there, seated by the bed and holding Jessica's hand in his. He stood when Connor came in and offered his chair, but Connor declined. Luce didn't miss the glower he sent his way.

"All right. I have a diagnosis." The doctor's light eyes landed on Jessica, whose gaze did not waver. "You have a brain tumor."

She bobbed her head, wincing slightly, but didn't look surprised. "What are my options?"

"We can operate, but there's only a slim chance of success. There's a good possibility you wouldn't survive any such operation."

Luce flinched at the words, but Jessica did not.

"The surgery itself could have life-altering effects."

Connor's fingers squeezed hers, and Luce sensed him drawing strength from her presence. "What are the chances of success?" he asked.

The doctor hesitated and consulted his clipboard again. "We need to run a few more tests to be sure, but it looks like . . . less than a twenty-five percent success rate."

Connor pressed a hand to his eyes, then dropped it. He let out a slow breath. "Mom?"

Jessica turned her head and looked at him, her lips quavering. "Oh, Connor," she whispered.

Luce hung back as Connor hugged his mom. They both cried, then Connor walked away and stared out the window. Jessica's eyes landed on Luce.

"Oh, sweetheart, I'm so glad you're still here," she said. "Connor needs you now. More than ever. Promise me you'll be there for him."

"I promise," Luce said.

Connor turned around and marched back to the bed. "Mom, you're not going to die. The doctor said we have options."

"Oh, yes, I heard my options."

"You should think about them," Dave said. "Don't dismiss them so quickly."

"I'll think about them," Jessica said, but even Luce knew she was lying.

Connor stroked his mom's arm. "We'll make a plan."

"I'm sure we will."

They talked a few more minutes before a nurse poked her head in and said, "Okay, that's all for now, guys. Only one of you can stay. But you can come back in a few hours. We'll be moving her out of ICU, and visiting hours start at ten."

"I'm staying," Dave said.

"I should," Connor said. "She's my mom."

"No, honey, be with Luce," Jessica said. "That's where you belong right now."

Connor looked like he wanted to fight Dave for the chance to stay, but instead his shoulders slumped and he gave in. "Okay." He kissed his mom's cheek and stepped back from the hospital bed. "See you in a few hours." He nodded at Luce, and she followed him out of the hospital room.

She expected him to reach for her again, but instead he scrubbed a hand down his face and stayed two steps ahead of her down the hall. Only when he got to the elevator did he pause for her to catch up.

"Thanks for coming." He shoved his hands in his pockets and leaned his head against the wall behind him. "I really appreciate your support."

Uh-oh. His voice was agitated, and his stance held a challenge in it. Luce's heart hammered out a note of warning. "Of course I came, Connor. I—"

I love you. The words were on the tip of her tongue, but he didn't give her a chance to say them. Instead, he straightened up and leveled his gaze at her.

"I'm sorry I drove off like that last night, but I had to think. I need to make this clear. I called you because it calmed my mom down to have you here. She loves you." His jaw clenched and he looked away for a second, then faced her again. "But you and I—I'm sorry. I just can't do it."

Luce gasped slightly, his abrasive honesty chilling her. "Just because—because I'm divorced?" Instantly she felt like someone had covered her in mud. Dirty, tainted, used, second-hand—all the things that made her want to hide her marital status in the first place.

"So you are divorced? It's final?"

"Yes!" she exclaimed, bristling slightly. What kind of person did he think she was? "I would never date you otherwise!"

"How am I supposed to know that?" he said softly.

"Because it's me you're talking to!" She stepped toward him, but he moved back. "You know me!"

He shook his head. "I don't think so."

She felt the panic creeping up, the hot flush on her face. "Just because I was married before?"

"That's not it."

"It sure looks like it from here!" She lowered her voice when heads turned their way. "What is it, then?"

"I just can't, Luce." His hand came out of his pocket and he reached for her, but then he let it drop. "I'll walk you to your car."

"Don't bother." She blinked hard against the tears threatening to fall, all of her hopes dashed to pieces on the scuffed linoleum. He'd needed her, no, his mom had needed her, that's why he'd been tender with her, and now it was over. No more pretending. She pushed past him, shoving her shoulder into his arm as she took the stairs to the parking lot.

The air held a chilly nip to it, and it bit her face as the tears escaped their confines and rolled down her cheeks. She climbed into her car and slammed the door, shaking with hurt and indignant anger. Connor had said he loved her. How could he throw her, their relationship, away so easily, as if she were an empty pizza box to be discarded? Was it truly just because she'd been married before?

A part of her knew it was better to know now how he really felt. The other part wished she could somehow have concealed the truth forever.

CONNOR

Connor stood by the window overlooking the parking lot, leaning his head against the glass, feeling like a broken mirror. Even if he somehow put all the pieces together, it would be forever shattered.

Luce didn't understand. He knew that. She probably thought he was the worst kind of guy right now, not wanting to be with her just because she'd been married. And that was an issue, he admitted, but he could have worked through it, if he'd been given the chance to come around to it while they dated.

Knowing she'd tried to hide it was what he couldn't work through.

He let out an exhale. There was nothing to do now. He couldn't sit with his mom yet and to hell with the shop. He sat down in the same chair Luce had been in before, the one where he gave in to his weak desire to be close to her and slept with his head on her leg. He looked up at the ceiling and told himself to stop thinking about her.

He awoke to the buzzing of his phone in his pocket. Surprised to see Dave's name, he sat up and answered.

"Dave. What is it?"

"They have a few more test results," he said. "We have a consultation in the chaplain's office in half an hour. Can you be there?"

Connor checked the time. Just after ten. "Yeah. I'll be there." He hung up the phone and hesitated. Should he call Luce?

No. The more contact they had, the harder this separation would be.

Half an hour later he sat in the chaplain's office.

The doctor's mournful eyes were all sympathy as he

steepled his fingers together. His focused his gaze on Connor's mom. "The tumor is entangled with the blood vessels in the brain. It would be impossible to remove without killing you. It's also growing rapidly."

"How did we not know about this?" Connor demanded. "Why weren't there signs? Couldn't we have caught this earlier?"

"There aren't any signs until it starts to press on the brain cells. And then the disorientation, headaches, lack of balance can easily be explained away by sleepiness, age, alcohol."

The words hit Connor hard in the chest. The symptoms had been there, all right. But like the doctor's suggestion, he'd brushed them off. "If we'd brought her in sooner, could we have helped her?"

The doctor shook his head. "This tumor is going to run its course no matter what you do."

"Is it cancerous?" Connor asked, his throat tight.

"We don't know yet. We would have to do a biopsy to see. And in this case, it may be a moot point."

He didn't like the sound of that. "If it's cancerous, we have to treat it."

"Yes, but even if it's cancerous, we can't remove it. So it would be a painful surgery of discovery."

His mom sucked in a breath. "What *can* we do?"

"We can try radiation for a few months, see if we can shrink it, but it's not going away."

"It won't go away?" Connor wrinkled his brow. "How can she live like that?"

"I can't," his mom answered, her tone steely. She directed her question at the doctor. "How long do I have?"

He shook his head. "Best case scenario, with radiation treatments, a year. Worst case . . ." He held her gaze. "A few weeks."

"A few weeks?" Dave said, as if the entire conversation had confused him. "A few weeks until what?"

Connor buried his face in his hands, his fingers raking through his hair. He felt his mother's light touch on his back, and he jerked his head up.

"It's not possible. She's young, she's healthy and strong. She can't be—can't be—" *dying.*

The doctor stood up. "We can start radiation treatments later this week if you decide to go that route, but you don't need to stay in the hospital anymore. Feel free to stay in this office as long as you need to."

The doctor walked out, and the three of them sat in an uncomfortable silence, as if they were strangers trying to figure out how to speak to each other.

Connor cleared his throat. "We should start the radiation treatments right away."

His mother looked at him, her eyes bright. "I don't think they're going to work, Connor."

He felt a flash of anger and shot her a scathing look. "They definitely won't work if you don't think they will. Half of this is a mental attitude thing. You have to believe you're going to get better."

"Connor's right," Dave said. "We have to fight this thing."

She lowered her eyes as more tears rolled down her face. "It's okay. If it's time, it's time."

Another moment of silence ensued, and then Dave cleared his throat and stood up. "I have to get to work. Connor, you're staying?" When he nodded, Dave continued. "I'll call later. But I trust Connor's judgment. You do what he says." He gave her a no-nonsense look, nodded at Connor, and walked out.

His mom reached over and took his hands. "I'm so relieved

you have Luce. That makes all of this bearable."

Her words were like a knife to his gut, twisting and turning his insides around painfully. "Mom, Luce and I—" What was he going to say, really? He had to tell her eventually, but—

"Connor," his mom said, apparently not noticing that he struggled to tell her something. "I know it's crazy, and I know it's asking a lot, but the one thing I really want, the thing I've dreamed of ever since you were born, is your wedding." Her fingers squeezed his, tightening their grip. "I hate to rush things, but it would mean so much to me—if there's any way that you can push the wedding up."

Connor's mouth dropped open, and he frantically searched for a way out of this. "Mom. You're not going to die."

"Maybe I'm not," she said fiercely. "But there's a good chance I am. And I don't want to miss it. Please think about it. Talk about it with Luce. It might not be the big grand wedding she's been thinking of her whole life, but I want to see it." Her eyes shone with unshed tears.

This was his chance to tell his mom, to let her know there wouldn't be a wedding, big or small, because Luce had already had her fairytale wedding, and it hadn't been with him.

"I'll talk to Luce," was what he said instead.

~Chapter Twenty-One~

LUCE

L uce did not want to go to work. If she saw Regina, she was likely to punch her in the face.

Yet life went on, something she knew better than most.

Melodee texted and invited her and Connor over for dinner on Friday, but Luce ignored the text. At some point she'd have to tell her they'd broken up, but not today. For another day, at least, they could be a couple, even if only in Melodee's thoughts.

There was no time to shower, but she had to go home and change her clothes. Her happy and bright polka-dotted scrubs seemed all wrong. So did the balloons and the puppies. She wrangled a pair of green ones out of the box, all wrinkled and smelly. They would have to do. She skipped the make-up and breakfast, too upset to consider food.

Surely she hadn't really lost Connor.

She started a text message to him, and then she recalled his words from earlier in the morning. He just couldn't do it. It was over.

How could he be so cruel? She was the same person he'd fallen in love with before finding out about her divorce. Couldn't he get past it?

The tears threatened again, burning behind her eyes. She threw on some sunglasses and headed to work. She slipped in the back entry and began pulling up files by the storage room, prepping for the appointments with lab work. Caroline joined her.

"Hey, this is my job today. You're assigned up front with intake."

"Where's Regina?" Luce asked, fighting hard to unclench her jaw.

"Working the pediatric desk." Caroline took a closer look at her. "Did something happen?"

"Yes," Luce hissed, swiveling to face Caroline. She yanked her sunglasses off, trembling, trying to keep her anger under control. "Regina followed me out to the parking lot last night. She told Connor about my divorce. She told him!"

Caroline's eyes widened, hiding the pastel green eye shadow she'd painted on top of the eyelids. "What did he do?"

"He broke up with me!" Luce's arm flailed out to the side in a gesture of despair. "Didn't ask me any questions. Won't give me a chance to explain. Just told me there's no way he can be with me now and it's over!"

"What?" Caroline's mouth dropped open, and anger flashed in her eyes. "I had no idea he was such a jerk. I'm sorry, Luce. At least you found out now."

Luce had tried to comfort herself with the same argument, but it didn't help the stabbing pain in her heart. "I love him, Caroline." She took a gasping breath, blinking rapidly and swallowing hard. "It hurts." The small admission was all it took for the tears to break free. She grabbed a tissue and shoved it against her face, hiding her eyes behind it.

Caroline moved in and rubbed her between the shoulder blades. "There will be someone else, Luce. Give it time."

"But what if the same thing happens?" she whispered into her hands. "What if the moment they find out I'm divorced, they don't want me? Do I need to wear a sign that says, 'Divorcee. Date at your own risk'?"

Caroline hugged her tighter. "No. You just need to find the right guy."

"Like you did?" Luce said. She didn't mean to be cruel, but Caroline wasn't a shining example of happily ever after. "When are you moving on?"

"I can't move on," Caroline said, her voice tiny.

"Why not?" Luce asked, her curiosity almost smothering her own pain. Almost.

"Because I'm still connected to him."

"What do you mean? By marriage?"

"I mean—he and I are still connected. That's all."

Luce furrowed her brow. "You love him."

Caroline did not respond.

"Luce?"

Another female voice broke through their reverie, and Luce stiffened when she recognized Regina. Caroline spoke up before Luce had a chance.

"We're good here, Regina." Her words came out clipped and cold.

"I need to talk to Luce."

Through her fingers, Luce watched as Regina's white sneakers stepped closer.

"Then talk to her right here."

"Fine," Regina said. "About last night, Luce. . . ."

Regina faltered, and Luce straightened up. She would rather have this conversation in private.

"It's okay, Caroline." Luce jerked her head at Regina. "Let's go out back."

Luce pushed open the back door. She stepped out into the deceptive sunshine and shivered, wishing she'd grabbed her jacket. Crossing her arms over her chest, she turned to face Regina. "What?" she said, keeping her voice and face flat.

Regina's eyes flared and then she looked away. "I don't even know what to say. I never should have done that. I was just jealous, and I guess not really over Connor." She bobbed her head. "I feel awful about it."

Luce tried to maintain her anger, but it faded rapidly under the other woman's apparent sorrow. "He hates me now."

"No, he doesn't," Regina said. She plucked at her scrubs. "He's just battling his own insecurities."

"Because I used to be married?"

"Yes, and—because of how he found out." Regina lifted her head and met Luce's gaze. "I didn't mean for you two to break up. It just hurt—and honestly, seemed a little unfair—that he would be with you when he broke up with me for the same reason."

Wait, what? Luce wrinkled her nose. "What are you saying? You're divorced, too? And that's why he ended it?"

"No," Regina said, shaking her head. "Because I lied to him."

Luce sucked in a breath, suddenly weak-kneed. "What happened between you two?"

Regina gave a short laugh. "It was really dumb. The problem is that Connor requires complete honesty, and I wasn't honest."

"Everyone wants honesty," Luce said, blinking hard. "I

knew I needed to tell him."

"Yeah, but it's worse with him. I don't know why. It's his tragic flaw, I guess."

Tragic flaw. Luce knew all about those from classic literature in her English classes. Luce could hardly breathe. She felt like someone had kicked her in the stomach. She had, then, as far as Connor was concerned, made the worst mistake possible. "I didn't know."

"No, you didn't, and I played that against you. I'm sorry for my part, but Luce? I learned a lesson. I'll never hold anything back in a relationship. They'll take me the way I am, the good, the bad, and the ugly."

Luce nodded slowly, understanding painting a gray tone over the scenery around her. "Thanks for telling me." She knew they would never be best friends. But Regina's admission had shed some light on their break up, and she accepted that the blame didn't fall on Connor; he hadn't broken up with her because he thought she was tainted or not as good. It was because of her own deception.

CONNOR

"You want me to do what?" Ty choked on his drink, sputtering a bit before Moki clapped him hard between the shoulder blades and got everything going again.

"Pretend to officiate at our wedding," Connor said, only the barest trace of annoyance entering his voice. He lifted the beer to his lips, feeling the tiniest bit guilty for dulling his senses at a bar while the hospice nurse sat with his mom at home.

"Fake wedding," Moki said, grinning, his eyes glittery like shiny beetles. "I'm keeping up okay."

"And how?" Ty demanded. "How do you expect me to

officiate at a wedding, fake or no? I'm not a minister."

Connor shook his head. "Don't you get it? That doesn't matter. Just tell my mom you got ordained online. No one's even going to care. Mom won't care, she just wants to see me in a tux and Luce in a beautiful white dress and feel like she's living out her fantasy." The visual image of Luce in a white dress brought such a churning of emotion, anger, tenderness, desire, that he fought back nausea.

"Whoa, there, boy," Moki muttered, sharing a glance with Ty.

Connor gave a slow exhale. He knew he was being a bit testy. "Sorry. This is not the most ideal situation for me."

Ty nodded, empathy in his eyes. "Have you talked to Luce about this?"

Connor ground his teeth. "Not yet. Not exactly looking forward to that one." Out of habit, he pulled out his phone. He'd blocked her number. A lot of good it did him; he'd checked the blocked number list at least once an hour. And at least once an hour, Luce called him.

This was killing him.

Ty shrugged. "See? We might be worrying for nothing. Luce probably won't even agree to this."

"She has to," Connor said. "It's my mom's dying wish. How could she deny it?"

"Because," Ty said, "Luce's crazy in love with you, and going through this charade is just going to make it worse. Imagining everything she won't have."

"Yeah, well, it's not just her," Connor snapped. "She took it all away from me too. Now she can see how it feels." He crossed his arms over his chest, feeling like a petulant child.

His friends glanced at each other again, and Connor wished he could read their minds.

"Maybe," Moki said, his voice uncharacteristically gentle, "you and Luce should talk things out."

Connor downed another gulp of the burning alcohol. "We are so done." He looked at them both as they stared at him, not liking the pitiful expressions on their faces. "I'm not crazy. It shouldn't be that hard. And it will make my mom happy."

"And you don't want to disappoint her," Ty finished. He shrugged. "I guess you better talk to Luce."

"Yeah." Connor dropped his arms and bobbed his head. "I guess that's the next step."

♥

Luce agreed to meet him at Mud Street Cafe after her yoga class the next day. Connor got there first and found a table for them. Then he sat and waited, sipping his hot drink while observing the groups of people around him. He'd rehearsed this conversation in his head and planned to keep it as dry and emotionless as possible.

He saw her step down into the lobby from the street, walking gingerly as if every movement took careful consideration. He sat up straighter. Even from here the pallor of her skin seemed too pale, her eyes ringed in darkness and her cheekbones more pronounced. He shoved down the concern that rippled through him. What did it matter if she wasn't well? She wasn't any of his business.

She still wore her yoga clothes, though she'd thrown a loose sweater over the top of the tank top. It fell just below her waist, and the tight black pants left her looking casually sexy and desirable. Connor redirected his eyes to her face and kept them there.

The waitress handed Luce a menu and directed her toward him. Her eyes scanned the room until they landed on him, and a timid, hopeful smile crossed her face. Connor swallowed, hating that he was about to destroy that hope. He lowered his gaze and swirled the mug in his hand.

"Hi," she said, dropping into the seat in front of him. "How's your mom?"

"She's home," Connor said, leaving the details for later. He needed them to help persuade her to this plot. "They released her yesterday."

"What?" Luce's eyes held disbelief, but she managed a smile. "That's fantastic, right?"

He shrugged and took another sip.

She lowered her eyes, and her right hand moved to her left.

She still wore the engagement ring. Slowly, as if hoping every second that he would stop her, she slid it from her finger and placed it in front of him with only the slightest of noises. "You should have this back."

Connor reached out and closed his fingers around it, the black hole of achiness spreading in his chest.

She leaned forward, clenching her fists together. "Connor, I —"

"Hey, guys." An older waitress with spiky blond hair appeared in front of them. "Know what we want to eat yet?"

Lifting his eyes from Luce, Connor said, "I'll have the Greek quiche."

"Um, yes, me too," Luce said.

"Anything to drink?"

"Just water," Connor said.

"For me too."

They sat a moment in silence while the waitress walked away, and then Luce tried again, her shoulders hunching forward. "I'm so glad you asked to talk to me. I've been trying to reach you since yesterday—"

"I know," he interrupted, unable to help it. "I've seen the

calls."

She flushed pink and fiddled with her napkin. "I know I made a mistake not telling you about my past." Her lip trembled, but she didn't stop talking. "I'm so sorry, Connor. But I hope that just because I'm divorced—"

"It's not about that," he interrupted, though there was no denying the burning in his throat at the thought of her being married before. "I could get over that. Eventually. It's the fact that you kept it from me. Would have kept it from me. It makes me wonder what else you would keep from me."

"I wouldn't!" she said, scooting her chair in and straightening her back. "I promise, I would tell you everything, every little thing. I screwed up, I know I did, but if you'll—"

"I can't trust you, Luce," he interrupted, cutting her off before she could get going. "I can't marry someone I can't trust."

She withdrew, rounding her shoulders and looking down, pulling into herself. Tears glistened unshed in her eyes, and he fought hard to maintain his cold exterior. She couldn't know how close he was to breaking, how much he wanted to gather her into his arms and tell her he loved her enough to try again.

The waitress arrived with their food and left just as quickly, probably sensing the tension between them. Luce lifted her eyes and swallowed, her face a blank mask, showing no sign of her earlier emotion.

"Why did you ask me here, then?"

To marry you. Connor almost laughed at the irony. "Mom's dying."

Her mask broke, her eyebrows lifting as her lips turned down. "Oh, Connor! Why didn't you say so? I'm so sorry! How are you holding up? Can't anything be done?"

"She has an inoperable brain tumor."

Luce's brow furrowed. "What about radiation? Can they shrink it?"

"Mom won't do it. She says it's a waste of money and it probably won't work." The bitterness crept out in his words. He didn't want her to die. He'd gladly pay thousands of dollars to prolong her life a few more months.

"What can I—what can I do?"

He leaned forward, his heart beginning to pound harder now. "There is something you can do. And it won't be easy but—it's what I need."

"What is it?"

"Marry me."

Chapter Twenty-Two

LUCE

Luce sat in stunned silence as Connor explained his plan for a fake wedding, a cold numbness slowly filling her heart and penetrating through the rest of her body. When he finished talking, she lifted one shoulder in a shrug.

"Sure." Why not? She'd already been married once. What did she care? She and Connor were through. She saw that very perfectly now.

"We'll have to get a marriage license, just because my mom has some silly frame for it. But Ty's not authorized to perform a wedding, so the license won't mean anything."

Just like she meant nothing to him. Luce took another sip of her drink and set it on the table. "It's fine."

"And then—" Connor hesitated, the first sign that maybe he doubted what he asked of her. "We can't both stay here. Or my mom will wonder why we're not together. Maybe I could take a trip back to Africa, go procuring wares—"

"I'll go." She didn't want to stay in this town any longer

than she had to. She'd sell her place and book it out of Arkansas. "My dad can help me get a job somewhere else."

He fell silent, lowering his head and dropping his eyes. "I'm sorry," he said quietly.

Luce stood up, shouldering her yoga mat and bag. "I've got to go. Just let me know what else you need me to do."

She turned to walk away, but Connor jumped up and grabbed her arm. Her eyes fluttered to his, for a brief moment a desperate hope rising that he would change his mind. But then he let go and took a step back.

"You need to think about what you're going to wear. Probably not a wedding dress, because, well." He cleared his throat.

Because it's not a real wedding. Because you already did that. Because you don't deserve to. But that, she decided, was exactly what she was going to do. He could let her go, he could force her out of his life, but he would at least see what he was losing.

"You don't have to tell anyone if you don't want to," he added. "We can keep it small."

She wanted to laugh. Wanted to cry. She could just imagine the scene with Melodee. "So, yeah, we're not engaged anymore, but we're pretending to be. Want to come to our pretend wedding?" The shame burned in her throat. Good thing she hadn't taken the time to tell her father yet. She gave a quick bob of her head and slipped away from him before he could see the tears fall.

♥

"I need another drink." Caroline raised her hand at the bartender, who brought her another shot. He offered one to Luce as well, but she shook her head.

"And you're just going along with this?" Her friend eyed her before downing the alcohol.

Luce shrugged. She deserved this. She'd caused it. If she could make something in Connor's life a little easier, she'd do it.

"What did your sister say?"

Luce gave a tight smile. "I think she wanted to kill him. But she's going to come. I begged her. I can't go through this alone." Then the tears came, making their way down Luce's face.

Caroline scooted her stool closer and put an arm around Luce. "When's the wedding?"

"In a week. We got our marriage license yesterday." Luce nearly choked on the words. Seeing Connor had been one of the most painful experiences of her life. She'd stood next to him at the registrar's desk, handing over their driver's licenses and signing paperwork and pretending like this was no big deal while inside she was dying, sobbing, crumbling into a million pieces.

"And then Poland? Why Poland? Why not Italy or Brazil or somewhere exotic?"

Luce exhaled. Her dad had really come through for her. Of course, he didn't know the reason for her sudden departure. "A foreign hospital doesn't have as many credentials as an American one, and they'll gladly take on a resident without as much experience. Italy wasn't an option, or believe me, I would have picked that." She smiled and ran her finger over the brim of her glass of club soda. "My dad found openings at hospitals in Poland, Russia, and Columbia. I chose Poland."

"Yeah, I probably would have too." Caroline stared into her empty shot glass and then shook herself. "So you want me to come?"

Luce met her eyes, tears clouding her view. "Could you? For

moral support?"

"I'll be there." Caroline hugged her tight. "But you might have to hold me back when I see Connor. I still can't believe he would do this to you."

Luce accepted the embrace wordlessly. She didn't try to defend Connor because she knew no one else would understand. But she did. And she had only herself to blame.

"Well, maybe I can believe it." Caroline gave a short laugh and pulled away, then flagged the bartender for another shot. "People are cruel."

"Your husband was cruel to you," Luce said, feeling a stab of anger toward this man she'd never met.

Caroline threw back the shot. "One, two, three, one, two, three."

"Caroline," Luce said softly.

"No," Caroline said, her voice too loud in the small space. "I was cruel to him."

Luce pushed back the ripple of surprise. "Do you want him?"

"Tell you what." Caroline stood up, her smile too big for her face. "I'll bring my husband to your wedding. And we can all be real together. It'll be dreamy." She headed for the door, and Luce jumped up.

"Let me give you a ride home," Luce said.

"You don't have to," Caroline said. She was crying, wiping her face. "Sorry. This was supposed to be your sob story."

Luce held her arm, helping her down the steep hill. "It's fine. We all have one."

CONNOR

Somehow Connor had managed to keep his communication with Luce to a minimum even while they planned their fake wedding. He explained her absence away to his mom by saying he didn't want to jinx it. And his mom, in an effervescent state of delirious happiness, didn't question him.

Now he stood hunched over his dresser, bow tie dangling around his neck, cursing himself for going along with this ridiculous plan. At least he hadn't had to throw away money at a crazy expensive venue for the wedding, but going through this charade was hurting his heart more than he wanted to admit. A part of him wanted to call the whole thing off, but that seemed rather silly, since none of it was real, anyway.

A knock sounded on his bedroom door, and he straightened as Ty walked in.

"Hey, Minister," Connor said, heaving his breath out loudly.

"How are you holding up?" Ty asked, giving him a sideways look.

Connor plastered on his best exaggerated smile. "I'm doing great! Getting ready to not marry the woman I love because it turns out I really can't trust anyone and I should probably just give up on any kind of real marriage anyway."

Ty shifted slightly, moving his weight from one foot to the other. "Maybe what you really need to do is give her another chance. I could get a real minister in here, we could make this a real wedding. You have a real license."

He nearly caved, giving into Ty's suggestion. There was no question he loved Luce still, and every time he looked at her, he felt a slice of his heart breaking away. Could he forgive her? He shook his head, clearing it. "No. I'm not bending on this." If he let this one incident slide, he would be opening himself up for more indiscretions. Some things had to be black and white.

"Are you sure? You're the one who gave me such great advice about Amber, and look what I've got now. I couldn't be happier."

Connor clasped his friend on the shoulder. "And I will just have to live my happiness through yours."

"She made a mistake, Connor. That doesn't make her the same con artist as your father."

Connor inhaled sharply, clenching his hands into fists. "Watch it, Ty." Tyson was one of the only people who knew the truth about Connor's dad. And it wasn't a topic to be broached thoughtlessly.

"Sorry." Ty adjusted Connor's bow tie. "Let's go."

They stepped out the sliding glass doors to the backyard, and Connor admired the way the wedding planner had decorated the terrace and yard. There were only two rows of chairs, all draped in white ribbons and bows. Instead of the typical arch at the end of the aisle, somewhere his mother had dug up two pillars and spun white curtains and flowers around them to meet in the middle. It was crazy beautiful, and he couldn't help the romantic mood it put him in.

"Come on," Ty said, taking his elbow and leading him up the white carpet laid between the chairs. "It's your time."

His mom beamed at him as he stepped in front of her arch, and he smiled back at her, reminding himself this was all for her. His grandparents were there, also, the Connors, who he had been named after.

"Granny," he said, stepping over to the chairs and stooping to give her a hug.

"Where is this girl of yours and why haven't I met her before today?" she sniffed, the same wounded arrogant attitude she always had. Her bluish gray hair all piled on top of her head, as usual. At least she'd subbed out her house dress for a flowery red one that matched her bright red glasses.

His mom rolled her eyes, but the familiarity made Connor smile.

"She better not be some uptown snob who thinks she's too good for us country folk," Granny said, and Connor remembered why he and his mom didn't spend too much time with the Connors.

"Now, Myrtle, don't get your panties in a bunch," Grandpa said, and Connor knew that was standing up to Granny, as far as Grandpa was concerned. She wore the britches in the house.

"Hi, Grandpa," he said, feeling guilty for dragging these old people out to a fake wedding.

"Can't wait to meet this pretty lady," Grandpa said, his eyes twinkling.

"You bring her by sometime so I can meet her proper," Granny said. "I'll bake some cookies. She better like sweet tea."

"I'm sure she does, Granny." Connor hid his smile and let Tyson haul him to the altar.

A few more familiar faces looked up from the chairs, mostly people he knew. He avoided looking at Luce's friend Caroline, who had brought a man with her, or at Luce's sister, both sitting in the front row, the only people who had agreed to go along with this. Even from here he felt the heat in Melodee's gaze. He took a deep breath and looked out over the forested hills, the colored leaves drifting off the branches.

The music started and Connor straightened, his heart giving a little tumble as the back door opened. Luce stepped out, accompanied by Moki.

All in attendance stood, but he didn't see them. He couldn't take his eyes off Luce. His breath caught. She wore a knee-length white dress that gathered at her waist, soft folds billowing around her legs as she walked. The bodice fit her curves as if made for her, elegant, lacy sleeves tracing her shoulders and down her arms.

Damn it. He wanted to marry this girl.

She lifted her eyes from the bouquet of pink flowers in her hands, her smile tremulous. Similar pink flowers adorned her auburn hair, tucked behind one ear in a loose bun.

She reached him and he extended a hand, taking her fingers and pulling her in front of him.

"You look beautiful," he whispered.

Her smile crumbled and she looked down, but not before the tears leaked from her eyes and fell on the bouquet in front of her. He squeezed her fingers, wanting to undo this pain, wanting to undo everything that had gone wrong between them.

Ty cleared his throat and started talking. A bunch of nonsense, bull, meaningless vows, and Connor tuned them out. Instead he studied the curve of Luce's jaw, memorizing the shape of her lip, the way her cheekbones added depth and shadow to her face.

Too much shadow. She'd lost nearly as much weight as his mom.

Ty cleared his throat again. "Do you, Luce Donovan—"

Donovan. Not O'Neil. He'd discovered when they got the marriage license that he hadn't even known her real name.

Connor lowered his eyes, barely hearing her response to the question. His own questions swirled in his head. In the end, did it really matter? Was he willing to lose her forever?

"—Connor Thomas, take this woman to be your wife?"

"I do," Connor said, cutting through anything else Ty might say. Get this over with.

Ty's hands visibly shook as he pulled out the pillow with

the rings, and Connor suppressed a grin. Apparently they were both nervous.

"Here," Ty said, handing Connor the rings. He watched them exchange their rings, and then Ty said, "You may kiss the bride."

It's all an act, Connor reminded himself. Not that that mattered. He had permission to kiss her. One last time.

Her lips were wet when he pressed his to them. Wet and salty. His hands slid around her back, kissing her harder than necessary, his own pent up anguish and desire urging him to take what he could get. But finally he pulled away, aware of their audience, aware of where they were.

Ty's eyes were wide, his lips slightly white. "I now pronounce you husband and wife."

Chapter Twenty-Three

LUCE

Jessica had outdone herself with the decorations. Connor had tried to talk her out of a reception, but she insisted. Luce stood beside him, angling away from him as they accepted the congratulations from the small crowd gathered in honor of their nuptials.

"Granny, this is Luce," he said, and Luce turned her body enough to send a vague smile in the direction of an older woman.

"Well, she's definitely nice to look at," the blue-haired lady said, somehow managing to put an insult in the words.

Luce gave up on the smile. "Excuse me," she said, then pushed her way past them to the punch bowl.

A slight breeze blew through the leaves, but she hardly noticed. The lacy sleeves on her wedding gown were enough to block any chill. She poured herself a cup of red punch, careful not to spill any on the dress. The plan was to return it.

What had she been thinking? That Connor would take one

look at her and change his mind?

A hand gripped her arm, and she nearly dropped her cup.

"Sorry, sorry," Melodee said, and Luce set the punch down before whirling into her sister's arms. Melodee stroked her back while Luce sobbed.

"It's okay. It's gonna be okay."

"Thanks so much for coming," Luce whispered, pulling away and wiping her eyes. She glanced around the crowd for Caroline. She'd seen her there, sitting next to a man Luce could only assume was her husband. Caroline had given her a hand squeeze after the ceremony, but she was nowhere to be seen now.

"You look stunning," Melodee said, her eyes sympathetic as she surveyed Luce. "The prettiest bride I've ever seen."

Luce trembled, her stomach twisting with nausea as anger and remorse ran through her veins. "I hate weddings."

"Since when?"

"Since two weeks ago."

"What are you going to do with all those gifts?"

Luce followed Melodee's gaze to the table covered in presents and a cheesy double-decker wedding cake. Now she knew she'd throw up. "Most are from Connor's mom. We'll hold onto them until—" *Until she dies.* Luce couldn't bring herself to say it. "For awhile. Then return them."

Melodee held her hand. "How long will you be in Poland?"

Luce shrugged.

"But you'll come for the baby, right?"

Now Luce attempted a smile. "That's why I moved here to begin with. To be close to you and the children."

Melodee pulled her into another hug. "I'll kill him if he keeps you away from me."

Luce laughed, and Melodee squeezed tighter.

"You think I'm kidding. I'm serious. You better come back."

Luce exhaled and stepped back. "I'm not very good at the starting over thing. Look what good it did me here."

"This was Connor's fault," Melodee all but growled.

No. It wasn't. Luce could have told him from the beginning about her divorce. But she hadn't, and then it was too late.

"Luce?"

They both turned as Connor stepped across the grass, his expression wary and reserved.

"We should go," he said. "Your flight leaves in a few hours."

"Can't miss that." She picked up her punch and downed it, wishing it were something stronger. Her throat and heart burned as if it were.

"You can stay long enough to feed each other your cake," Jessica said, intercepting them in the hall. "I know you're in a hurry to be alone—" she beamed at them— "but this is tradition."

"Oh, no," Luce protested, "I've always hated that part."

Connor glanced at her, and her face warmed as she could practically read his thoughts: did she hate that at her last wedding?

"I think we've got time for it," Connor said

Luce faced him in surprise, her heart giving a little tumble. Was that a smile playing about his mouth? For a moment his eyes seemed to twinkle with warmth, and then he looked at his mom, and her heart sank.

Still part of the act.

Jessica clapped her hands and called for the crowd to gather around, and then she hovered close with her camera, snapping pictures as they cut the cake.

"You first," Connor said to her.

She eyed the big piece of cake he'd cut and shook her head.

"No, you."

"If you insist."

He sounded so like his normal self, like he was laughing at a running joke all the time, that Luce didn't even have to act. He shoved the cake at her face, and she laughed as small bits of the sugary icing made it into her mouth while the rest clung to her skin.

"Did you even try to get my mouth?"

"A little."

She used a napkin to clean off the majority and then cut a bigger slice of cake. "All right, you asked for it."

Luce took aim for Connor's face, wiping the icing over his nose and chin before placing a small piece on his tongue. The touch of his mouth sent shivers through her body, and she let her fingers linger, smearing the fluffy white confection over his lips.

"Kiss her, kiss her, I need a kiss!" Jessica said, camera poised.

Connor gripped Luce by the elbows and drew her nearer, and Luce thought he would comply.

Then, as if remembering himself, he let her go. He grinned at his mom and shook his head. "I think she'd rather I didn't get this all over her face."

Luce swiveled away, the tears clogging her throat again. "He's right. Let me wash off and we can go." Head down and eyes averted, Luce made it to the hall bathroom before breaking into renewed sobs.

CONNOR

Connor stood at a window in the lobby of the Crescent Hotel where Ty had arranged a suite for them, watching Luce's car pull out of the parking lot. Well. That was done. The fake wedding, the fake reception, and now the fake honeymoon. Her flight to Poland was in two hours, and she'd stay there until they could drop this farce and go about their lives like normal, uninvolved people.

Her engagement band, as well as the wedding band studded with little diamonds, sat like a rock in his pocket. She'd given them to him, told him to get his money back.

He undid the bow tie and headed up the stairs to their suite. The whole affair had left a bitter taste in his mouth, like taking a handful of chocolate raisins only to discover they were coffee beans.

He unlocked the door and paused in the doorway, taking in the over-fluffed king-sized bed and the two-person bath with the cascading waterfall. He groaned and leaned his head against the door jamb. It was a good thing Luce hadn't come upstairs, even for a minute. Because the sight of this room, coupled with his desire for her, would have undone him.

He blinked against the burning in his eyes, swallowing hard. The what-ifs circled around and around his head like relentless vultures, certain something had died but not sure what. He closed the door and threw himself face-down on the bed.

He wasn't sure how long he lay like that before someone knocked on the door. He sat up, a traitorous flare of hope igniting in his chest. Had she come back? But he didn't want her to come back, he reminded himself.

The knocking came again, rising in volume until it was an insistent pounding, followed by Ty's voice. "Connor?"

Connor dragged himself to his feet and stumbled to the door with all the grace of a drunkard. He threw it open. "Hello, friend," he said, bitterness lacing his words.

Ty stood in the doorway, regarding him. "Are you drunk?"

"I wish."

Ty pushed his way into the room and took a quick look around. "You're alone," he said, the disappointment heavy in his voice.

Connor sat down on the edge of the love seat in front of the television. "You knew I would be."

"But I hoped you wouldn't." Ty shoved his hands into his suit pants and shook his head. "I didn't think you'd actually let her go."

"I had no other option."

"You had lots of options!" Ty fired back, surprising Connor by raising his voice. "You could have forgiven her, Connor! You had the perfect chance. The perfect set up." He softened his tone. "Don't you love her?"

"Yes." Connor shook his head. "It's not enough."

"Pete's sake, man! The love you two have, it's a shame to throw away! Go after her, Connor. Get her back."

For a moment, he was tempted. He could hop in the car and get to the airport before she left. But then what? What could he say that would undo the mess between them? "I've already accepted that I'll be a bachelor the rest of my life."

Ty groaned and pressed the palms of his hands to his eyes. "You have to go get her, Connor."

Connor frowned at him. "I appreciate the loyalty and the desire to see me happy, but aren't you getting a little too involved? You're going too far."

With an abrupt laugh, Ty dropped his hands. "I definitely went too far."

Icy prickles of warning fingered their way along Connor's spine. He sat up straighter. "What do you mean?"

Ty spread his hands wide, an expression of resignation and

helplessness on his face, like one walking to the gallows. "I married you."

"I was there," Connor snapped. "What's wrong?"

"No, Connor. I *actually* married you."

For a moment Connor could only blink at him in confusion, and then understanding crashed over him. "You *what*?" He jumped to his feet. White hot rage blinded him, and his body shook with the effort to keep from pummeling Ty to the ground. "Tell me I misunderstood."

"You didn't." Ty hooked his fingers in his pants again, eying Connor warily. "It seemed too easy. You told me to tell everyone I got my license online, well, I decided to just do it. You're so freaking stubborn. I thought if I could get you two married, it would—"

"Force us together? Force us to deal with our problems? Well, it doesn't, does it? All it does is force us to get an annulment!" His breathing came too fast, and he gripped the wall, concentrating on slow inhales and exhales. "How could you do that to me? If I get married someday, I want it to be because I chose to!"

"I'm sorry," Ty said softly. "I should not have done that."

"Hell right." Connor grabbed his suit jacket and car keys, jamming his feet into shoes and pushing past Tyson.

"Where are you going?" Ty asked, spinning around.

"To the airport. I have to tell Luce."

♥

Connor drove faster than safety required, taking the switch-back curves out of Eureka Springs nearly on one tire. He considered calling Luce, but what would he say on the phone?

"Don't get on the plane. We just got married."

No, he needed to talk to her in person, they had to figure out where to go from here.

He made it to the regional airport in Bentonville in just over an hour. The closer he got, the more anxious he became. How would he explain this to her? What would he say? She wouldn't be able to leave right away; they'd have to take care of this. But if she stayed—if he spent any more time in her presence—

Connor couldn't think of that right now. She above all people had the right to know.

He squealed into a spot in the short-term parking and slammed on his brakes. Her flight left in forty minutes, and if he didn't catch her before she went through the security gate, he wouldn't be able to.

Still in his tux, the undone bow tie flapping around his collar, he ran through the crosswalk, barely glancing to his right to check for cars, and barreled into the ticketing terminal. A glance at the monitor showed that her flight would be boarding in five minutes. Something sank in his stomach. No way would she still be out here. He scanned the security lines anyway, hoping to catch a glimpse of the girl with reddish brown hair.

She'd already gone through. Connor realized he only had one option. Finding an open line, he hurried forward to the airline attendant.

"How can I help you?" she asked, all politeness, if not distracted.

"I need a ticket."

"To where?"

"Anywhere. The cheapest you've got, even if it's one-way. And quickly."

She arched an eyebrow as her fingers typed away at the keyboard. But she didn't ask any questions, so maybe she'd heard it all before. "I can get you a one-way ticket to Dallas this afternoon for three hundred and seventeen."

"Done." He slapped his credit card on the counter, and she booked his flight to nowhere.

"Thank you." He slipped his card into his pocket along with the boarding pass and turned, ready to sprint for the security line.

"Any bags to check?"

"Nope!" he hollered the last word over his shoulder as he ran.

The line moved at a snail's pace, and Connor tapped his foot anxiously, doing a dance similar to the little boy in front of him who kept whining about needing to use the bathroom. He checked the time. Her flight was boarding now. His heart rate sped up. If he didn't get there before she got on the plane . . . He didn't finish the thought.

He'd have to call her. She couldn't leave. He pulled his phone out and dialed her number.

"Hi, this is Luce," her voicemail greeted him, and he swore as he shoved his phone back in his pocket. She must've put it on airplane mode already.

Then he was through the line, and again he was running through the airport, grateful for once that there were only two terminals and the A gates were nearby. He wracked his brain, trying to remember her connecting stop before continuing to Poland. Probably Dallas, as nearly everything rerouted through there.

He skidded to a halt near a long line of people boarding a flight to Dallas. He took quick breaths, trying to gather his thoughts.

There she was. Luce had changed out of the soft white dress she'd worn for the fake wedding—no, the real wedding—and put on a pair of tight gray slacks with a loose fitting maroon tunic. Her hair remained in the artful bun with carefully planned curly tendrils framing her face.

His heart stopped beating, his breathing halted. It was as if time stood still.

He didn't want her to get on that plane. He didn't want her to leave.

Time started up again and Luce stepped forward in the line, pulling out her phone and scanning the boarding pass.

It was now or never. He'd found her. He needed to tell her. He needed her in his life. And yet he was still torn, torn by the thoughts of not giving in, of holding strong to his principles.

The attendant smiled at her and Luce walked past, through the door and down the connecting hallway.

Connor squeezed his eyes shut and leaned his head against the wall. As the gate closed and the plane readied for take off, he realized, too late, what held him back. And it wasn't righteousness or a stronger moral code.

It was stubborn pride.

Chapter Twenty-Four

LUCE

Luce's hands shook as she settled into her seat in the middle of the plane. Her mind kept replaying the kiss Connor had given her at the altar. The one that told her, more than anything else, how much he loved her and wanted her. Yet he would not allow himself to be with her.

She pulled her carry-on into her lap and felt around inside for the tissue-paper wrapped frame. There it was. She hauled it out. Someone with a Polaroid had snapped a photograph of the wedding party, and Jessica, thoughtful person that she was, had immediately framed it for them to take on their honeymoon. Luce had shoved it into her bag without a second glance. Such a big joke, that the most important memory of her life so far was a fake one.

Now Luce peeled back the tissue paper over the top of the frame. She didn't look at Connor, but instead at the small crowd they'd invited. Her sister, not even trying to smile. Ty and Moki, making goofy grins like typical boys. Caroline, who had brought someone—her husband? And Luce knew she'd have to talk to her to get some answers.

Finally she let her eyes land on Connor. Instead of looking at the camera, his gaze was on her. His expression was one of awe, one of total adoration. She shook her head. How had he managed to fake that emotion so well? She'd been close to tears the whole time, but lots of brides cried, so that wasn't such a big deal, either.

She looked again at the boarding pass. One way to Poland. She exhaled slowly. How long would she stay? Who knew? This would be a good opportunity to regroup. Maybe she wouldn't come back.

In fact, the idea of settling down and finding her own getaway held a lot of appeal.

♥

The first week in Lodz, Poland, passed in a blur of confusion. Poland was frigid this time of year, rarely getting above freezing and only getting colder. She didn't speak the language, her studio apartment hadn't changed much in the past two hundred years, and the meat was much too fatty and flavorful for her preferences.

But by the second week, she fell into a routine. The public hospital was only a thirty-minute bus ride from her flat, and they put her to work in every ward, rounding out her experience as a nurse and giving her more opportunities than many residential students.

But when they sent her on rounds to the local children's home, the term for an orphanage, Luce's broken heart found something else to latch on to. Somehow caring for the children who had no parents and no one to love them opened her up to moving past both her failed marriage and her failed almost marriage.

Despite the chill, the Polish people didn't hole up indoors, and Luce found herself investing in winter gear that didn't even exist in Arkansas. Soon she could walk the streets with the best of them, wearing three layers beneath the ankle-length wool coat and scarf.

In the middle of the third week, she stumbled upon a small market. Lean-tos and blankets covered the sidewalks in between aisles for pedestrians, with vendors selling everything from fruit to jeans. But what caught Luce's eye was a pie plate, glazed white with intricate blue circles designed across the entire surface. She made a bee-line for the stall and picked up a cow-shaped butter dish, also beautifully decorated.

She'd never really been one to paint her pottery. She preferred to use a stain or colored glaze and let the natural beauty shine through. But perhaps living here in Poland, giving herself a second fresh start, made her feel an affinity for the pieces. This was her home now. She picked up a salt and pepper shaker next, then a canister, all with the blue circles and red accents.

The old lady behind the table immediately spouted off at Luce in Polish.

Smiling apologetically, Luce said her favorite Polish phrase: "I don't speak Polish."

The woman clucked her tongue and yelled at the lean-to behind her. A moment later a man stepped out, graying hair around his temples the only thing to mar his youthful image. He spoke to the woman while Luce admired his broad hands and wavy blond hair. Maybe she needed to find a handsome Polish man to take her troubles away.

He looked at her now, eyes so blue they were almost transparent. He offered a smile. "English?" he asked with a thick accent.

Luce perked up. "Yes! You speak English?"

He rolled his hand. "Somewhat. How you like?" Another smile followed his words, as if embarrassed by his broken speech.

She smiled back, trying to put him at ease. "I didn't mean for her to call you. These are beautiful." She gestured to the bowls and canisters, a longing spurting up within her chest. "I used to make them."

"You make?" He picked up a bowl and handed it to her.

Luce caught her breath at the artistic care taken. Small etchings decorated the inside of the bowl, and the blue pattern wove into a green one. This was new to her. "Not like this. I'd like to learn it." She looked up at him, cheeks warming at her own brazen suggestion. "Could she teach me?" She inclined her head toward the woman.

"Teach you to do?" He looked a little confused as he took the bowl back.

"Like this." She traced the etchings and patterns. They lent a definite Polish flavor to the pottery, and an idea formed in her head. Maybe she could throw pottery that represented different countries. People didn't have to go to Poland to have a handmade Polish set. Or Spain, or Morocco. She could have a whole line of foreign stoneware. And if she concentrated on the online business, she could do it from anywhere.

She could do it from here.

Luce looked at the old lady again. "Can she teach me?"

He patted his chest, smiling at her again. "I teach you." The corners of his eyes crinkled, and despite the graying hairs, Luce realized he couldn't be much older than thirty. "Come back tonight. After market closes."

"Okay." Luce's lips drew up in a matching smile. "I will."

She walked to the bus stop empty-handed, but she noticed a certain lightness in her step.

CONNOR

"How's Luce?"

Connor finished adjusting the temperature of the space heater and rearranged the cushions on the bench beside the bed, taking his time before turning to face his mom. She'd lost the ability to walk a week ago, and her body languished, giving up its will to live.

A lump formed in his throat. "She's fine. She emailed me yesterday, sent me pictures."

His mom's smile lacked its usual luster. "Can I see?"

He was prepared for this. Connor pulled out his phone and opened the file with pictures of her in Poland. She'd started a blog just for him, a place where she could post photos and he could download them as if she'd sent them to him. He swept his eyes away, not wanting to look again at Luce smiling next to the hospital sign, the picture of the skinny children, the beautiful pottery she was making.

"She looks lovely." His mom sighed and handed back the phone. "When is she coming back?"

"We're working on the arrangements. She has to get special permission to get time off from the hospital. She didn't know she'd be getting married when she accepted the post."

"Of course." She chuckled, some warmth returning to her eyes. "You could have gone with her."

"And leave you?" He shook his head. "No way."

"It was a beautiful wedding."

"It was," Connor agreed, his tone wistful. He thought of the way he'd kissed Luce, of the honeymoon suite they didn't use.

And could have, and should have, because they'd actually gotten married.

"Well." He bent and kissed his mom's forehead. "I saw your nurse's car pull up. I'll go open the store, okay? Just call if you need me."

Her hand plucked at his fingers. "Any word from Dave?"

"No." Which meant Connor might have to go dig up the douche and drag him to his mom's side. Dave hadn't stopped by in over a week. No way was he going to vanish while his mom lay dying. "Granny will be here in an hour. I'll see you later."

He threw on a leather jacket and shouldered his bag, phone already in hand as he headed to his car. He couldn't be here when his grandmother arrived; all she did was nag him about Luce.

"What's up?" Ty said, answering on the first ring.

"Meet for lunch today?"

"Yes," Ty said, sounding a bit more wary now. "You have the paperwork done?"

"Yeah," Connor said shortly. "It's done."

♥

They met at the Italian restaurant on Spring Street.

"Still can't step into Mud Street Cafe?" Ty said, grimacing slightly as he settled into the seat across from Connor.

Connor only shrugged. Every time he thought of the cafe, he remembered Luce's expression when he'd told her she needed to pretend to marry him.

Ty glanced at the Basin Park Hotel looming over the street. "Think they're hiring?"

Connor sipped his lemonade. "Still haven't seen a ghost?" Ty only took the job at the Crescent Hotel because he hoped to catch a glimpse of the paranormal. He threatened to quit every week, but since it was getting him through law school, he'd need a back up first.

"Nope." He raked his hands through his hair. "So I guess you brought the papers?"

"Yes." Connor opened his messenger bag and placed the bundle on the table, stuffed into an envelope.

Ty picked up the envelope and tapped it on the table. "I'm sorry. If it weren't for me, you wouldn't be filing for an annulment. I'm not an attorney yet, but I'll help the best I can."

Connor focused on his lemonade. "Read the papers," he said to the ice cubes.

"Why?" Ty sounded puzzled. "Are you still using me as a witness?"

Connor didn't answer. Ty would know in a minute.

Tyson opened the envelope and pulled out the sheets of paper. He shuffled them around, then slapped them down and stared hard at Connor.

"They're blank."

"Yep." Now Connor met Ty's eyes and leaned back in his chair. "I don't want to file."

Ty's mouth fell open. Like, cartoon-perfect, jaw-dropping expression. "What?"

The waitress served their pasta, but Connor ignored it. "I married her. It might have been an accident, but I love her. I want to fix this with her."

Ty whooped, then laughed, then dug both hands into his hair. "I can't believe this! Really?"

"Keep it down," Connor murmured. He still hadn't touched his food. "It's not so easy, though. I have to get her home. And I have to tell her."

"Just tell her, man. That will get her home."

"Yeah, but—" He shook his head. "I don't want to do it like

that. I don't want her to think I feel forced into this. I want to apologize to her. I want to tell her to her face."

Ty was grinning like a madman. "Holidays are coming."

"She didn't come home for Thanksgiving." Connor knew. He had checked with Melodee.

"She will for Christmas. And if she doesn't, maybe you need to go to her."

Connor let out a deep breath, feeling a semblance of calmness at Ty's logic. "Maybe I should tell her sister." Her sister. She was having a baby in January. He knew Luce wouldn't miss that.

"No way, man. You don't want her to hear it from someone else."

His phone vibrated, and Connor pulled it out of his pocket. It was his mother's landline. His anxiety ratcheted up a notch, and he answered. "Hello?"

"Connor, it's Josie," his mom's nurse said. "I think you better get over here."

Chapter Twenty-Five

LUCE

"No, no, like this."

Luce started in surprise when Henryk put his hands on hers and began massaging the clay around her fingers. In the two weeks that she'd been coming to his shop, Henryk's English had improved significantly.

The flames in the fireplace warmed the small workroom, chasing away the cold air outside. Or was it the man in front of her that warmed her?

"You must caress it," he said, lifting his eyes to hers. "Love it."

Luce caught her breath at the intensity of his gaze. He leaned toward her, and she turned her head enough that Henryk's kiss planted on her cheek.

He didn't comment on it, just removed his hands from hers. "There. You try."

She kept her eyes on her clay, face flushed, willing her heart to slow down. Henryk and his grandmother had welcomed her openly. They had so much to offer her. They told her she could move into their guest bedroom and stop living in the dumpy studio room passing for her house. They even offered her a job at the shop during her off hours, selling any pottery she made.

And there was Henryk, whose crystalline eyes and inviting smile offered something else entirely.

It was perfect, really, the exact chance she needed to start over.

Yet something held her back, and she hated to dwell on what it was.

She stood up and went to the sink, where she washed the mud from her hands. She moved to the shelf where the pieces they'd put in the kiln the day before waited to be painted. "I'm getting better at the designing." Her fingers were skilled in shaping, not painting. Luckily a lot of the designs were made with stenciled sponges. All she needed was a steady hand, and that she had.

"You are, indeed," Henryk said. "Perhaps you can do the next ones by yourself."

She turned around to see his eyes on her. "I would love to try."

In the purse she'd deposited against the wall, her phone began to ring. Both she and Henryk turned toward it, and she imagined the surprise on his face was also etched on hers. No one ever called her. Ever. Melodee and Caroline messaged her using the internet, and her dad only emailed.

Maybe Melodee was having the baby! No, no, that couldn't be it, she wasn't due until January.

It couldn't possibly be Connor.

The hope hurt her heart as physically as a wound, and she staggered to her purse, trembling as she removed her phone.

It was. It was Connor.

She stopped a moment to take a deep breath. She ran a shaky hand through her hair, and only after her fingers got stuck did she realize they still had mud on them. She answered the phone, knowing she'd have to scrape the clay off when it dried.

"Hello?" she said, trying to sound calm.

"Luce? It's Connor."

"Oh, hi, Connor." Like she hadn't known.

He hesitated, then said, "How are you?"

He was calling to chat? Luce glanced around and found a rusty metal folding chair. She collapsed into it, trying to ignore Henryk's eyes as they slid toward her while he worked. "Good. Great, actually. Things are really well here."

"Yeah? You like it? In Poland?"

Why did he sound so surprised? "Yeah. I've been learning some new pottery techniques. And—" she hesitated, but then decided to let it spill. "I met someone."

"You—you what?"

She could tell from his voice that he had not expected that.

"Yeah. Yeah, I did. He's really nice."

He made an odd noise, almost like a strangled cat. "Luce, I need to tell you something."

"What is it?" She straightened up, suddenly dreading his news. "Is it your mom?"

He paused, and then he said, "Yes. Will you come home?"

Home. Like his home was hers. She closed her eyes, wanting nothing more than to see him again. She should play hard to get, make him think she didn't want to come. A dozen arguments flitted through her head, how she was establishing a life here, how she wanted nothing more than to forget him and what they'd almost had, how she couldn't afford a plane ticket to Arkansas and then back again. But the arguments died before they reached her mouth. She loved his mother, and the thought of seeing Connor again, even if only to support him in his time of need, left her anxious. "Yes. I'll come. When?"

He let out a slow breath. "I hope you don't mind, I booked you a flight. Tomorrow."

Tomorrow! "But the hospital—" she began, and then she cut herself off. It must be urgent. They'd managed without her before; they could get by again. She'd have her father work it out with them.

"Do you need more time?" he asked, his tone somber. "More time to explain it to your—boyfriend?"

He nearly choked on the word, and Luce covered her mouth to keep from giggling. If she needed any more evidence that he still cared for her, there it was. He was jealous.

"No, I got it. Everyone will understand."

"Okay. I'll email you your flight itinerary."

"Thanks," Luce said. "Should I have Melodee pick me up?"

"No. I will."

Connor would. She pressed her hand to her chest, the hope so real it physically hurt. Why would he? He couldn't stand her.

Unless something had changed.

"Okay. I'll see you soon."

"What was that?" Henryk asked when she hung up, but she could tell from the resignation on his face that he already knew.

"I have to go." She brushed the now-dry clay off on her khaki pants. "My friend's mom is dying, and I need to be there."

"Of course," he said softly. "I will finish teaching you when you return." He lifted his chin, offering her once again the promise of a future.

"I look forward to it," she said.

What a liar.

Connor was waiting for her at the baggage claim in the small Northwest Arkansas Regional Airport, dressed in a brown sweater and jeans.

"Hi," she said with a small wave. She felt stifled in the heavy wool dress and tights with knee-length boots she'd worn to the airport in Poland. Her coat she had draped over her arm. At least if it was cold outside, she was ready.

"Luce." He reached for her and then stopped. "You look amazing," he said, stuffing his hands in his pockets instead.

"Thanks," she said, turning to hide her disappointment. What had she been thinking, really, that five weeks away would make him change his mind? No, the only person who could change his mind was herself.

And she had time. He hadn't purchased her a round-trip ticket.

Her bright purple bag appeared on the conveyor belt, and Connor lunged forward. "I'll get that," he said before she could reach for it.

Luce shifted her carry-on and treaded behind him. "How's your mom?" They stepped through the automatic glass doors, and for once the cold didn't even faze her.

He shook his head and waited for her to catch up before heading to his car in short-term parking. "Any day now, Luce."

"I'm sorry." She hugged herself, wishing she could hug him.

"You're cold." He wrapped an arm around her, pulling her into his side.

Actually, she wasn't. But she didn't contradict him.

"How was Poland?"

"Beautiful," she murmured. "I didn't think so at first. It's different than I expected. But I love it. It's so old and just lovely."

"Did you like it?" He let go of her when they reached his car.

"I was learning a new way to do pottery." Luce watched him place her luggage in the trunk. "Henryk said I could sell my wares in his shop. He and his grandmother own one. Not a lot of money, but they are artisans. It's amazing."

"Henryk." Connor shot her an undecipherable look. "That's the guy?"

Luce ran a hand over her fingers, remembering the feel of Henryk's strong, firm grip as he helped her mold the clay. The expression in his eyes when he'd leaned in to kiss her. "Yes."

Connor didn't say anything else on the drive, and Luce remained silent also until she realized he'd passed her condo. "Are we going straight to the hospital?" Was his mom that bad off? Had Luce barely made it?

"Um, no." Connor kept his eyes on the road, but his fingers tapped the steering wheel, belying his nervousness. "I thought you could stay at my house. Just for now. Just for appearances. My mom—she's there."

"Oh," Luce said softly. "She's on hospice care?"

"She's on comfort care. We're just waiting."

Luce sank back into her seat. There was nothing more they could do for her.

Connor pulled into the driveway and came around to her door as she climbed out. "One more thing, Luce." He opened his wallet and pulled out a ring.

Her engagement ring, soldered now to the wedding band.

She inhaled and swallowed against the lump in her throat. Wearing the ring for the few hours of their fake wedding had been like taking a knife and prying off her fingernails one by one. A sharp reminder of what she'd almost had and never would. She shook her head, and tears tumbled down her cheeks.

"I know. I know, Luce." His tone was gentle as he took the ring and slid it on her finger, and then grabbed her face in both hands and pressed his lips to hers. He let go of her face and gripped her shoulders, staring at the concrete and exhaling deeply. "I hurt too."

They stood like that in silence, Luce blinking hard to stop the tears, her chest constricting painfully. It didn't help to know that Connor was still broken up about them; it only reinforced her own guilt in their break up. If she hadn't screwed up so badly. . . .

He lifted his head and gave her a weak smile, then wiped the tears from her cheeks. "Let's pull ourselves together. I'll bring in your bags. You check on Mom. She's in the guest bedroom."

Luce nodded, a frown pulling at her lips. She'd assumed *she* would be in the guest bedroom. But if Jessica was in there, where was Luce sleeping?

Pushing that worry aside, she worked to turn her lips into a smile as she entered the bright and cheerful yellow room. "Jessica? It's Luce."

Jessica shifted her head from its spot on the low pillow. She'd lost a lot of weight and looked tired, but otherwise not any worse for wear. "There's my elusive daughter-in-law. I'm so glad you're back. You chose a rotten time to leave."

"I know." Luce stepped to her and squeezed her hand, then bent and kissed her cheek.

Death. The smell lingered on Jessica, coloring the pastel blue pillows, swirling in the air around them. No matter how she looked, the end was near.

"Poland would make a nice honeymoon. I hope you two take one soon. Don't let work get in the way. Or me." Jessica winked at Luce.

Luce tried to smile, but at the moment she could find nothing to be joyful about. Nothing at all.

"Don't cry," Jessica whispered, touching a tear that rolled down Luce's face. "This is part of life. I couldn't be happier. You and Connor bring me such happiness."

Luce bit down on her lip. "Where's your nurse?"

"She's probably in the kitchen. She keeps herself busy when she's not changing my catheter or putting calories in my veins."

Luce finally laughed. "And Dave?"

Jessica shrugged, a shimmer of disappointment darkening her gaze. "I don't think I'm as much fun as I was."

Luce squeezed her hand. "Don't worry about him."

"Soon I'll be dancing with the angels. They better be hot."

"You know it." Luce spotted Connor then, walking down the hall with her bags. She let go of Jessica and joined him. "Where are you taking my things?"

Even as she asked, Connor reached his bedroom and pushed it open. "Oh. In here." She watched him deposit her luggage and carry-on onto the full bed in the middle of the room. She glanced around and spotted a separate bathroom, a dresser, and a TV, but no other bed. " And where am I sleeping?"

Connor returned to her, his expression unreadable. "My mom thinks you're sleeping in here."

Luce gave a startled laugh. "Of course she does. But where

am I really?"

Connor hesitated. "I can pull out the sofa bed in the living room. But I'll sleep there. You take this bed."

No way. "I'm not taking your bed." She would never in a million years get his scent out of her head.

"I can't have you sleeping on the couch." He lowered his voice. "Tell you what. I'll take the floor. I've got my own bathroom, it doesn't have to be awkward."

Not be awkward! What part of this *wouldn't* be awkward?

"If the nurse sees one of us on the couch, she'll know something's wrong," Connor added. "She might say something to my mom."

"Fine," Luce snapped. "But I get the floor."

"Luce—"

"No. I will not sleep in your bed." She snatched a pillow from his bed and threw it on the floor as if to claim her place. "I'm going to talk to the nurse." She turned around and marched out the door before he could see her tears.

CONNOR

She had a boyfriend.

This was an unexpected and unwanted twist. When Connor called Luce, he'd fully intended to tell her everything in the airport. Apologize, beg forgiveness, and ask her to be his wife for real. Tell her he didn't care anymore, that he'd missed her like crazy, that he loved her.

But she had a boyfriend. It wasn't fair to her to ask her to be his wife just because they were accidentally married. She had as much right as him to decide this was what she wanted.

Every part of Connor's soul trembled to be so near her but not have her. The irony of the situation—that she thought she pretended to be his wife while in reality she was—wasn't lost on him.

But even worse was seeing her anger at him, her disgust, her wanting nothing to do with him.

He wasn't sure what to do now.

He stared at the door she'd just walked through and debated going after her. But she looked ready to bite his head off, and the last thing he wanted was to fight in front of his mom. He couldn't disillusion her about their wedded bliss.

He'd already cleaned his room, but if Luce insisted on sleeping on the floor, he'd have to make it more comfortable. He stepped into the bathroom and searched through the closet until he found the blow-up mattress. Now he needed a blow-dryer.

His mom was asleep when he tiptoed past the guest bedroom and into the master room. All of the machinery hooked to his mom required an empty room; the master was too full of dressers and ottomans and decor.

What would he do with it after she was gone? Have an estate sale so someone else could buy it and sell it in their store?

It only took a moment to find her blow-dryer, but she was awake when he passed the guest room again. She had her eyes open, and they fell on him when he walked by.

"What are you doing?" she murmured.

"Oh, just grabbing this. Luce might need it." He brandished the blow-dryer.

"She doesn't have one?" his mom whispered, as if every word took her breath away.

"She probably does. I didn't ask. I want to make sure she has everything she needs."

"You're such a thoughtful husband." She sighed, closing her

eyes and slipping off.

If only that were true. Connor tiptoed out of the room, guilt twisting around his insides like something rotten.

♥

After he blew up the mattress and laid blankets across it, Connor made his way to the living room and kitchen. Part of him hoped to find Luce, to somehow break the ice and get a conversation going, while the other part was terrified to. He had to convince her not to go back to Poland. Even if he was unable to do so, he couldn't let her go without telling her the truth.

He had no idea what would happen after that, but he knew it wouldn't be pretty.

Especially with this other guy in her life.

He had no right to the angry jealousy that reared up like a Chinese dragon, knew the hapless man didn't deserve Connor's fury. But he wanted to punch his lights out.

Connor followed the soft whisper of voices to the patio and found Luce and Josie talking softly.

"It won't be long now," the nurse said. "She's lost so much weight. Her body is shutting down. It's a good thing you came when you did. She talks about you nonstop."

"I'm sorry I was gone so long," Luce replied. "If I'd known how bad off she was. . . ."

"You're here now. That's what matters." Josie turned slightly and spotted Connor. She nodded and started past him, but Connor stopped her.

"How long?"

She cocked her head. "A few days. A week at most."

His throat clenched, aching at the reality even though he'd known. "Is she comfortable?"

"As much as I can make her."

"Thanks." Connor exhaled a breath and stepped aside.

"Excuse me," Luce murmured, making to follow the nurse.

"Hey." Connor put his hands on her forearms, but she jerked away from him. "Sorry," he said, throwing his hands up. "I just thought maybe we could talk."

"There's nothing to talk about," she said stiffly. "We both know where things stand."

You have no idea. But Connor backed off. He'd need to soften her up first, get her to come around to him. "Okay, no talking. How about some lunch? You've got to be hungry. I've got peanut butter and jelly. Frozen pizza. Or we can go out, get a bite somewhere."

"I am hungry," she admitted, crossing her arms over her chest. "But I can get myself something."

She wasn't going to yield even an inch to him. "Do you mind if I eat at the same time?"

"It's your house."

Not for long. In a matter of days, when his mom died, both he and his wife would inherit it.

♥

His mother rallied for a bit in the afternoon, using Josie and the walker to come out to the dining room. Luce had holed herself up in a chair with her laptop, completely ignoring Connor as she updated her blog or emailed her boyfriend or who knew what. Connor took the time to write an essay, seated in a corner as far away from her as possible. At the sound of his mother's footsteps dragging down the hall, he jumped to his feet. Luce did as well, and they both glanced at each other before moving subtly closer.

"There you two are," his mom said, a fragile smile crossing her lips as she came around the corner. She breathed so noisily that Connor could hear it from where he stood. "My favorite people in the whole world are here. I'm not staying in bed."

Luce moved to her side, tucking a few strands of hair behind his mom's ears and patting her arms. "Are you sure you should be up?"

"Josie said it's fine," she said, indicating her nurse with a nod.

"It won't hurt her none," Josie said, her eyes sympathetic.

"What do you want to eat, Mom?" Connor asked. He reached the fridge in two strides and surveyed the frozen dinners there. His diet as of late hadn't been particularly healthy. "Want me to order out?"

She waved him off as Josie helped her sit down. "I'm not very hungry, sweetie. Whatever you and Luce have." She fixed Connor with a stern gaze. "You know you can't hang around here all day keeping an eye on me. Who will take care of the store?"

He hesitated, thinking for sure he'd told her. "I closed it, Mom." At the look on her face, he added quickly, "Just for now! I want to spend my time here with you—and Luce." He managed to say her name straight-faced, keeping his gaze on his mom.

"I can go to the store," Luce offered.

"No." His mom took her hand and held it. "You stay with me."

"Ha!" Connor joked, though it warmed his heart to see his mom smiling. "You like her more than me."

"He wasn't supposed to figure that out," his mother whispered, and Luce laughed.

Connor closed the fridge, grinning at both of them. "Forget this stuff. I'm ordering sushi."

"You don't need to do that," his mom protested.

He held up a hand. "Luce loves it. Don't you, Luce? And I

bet it's hard to find in Poland."

Luce met his eyes briefly before looking away again. "They do have it. But it's not the same."

"Nothing's the same as Arkansas sushi," Connor said, and she gave the tiniest of smiles.

"No," she agreed. "It's not." She settled back in the chair, relaxing slightly.

Chapter Twenty-Six

LUCE

Jessica's energy didn't last long, and Josie helped her back to bed after only a few bites of sushi. That left Luce and Connor alone at the table, picking through what remained.

"How was the food in Poland?" Connor asked.

"Heavy," she said. "Not a ton of vegetables except beets and potatoes. I didn't enjoy it much."

"You look like you've lost a lot of weight."

She picked at the fish eggs on top of a sushi roll and didn't comment. That probably had more to do with her lack of appetite. Her eyelids drooped, and she put the food down with a sigh.

"I don't think I'll even need my sleeping pills tonight. I'm exhausted from the flight."

Connor lifted his eyebrows. "How often are you taking those?"

Every night. But she didn't answer. She was supposed to be over him, right?

But how could she get over him? She'd lost a loved one. Except he wasn't dead, just—gone.

She stood and pushed away from the table. "I'm tired."

He followed her, staying right on her heels all the way to the room, and her irritation flared. Why couldn't he leave her alone?

"How am I supposed get ready with you here?" she asked when he closed the bedroom door. "Your mom's out for the night. You can go away."

For the briefest moment, hurt flicked across his face. And then it was gone. "I'll stay in the bathroom. Just go to bed, Luce. I'll leave you alone."

She glared at him until he disappeared into the other room. Then she simply lay down on the mattress and pulled the blanket over her, wool dress and all. She closed her eyes and didn't move, made her breathing deep when Connor finally came out. She heard him open the dresser drawer, the jangle of his belt and pants as he dropped them to the floor. Her heart rate quickened, and she willed herself to keep her eyes closed.

Perhaps she should have taken a sleeping pill after all.

♥

A soft sound, almost like a kitten mewing, woke Luce.

She blinked into the darkness, disoriented for the briefest moment before she remembered she was back in Arkansas, sleeping on a bumpy air mattress in Connor's bedroom.

The sound came again, and this time she identified it: a choked sob, the muffled sound of something crying, swallowing tears.

"Connor," Luce whispered.

The sound cut off abruptly. A moment later his voice whispered back from the direction of the bed.

"I'm sorry, Luce."

She held her breath, her heart instantly pounding in her neck. Would he actually apologize for dumping her the way he had?

"I didn't mean to wake you," he continued, and she resisted an eye roll.

"Are you okay?" she asked.

He didn't answer for a long moment, and when he finally did, his voice was tight and closed. "She's really going to die. She's been the only steady thing in my life. My whole life. Sure, she makes me crazy and acts like she's twelve sometimes, but she's my mom. She's mine."

"I understand," Luce said, and the tears swam in her own eyes. "My dad was never really there for me. After my mom died, all I had was Melodee. I don't know what I'd do without her."

"How did your mom die? You never told me."

"Car accident," Luce whispered. "We were all in the car, coming home from Melodee's dance practice. My mom ran a stop sign—she wasn't paying attention, just talking to us—and another car hit us."

He leaned over the edge of the bed, facing her. "That's awful."

"It was." Luce wiped at her own tears. "I was only twelve. But we heal, we move on. My dad too much. He threw himself into his work. Couldn't bear to be the only parent."

He reached his hand out to her, extending his fingers in invitation. She hesitated only a moment before accepting. His thumb caressed the backs of her fingers, sending little shivers through her midsection. "I'm glad you didn't have to go through that alone," he said.

"You don't either." She squeezed his hand. "I'm here with

you." But was she really capable of only being Connor's friend, if that was what he required? She thought of Henryk and the promise of a future he offered, but conjuring his face in her mind didn't make her feel anything. Nothing like what Connor's thumb on her skin was doing. She changed the subject, trying to distract herself from his touch. "What about your dad? You never talk about him."

For a moment, Connor's movement stopped. And then his grasp tightened, almost painfully. "My dad." He heaved a sigh. "He left when I was a kid. I missed him. I loved him. I hated him."

"Where did he go?"

He released her hand, the sudden lack of pressure sending a cold sensation through her fingers. "Back to his wife and family."

"What?" Luce couldn't resist the gasp of surprise. "He was married?"

"To someone else. Yeah, my mom didn't know either. Apparently he'd left her too. Then he changed his mind and went back."

"What?" she whispered again, her mind reeling. Suddenly pieces were falling into place. Connor's demand for absolute honesty. His inability to deal with her deceit about her previous marriage. She had unwittingly stepped directly into the mire of Connor's biggest wounds.

Now who had the tragic flaw?

"So your parents were never actually married," she choked out.

"Right."

Luce moved her hands to her face, covering her eyes so he wouldn't see her cry.

"Tell me about your ex-husband," he said, the words so soft

Luce almost thought she imagined them.

She caught her breath, disbelief making her ears ring. Why would he ask that? It felt too personal, and at the same time, nobody deserved to know more than he did. She exhaled and lowered her hands. "What do you want to know?"

"I don't know. Anything you want to tell me."

Nothing. She wished Connor didn't have to know about him at all. "He flattered me. Told me my pottery was beautiful. I had a good business, and he convinced me he could make it better. We—" she strangled on the words "fell in love" and left them out. "We got married. Then he took all my money, my capital, my savings, and gambled them away."

"That's why you quit making things."

"Yes."

"Do you hate him?"

"I did." Luce shook her head. "I feel nothing for him now. It's like a chapter out of someone else's life."

"And what about your boyfriend now?"

He said the words in a rush, like it took courage to get them out. Luce almost laughed. He thought Henryk was her boyfriend. "He's a nice guy. Helping me learn Polish pottery. It's nice to feel like someone cares."

Connor's fingers grazed the air mattress before finding her hand and stroking her forearm. "I care, Luce."

A salty tear dripped past her lips. She licked it away. He cared. Just not the way she wanted.

♥

She couldn't stay in this house another hour.

Luce had awakened with her fingers clenched in Connor's, his body draped over the edge of the bed and his hand outstretched to her.

The sight of him opened up a well of desire inside her, and

the love she felt was so strong and so sharp that she knew it would wrench her in two. He'd acted genuinely interested in her last night, and she'd felt the warmth of friendship between them.

Today she felt only loss.

Finding her suitcase, she pulled out a long sweatshirt and jeans. She changed in the bathroom quickly, planning to shower at Melodee's. She needed to get out of here before Connor woke.

No such luck. He was up when she came out, and he'd already dressed for the day in casual slacks and a polo shirt.

"Want to grab some breakfast?" he asked.

She shook her head. "I'm going to see my sister." She stuffed her wool dress back in her suitcase, zipped it up, and stood, pulling the suitcase up so the little wheels tracked on the ground.

His eyes followed her hand to where she still held onto the handle. "How long are you staying?"

She shrugged, averting her gaze. "A day. Maybe two."

"You can't be gone that long."

"I can't not see her."

"Then go for an hour and come back."

The irritation rose up in her, and she welcomed it, because it was so much easier to face than her affection for him. "I'll stay as long as I want."

Bewilderment flashed across his face, quickly replaced by his own anger. "The whole reason you're here is for my mom! She's going to die, Luce. I know it's a major inconvenience, but can't you stick around for that?"

"I know that's why I'm here," Luce snapped. "You think I have delusions that maybe I'm here for you? That you wanted me here? To fix things? I'm not that stupid. I'm not going to sit around here while you act like we are something to each other. So figure out something to tell your mom."

"Luce," Connor said, taking a step toward her. "I didn't mean—"

"Don't, don't, don't," Luce said, holding up her hand. "Don't apologize. You can't give me what I want."

CONNOR

"Where did Luce go?"

His mother's voice came quietly from where she lay in the bed as Connor pulled back the curtains and repositioned the ties.

"To see her sister," he said, stopping to stare out the window. She'd left yesterday and hadn't come back yet.

The heaviness in his heart had very little to do with his mother. Getting back into Luce's good graces would be harder than he thought, especially since every word out of his mouth seemed to screw it up.

But the memory of the other night still warmed him, the way she'd confided in him and how they'd whispered. He'd felt so close to her, talking about his fears, his past, listening to her talk about her life. There had to be a way.

He still hadn't told her they were married. Somehow he was finding it very hard to broach the subject. It just didn't feel like the right moment. But when would it?

Was this how she'd felt about her divorce? Knowing she needed to tell him, but unsure how to do it?

The moment he thought it, he was one hundred percent sure he was correct. He'd become so familiar with the guilt living in his chest that he hardly noticed it flicker to life and spin around. What he kept from her was a whole lot worse than what she'd kept from him.

His mother cleared her throat, and he realized he'd lingered too long in silence. He turned from the window and attempted a smile.

"Are you and Luce okay?" she asked.

"Of course we are." He stepped to her side and kissed her forehead. The skin crinkled like paper beneath his lips. "She's just been away from her family for a few weeks and they want to see her. She'll be back soon."

"Tonight," his mom whispered, closing her eyes. "Tell her to come back tonight."

"I will."

When Luce hadn't returned by lunchtime, Connor sent her a quick text.

Mom's asking for you. Can you come back?

She didn't respond right away, and he tried to focus on his schoolwork. But his thoughts kept going back to her, and he knew he wouldn't be able to think until he talked to her. Giving up, he dialed her number.

She answered on the third ring. "Sorry, Connor," she said. "I just now saw your text."

"That's all right," he said, relieved she hadn't been ignoring him. "She wants you here, Luce. What can I do to make this more comfortable?"

There was a pause, and then she said, "Nothing. But I'm a big girl. I can put on a happy face. I'll be there soon."

"Thanks," he said, and hung up. Because what else could he say? He didn't make her happy. He'd blown that one.

She showed up an hour later, wearing the floral dress he loved and smelling like lavender. Just as promised, she came in like a breeze, all big smiles and cheer. She sidestepped

Connor and went down the hall.

"Jessica," she said, entering the master bedroom and greeting her with a kiss. "Did you miss me?"

"So glad you're here," his mom whispered.

Luce shot Connor an alarmed look where he stood in the doorway, and Connor knew she saw what he did. It wouldn't be long now. His mother looked like she'd aged ten years in the past two days. "What can I get for you?"

"It's time for vows," his mom said with a hint of her former wicked grin.

"Vows?" Luce repeated, looking panicky.

"Connor," his mom called.

"I'm here." He joined them, standing on the opposite side of the bed of Luce. "What do you need, Mom?"

"A glass of wine," she pronounced.

Luce looked startled, but Connor burst out laughing. "Will that make you happy?"

"Immensely," she replied, grinning. "Josie hasn't let me drink, but it doesn't matter now."

Connor looked around. "Where's Josie?"

"Taking a shower. I wanted a moment alone with you two before my parents get here. But first—" she cocked an eyebrow at Connor. "My wine?"

"Right," he murmured. He swallowed past the thickness in his throat and left the room. Wordless thoughts and emotions swirled through his mind as he poured her a glass.

He returned to the quiet room, the atmosphere somber and tense. "Mom." He helped steady her hand as she sipped the wine.

She smacked her lips and let out a satisfied sigh. "Thank you. Now I'm ready to talk."

Connor set the glass down and scooted a chair over to her

bed. "Go on."

"Luce, help me sit up?"

"Sure." Luce moved the pillows around until his mom was nearly straight.

"My last words," she exhaled. She smiled at them, and Connor saw how Luce attempted a smile back but failed. "Connor. I owe you the biggest of apologies. After your father left, I became a very deficient mother."

"Mom," he protested, but she bowled right over him with a growl.

"Don't defend me just because I'm dying. You know how it was. You're a wonderful, kind, respectable son, but not because of me. On that note." She swiveled her eyes to Luce, chin barely moving to follow the motion. "You married a fantastic man. But he practically raised himself. Don't blame him when he screws up; blame me, I won't care." She squeezed both of their hands, eyes still on Luce. "Forgive him when he falls short."

Connor found himself holding his breath, waiting to hear Luce's response.

"I will," Luce whispered, never breaking eye contact with his mom.

He let out a tiny breath. But did she truly mean it? Or was that promise as empty as the ones they'd made at the altar a few weeks earlier?

"And you," his mom said, focusing on Connor now, "she's the best thing that ever happened to you. Love her always."

"Always," Connor promised. And his was not an empty one.

A smile pressed to her lips as her eyes closed, and Connor half expected her not to take another breath. But her chest continued to rise and fall, however lightly. He held her hand in his and avoided looking at Luce, unsure of what he'd see in her expression.

Footsteps padded across the hardwood floor, and Josie came in, already back in her standard blue scrubs, short blond hair dark with water. "What's going on, guys?" she asked, taking in their positions.

Connor turned to face her. "She thinks she's going to die tonight." He studied Josie's face, hoping for an indication that it wasn't true.

She stepped forward and checked his mother's blood pressure. "Sometimes they know before we do," she said. She took a few more measurements, writing things down on a clipboard, and then settled into the padded bench in the room. "I won't leave her side."

The front door opened just seconds before Connor heard Granny's voice.

"Hello?" she called. Her tone lacked her normal boisterous confidence.

"Granny. Grandpa." Connor accepted their hugs and wished he felt closer to these living relatives. Maybe it was time to get to know them better, even spend time with Lilly and her family.

Granny brushed tears from her eyes and clung to Grandpa's hand. "I never thought I'd out live her. She's always been so stubborn and determined."

"Just like you," Grandpa said, his tone somber and affectionate.

Granny turned to Connor, leveling her gaze on him behind her red glasses. "Don't think I don't know what you've been doing with that store."

Surely she wasn't going to make an issue of it now. He just stared at her, not quite sure what to say.

She softened her tone. "It will be yours now, once she's

gone. You can do what you want with it."

He exhaled and put his hands in his pockets, feeling the weight of defeat. "I'll make sure it doesn't change. I'll keep it going just like you had it, like your mom did."

"Why would you do that?" She scowled at him. "The things I've seen you put in there add such a vibrant touch. You should fill the store with them."

It was all he could do not to let his jaw drop. "You like my things?"

Granny chuckled and patted his cheek. "I always told Jessica you have a good eye. That she should give you more control. That's probably why she didn't."

Connor blinked, and then gave a short laugh. "You mean Mom kept the store the same to spite you? Not because it's what you wanted?"

Granny laughed also, her shoulders quaking. "Your mother always had to have the last word." She sniffed, eyes reddening. "I thought she always would."

Chapter Twenty-Seven

LUCE

Luce started slightly when Josie ushered Mr. and Mrs. Connor into the room. Though Luce had only met them briefly, Jessica's illness had done a number on them. Mrs. Connor's blue hair rinse had faded out, and the resulting white aged her by decades. The glasses didn't hide the bloodshot eyes.

Luce stood up, offering her place to Mrs. Connor, but the old woman shook her head.

"Stay," she said, her voice cracking. "You're the daughter she never had." Mr. Connor put his arm around her when her shoulders began to quake, and Luce looked away, their grief making her throat close. She took Jessica's hand again, watching her chest rise and fall in quiet breaths.

Connor came in behind them, and Luce didn't look at him as he settled in the chair on the other side of the bed. But she was hyper aware of him. Of his eyes on her.

She was past feeling, past hoping that he loved her. His

promise to his mom to always love her stirred something inside her, but she wasn't sure what it was. She couldn't even drum up the energy for indignant anger.

She wished he would give her another chance.

The tears slipped down her cheeks, landing softly on the bedspread, soaking the skin of Jessica's hand. Jessica didn't flinch, didn't wake. Connor's hand released his mom's and crept across the blanket until his fingers brushed hers. He turned his hand upward, but she didn't accept it this time. Instead she let go of Jessica and left the room.

Maybe she would try some of that wine.

She had just poured herself a glass and leaned against the counter, taking tiny sips, when Josie came into the kitchen.

"Her heart rate's slowing. It's now."

Luce put down the wine, her face flushed, and followed the nurse back into the guest room. Josie stood by the machine, charting its course, and Luce resumed her spot next to Jessica. Mrs. Connor stood at Jessica's head, crooning softly while she caressed Jessica's hair. Tears rolled silently down her face.

Jessica didn't open her eyes. Her breathing slowed, the chest rises becoming shallow. And finally they stopped. The machine let out a warning beep, then an alarm sounded. Josie turned it off and wrote a few things down.

"Time of death: One-fifteen in the afternoon," Josie pronounced. "If you've got anything else to say to her, guys, do it now. I have to call this in."

Luce let go of Jessica and followed Josie into the kitchen. She listened as the nurse called the hospital and arranged transportation for the body.

"What do we need to do now?" she asked when she got off the phone. "What about the funeral?"

"Jessica was prepared," Josie said. "She left all her

documents in a folder and prearranged her funeral with the funeral home. You'll need to go in with Connor and sign some papers, but it should be fairly easy." She touched Luce's arm, her eyes sympathetic. "Go be with your husband. He needs you."

Husband. Luce nodded, the word leaving a bitter, thick coating on her tongue.

Luce returned to the guest room and made her way to Connor's side of the bed. She sat stiffly beside him. He didn't hide his tears, though he kept his head down and wasn't noisy about it. His grandparents sobbed openly, holding each other tight.

"What now?" Connor asked, lifting his head.

Luce's heart melted at the sight of his distress, the swollen skin around his bloodshot eyes. She touched his arm, then rested her hand there. "Josie said almost everything's been arranged. We'll have to go to the funeral home and sign some papers, but the decisions were already made. Jessica already outlined what she wants for the funeral." Luce attempted a smile. "Kind of her."

He didn't smile back. He simply bobbed his head, then pushed his hands against his thighs and stood up. "Can you find out what we need? I can't think. I need a moment." Without waiting for her response, he went to his bedroom and closed the door.

"Yes," Luce answered to the closed room. So much for needing her.

♥

Josie tried to give the papers to Mrs. Connor, but she declined, saying Jessica would want Connor and Luce to make the final arrangements. So Josie provided Luce with the documents they'd need at the funeral home. When the ambulance arrived to transport the body, she and Connor got in his car and followed it. Connor stood by in absolute silence while Luce spoke with the director.

"This is the casket she picked," he said. "And she wanted these flowers. We'll do the embalming tomorrow and be ready for a funeral the day after. Does that work for you?"

"Connor?" Luce asked, turning to him. "Is that enough time to get a guest list together?"

Connor simply shrugged and ran his hand over one of the sample caskets in the room.

"That sounds good," Luce murmured to the man.

"Sign here, please."

Luce hesitated only a moment before signing her name. Luce Donovan. The one and only.

"Come on, Connor." She gripped him by the elbow like he was a toddler and guided him out. "Let's go home."

The moment they stepped back into the house, Connor disappeared down the hall. Luce wondered where he'd gone. His room, to have another moment alone? Or maybe his mom's room, to remember her alive? Or even the guest room, to relive the last few moments with her? There'd been no one else he'd been able to rely on for the past few years.

Luce felt her own guilt over that. It could have been her, comforting him, caring for him, being here for him.

She walked to the kitchen counter and set down her purse. The house was empty, so his grandparents must have gone home. Her wine still sat there, and she dumped it down the sink. Their checklist sat by the toaster. She ran her finger down it. The body had already been taken and the doctor notified. She needed to contact the closest relatives. A date had been set for the funeral. The funeral home would take care of the death certificate, as well.

They still needed to take Jessica's will to the city office. But that could wait a few more days.

Only the formalities remained: order the flowers, invite the guests, print an obituary in the newspaper. The flowers she could do; she'd need help from Connor to do the guest list.

She walked to their shared bedroom to get her computer, realizing as she did so that she didn't need to stay in his room anymore. There was no one around to fool. In fact, she could go back to her condo.

The thought didn't bring her comfort. Leaving would sever the last tie she and Connor had to each other.

The bedroom door was ajar, and Luce pushed it open. She stopped when saw Connor standing with one arm leaning against the window frame, head down, gaze on the floor.

"Connor?" she murmured, stepping closer. Her heart squeezed in sympathy. It had been twelve years since her own mother's death, but the pain never quite went away. She walked to his side and rubbed his back. "Are you okay?"

He shook his head, then swiveled his body and took her in his arms. He crushed her against him and cried into her neck. There were no words, hardly even a sound, just the shaking of his shoulders and the wetness on her skin.

"Come, let's sit," Luce whispered, pulling him to the bed. He let her lead him. She rearranged her positioning so he leaned against her and she held him. She closed her eyes as he relied on her, grateful for the closeness. Maybe he wouldn't lock her out of his life completely.

He straightened up and studied her, the vibrancy and luster of his light brown eyes hidden behind a shimmery curtain of tears. "Luce, thank you for being here," he said, his breath whispering against her face. "I know you didn't have to come, you've gone through this whole charade for my mom, and you've gotten nothing out of it—"

"Hush." She pressed a finger to his lips. "Don't you know why I did this? I did this for you. I love you. I'm so sorry for your mom, so sorry I hid the truth from you, that I lost you. If I could . . ." Words failed her as her anguish got the best of her, and she shook her head. "But I can't," she finished with a broken sob. "I can't."

Connor's thumbs wiped the tears as they trailed down her cheeks. He leaned forward and kissed her ever so tenderly. Luce gripped his wrists with both her hands, returning his kiss with the longing and despair she'd felt these past few weeks. The kiss deepened, and Connor's hand moved behind her head to hold her in place while he pressed his mouth to hers, opening her lips with his, his tongue pulling her into him.

Luce caught her breath and turned her head, feeling how her heart pounded, how her skin warmed with the expectation of what came next. She hadn't been kissed this passionately in a long time.

Connor did not wait for her. His mouth moved to her jaw, and she closed her eyes, lengthening her neck as his kisses traveled downward.

She wanted more. But just as he hadn't when they were dating, Connor didn't push her. He didn't try to undress her or slide his hand under her clothing.

Luce pulled back, reaching her hand behind her head to grip the zipper of her dress. "Help me with this," she whispered.

His eyes didn't waver from her face, intense as he studied her. "Are you sure?"

"I want this," she whispered, guiding his hand around her back. "I want you." She wanted to feel the strength of Connor's love, his desire, his acceptance. Even if only once.

He brought his hands back to her face, caressing the hair

around her temples before kissing her again. "I never stopped loving you, Luce."

His words warmed her soul. If nothing else, they would always have this. She responded by returning his kiss forcefully, her hands moving to his waist and then to the bare skin under his sweater. This time he didn't hesitate, his fingers fumbling with the zipper and slipping the dress off her shoulders, his hands strong and sure. Just as she'd always imagined they would be.

♥

Connor cried again after they slept together. Maybe he thought she didn't notice, since her head was on his bare chest and he stroked her hair, but she heard it, the shallow, shaky breaths beneath her ear. His fingers wrapped around the hair close to her scalp and tightened, then unwound and stroked, then repeated.

She lay there with her eyes open, feeling the rise and fall of his chest, staring at the light blue paint on the textured walls. Where the guest room was pastel yellow with blue accents, this room was sky blue with navy accents. She wished she could read Connor's mind. Did he regret what just happened between them?

After a moment his hand stilled, and then his breathing deepened. He'd fallen asleep. Luce didn't move, waiting a full five minutes to make sure Connor was really asleep. Then she slipped out from under his arm and put her clothes back on.

A wave of shame washed over her. Funny how she'd been so worried about Connor's regret, she hadn't considered her own. What was she thinking? She'd never slept with someone she wasn't in a relationship with. Never something so impulsive. They hadn't used protection and she wasn't on the pill. It was a little too late for prayers, but she uttered one anyway, praying there would be no lasting consequences for their passion.

Finding her laptop, she set it up on the dresser and opened a web browser. She needed to get out of here. Already her heart hurt from their intimate moment. Anger added to her shame, and she pressed the keys on the keyboard a little harder than necessary.

The airlines website pulled up, and she pondered a moment before putting in the dates for a return flight. She needed to stay here though the funeral. Then she'd return to the hospital in Poland. She'd move there permanently, and this time she wouldn't hold back when Henryk offered her something more lasting. Maybe, maybe she would even find love again.

A tear fell on her keyboard, and she sniffled. She hadn't even realized she was crying. She closed her eyes, allowing herself for a brief second to remember the feel of Connor's lips on her body, the touch of his flesh on hers. Warmth shimmied up from her belly, and then she banished the memory. Never again.

"Luce?"

Connor's voice came as a quiet whisper from the bed, and she turned, avoiding looking directly at him.

"What are you doing?"

She forced a smile that dropped from her lips just as quickly. "I'm booking my flight back to Poland. Back home." There. She may as well begin to think of it that way.

Connor sat up and pressed the palms of his hands to his temples. Then he looked at her. "I thought maybe you could stay."

She shook her head, and tears danced away from the corners of her eyes. "I can't." She gestured from him to her. "This— between us, I don't even know what it is. But it will kill me to be so near you and not be with you. It's killing me."

He uttered a long sigh and then reached for his jeans. Luce averted her gaze while he dressed and then looked over again when he sat down heavily on the bed.

"There's something I need to tell you," he said.

He'd said that when he called her in Poland. What more was there to say? She cocked her head and waited.

Connor licked his lips and looked away from her. "When Ty did the wedding ceremony, he—he married us." Finally he met her eyes. "Like, for real."

His words made no sense. "It was a fake ceremony."

"No. We only thought it was. We're actually married."

Luce gasped as the implications began to sink in. "But how? How could Tyson marry us?"

"You can get ordained online. He did it."

Luce shook her head, her mind flashing back to the simple backyard ceremony. It had been real? "How long have you known?"

Connor's eyes roamed around the room, anywhere but her face. "Since that day."

"But that was—that was before I went to Poland!" Luce clenched her fists together. Connor had known they were actually married before she left. That he hadn't told her revealed his thoughts as clearly as if he'd stated them: he didn't want to be married to her. But more than that, he hadn't even thought it important enough to tell her. Her thoughts flew to Henryk, to the flirting and the kiss they'd almost shared, the relationship she almost had with him. Something she could never do, not if she was already married! Fury slashed through her like a forest fire. "You knew. How could you keep that from me?"

"I'm sorry, Luce. I'm sorry."

"You realize that I was starting a new life in Poland? If I'm a married woman, I have the right to know!" She marched toward him, fists still balled up.

"I know." He held up his hands as if to ward off an attack. "I wasn't sure what to do about it, I wanted to think it through."

"This had to do with me, too!" she shouted, thumbing her finger into her chest. Her whole body shook with anger and hurt and rejection.

She couldn't talk anymore. She had no more words. Instead, she turned and yanked open the bedroom door.

"Don't go," Connor said, bolting from the bed.

Oh, no, she wasn't falling for that pitiful act. She whipped around, hoping he could see the rage in her eyes. "The full extent of your regard for me is quite clear now." Spotting her laptop, she scooped it up and left the room.

Connor trailed behind her. "Where will you go?"

"To my house."

"But will you come back? For the funeral?"

She gathered her purse from the kitchen and shoved her laptop inside. "You're on your own, buddy." She lifted her gaze and met his eyes. "I'll be back tomorrow to get my things. And I'll bring annulment papers." She spun on her heel.

"How will you get home?" Connor asked, still following her.

"I'll take the trolley!" She let herself out the front door and slammed it hard, praying he wouldn't follow her out here. If he did, he'd see her break. The righteous indignation that had fueled her departure was rapidly dissipating, leaving her feeling more wounded and broken than she could ever remember.

She needed a good strong drink.

Retrieving her phone, she dialed the number of her only friend. "Caroline? I need you."

CONNOR

It took Connor all of five minutes to pull on a shirt and get shoes on, but in that time, Luce had vanished. He hopped in his car and drove to the trolley stop, but she wasn't there. It was possible she'd gone to another one. Or maybe the trolley already came.

He tried her phone for hours, driving through Eureka like a madman, as if hoping to somehow ping off her location by calling her over and over. She never answered, and he began to wonder if maybe she'd blocked him.

All he wanted was to be with her. To share the same space. To breathe the same air. Was that too much to ask?

He parked himself in front of her condo, tapping impatiently on the steering wheel, alternating from checking his clock to checking his email and back again. He started a million text messages but only sent a few of them. Last thing he needed was for her to put a restraining order out against him.

The sky began its lazy color change as night approached, and still no sign of Luce. Maybe she was at her sister's. He drove to Melodee's house, bracing himself. Certainly Melodee wouldn't be happy to see him.

"Melodee?" he called, knocking lightly at the door. A TV blared within, and the happy chatter of children and pots banging came through the door. Maybe he hadn't been loud enough. "Melodee!" he called again, pounding a little harder.

Connor took a step back when he realized he was banging. What now? Maybe it really was time to camp out on Luce's doorstep. Make her listen to him. If she went back to Poland, he was following her.

The door swung open and Melodee stood there, looking twice as large as the last time he'd seen her. And all Connor could think was that could be Luce someday, round with his child, and his whole body ached to make that a reality.

"I've made a horrible mistake," he spurted.

Melodee lifted an eyebrow. "That's quite an opening."

He shook his head. "If anyone can help me, it's got to be you. She'll listen to you."

Melodee crossed her arms over her chest, resting them on her bulging belly. "You've made lots of mistakes, Connor. What did you do this time?"

"I let her go," he breathed out. "The biggest one, the worst one of all. I had her, I loved her, and I let her go. No, no, it's worse than that. I made her feel like she wasn't good enough. Like she fell short somehow. That. That was my mistake."

"Yeah, that's a big one," Melodee agreed.

"But it was me, it was me the whole time," he went on, unable to stop now, as if sitting in the confessional at church. "I was the one who wasn't good enough, and I compensated for my own inadequacies by finding fault in others. It was my security blanket. Somehow it made me smug in my misery."

"Connor—" Melodee began, but he kept going.

"Then I lost her." He bowed his head as tears stung his eyes, and he blamed his overly emotional state as much on Luce as on the death of his mom. "I lost her, Melodee, and I've got to get her back." He lifted his face, blinking hard. "You have to tell her. She won't talk to me. And I can't, I can't—I can't do this without her."

"Do what?" Melodee asked.

"Anything." He dropped his head again, suddenly spent from his outburst. "I can't do anything."

She dropped her arms and heaved a sigh. "I shouldn't do

this."

His heart skipped a beat and hope flared. "Do what?"

"Come in. You're letting in the cold."

Connor followed Melodee into the kitchen, where she snagged a piece of paper and wrote down a number.

"That's her friend Caroline. Try her."

He reached for the paper, hands shaking with anxiety. But Melodee didn't let go.

"And Connor? Don't screw it up again. I can pretty much guarantee this is your last chance."

He met her eyes, gave a nod. "I won't."

Chapter Twenty-Eight

LUCE

Caroline sat with her mouth wide open as Luce finished up her tale.

"Oh, my gosh," she said, grabbing her shot glass and downing it. She banged it on the counter for a refill. "I can't even believe it."

"Yeah. Me either." Luce picked up her own, making a face as she tipped back the strong alcohol. She let out a short laugh. "I'm a married woman. But my husband doesn't love me. Again." Then she burst into tears.

"Luce, honey." Caroline shifted closer and rubbed Luce's shoulder. "Maybe it's more complicated than that. You guys have had nothing but drama for weeks."

Luce shook her head. "He wasn't even going to tell me. How could he not tell me? Like he thought if he ignored it, it didn't happen?"

"I'm going to kill Tyson," Caroline growled.

Luce picked up her napkin and shredded it. "I slept with

him."

"With Tyson?" Caroline gasped.

"No!" Luce snapped. "With Connor!"

"Oh. You did?" Caroline squealed. "Well, that means something!"

"It means he was lonely and wanting comfort and I was available."

"Did he say that?"

"No."

"What did he say?"

"He said he loves me. That he never stopped." The words fell bitterly from Luce's mouth. "Just like every other guy who's tried to get into my pants. This one I actually believed."

"Maybe he does." Caroline gave her a squeeze. "He's not the first person to keep an important secret from their significant other."

"Yeah, but I think me not telling my fiance that I'm divorced falls quite short of not telling your ex-girlfriend you accidentally married her."

Caroline giggled. "Yes, he takes the cake. But what if you can forgive him?"

Luce shook her head. "No. This is about trust. I can't be with someone—"

"Who you can't trust." Caroline sat back, a smug look on her face. "Pretty sure those were Connor's words."

Pretty sure Caroline was right. Luce fell silent, thinking.

"What do you really want, Luce?" Caroline whispered. "Do you want to be Connor's wife? Or do you want to go back to Poland?"

"I want to be his wife," she answered, fingers trembling. The ring on her hand caught the overhead light, and she stared at it.

"Then you already are." Caroline lifted her chin. "Find a way to fix this."

Luce grabbed up one of the waxy napkins and wiped her face. "You've been avoiding my questions for weeks now. Was that your husband at my wedding?" She hiccuped on the word.

"Yes," Caroline said, and suddenly her face had a timid quality to it. "We've been talking."

"Are you back together?" Luce looked at her through watery eyes.

"No. But we're communicating. Pushing through."

"What does he do?"

Caroline picked up a peanut from the little bowl on the counter and flipped it down the bar. "He's a cop."

Caroline with a policeman. Luce wouldn't have guessed.

Caroline's phone rang, and she frowned at the number. "Give me a sec," she said, then pushed off the stool and went around the corner.

Luce balled up what remained of her shredded napkin. Now what she needed was liquid courage if she was going to face Connor and really talk through these feelings. Except her head already felt fuzzy from the two shots she'd had.

Caroline was back, grabbing Luce's hand and tugging her off the stool. "Let's go back to my place."

"Good idea." Luce sighed and shouldered her purse. "Drinking does not agree with me." She settled her tab and let Caroline guide her to the car. "Thanks for coming for me, Caroline. I appreciate it."

"No problem, girl. I was glad to claim a family emergency and take off from the clinic." She backed out of the parallel parking spot, and the engine revved as it worked its way up Spring Street.

CONNOR

Caroline's house was closer to Holiday Island, and it took Connor fifteen minutes to get there. But she'd been friendly on the phone, agreeing to meet with him and advocate his side to Luce.

Caroline answered the door before he even knocked. He attempted a smile, but she pressed her lips in a firm line.

"You're quite the hypocrite."

Okay. He should have expected an attack. "I guess she told you?"

"I'm waiting to hear your lame excuses."

"Excuses?" A sardonic laugh escaped his lips. "I don't have any. I pushed the woman I love away from me and I want her back. She's all I've got."

"So you just want someone to comfort you and warm your bed."

Heat rushed to his face. He hadn't expected Luce to tell her *everything*. "I want Luce. I love her. I want her to be my wife and the mother of my children."

"Maybe she doesn't want kids."

Had she said that? Connor floundered. "Then—then we'll work something else out. Can you just talk to her for me? Tell her I love her."

Caroline crossed her arms over her chest. "You love her? Really? You reject her because she married another man, make her fake marry you—which turns out not to be fake, but you don't tell her that—and then you use her and decide you love her?"

His sins flashed before his eyes like she was Saint Peter at judgment day. He gripped the edge of the door, feeling if he could just convince Caroline, maybe he could convince Luce.

"I never stopped loving her. It was stupid of me, stupid arrogance, pride, it made me think I could judge her, I know I was wrong. She's so much better than I am. And what happened between us—" He hated discussing this with someone else, but he had to make her see— "I wasn't using her. That was the first time—the first time in my life—that I actually made love to a woman." He was never going to live that statement down. "I don't know if I can ever deserve her, not after what I did. But if you could talk to her . . . Tell her I'm sincere . . . I just want the chance to prove it."

"Connor."

It wasn't Caroline's voice, and his eyes shot over Caroline's shoulder as she pushed the door open wider. He sucked in a breath and took a step backward as Luce moved in front of her friend.

"You're here," he said dumbly. "You were here the whole time."

"Yes," she said, and though she didn't smile, her eyes crinkled just a little. "I heard everything."

"I meant every word," he breathed. "I love you, Luce. I tried to tell you before you left for Poland—I followed you to the airport, I bought a ticket just to get through security. I went to stop you from boarding your flight. But I got scared. Scared of proving myself right, scared of proving myself wrong. Basically I set myself up for failure."

Luce glanced at Caroline and then stepped onto the porch, closing the door behind her. "You were horrible."

"The worst," he agreed.

Tears pricked her eyes again, and she hugged herself. "I felt lower than cat puke."

"That's pretty low."

Her lips curved as if fighting a smile. "But I did keep a huge secret from you."

"I understand why. And I'm sorry for not understanding before."

"You kept the fact that we got married a secret," she whispered, her voice choking on the last word. "That's bigger."

"I know." He swallowed hard. "I screwed up. Big time. I'll do what you want. If you want to get the marriage annulled, okay. But if not." He took her hand, his fingers shaking. "We can do over if you want, have a nice wedding. Make it really real this time."

"It was real last time," she said, and the tears overflowed. "I've never loved you any less. I've just been terribly, terribly angry with you. And quite a bit hurt."

That sounded a lot like forgiveness. Hope sprouted in Connor's heart, and he used his grip on her fingers to pull her closer. "Are you still? Terribly, terribly angry? And hurt?"

She lifted one shoulder, allowing him to tug her forward. "Maybe not so terribly terribly. Just terribly."

"Give me a chance to win you back," he begged.

"The same chance you gave me?"

Her words slashed at his heart, not because they wounded him, but because he knew how badly he'd wounded her. "I'm so sorry."

She took a deep breath, then another, and then her shoulders quaked as she cried. Connor ushered her into his embrace, kissing her face, wiping the tears with his fingers. He had caused this, and he deserved to share the burden. "I love you," he whispered between caresses. "Forgive me, Luce. I'm learning. I'll be the husband you want."

She turned her face upward and he met her lips with his, kissing her soundly.

"Let's not hurt each other any more," she murmured.

"Let's not," he said, and her words flooded him with a lightness, a joy that made him think maybe he could fly. "I don't expect you to put this behind you overnight, but when you're ready to come home—to be my wife—"

"I am your wife," she interrupted. "I want to live like it."

He hugged her tight, holding her in the deepening darkness, treasuring her nearness. "Okay. Then let's go home."

~ Chapter Twenty-Nine ~

L uce had just straightened the display case and sat down behind the computer when the shop door opened, bringing with it a blast of chilly January air.

"My, my, you've been busy," Melodee said with a cluck of her tongue. The thick winter jacket nearly obscured her large girth, but not quite.

Luce smiled at her and came around the counter to hug her sister. "Seems my muse is back."

"And better than ever." Melodee eyed the Poland-inspired pieces behind the glass wall. "Venturing out, huh?"

Luce shrugged. "Turns out there's more than one way to throw pottery."

Melodee turned to her. "You look well."

Luce could only smile again. "I've never been happier."

"Well, I'm just glad I didn't miss your wedding."

Luce laughed. It had been a bit of a shock when she confessed to her father that she'd gotten married. She'd let most people assume it was an elopement, though of course Melodee knew the truth. "Maybe next time."

Her sister gave her a stern look. "There will be no next time. Connor's a keeper. Hold onto him."

A fuzzy warm feeling came over Luce at the mention of Connor's name, and she knew she probably looked like a love-smitten school girl. "Yeah. Yeah, he is."

"I bet you're excited to get that honeymoon in Italy."

Luce focused on Melodee now. "Yes. So could you hurry up and have that baby already? You're the only one we're waiting on."

Melodee groaned and ran a hand over her belly. "I'm working on it."

The shop door opened again, the bell jangling as Connor came in. His cheeks were flushed, and he wore a red scarf over a dark brown sweater, even though she knew he'd only walked across the street from his mom's—no, his—store.

"Winter's here," he breathed out, rubbing his hands together. "Good time to set up your shop. By the time we open for the spring, you'll be ready to take this place by storm. Hi, Melodee."

She waved. "I just came to say hi. My car's parked up the hill and it's cold, so I better get going."

"Call me at the first sign of that baby," Luce said.

"Oh, I sure will."

She let herself out, and Luce turned back to Connor. Normally winter hours also meant less money, but not this year. "Good thing business is booming." Luce turned her computer around to show him the data coming in from her online website. "Looks like Christmas orders put us in the black."

Connor leaned in close and whistled. "Good job."

She lifted a shoulder. "Who knew the Polish theme would be such a big hit?"

"Perfect time to expand. Let's get to Italy for that business trip and add your Italian line."

Luce slid the computer away and leaned toward him. "Honeymoon."

He bent his head, his nose nearly touching hers. "Tax write-off."

"Honeymoon," she whispered.

His lips met hers in a gentle kiss. "Call it whatever you want. As long as I'm with you, I don't care."

She intertwined her fingers with his. "Good, because I'm planning several lines of cultural pottery. We might have to travel a lot."

He kissed her again. "Can't wait."

This time the kiss lingered, and Luce twisted her fingers into his thick, wavy locks, unable to believe the turn her life had taken. She never would've married Brian if she'd known Connor was in her future. And yet, if she hadn't married Brian, she never would've come back to Arkansas and dated Connor.

Funny how life could turn something awful into something wonderful.

Don't miss the other books in the Eureka in Love Series!

Find out Kerri's story, Connor's friend from down the street, in *Chocolate Kisses*!

Chocolate Kisses

With only one semester of college left, Kerri Manning returns home in pain and defeat. She needs to figure out how to deal with a diagnosis that will change her future. It's hard to dream of happiness, but the new guy in town manages to make her laugh. Can she take a chance he'll stick around?

Eric Hunt is an up and coming sculptor who has grown tired of his fake friends in New York City. He finds himself in the small town of Eureka Springs looking for the passion he used to have for his art. Could Kerri be the inspiration he needs?

Landscape Love

Landscape Love

Nathaniel Pierce ran away from home and the painful memories from his past. He recreated himself in Eureka Springs. No longer a veterinarian, he's Nate the landscaper. When old Lilly Connor dies, the whole town turns to him to watch out for her estranged granddaughter.

Lilly Ramirez never knew she was named after her grandmother. In fact, she didn't know she existed. The small town isn't anything like she expected, it's way better. The only downside is the good looking man that keeps tying her in knots.

Can they work out their issues to find love?

Ready to know Caroline's story? Coming in 2019!

Bridging the Divide

Chocolate Kisses
by River Ford
Chapter 1
Eureka Springs, Arkansas

Kerri Manning sighed in relief when they turned down Spring Street. Her knees and hips ached from sitting for the last hour, and she couldn't wait to see her mom.

"Almost there, Sweet Pea," Her dad, Ken Manning, patted her hand. He hadn't called her by that nickname in years, and she found it comforting to hear now. "Your momma's been looking forward to getting you home."

She appreciated his attempt to keep things light and positive, but the truth remained. She was returning home in defeat. Her dad had driven down to Fayetteville to bring her home from the University of Arkansas with only one semester left to graduation. For the last year and a half she'd been exhausted and achy without knowing why. The doctors ran test after test trying to figure things out while she suffered through her day to day life.

Finally, a little before fall semester started, she got a diagnosis. She still hadn't recovered from the shock. Even though she pushed her way through one more semester, she couldn't handle the constant pain, exhaustion, and the pressure of school anymore. It made it next to impossible to attend classes and pay attention.

They pulled into the drive. Kerri prepared herself mentally for the task of unloading her belongings and carrying them up the stairs to her room. You can do this.

Her dad popped the trunk. Kerri opened the back door and hauled out her suitcase. She was halfway to the porch when her mom ran out and pulled her into a hug. Even though the January weather was a mild fifty degrees, her mom's warmth was exactly what she needed.

"Finally! I was getting worried." Cheryl Manning squeezed her tighter.

"Sorry. I asked Daddy to stop in Rogers so I could stretch and get some hot chocolate." She dropped the bag and clung to her mom.

"Good. There's nothing like cocoa with—" she paused expectantly.

"Extra whipped cream." Kerri finished with her mom's motto. "It's good to be home."

"Why didn't that man of yours drive you home?"

Kerri finally backed out of her mom's arms. "He had more important things to do."

"Nonsense! I'll have a good talk with him next time—"

"We broke up." Kerri kept waiting to feel devastated about her ex-boyfriend Steven, but she'd only suffered mild sadness to this point. She wondered if it was shock. Surely the man she'd spent two years with should have garnered a stronger response?

"Why?" Cheryl's brow rose.

"He...he didn't want to be stuck with my problems." Kerri chewed on her bottom lip, but stopped short of twirling her hair around her finger.

Her mom gasped. "He didn't say that did he?"

"Yes." Kerri reached for the suitcase, determined not to revisit her last conversation with Steven. "I really don't want to talk about it."

"Okay, but I'm here when you do. Come on, I've got your room all ready." Cheryl took the suitcase from her and walked through the front door. "I hope you don't mind, but we're putting you in the downstairs guest room. It's got its own bathroom and you won't have to climb the stairs."

Kerri swallowed the lump in her throat. Her family had made changes for her. Would her disease affect everyone she met? She felt so tired all of a sudden. Her body had become the cement block that would pull her to the bottom of the lake, never to surface again.

"Kerri?" Her mom touched her shoulder. "Is that okay?"

"Yeah. Thanks," she nodded.

"Well, go on and make yourself comfortable. Oh, and I saw Jaya the other day. She's back in town with her fiancé."

"Really? I didn't know she was coming home so early. I bet she's working on wedding stuff. I'll have to give her a call sometime." Kerri didn't want to think about her high school classmate's upcoming nuptials. Was it jealousy, or just regret?

If she hadn't gotten sick, would she still be with Steven planning a wedding some time after graduation? It doesn't matter, get over it.

Kerri had to admit she was more in love with the idea of marriage and stability than she ever had been with Steven. In fact, she could now admit she'd never dated a guy that she missed after he left. She looked around the room in an effort to stop dwelling on the pathetic state of her love life. Her mother had redecorated the guest suite. The room had a fresh coat of pale blue paint that matched the tiny flowers in the quilt on the bed. The furniture was her grandma's cedar set. The rich red wood streaked with lighter veins had filled this room for most of her twenty-three years. The scent had grown faint over the decades, but if she pressed her nose close she could still smell it.

A large, rounded mirror hung over the dresser. The two bedside tables had brass lamps with fringe-ringed shades on top of lace doilies. It wasn't that her parents were old fashioned, they just believed in using things until they stopped working. They rarely threw away anything. It was comforting in a way.

Her dad returned with another box from the trunk. He set it on the foot of the bed and sat beside her. "Come on, Sweet Pea. Chin up. Remember what the doctor said. A good attitude will go a long way in keeping this beast under control."

Kerri sighed and leaned over to rest her head on his shoulder, content to be his little girl for the moment. "I know, Daddy, but I feel like my life has ground to a halt. What am I supposed to do?"

He shifted to wrap his arms around her. "Maybe this is God's way of telling you to look for new dreams."

She groaned.

"No, hear me out. You went to school and changed a lot of things. What you wanted to do, where you wanted to live. Every time you came home I wondered what happened to my baby. Perhaps this will help you find that carefree, happy girl again."

She wiped at tears. "I don't know where to start. I think I'm too scared to hope for anything."

"Ah, Sweet Pea." He squeezed her tighter. "Your mom and I will hope for you until you can do it on your own again."

"I missed you calling me Sweet Pea."

He chuckled. "Well, I'll forget your name is Kerri if that'll help you feel better."

"It just might." Coming home always made her feel better, and maybe her daddy was right. She needed to find out who she was again.

Her phone rang as her dad stood. "That's my cue to grab some more stuff."

"I'll help if you give me a minute." Kerri's nerves rumbled. Please don't be Jaya. She searched in her purse for her cell, relieved to see her roommate Jen's face smiling up at her. "It's Jen."

"That didn't take long. You only left a couple hours ago. Tell her I said hi." He closed the door behind him.

"Hey, I just got home." Kerri leaned back on the bed, enjoying the way it felt to stretch out.

Jen had been her best friend for as long as she could remember. The two of them, along with Jaya, Mic, and Brynn survived high school together. However, Jen was the only one Kerri had roomed with at U of A.

"It's already lonely here." Jen tried to sound pouty, but she was one of those perpetually happy people. It's one of the things Kerri loved about her. "Guess what?"

"What?"

"I'm coming home in three weeks!" Jen screamed into the phone.

"What? How did you get off work?" Kerri couldn't believe it. Jen was always working. It's actually how they moved from friends to besties. When they were in middle school, Jen didn't have any money for candy or sodas, so they started their own cookie business. They never got rich, but they both learned to work hard. "Wait, why are you coming home in the middle of the semester?"

"In a minute. I have a favor to ask you." Jen paused and Kerri could hear her tapping her fingers on something.

"Why do I get the feeling I'm not going to like this?"

The fingernails on the other side of the line quieted. "Because you're probably not, but I want you to think about it."

"Uh-oh. Okay, spit it out." Kerri felt a wave of tiredness wash over her, but she knew if she could help her friend she would. Jen never asked for anything too hard anyway.

"I'm coming home Valentine's weekend." Another pause that lasted longer than normal. "For the chocolate festival."

"Oh." A spike of excitement jolted through Kerri before fizzling out. She hadn't thought about the annual chocolate contest since Steven laughed at her over it. That memory haunted her as much as the pain that never really went away. "I don't know Jen. Working the chocolate might be too hard for me. Remember how much it hurt at Christmas."

"Come on, girl. Remember, use it or lose it. Even if it hurts, it could help. Don't give up. Just think about it. Plus, without the cost of school, you can afford all the medicine, right?"

"I'm still paying for school. My classes will just be online instead of on campus."

"Oh, yeah." Jen paused before bouncing back even peppier than before. "At least we can graduate together. You'll come back for that, right?"

"Yes, I wouldn't miss it."

"Good. Well, you've probably got a lot of unpacking, so I'll let you go, but promise me you'll think about it for more than five minutes?"

"I promise, but don't get your hopes up."

New York City

Eric Hunt hid by the catering door watching the crowd mingle. They laughed, toasted his success. Few of them looked at the sculptures on display. They were more interested in being seen than seeing. He should have been used to it by now, but even two years in New York City hadn't erased his fond memories of gatherings at home. Life had been different there. More relaxed, and he knew who his true friends were. Don't be the country boy tonight.

He turned his thoughts to his latest work and cringed. The only thing he could say about the sculptures was they were larger than life. That's what his agent, Julie, had wanted. A statement as big as New York City. The twelve pieces on display represented various aspects of the Big Apple. The largest of the series filled the middle of the room. Skyscrapers grew upward and outward in a skewed version of a skyline. The buildings were larger at the top than the bottom. The details were good. He even had the illusion of people behind the windows, but it didn't make him feel anything. None of these city pieces did.

A glance at his watch showed half past eleven. Perhaps he could slip away without causing too much ruckus.

"Eric, there you are." A perfectly manicured hand brushed

his arm. Long blonde hair draped over bare shoulders. The dress was practically sewn onto the woman's body. "I've been looking everywhere for you."

"What do you need, Candace?" He didn't move from his spot even though she tried to pull him into the open room.

"I need you..." She fluttered her eyelashes.

It took all he had not to roll his eyes. Candace wasn't the biggest fake in his life, but she ranked pretty high. She was a great agent, but she flirted constantly. Eric never knew whether to take her seriously or not.

He felt the same about most of the women he'd met since gaining a bit of fame. They all flirted. Said they wanted him, but they only wanted their picture in the papers. They wanted to know who he knew, who could help them with their ambitions. He learned his lesson the hard way, and even if Julie hadn't been his agent, he wouldn't give her the chance to break his heart like Vanessa.

"We agreed to keep things strictly business." He nodded toward the room.

"You're no fun." She waved toward the gathering with a small pout. "Come out and be seen at least."

She tugged on his arm again. This time he walked with her toward the middle of the gallery and his artistic interpretation of the New York City skyline. Photographers surged toward them. The staccato of flashes nearly blinded him.

"Try to look happy." She whispered.

Her beauty-queen smile was in full force for the cameras. The games women played for attention pushed him over the edge. He didn't care if she was his agent, he was done.

Eric held up his hand. "Everyone, thank you for coming tonight. I hope you've enjoyed the exhibit. Please excuse me, I have another engagement to attend tonight."

He retreated toward the door, Candace still clinging to his arm.

"That's not going to help you sell anything. Where are we headed?" her sickly sweet voice grated on his nerves.

Eric paused long enough to pry her fingers loose. "I need some time alone. Find my creative vibe again. Get started on the next set of show pieces."

"So there isn't another place you have to be? Looks like I'm finally turning you into one of us. I'll let you get away with it tonight." She ran her finger down his chest and stepped closer. "Especially, if you let me help you with your creativity."

"Seriously, back off. Do I need to find another agent?" He turned his back on her and grabbed his coat and gloves from the valet.

"You're stuck with me until our contract is up." She dropped the sweet tone. "And trust me, if you try to get out of it, I'll slap you with so many lawyers you'll never find that vibe again."

Eric bristled, but knew he had to keep calm. "I don't want out of our contract. I simply want you to be my agent and stop all this flirting."

"Why didn't you just say so?"

Eric rolled his eyes and walked out to the busy street. The temperature hovered just below freezing. The wind bit into his face and he pulled the scarf up higher, covering his mouth and nose. At least it wasn't sleeting. The dirty snow from the day before crunched under his feet as he hailed a cab.

"308 Mott Street in SoHo, please." Eric settled in the back and rubbed his hands together.

New York blazed with lights. Traffic was the only thing that moved slowly here. When Eric had first come to the city he had been dazzled by it all. Everything had been exciting. Now he just saw the dirty snow piled along the side of the street. It was starting to affect his art.

"Maybe it's time I get out of here." He mumbled to himself.

"What's that?" the cabbie asked.

"Nothing."

Once he reached the apartment, Eric opened his laptop and Googled artist communities in the US. He scanned a list of websites. There were lots of up and coming cities, but he was sick of the run around. He wanted something quiet. Somewhere he could hide from his fake friends and work on creating art again.

"Top 25 small cities for art." He clicked the link and skipped the top ten entirely. "Eleven—Corning, New York. Too close. Twelve—Eureka Springs, Arkansas. Thirteen—" His gaze went back to number twelve. "Arkansas? They have art communities in Arkansas? You can't get any more remote than that."

Chapter 2

After a week, Kerri's life fell into a new routine. Sleep, study, email her assignments, then head to the store to help her mother. She had successfully avoided most of her family, and her friends. Even Mic, although she didn't think that would last much longer, since she was the only one of their group that would cook with him. However, the thought of smiling and acting happy for all of them weighed her down. It wasn't fair they still had their whole lives in front of them—jobs they loved and relationships that could lead somewhere like weddings and babies. She had no idea what her future held.

Nothing. There's nothing.

Thursday morning, Kerri sighed and got out of bed. Her body ached and complained about every move she made. She needed to email a paper to her professor by nine o'clock, but she would soak in a hot bath first. She was grateful her teachers were willing to help her graduate on time, typing made her wrists hurt and put her in a bad mood. It was a hundred times worse in the morning when she already felt like a zombie.

When she finished her homework for the day, Kerri grabbed her coat and walked down the hill to the shop. Dr. Dahler told her to walk as much as possible to keep her knees healthy. He'd been her doctor all her life, and now he would help her survive this new challenge.

She lived a mile and a half from the shop. On a good day, it only took twenty minutes to walk down the steep streets. Kerri's family owned a little store on Spring Street selling handmade jewelry and beads. Mostly beads. Thousands and thousands of colored beads of every shape and size imaginable filled boxes and trays along the walls of the narrow shop. She used to help her mom make dangly earrings and necklaces to sell.

"Hey, Mom. What do you need me to do today?" she nodded to her mother who sat behind the counter.

"Take over here so I can work on the Mardi Gras stuff."

"No problem." Kerri took her place and switched on a small space heater behind the cash register. Hours passed. She greeted customers, but mostly she huddled behind the counter trying not to think.

"You're sulking again. If you don't want to be here, do something else." Her mom shooed her off the chair.

"Like what?" Kerri rolled her shoulders and flexed her hands. The dull ache hadn't left her alone today.

"If you won't visit Jaya, call Mic or someone."

Kerri made a face.

Her mom wisely ignored it. "If you won't be social, at least get in touch with your creative side."

She headed for the back room. It was a five by five space as familiar to her as anywhere in the world. She took a moment and breathed it in. The building was old and this room really showed the age. The paint peeled in the corners and the floor dipped in the middle. Nothing could hide that old dusty smell either. She didn't know if it was in the wood or the threadbare carpet, but she had missed it.

She ran her hand along the high-back wooden chair that sat by a bench built into the back wall. As a teen she'd hated the stiff slats even when she loved making jewelry. Now she slid into the seat and allowed herself to appreciate how straight it made her sit. That was supposed to be good for her, but making jewelry would have her slouched forward in no time.

"Do it anyway." She whispered, pulling strength from the familiar surroundings.

The Eureka Springs Mardi Gras celebration needed quality necklaces. They couldn't have any of that cheap plastic junk for the royal court. She opened a box of bright pink beads and another one full of silver antiqued ones. It was time to take back her life and find something to make her happy.

***

After driving the length of Eureka Springs on Hwy. 62, Eric turned around and returned to Main Street and the Historic Downtown area. The artist in him thrilled at the way the streets climbed their way up the hillside. The buildings had character, history. Old brick, faded advertisements. It had the opposite affect on him as the steel and glass he'd grown accustomed to in the city.

He pulled into one of the public parking lots and squeezed a few bills into the payment booth. The weather was mild for the last day of January, but cool enough he was grateful for his coat and gloves. He decided to browse the shops along Spring Street to get a feel for the community. There were all kinds of things being sold—Christmas stuff, quilts, wind chimes of every size and variety you could imagine, an art gallery, handmade soaps, nuts, clothing, faeries, candles, and a decent sized bookstore.

The next shop was smaller than some of the others and full of beads and jewelry. Both sides were lined with tables loaded with bins of beads, and the middle had a display of tools and other gadgets needed to make jewelry. He was about to turn around and walk out when a dark-haired woman, with a touch of gray sprinkled throughout, called to him from behind the counter.

"Hello, welcome to Beads and Baubles. Are you looking for anything specific?"

Before he could answer, he heard a thump followed by a clatter and the sound of something spilling. An angry mumbling ensued. The woman at the register jumped up and hurried to the back corner of the store. It took her less than ten steps the place was so small.

"Are you okay?" she asked the person entering from a side room. The second woman knelt to the floor.

"Yes." An angry voice drifted to him.

The air fairly crackled with tension. Eric hovered just inside the door, not sure if he should help or leave them alone.

"Don't worry about it." The first woman tried to help. "Let me do it. Why don't you go get some air?"

The second woman stood, giving Eric his first real glimpse

of her. Her profile showed the same delicate bone structure as the first woman. She also had smooth skin, and hair a shade darker than the woman who had welcomed him. It's soft curls fell around her shoulders. She wore a dark green sweater, a couple sizes too big for her slender frame, that reached almost to her knees where thick striped tights covered her legs. None of the women he knew would be caught dead in the bright leggings or the loose sweater. This woman wouldn't know a Versace from a Dior.

"Let me clean it up." Her voice softened but carried the bite of frustration.

Eric crossed the store, pulled forward by the need to see her entire face. It was the kind of face he might want to sculpt. The woman spun around when he cleared his throat. He came face to face with the most amazing brown eyes. They glittered with unshed tears. The rest of her countenance was open and expressive. Everything about her screamed real.

She sucked in a shuddering breath. "Oh!"

"Hi, can I help?" He felt a surprising need to comfort the fragile looking girl in front of him. She had to be close to his age, but the wide eyes that sparkled in the light made her appear younger.

She blinked a few times and rubbed her wrist.

"It's just beads." She glanced up through her lashes.

Attraction shot straight through him. She looked like a broken angel. That one simple look through misty eyes made him want to scoop her up and hold her until her wings healed. Eric directed his gaze to the floor, surprised at the effect that vulnerable expression had on him. He hadn't felt this way since Veronica left him. It took a moment to focus on the pink and silver dots. "Well, an extra pair of hands couldn't hurt."

"What?" She squeaked and glared at the older woman.

"Does he know?"

"Know what?" Eric took a step back.

"Of course not. He just walked in. Believe it or not, I don't know him." The older woman stood up and held out her hand. "Sorry. I'm Cheryl and this is my daughter Kerri. She thinks I'm a busy body determined to set her up with every available man in town. Are you?"

"Am I what?"

"Available?" Cheryl asked.

"Mom!" Kerri turned almost as pink as the beads in her hand. She looked at Eric with those big eyes, dropped the beads and hurried toward the door.

"Kerri, wait." Her mom called after her, but she had already fled. "I'm sorry. You must think I'm horrible, but I was only trying to make her smile. I didn't think she'd take me so seriously."

Eric wondered why spilling a few beads would make a grown woman freak out. "Will she be okay?"

Cheryl nodded once, then shook her head. "No, she didn't take her coat. The cold will probably make her joints hurt worse."

He watched her put the beads in a box and walk to the counter. A thick wool coat hung on the chair behind it. It seemed a bit excessive for the mild weather outside. The day had leveled out around forty-five, but the wind was chilly.

"I'm sorry, I'll have to close up so I can take this to her."

"I could do it." Eric bit down on his tongue too late. What was he thinking? He'd only been in town an hour and he was offering to chase some girl through the streets. She was beautiful, but from the look of things she was a drama queen. That was the last thing he needed.

"What was your name?" Cheryl asked.

"Eric Hunt. I'm staying at the Grand Central Hotel." He held out his hand to shake hers.

"Billy can keep an eye on you." She nodded and handed him the coat instead. "She probably went up the street to Frank's store. He's at the top of the hill. Head on up, around the corner and then he'll be on the right hand side. If you get to the post office you've gone too far."

"Top, right. What kind of store?"

"He's a sculptor. Kerri loves it there."

"Really? So am I." Eric thought it strange she would trust a stranger to look for her daughter. "Are you sure about this?"

"I have a good feeling about you. Plus, we know all the shop owners between here and Frank's. I've got eyes everywhere."

"Sure." Eric wanted to make sure she knew she could trust him. "If it makes you feel better, you can look me up online."

"I think I will." The woman smiled and shooed him out the door. "Go on. I'll see you when you bring her back."

Kerri's heart pounded. Her emotions flew in multiple directions at once as she ran past shops on her way up the hill to Frank's. She was angry that her fingers had refused to work and embarrassed by the failure. Then she'd turned to see an amazing pair of aquamarine eyes staring at her. It was hard to name the sensation she'd experienced as she took in the rest of the man.

Something jittery had moved into her stomach when she met that gaze. He had the kindest eyes. Time had frozen. She was well on her way to getting lost in their depths when he offered to help. Those few words sounded like pity to her, and she'd put her foot in her mouth. Why did she always talk before thinking? Of course he didn't know about her problems. He did see her over react and run away like a child.

So much for making a good impression.

She pushed the thought from her head. Why would she want to make a good impression anyway? She wasn't the kind of person someone that gorgeous would be looking for, even if she were healthy. He had that manicured Hollywood stubble going on, making him look like a GQ version of a lumberjack. One that wore designer jeans and polo sweaters. The kind that needed a beauty queen hanging off each arm.

Stupid men!

Her steps slowed and her body ached by the time she made it to the top of the hill. It only took a couple of minutes, but she hadn't run in months. Her hips and knees screamed at her. She stepped into Frank's shop. Instead of the traditional bell or wind chimes others had over their doors, Frank had placed a cowbell. It was one of the ways he had made this place his.

"Be with you in a minute." A voice called from the back.

"Frank?" she headed for his workroom.

"Kerri, is that you?" A white haired man in his late sixties poked his head around the door. "You're home." He gave her a big hug. "You're shivering. Where's your coat?"

"I left it at the shop. Do you still have that little space heater?"

It didn't take long for her to get cold, especially since she'd lost so much weight since she'd become sick. Kerri had often huddled over the vents at school soaking in the warmth after walking across campus. She tried to catch her breath while she waited for Frank. Running had moved the ache deep into her chest. Was this a new symptom? Or was she just out of shape?

Just breathe. She tried to calm herself, but every little thing made her worry something else was going wrong with her body.

Frank pulled a small heater from under a table and plugged it in. "Why haven't you been up to see me yet?"

Kerri sat on the floor and let the heat seep in. The tears she thought she had under control threatened to spill over again making it even harder to breathe normally. Get a grip!

"Hey now, what's going on?" Frank patted her shoulder. "Mic was in yesterday and said you've been avoiding him too."

The bell over the shop door clanged again.

"Kerri?" A male voice called her name.

"Back here." Frank answered for her.

The stranger appeared in the doorway. Kerri couldn't believe he'd followed her. Maybe he really did think she was incapable of taking care of herself. It hurt more than she thought it should. Why couldn't she start over and make a better impression?

She took the time to look him over again. His brown hair had a little wave to it and curled around his ears. Her eyes were drawn to his hands. They looked strong and capable clenching her coat. Her coat?

"That's mine." She blurted out and tried to stand. Her body didn't respond, but sort of flopped. She still sat, but now her arms were the only thing keeping her in that position. The run had been too much. Shame and embarrassment washed over her.

"Your mom asked me to bring it to you." He watched her carefully, his gaze full of something she didn't understand.

"I'm Frank." The older man held his hand out.

"Eric Hunt." He shook Frank's hand but kept kept glancing at Kerri. "I'm a sculptor too. Just came in today from New York City."

"Really? How do you know Kerri?"

"I don't. I mean, we just met and her mom wanted to make sure she got her coat."

Frank grunted and mumbled something about her mother before addressing Eric again. "Are you visiting or looking for a change?"

"A little of both." Eric shrugged.

Frank laughed and moved back to the piece he was working on. He chipped at the wood as he talked. "I came eighteen years ago for a change and never left. Life's simpler here. Slower. You have time to be yourself."

The words sank deep into Kerri's soul. They might have been aimed at Eric, but they were what she needed to hear. Her breathing eased. She pushed herself up a little higher and finally let go of the cold floor. Now she simply had to figure out who she was or who she could be with her prognosis.

"That's what I'm hoping." Eric smiled and a dimple appeared on his left cheek.

Kerri's stomach flipped. She could die of mortification. Here was an attractive man, with dimples no less, holding her coat and she couldn't get off the floor. Perhaps if she sat still he'd forget she existed.

No such luck.

He turned that smile on her. The fluttery feeling threatened to explode right out of her. Seriously, she would throw up if he kept looking at her like that.

"Your mother was worried and sent me to find you." Eric extended his hand.

Heat crept up her neck. She shouldn't have run out on her mom, but looking weak in front of this man felt like the worst thing that had happened in a long time. Even worse than the time she started her period while on a school field trip unprepared. She'd hid in the bathroom until her mom could pick her up, but everyone knew what had happened. Mic called her Spot for months until Brynn made him stop.

"Kerri?" Frank stared at her. "Are you okay?"

She looked away from the two men standing over her to glare at the heater. "Yes, I'm just tired. I need to rest a minute before heading back to the shop."

Frank knelt beside her. "Honey, I don't understand."

"It's nothing." Her eyes flicked to the stranger. His gaze was glued on her, completely undoing any sense of peace. She had to put distance between the irrational hope those blue eyes pulled from her. There was one way to do that, but she couldn't bring herself to say the words. She focused on Frank and glossed over the problem instead. "Doctor Dahler figured out what's wrong. I just need to rest, and then I'll be okay."

"What did he say?" Frank asked.

"Can we talk about it some other time?" Every inch of Kerri's skin felt warm from his gaze.

Frank glanced at Eric and nodded. "No worries, but let me help you up." Frank bent half way down and winced.

"You'll throw your back out. Just give me some time." Kerri waved him away.

"I can help." Eric reached for her again.

Kerri sat on her hands. "No, really. I just need a minute."

"You're mom will think I kidnapped you." He bent down, slipped his arms under hers and lifted her to her feet.

She stood in his embrace. Warm from head to toe. Her hands grasped his shoulders of their own will. The muscles of his arms felt solid under his shirt as her fingers skimmed downward to rest in the crook of his elbows. The churning in her stomach turned into a cyclone. Trembling from the current running through her, she lifted her gaze from his chest to his eyes.

"Thank you." She whispered.

"Any time." He whispered back.

About the Author

Tamara Hart Heiner is a mom, wife, baker, editor, and author. She currently lives in Arkansas with her husband, four children, a dog, and a bird. She would love to add a macaw and a sugar glider to the family. She's the author of several young adult suspense series (*Perilous*, *Goddess of Fate*, *Kellam High*) the *Cassandra Jones* saga, and a nonfiction book about the Joplin Tornado, *Tornado Warning*. This is her first foray into romance, and she'd love to hear your thoughts!

Connect with Tamara online!
Twitter: https://twitter.com/tamaraheiner
Facebook: https://www.facebook.com/author.tamara.heiner
blog: http://www.tamarahartheiner/blogspot.com
website: http://www.tamarahartheiner.com
Thank you for reading!